THE WILD ONE

'My father was a drunkard, and my mother was a whore.' So begins the story of Judith Perryn, the Cornish girl who would marry the wild sea captain, Matt Thomas and become housekeeper and mistress to Squire William Pendruggan. Finally, her career reached its explosive crescendo in vengeance and passion with arrogant Venn Ettyn, master of wild and remote Thorncarne.

The Wild One

by

Mary Williams

Magna Large Print Books
Long Preston, North Yorkshire,
England.

British Library Cataloguing in Publication Data.

Williams, Mary
The wild one.

A catalogue record for this book is available from the British Library

ISBN 0-7505-1386-1

First published in Great Britain by Futura Publications Ltd., 1979 under Marianne Harvey

Published in Large Print 1999 by arrangement with Mary Lewis

Magna Large Print is an imprint of
Library Magna Books Ltd.
Printed and bound in Great Britain by
T.J. International Ltd., Cornwall, PL28 8RW.

CHAPTER 1: 1880

My father was a drunkard, and my mother was a whore. That's what my grandmother told me when I was old enough to listen. From other remarks she made I gathered they were both dead, which was why I lived with her in the fishing cottage overlooking Port Einack harbour. Her husband, my grandfather, had died in a wreck off the Scillies, and her two sons had taken off to America. In her younger days she had worked in the kippering sheds, where herrings were smoked and packed for sending up country. But following my mother's—her daughter Lucy's—misdeeds, which were to have such a dark end, the cottage was turned into a boarding house for 'sea-faring gentlemen', and there, from the age of two, I spent my youth and adolescence.

The cottage was really quite a fair-sized place, with rooms in the basement where we lived and two floors above for her 'gentlemen', who came and went with amazing rapidity and were mostly far more colourful characters than the notice in the front parlour window suggested they should be.

My grandmother, despite her stern character, *had* an astute business sense, shutting her eyes to much that she, with her professed principles, should have condemned. And her advice to me from an early age was realistic.

'If you've got to have a man,' she said more than once, 'see he's rich enough and you've got enough brains to keep him guessing. The rest doan' matter.'

Life was hard for both of us. I worked early, from six in the morning till six at night, and though I tried to keep my grandmother's advice in mind, it seemed to me, as I reached my early teens, that the prospect of meeting a rich man was very unlikely. Our boarders fo the most part were sailors from the ships that berthed in the harbour for a few days and then were off again; they were frequently a loud-mouthed, rough lot, returning to the house at night too full of liquor to resemble gentlemen and too inclined to nip my bottom if I passed, unless I was careful with a tart reply on my lips and a sharp slap of my hand ready for any man thinking he could take liberties.

I admired my grandmother for the way she handled them. She was as strong as any man, with a bony, hawk-nosed face, jutting chin and a long upper lip with a fine sprouting moustache.

Her vocabulary equalled any of her boarders and had long since frightened away any holy-minded Evangelist stupid enough to come preaching at her door-step. She was handy with her fist, too, and quite capable of knocking a man twice her size flying, if she had reason.

She was always neat about her appearance though, wearing a white apron about the house in the mornings and later changing it for an embroidered black satin one that had belonged to her mother, a fisherman's wife. Her name was Hannah Perryn, and as I didn't know my father's name—anyway it was doubtful he'd ever sired me legally, according to her—I was known by it, too: Judith Perryn.

When I'd time to think about things at all, which wasn't often, I'd wonder about my parents, as any young girl would; my father especially, because there was nothing about my grandmother in my looks. I was tall for my age, chestnut-haired and small-featured, with a pert nose, green eyes and a good figure.

On the rare occasions when I had an hour off, I'd climb the hill at the back of the harbour to the high moors leading westwards to Penzance, where the air was tangy with heather and gorse and the wind blew fresh from the sea; there I'd wonder, imagining myself a fine madam like Lady St Heriot, whose husband, the Lord, owned much of the land round abouts and several mines Penjust way. Their house, Castlegwarran, stood in a wooded valley cutting from one coastline to the other, and when I looked down at its turrets stretching from the trees below, I knew that my grandmother's advice about marrying a rich man made sense.

I always left the moor with a feeling of distaste, more reluctant each time to meet the sour, salty smell of fish rising from the town where 'long-liners' were thick about the harbour and the air was often filled with shouts of excitement when some merchant vessel moored by the quay.

My grandmother's voice was always harsh upon my return.

'Where you bin, girl? There's money to be had tonight, so make yourself tidy, sharp. An' doan' be long 'bout et, or I'll tek my hand to your backside same as ef you wuz a nipper.'

I knew she meant it. Many's the thrashing I'd had in former days when I'd run truant or not done as she said. On the whole though, she was kind to me and did the best for me she could.

I was just sixteen when Cap'n Matt Thomas came to stop for a few days as one of our lodgers. He was about thirtyish, I guessed, tall and broad-shouldered, with black hair, a handsome face browned by sun and wind, and a way of looking at me, from black eyes under bushy brows, that sent shivers down my spine.

He had an air about him that was different from the usual kind of visitor to our establishment, who were mostly common sailors, at the best a mate or two. To have such a fine gentleman as a Cap'n was a rare honour, my grandmother said.

'You attend to un,' she said. 'Mek yourself agreeable, but no familiarity, mind. Familiarity was the death of your sinful ma. Jus' smile an' keep yourself off. That's the way a real man with money in his pocket wants a wumman.'

I did as she said, and Captain Matt seemed to take to me. Before he left again for the East Indies a week later, he bought me a present of a splendid red cloak with a hood, embroidered fantastically with dragons and flowers worked in finest cream silk.

I could hardly bear it when he left, wishing for a moment I'd not kept him *quite* so much at arms' length. But my grandmother approved.

'You wait, girl,' she said. 'He'll be back.'

And he did come again. Just three months later, with bottles of brandy and rum for my grandmother, a necklace and yards of silk and lace for me, and a look on his face that told me the time would come when he'd be asking for something for himself. It didn't worry me. In fact, I wished I didn't have to wait.

My grandmother, being a wise woman, knew the way my thoughts were running.

'Next time,' she said, 'he'll be nibblin' after you, an' doan' 'ee say yes at first. Et's good, as I've told ye times 'nuff, to keep a man wonderin'.'

But the next time Captain Matt arrived in Port Einack, my grandmother was dead—through overwork and a cold in the lungs, the doctor said.

I knew what loneliness was then. In spite of her rough tongue and often hard ways, she was all I'd had of my own and I'd been fond of her. But the house was mine, along with what bit of money she had left, so I had to go on running it in the best way I could, with the help of a girl, Carmel, who'd grown tired of the smoke sheds and fancied herself more in gentlemen's company.

Gentlemen! I could have laughed in her face, if she hadn't been such a plain, puny-looking creature, with her tow hair and long nose. She was strong though, despite her poor looks, and I saw she did her fair share of the rough work. Perhaps I was a bit hard on her there, but I knew I'd be a better advertisement for the lodgers if they saw me clean and tidy and in pleasant attire rather than looking too much like a working woman with pail and brush and my hands all red and chapped.

Still, though Carmel was handy enough, most days I was rushed off my feet, what with the bedrooms to attend to, meals and washing, and accounts to keep. I hadn't had much schooling and was cheated twice by unscrupulous seamen who distracted my attention with sly compliments so I was confused into believing I was being paid properly when they were giving me less than half of what it should have been.

After that I was careful, putting on a prim, stern air, referring even at times to a fictitious friend who was in the police. That always seemed to subdue them.

The evening Captain Matt returned was a wild one in late February, when the port was lashed by rough tides and high winds, with the moaning of ship's sirens and the screaming of gulls round the quay.

A cargo of silk and liquor from the East had been landed, and I'd had a bit of trouble turning 'gentlemen' away who'd insisted on coming into the house with a good deal of drunken swearing and bawdy remarks. Carmel, shaking and shivering, fled downstairs to our kitchen, where she hid herself like the scared rabbit of a creature she was, beneath the table. I was wearing black, with my best satin apron, and my hair taken trimly from my face in a knot secured by combs and a ribbon, to give a dignified, stern look. Grandmother, I knew, would have done better. A rolling pin would already have been in her hand, and she would have given forth a flow of language loud and abusive enough to put the fear of God—or the devil—into the whole bawdy company. But my show of temper seemed only to amuse them, and when one drunken oaf caught me by the shoulders, pulling my body against his fat stomach with his hot whisky breath and wet mouth against my cheek, I'd have done anything at that moment to have my grandmother's stiff moustache and bony fist in his face. All I could do was kick his shins and struggle wildly, while the others laughed and jeered and attempted to get a look in themselves.

It was then, praise heaven, that the door opened, and the hilarity suddenly died to a muffled chorus of muttered oaths. A great arm swung out to send my attacker sprawling backwards to the floor with the blood streaming from his mouth, both eyes blackened and shut, and limbs writhing as though all the fiends of hell had got him.

'Cap'n,' I heard one man say. 'Et's the Cap'n 'isself, darn 'is guts ...'

I looked up, and there he was—Matt Thomas, in sea-faring uniform, but hatless, with black curls tumbled loose about his forehead.

One hand wiped the sweat from his brow as

he said after one look at me, 'Get out, you bastards, and never put a foot inside this door again or I'll have the guts and hides of every one of you. Be off ... d'ye hear, and take this drunken pig with you.'

A booted foot was driven heavily against the groaning hulk on the floor. He attempted to get up but staggered back again and fell, with a yell of pain, only to feel Matt's boot again and to hear a contemptuous laugh from the Captain.

Brought to their senses, the rest of the sailors dragged their companion to his feet, and half-carrying, half-pushing him, between them they got him outside on to the cobbled wharf.

I stood quite still for a moment, letting my heart steady against my ribs till the breath came back, then I turned and saw Matt coming towards me, having secured the door firmly, holding the key in his hand.

'Well,' he said, pushing me into the parlour, 'so this is what happens when I go journeying to foreign shores.'

I sat down, still trembling, noting with distaste a trickle of blood on my hand and my torn bodice revealing flesh marked by long scratches from the fight.

'Yes,' I said. 'But not often. Never like this ... before.'

'Where's your grandmother?'

'Dead,' I told him.

'Good God!' He paused before adding, 'And you alone, running a place of this sort for men so starved of women they'd rape any toothless biddy rather than nothing ...'

'I'm not alone,' I said, with a rush of faintness suddenly blurring my sight. 'I've a girl, Carmel ...'

'A *girl!*' His voice was contemptuous. 'And where is she then?'

'I don't know. She's only young. In the kitchen, I s'pose.'

He took a flask from his jacket and pressed it to my mouth. The spirit was very strong, burning my throat, but I soon felt better and got up, still a bit muzzy headed, saying, 'I'll get you something to eat. And your face is filthy with muck an' blood. Oh, Cap'n Matt, I'm glad to see you.'

His arms went round me and his lips pressed to mine, then to my hair, and neck, almost throttling me, then back to my mouth again. I could feel the thudding of his heart in his deep chest, and my own racing quicker than a frit bird's but wild and strong with needing him. I knew then that Matt Thomas was the only man for me, whether he'd wealth or not, property or nothing in his pocket save a few bawbles and a ha'penny or two.

He lifted me up and held me close, then carried me to my bed, where he laid me gently, more gently than I'd thought any man could do, and fetched a bowl of water and a cloth to wash me with.

'We'll be married, Judy,' he said presently. 'An' I'll take on here where your grandmam left off—but with differences, o' course,' he grinned wickedly.

'Who says so, Matt Thomas?' I asked, just

for devilment. 'And what about your ships and those foreign places ...?'

'Those times are over, Judy love,' he told me, stroking the hair from my forehead with one hand while his other hand slipped down the bodice of my torn best dress and enclosed a breast; he put his lips to it as though it was a ripe fruit to nibble. I snuggled close, giggling, and wondered what my grandmother would say.

There was nothing else between us then, though. Cap'n Matt was an honourable man and didn't take me until a month later, when all was in order and he had a licence in his pocket from the minister, who married us at the grey, squared, Bethlehem Chapel at the back of the harbour, where it was said that John Wesley had once preached.

Afterwards we went back to my house, and that night I became the true wife of Matthew Thomas.

CHAPTER 2

From the beginning, my life with Matt was not only entirely satisfying but exciting in a way I'd never dreamed.

For instance, instead of the 'sea-faring gentlemen' notice of my grandmother's day, Matt put up a different sign in the window, saying, 'Guests Welcome'.

'I've heard it said artists and rich folk are beginning to come here these days,' he pointed out. 'We can charge more and have less trouble on our hands. Besides, I'll not have you working your fingers to the bone for a handful of filthy mariners. You're a married woman now, my girl, and as good a lady as any in the land. You must get yourself some fine clothes and stop labourin' when you feel like it. We'll get a boy in, and a new smart girl to help that slut Carmel! I'll get myself a small boat for fishing, too, and when they feel like it, maybe some of our folks'll like a trip out.'

It all sounded so easy. Matt really did take my breath away, although I wondered where the money was coming from.

'Don't you fret about that, love,' he said. 'I've a bit saved up. We'll put the whole lot, and what you've got, into the bank and arrange for a joint account, so's either of us can draw something when we want, on a cheque.'

A cheque. Matt really *was* well versed in the affairs of the world, I thought. And who'd have thought of putting money in the *bank,* which seemed to me a way of life reserved only for the gentry and rich merchants.

The hundred or two my grandmother had left me from her lifetime of stinting and scraping lay in a box under the floor boards in the kitchen, where she'd always kept it, and I felt a pang when I took it out. Matt grinned and squeezed my waist.

'It'll be safer under lock and key,' he said. 'I know all about these things. It'll be doubled after the summer, don't you fret. Don't you trust me, Judy?'

Not trust him? The idea! Of course I did. But the fact was that, as the weeks passed into months, his bursts of gaiety and extravagance *did* puzzle me a bit. Our guests were pleasant and more genteel, it was true, and for the most part paid a little more. But there were losses, like the occasion when Mr Charlesworth, a 'foreigner' from up country and a painter, found at the end of the month he was temporarily out of funds. I wanted to get the police, but Matt had a soft spot for artists.

'Police?' he said. 'Never have anything to do with them unless you're forced to. A mean lot they can be. Narrow. And always after the ones who can't speak up for themselves. If we took a case, what'd we get out of it if the poor devil hadn't a penny to his name?'

'How do you know he hasn't?' I said stubbornly, recalling my grandmother and her strict attitude to debtors of every kind, who, in her opinion, were no more than worthless vagabonds out to deceive women and folks too old or helpless to look after themselves.

'Now, Judith ...' I heard my husband say, swinging me round, with just a tinge of anger in his voice, ' 'tisn't like you to argue. Not going to turn into a shrew, are you?'

I pulled myself away, facing him with my chin up, the hot blood rising in two bright spots of flame to my cheeks like it always did when I was angered.

'And if I am? What then?' I retorted. 'Seems to me you've always had *your* way, Matt Thomas. What about me?'

'Yes. What about you?'

His smile had died. One arm was round me again, a hand travelling to where it shouldn't have been at that time of day, the other tilting my chin upwards to meet the hot stare of his grey eyes. I'd never noticed how clear they were before, yet glowing, like cold ice lit to flame from inside.

'Yes, you,' he said. 'Never satisfied are you? Always wanting more.'

I didn't answer. I didn't have to. He lifted me up just as though I was a sack of feathers and carried me to the bedroom, where he pulled off my dress and frilly underskirt and new-fashioned, fancy bloomers he'd bought me on a jaunt to Plymouth, while I shook and giggled as though it was the first time, until we were both panting, all the stupid talk of expense and money forgotten.

It was mostly like that: fun, hard work and love. I was content generally to leave everything else to Matt, who did all that was necessary at the bank, telling me such dealings were a bothersome business for any woman and that as long as I had him to look after me, I'd be all right.

There were times, though, when I fancied a kind of shadow on his face. He looked different then, morose and far away.

'What's the matter, Matt?' I'd ask. 'Is anything bothering you?'

Most times he'd answer, quite roughly for him, 'Nothin'. What should there be? You get to your kitchen, Judith, and leave me alone. Sometimes a man has to think.'

I felt chilled then, like a child scolded, and walked away sharply, head up with my heart sunk like a pebble down a great well. Then suddenly he'd be after me again, all soft and loving, and I'd forgive him as I always did, telling myself I was the silly one and there was nothing to forgive.

Once, when he was much later than usual returning from taking two or three passengers out for an afternoon's fishing in his boat *The Girl Judith,* I went down the slipway to see if he was about. The tide was halfway up by then, creeping closer to the end of the pier where the long-liners were massed dark, in readiness for a night at sea. A schooner or two and a merchantman were anchored nearby. It was a fine evening, with a thin mist hanging over the water and already a queer, greenish light about the sky predicting a rising moon later. I didn't know why, exactly, but a strange feeling of unease crept over me, a sort of foreboding, just like I'd had when I was a child before something unpleasant happened, like a wreck or a drowned man washed up on the rocks.

My grandmother, though such a commonsense body, had understood. 'It's the sight,' she said. 'Somethin' only us fishin' folk have—if they're the right sort ... Cornish.'

So I'd accepted my odd gift—if gift it was—as a perfectly natural sense, like breathing or smelling. As I'd grown older, it had seemed to fade, except for rare occasions when it resurfaced and I'd toss it aside, refusing to accept or listen.

This time, though, it was different; perhaps the extreme quietness of the evening and the dying light with the milky mist over the pale sand emphasized the rising fear in me that I couldn't get rid of. Matt, I thought. Something had happened to Matt, and I recalled how, with just such calm tides, there could be dangerous undercurrents and whirlpools about the rocks, ready to suck under any man or small craft that got too near.

I lifted my skirts to my knees and rushed towards the sea, forgetting I was a married woman running an establishment, hearing only the warning of my own brain and heart—fear for Matt.

Then, suddenly, I saw him, ambling towards me, with a man of his own size; a seaman, coloured, like many of them were who docked from merchant craft, and over-matey from the look of him with my husband.

Relief brought a spate of words to my lips.

'Where you bin, Matt Thomas?' I shrieked, with my voice shrill and abusive, even to my own ears, just as though my grandmother was talking. 'Two hours late—*more,* you are—and here was I scared stiff ...'

On I went, on and on ...

Then I broke off in quick shame, seeing the hot blood suffuse Matt's face and the dark man grinning in amusement. For the first time I noticed my hair was tumbled on my shoulders and my neck bare where the buttons had come undone.

I was breathing quickly and hardly heard Matt when he said, 'This is a friend of mine, Mr Jago. Hope you've a decent meal ready. We'll have company this night. Nick ... my wife.'

I don't remember what I said, realizing only how angry Matt was. Wilder under his cold calm than I'd ever known him to be. I made an attempt to pin up my hair and smooth my clothes, walking with as much dignity as I could muster, between them to the house. First I went to the kitchen to see that the meal was still ready in the oven and then I ran upstairs to get myself neat and clean.

Matt came in as I was changing my skirt and shut the door sharply before saying coldly, 'What the devil did you mean by that?'

Not turning, I answered, trying to keep my voice controlled, 'I'm sorry. I was worried.'

His hands were on my shoulders, swinging

me round to face him, and what I saw in his eyes for those few seconds wasn't pleasant.

'Remember ...' he said, 'if you ever do such a thing again ... screaming like a shrew at me in front of any mate of mine, I'll give you the beating of your life. So button your skirt quick over your so charming bottom, or I'll forget myself and start on you now.'

He tossed the garment at me and strode out, slamming the door.

I stood for a moment, hot-cheeked and humiliated, hating him briefly for his rage and way of showing it. Who was *he?* I asked myself, with my heart thudding savagely, thinking he could come into my own house and treat me as though he was God Almighty, orderin' and threatenin' into the bargain? But I'd show him. Oh yes, I'd show him all right.

When I went downstairs, changed into the scarlet dress, gathered back into the bustle thing, he'd bought for me in Truro only a week before, I knew I looked as fine as any great lady in the land, with my hair pinned in curls on the top of my head and two necklaces he'd given me blazing round my neck.

We had rabbit pie, followed by figgy pudding that had gone a bit harder than it should through waiting on the oven too long. I behaved proudly, only speaking when I had to, putting the two men into their places properly, I hoped, though I noticed at moments Matt's grey eyes blazing at me. It wasn't an enjoyable occasion. The dark man, Nick, seemed uncertain and a bit embarrassed; Matt was over-jovial when he spoke to him and extra polite with me, addressing me as Mrs Thomas, which would have sent me into fits of laughter if I hadn't felt so mad.

Carmel served us at table, as the other girl, Jane, had an evening off. She knew very well what was going on, I thought, uncomfortably; she had probably heard every word of the undignified bedroom scene. I could tell it from her sidelong look and the way her mouth turned down, as if she could hardly control a smirk. She was a real one for listening with her ear to the keyhole, and I decided that the next time I caught her at it I'd send her packing.

I wondered whether Matt's friend would be thinking of staying the night and relished the thought of telling him we'd no room, which would be true enough, as our three bedrooms were already occupied by a husband and wife on holiday and a traveller from Birmingham, all who'd eaten two hours since and either gone strolling about the harbour or off to bed.

He didn't ask though and, after chatting for an hour with Matt in the parlour, went back to his ship, leaving me and Carmel to clear up.

I went to bed soon after and was between the sheets when Matt came in. He didn't speak, and I feigned sleep, occasionally glancing at him from one eye when his back was turned. As he took off his clothes, I couldn't help thinking even through my lingering anger what a fine figure of a man he was.

For quite an hour, maybe more, we lay side by side in the wide bed he'd bought at a sale in Penzance. I was miserable and lonely, longing suddenly to have him close yet remembering my grandmother's words about keeping myself off and the way a man 'wanted a wumman'. So I pretended indifference and, as time ticked by, it was a battle between us, a battle I could've won if I'd fought hard enough. But suddenly I didn't want to. I'd behaved badly on the beach, why should I want to shame him more?

So I turned quietly and touched his cheek. Quick as any wild thing he was on me and in me, and we were pulsing together in the sweet wild ecstasy of lovers—man and woman—made one again after a long strain. Afire under the hot pressure of his body, I was wanting more, still more, as his hands travelled over my breasts and thighs, giving and taking and moaning between words of endearment that came and went in gasps of delicious pain.

When it was over, with one of his arms lying across my breast, he said, 'This is for ever, Judy. Nothing on God's earth's going to part you and me. Maybe we'll have words sometimes, maybe I'll have to teach you a thing or two, but you're mine, see, and mine only.'

And I agreed, with only a frail shadow of fear at the back of my mind. How could things be for ever? Nothing was that. Even my grandmother, who'd seemed indestructible, had gone. And one day ...

But I didn't want to think of it and wished fiercely I could dispel for good the insidious warning voice of my heritage, that uncanny sixth sense of seafolk born in me, so deep in the blood it was as much a part of my living self as my lustrous, thick hair, green eyes and tidy, slim waist below the full breasts.

'What you thinking of, Judy?' I heard Matt saying presently.

'Nothin',' I told him. 'Just idle things that don't make sense.'

He kissed me on the temple, muttered something unintelligible, and the next moment was breathing so heavily I knew he was asleep. A little later I, too, was lying quiet beside him, forgetful of the day's events.

The following morning was bright and clear, and I was relieved to see, quite early, Nick's ship setting off again for Jamaica or some such place. He'd been pleasant enough, I had to admit, but I couldn't help connecting his presence with the niggling forebodings of the night.

However, I soon forgot—or almost forgot—any passing worries, and when Matt suggested we take a trip into Penzance that very day for a bit of a holiday, my pulses danced with anticipation, though I pretended to be dutifully concerned about the visitors.

Matt laughed, put his arm round my waist, swung me round and said, 'Let the furriners know what they're missing for once. Have Carmel make one of her obnoxious stews or pasties. It's Corpus Christi Fair, love, and we both need a bit of fun.'

So he arranged with Billy Trevean, who was driving a cart of young suckling pigs for sale, to take us along with him.

What a ride it was, with the 'slips' screaming

their heads off, Billy cracking his whip to make the old nag go faster, Matt singing a wicked old sea-faring song, and me so convulsed with happiness and laughter I could feel my new corsets cracking against my ribs.

I was wearing the red dress I'd had on at supper the night before, with a shawl round my shoulders and a silly bit of a flowery hat Matt had given me perched on my curls. Once the wind blew it and would have sent it flying hadn't Matt caught it and jerked the ribbons from the brim to tie under my chin. A lively occasion it was, with nothing to spoil it but the smell of the young pigs and their frightened yelling that made me sorry and a bit sad because they were so plump and tiny and needing a mother's care.

We spent the first few hours on the fairground itself, visiting the penny peeps, gingerbread stalls, boxing booths and shellfish stannins. There were sideshows of every kind, including a conjuror juggling balls on his nose, a tent showing a monstrous fat woman with a fish's tail, and a larger place covered with tarpaulin where a group of players were performing on a platform. It was then, when I saw the name Moody and Hackett's Theatre Company in bold gold lettering outside, that I had one of my 'feelings'. Matt didn't notice, but I felt, for a few seconds, an odd lightness in my head, as though the ground had shifted ever so slightly, making me giddy and suddenly apprehensive, wanting to go in yet fearing to. Just then the weather decided things, bringing a spattering of rain from the west, where clouds were gathering.

'Come along,' said Matt, pushing me ahead of him. 'We'll have a peep at the actors, then go and have a bit to eat somewhere.'

I don't remember much about the play, only that it was in costume, with a good deal of proclaiming, and that the heroine was far too old for the part, wearing a yellow wig that sat incongruously over her raddled face. These were mere details though in comparison with the rest, which resolved itself into just one figure—a man's; quite old he must have been, nearer fifty than forty, but magnetic somehow, moving proudly about the platform with his head held high and speaking his lines in the manner of a king.

Unaware of Matt's hand trying to stop me, I stood up in my seat, which was near the front, and for a few seconds our glances—the actor's and mine—met and were held as his speech failed momentarily, a brief pause during which a hand went to a pocket and drew out a small flask. He put it to his lips and the spell was broken. He turned, breaking once more into oration.

The confrontation was over. But I'd seen enough. His eyes were green, tilted slightly above high cheek-bones; his thick hair, greying at the temples, was still a rich chestnut where it waved behind his ears to the level of his upstanding, starched lace collar.

As I sat down again, the words of my grandmother once more rang through my head:

Your father was a drunkard, and your mother was a whore.

But my mother didn't seem to matter just then. I was thinking only of my father.

CHAPTER 3

Most days during that long hot summer with Matt brought excitement, fun, work and love, filling me with wonder when I thought back to the hard times I'd spent slaving for my grandmother. Sometimes, of course, we had tiffs, when I rebelled or put on fancy airs just to goad him, knowing that when his anger was spent how sweet the making-up would be.

Every day I'd notice something new about him, like the way his eyes lit up to golden specks when he was needing me or darkened to glowing black-grey if he was crossed too much and wanting to show he was master. I was careful never to let him be too sure. He was jealous, too. Once when we'd gone up to bed for the night after a lively evening and I was properly attired in a new fancy shift I'd spent all my spare money on in Penzance, he pulled it off me suddenly and, before I knew quite what he was doing, had ripped it from seam to seam and then across until it was just a ragged thing on the floor.

I was wild and sprang at him, scratching his face.

'What you done that for ... you great big hulk you? It was mine. *Mine.* Get out. Go away.'

The tears were thick in my throat. But Matt didn't know, of course. He stared at me for a moment, one hand to his face, while I stood naked watching him, in a streak of moonlight from the window. His eyes had gone from grey to black. They had a cold, searching look in them, almost calculating, that frightened me, until I said, seeing the blood trickle through his fingers, 'I'm sorry, Matt. I ... I ...'

'Sorry?' he echoed. 'An' so you should be. Remember what I said at the beginnin', 'bout not having a shrew around? Nor havin' you throwing your eyes about on any Tom, Dick or Harry? Remember, Judy?'

'I ... I ...'

'Think I didn' see you tonight primpin' yourself before that new fancy lodger from London?' He approached me steadily, and though I shot round the side of the bed and under it to avoid him, he had me out and over the sheets, pinning my hands across my back while his own great palm was stinging my flesh.

I'd had beatings before. I'd grown used to them in childhood. But this was different. I was so humiliated and angry, so burning with pain, I could've killed him.

When it was over he pushed me round on my back, where I lay glaring at him as he went to the wash basin, poured water and bathed his face. Then he slipped off his shirt and breeches casually, ambled towards me and got me under the sheets beside him.

For some time neither of us said a word. I could hear his heart thudding, and presently a thigh touched mine. I edged away. He laughed with a sort of sensuous amusement in his voice, then said in that maddening, cock-sure way of his, 'So now you know, love.'

I lay rigid and silent, refusing to acknowledge defeat.

'Come on now,' I heard him continue. 'Don't say you didn't like it? A real wild-cat you are, born and bred, and wild cats need taming.'

I turned my face away stubbornly.

'Judy,' he said more sharply, 'enough of that.' And when I still didn't reply, 'Judy ... *love.*'

I don't recall now just how things happened, but suddenly I was panting and moaning beneath him, with his lips warm and demanding on my temples, lips and breasts, and our two bodies pulsing together in the wild leap of fulfilment that was darker and more savage than any I'd dreamed of before, yet entirely physical, with nothing in it of tenderness or understanding.

Looking back now I think it was from that moment that things became a little different between us. Passion became intensified and yet in a queer way more objective. I'd no illusion about Matt any more. We were as necessary to each other as rain and storm to the earth, and winter to summer. But some of the magic and mystery of mutual discovery had gone. I knew what to expect; so did he. I really believe that everything he had to give a woman was mine. But there were secret places in his life I couldn't share. I realized this instinctively, and though I'd have resented it earlier, I didn't any more.

I loved him, of course. He was my husband, my man. But sometimes, just occasionally, I found my thoughts taking a more romantic turn, recalling youthful wanderings over the moors in bluebell time—pictures that rekindled the vision of being a fine madam like Lady St Heriot living in her splendid mansion, Castlegwarran.

Marry a rich man, my grandmother had said. Well, I'd done the best I could, but not for riches, since Matt, I was beginning to discover, was becoming increasingly cagey over monetary affairs. In any case, being the type of woman I was, I could never have tied myself up from mercenary motives. All the same, as high summer turned to autumn, Matt's increasingly silent moods frequently made me uneasy. With dispersal of the guests, he seemed to lose interest in his boat and spent much of the daytime on the beach or looking out to sea from our cobbled front yard, as though expecting something.

By the end of October I began to resent his apparent indifference. We'd got rid of the girl Carmel by then and I'd only Jane to help me. There was a great deal to do in the house, and when Matt suggested we started taking in night lodgers once more I questioned tartly, 'You mean sea-faring gentlemen?'

He shrugged. 'What's the matter with them? You married one.'

'I know. And sometimes I wish ...'

'You hadn't?' he interrupted. 'Well, I don't blame you. I suppose a man's always what he was born to, underneath, and I can no more get the salt out of my blood than stop breathing.'

Feeling as though my heart, like a great stone, had fallen into my boots, I said practically,

'I should've thought there was enough salt about here. You couldn't live nearer to the sea anywhere. And you've got your boat, haven't you? Why can't you go out and do a bit of fishing?'

His eyes, when he looked at me then, were those of a stranger, remote and questioning, with a sort of sad inevitability in them that chilled me.

'Boat?' he said. 'Call that puny smack a *boat?* and *fishing?* What would I want paddling about in the waves for a few measly herrings?'

'Measly,' I echoed. 'You don't call them that, Matt Thomas, when you're sitting to eat a good meal of them *prepared* by me, dished up all tastily with a nice clean cloth before you washed and *ironed* by me, on top of all the rest of the work I do. You say you didn't aim to marry a scold. But what do you expect when you do nothing but stare and mooch about most of the time, longing to be away. Oh yes ...' I continued breathlessly, 'I've seen it in your face, and in your walk when you stride off down the pier every time a ship's expected. You're sick of it, aren't you, Matt? Of me, and life here, and having each day the same ...'

I broke off breathlessly with the blood hot in my face, each nerve in my body quivering with disappointment and a dread of what his answer would be.

I needn't have worried though, not then. Suddenly he came and took me in his arms again, all warm and caressing, with one hand travelling from my shoulders to buttocks, where it stayed briefly, pressing me against him. His voice was gentle, a kind of rich whisper, when he murmured against my ear, 'Not you, Judy. Never of you. Whatever happens in the future, love—and no one can tell what's ahead—you'll be a part of me, in me, and of me ... just as ...'

'Yes?'

He laughed. 'Just as that little black mole in your groin is part of *you.*'

'Oh Matt,' I said, relaxing. 'What a thing to say. Comparing me with a mole. Really.'

Releasing me sufficiently for him to have a good look at my face, he said reflectively, 'No. I reckon that mole's a kind of guarantee.'

'Guarantee?'

He nodded. 'Of faithfulness. Something only you and I know about. It's true, isn't it, Judy?'

I sighed, wishing for once that Matt's jealousy didn't always have to come up, spoiling things.

'You know it is,' I said. 'Why must you always be doubting me these days. You didn't at first.'

'It was different before,' he said shortly. 'You were a child—almost. Now you've come to full blossom I wonder how in hell sometimes I'm going to be sure of you. 'Specially if I take off again.'

'Take off? What do you mean?' I asked, with my voice shrill in my own ears.

He released me and walked to the window, staring out across the grey sea under the lowering yellow autumn sky. There were no large vessels in harbour, only a few long-liners and Breton fishing smacks with the dying light throwing a dull glow on their coloured sails.

'Yes?' I prompted him. 'Well?'

He turned.

'I may have to, Judy. We've got to live. The season here didn't pay as I thought, and I'm a qualified Captain. Good Captains are wanted for valuable cargoes. It seems commonsense I should take advantage of it.'

'You mean you've been planning something all along?' I queried with a risk of anger. 'Letting me think our life here was settled, and all the time you were aiming to be away ...?'

'No, no, love,' he assured me. 'Nothing's planned. And when—*if*—it is ... you'll know.'

In the long pause following, my mind darted this way and that, trying to puzzle things out, to find an answer, before Matt took everything into his own hands. At last I said recklessly, 'If you *do* go to sea again, couldn't I come with you? I'm tough, Matt, and used to hardness. I wouldn't be an encumbrance. I could help. Cooking perhaps, and doing things for the crew only a woman knows how.'

He laughed, not derisively, but like someone humouring a child.

'You don't know the first damn thing about men months away without the sight or feel of a woman around,' he said curtly. 'I wouldn't trust you or any of them an inch, and I wouldn't have time to be forever on your tracks seeing you didn't flash your skirts about. Women at sea are a curse, and that's that. Understand?'

'No,' I said coldly. 'But then I don't suppose that matters to you.'

'It doesn't,' he agreed. 'I've never been one to worry what goes on in a woman's mind, especially yours. So forget all this, Judy love. Come here ...'

Because of his manner and a certain note in his voice, I did what he said, and the next moment his lips were hot on mine and I surrendered myself to the inevitable truce of physical assuagement, though for the first time I found in it no peace or reassurance.

I knew I loved Matt as much as ever, but his changing moods gradually put a kind of shadow on me. I didn't feel sure any more of what the next hour or even the next moment would bring; it was as though, with the approach of winter, something seemed to be ending. It would have been easier if I could have questioned him more, tied him down. But Matt wasn't that kind of man. I never forgot what he'd said once shortly after our marriage: 'Don't try and handcuff me, girl. If you do, I'll be off quick as a puff of air. You got to trust me. See? If you don't, then there's nothing ahead for either of us.'

I'd tried to do as he'd said, and in those early days nothing had mattered except to have Matt near me with the hot, strange look in his grey eyes, his laughter rich about the house, and his lips pressed warm against my cheeks. I hadn't cared that the only security I had was in his hands; all I needed was just belonging to him and being able to forget the bothersome business of money and livelihood. But when

I discovered later what was going on in his mind about leaving, things gradually changed. I'd steal sometimes to where the little pile my grandmother'd left me had been hidden under the floorboards, and be filled with a sudden, quick panic. Guilt, too. She'd striven so hard to scrimp and slave so I'd have something to my name. Commonsense told me I should've kept my own fist on it. I could almost hear her saying in her harsh voice, 'You fool girl. Didn't I teach you nothin' after all? Did I work my guts out for 'ee to throw et all away on a man? Like your mother you are—an' you'll end up same way ...'

Of course it was all in my mind. But the gulls screaming overhead seemed to echo my own thoughts, whirling and crying over the harbour and chimney pots, filling me with a dread sense of foreboding; and I'd turn and rush away, determined to visit the bank the next day and find out how our joint account stood.

I never did though. Once I was back in Matt's arms, all doubts of him were swept aside and I'd tell myself to go prying into our affairs would only prove I didn't trust him. Besides, about that time something else happened that made me think my morbid premonition had nothing to do with Matt at all but were due to that extra sense of the Cornish, so often heralding great disaster.

There was a wreck.

The day had been cold but calm, giving no indication of gale ahead. The fishermen had been wary though and stayed mostly inshore, knowing as I did that waters so still and glassy under a windless sky could predict storm later. All the morning I'd found myself glancing out of the window inwardly tense and on edge. Matt, too, was restless.

'Gale coming, I shouldn't wonder,' he said once, staring out to sea. 'Think I'll take a stroll round the harbour. Such stillness isn't good.'

Although it was then afternoon with the meal cleared away, he didn't ask me to go with him or throw me a single glance. For all he cared, I thought with a stab of irrational jealousy, I mightn't be there—and the knowledge hurt. But I'd learned when to hold my tongue so I kept silent and presently saw his sturdy shape swinging down the wharf towards the Seamen's Lodge.

At five thirty he hadn't returned, and by then the wind was rising, driving the waves with increasing speed to a fury of darkness and spattered foam about the rocks and ancient quay. The twilight sky blackened suddenly to deepest night, lit only briefly by an occasional break in the sullen clouds.

Then the rain came, sweeping, slashing, blurring the wild vista to tortured, wanton uniformity. Immense breakers pounded the sea wall and over it, hurtling against windows and walls of cottages. Small craft in the harbour were tossed from their moorings and taken as so much flotsam by the greedy tide. Behind the window of his cottage at the corner of Fish Street, old Abraham Daniels, white-bearded and stern-eyed, prayed from the Bible before him. During his ninety-nine years he had seen many other such storms, few without claiming one victim or many.

About six the tragedy happened. A merchant-man from Liverpool was swept off course and crashed on to the jagged Black Sisters rocks only a mile to the north-west of Port Einack. She was a vessel of about 300 tons, carrying, besides a crew of sixteen, a number of passengers. As soon as the vessel was sighted, activity started in the harbour, and the sound of men's voices mingled with the wind's roar and crash of the waves. From the front window I watched the crew of the small lifeboat board it, then saw it launched determinedly and taken by the oncoming breakers before properly afloat. It was righted again with assistance from the shore, and on the moment of taking off Matt's figure was on the scene, being helped over the side.

Panic rose in me as I rubbed the window frenziedly. Then, in a rush of fear, I flung a shawl over my head and ran out into the rain. There were others there, some already praying for rescuers and the rescued—if any.

Lights bobbed and dazzled briefly through the watery inferno, and the anxiety in my heart was as frenzied and desperate as the wild onslaught of the elements. My lips moved automatically with those of the others whose sons and husbands had undertaken the desperate mission. But prayer, I felt, could be meaningless in such a holocaust, which demanded first of all sufficient skill and courage to keep such a comparatively puny craft afloat.

Later—how much later I didn't know—the lifeboat returned, followed by a fishing smack that had set off with another on the tail of the rescue operation. There was no sign of the second, or its brave little crew, and I guessed without having to be told that there never would be again.

When the sky lightened a little, the hulk of the vessel could be glimpsed as a black shape stark and half submerged by the teeth of the dreaded Sisters. Bodies were being carried ashore and brought speedily to the inn and surrounding cottages for sustenance and immediate emergency treatment.

Of the seven passengers four were saved, though two died later. Ten men of the crew's sixteen survived. And Matt was there ...

'Matt ... oh Matt ...' I cried, rushing towards him as his dripping figure emerged through the crowd carrying something that looked like a woman in his arms. 'You're safe ... Thank God ...'

His voice was harsh and cold in the wind when he shouted, 'Many aren't, so have done with your thanks, girl, and go get drink and food ready for this poor sick creature. And a fire. Stir your stumps, for the love of Pete ... Hurry.'

I saw through the bad light that his eyes stared hard in his dead white face. Blood flowed from one temple to his jaw. The whole air seemed to reek of it—blood and salt and a terrible dark despair.

I fled before them to the house, poked the fire and brought brandy from the cupboard with biscuits, a cheese and some broth from the hob.

When Matt struggled through the door and laid his bundle down I saw I had been right. It was a woman he carried, quite elderly, with a sunken, yellowish face under a bedraggled matt of grey hair. At first I doubted she'd survive another hour, but miraculously she did. After a night in our house, between blankets heated by hot bricks, with stimulant and a little food inside her, she was taken next day to the nearest hospital for a time of necessary convalescence. I never knew her name or who she was. Her memory had gone. Whether she recovered it or not was no longer our affair. I'd lived far too long by the sea to fret over its secrets, knowing that whatever the will of man it would retain its own and that there was no power on earth able to quell it once its course was set.

Following the tragedy the weather settled down to calm and quiet again but Matt seemed overstrung and ill at ease. He helped salvage some of the cargo of the wrecked boat, which included calico, silk, wines and bacon, and during that brief period he seemed almost his old self again. Afterwards, though, a curious, remote air of retrospection settled on him, a mood I somehow couldn't penetrate or fully understand.

'It's no use, Judy love,' he said one afternoon, crossing to the parlour window with his eyes once more turned as they so often were on the grey sea. 'It's there I should be ... I belong to it. Not here spreading the blarney among sightseers or playing at boats like a child. What have you done to me, girl? Eh?'

He turned, placing both hands on my shoulders, with his black eyes staring darkly into my own.

'Oh Matt,' I murmured, 'please don't. Don't talk that way.'

His lips came down on mine, soft yet demanding, draining all life and energy from me. Then he carried me upstairs and made love. But somehow it was not the same.

We got a few night-boarders that November, although the regulars we used to have in my grandmother's day had found lodgings somewhere else when we took to the guest house business. I knew this depressed Matt, and he was itching for more company and contact with fellow sea-farers. He began to drink more than he used to, and sometimes when he came back at nights there'd be the hot stench of spirits on his breath. At those times I prayed he'd let me alone and go straight to bed before the thought of wanting me got into him. But it never happened like that. The rum only seemed to put the fire into his blood so he'd pull my skirt when I tried to avoid him, saying, 'Come on now, Judy. You're mine, aren't you?' And when I didn't answer, he'd said, 'That's right, love. See you remember.' I'd hold myself stiff then until he'd got me close, smothered against him, with such a mixture of feelings in me, he soon had his way.

The next morning, looking a bit shamefaced and somehow curiously young, like a great overgrown boy, he'd apologize and ask me to forgive him.

Naturally I did. I always forgave Matt, until the last time. The time Topaz appeared.

Matt was out somewhere, seeing to his boat he told me, though I guessed he'd look in at the Kiddleywink before he got back. Jane had the afternoon off, and the early evening was closing to twilight when I heard a thump on the front door. Knowing a merchant vessel had put into harbour less than an hour ago, I ran from the kitchen, thinking it might be a sailor wanting a room.

I got a shock. A rather large woman wearing a thick blanket sort of thing over a flowered dress stood there, holding a small boy by the hand. On her head was a bonnet, and although the light was poor I saw at a glance she was dark-skinned, stout and smiling affably as though we were old friends.

'Well?' I said sharply, annoyed at the intrusion because I had been in the middle of baking.

'Mas Thomas live here?' she questioned in a deep voice that had a certain accent about it I'd noticed in some of my husband's friends. 'Cap'n Matt Thomas?'

'That's right,' I answered shortly. 'What do you want? Can I help you? I'm ...'

'Oh no, ma'am. Not you,' she interrupted before I could finish. 'It's the Cap'n. Very important business, ma'am.'

'Oh,' I paused before adding, 'he's not in.

If you came back later, in an hour or two, he should be here. I'll tell him you called ...'

'Can't we wait, ma'am? We've come a *long long* way, me and Wellington. We's tired an' hungry. I pay you, see ...?'

I hesitated, 'Oh, I don't know ...'

'Please, ma'am.'

In the end I agreed, knowing that if she really was a friend of Matt's he'd be annoyed if I turned her away.

'Come in then,' I said grudgingly. 'I'll make you a pot of tea and you can sit in the front parlour. What's your name, by the way?'

'Topaz,' she said.

'Topaz what?'

She smiled broadly but with a knowing look to her black eyes that mildly discomforted me.

'Jus' Topaz,' she echoed. 'An' this is Wellington.'

The little boy was staring up at me with huge solemn eyes, so dark they were almost black; a good-looking child, paler skinned than his mother, with an old-fashioned air about him that slightly irritated me. And Wellington! What a stupid name, I thought as I ushered them into the parlour. But obviously Topaz had decided on the grandest name she could think of, hoping her offspring would one day merit it.

Before I went to the kitchen I lit the lamp and had a clearer look at the odd couple. Topaz was certainly striking and in her first youth could have been a beauty. But her figure had gone ponderously to seed, and a double chin marred the fine structure of her cheekbones and jaw line. Her hair was coarsely lustrous and black and her lips, though thick, firmly carved. As for her eyes, there was something in them I didn't like; something shrewd and covetous despite her apparent naïvety which didn't fool me for one moment. I knew, without being told, that her business with Matt would be very much to her own advantage if she got her way. And I resented it.

'Sit down,' I said abruptly. 'If you want a paper to look at ...'

She didn't let me finish but with a gust of laughter and jangle of her immense dangling ear-rings said heartily, 'Lor', ma'am. We don't go in for reading, Wellington or me. Just a cup of tea, ma'am, that'll sure be 'preciated.'

Beneath the cold, darting stare of her black eyes her sensuous lips widened into a huge grin, displaying a flash of incredibly white teeth.

I turned quickly and left them sitting there, almost running to the kitchen before my temper get the better of me and I ordered her out with a flurry of hot words I'd learned from my grandmother. She'd no right in my home, I told myself stubbornly as I put the kettle on and prepared a tray with saffron cake, a jug of milk, cups and saucers, and had the teapot ready by the stove. What did she want with Matt anyway? For that matter, what would *any* woman want of my husband except the one thing she couldn't have?

I tried to make light of the matter in my mind, but underneath a niggle of doubts and tormenting thoughts haunted me. Half an hour later, when Matt arrived, I knew I had cause.

His face looked blank at first when I told him, but I could sense his brain darting this way and that behind the narrowing grey eyes, like an animal searching for escape, when he echoed, '*Topaz?* Did you say *Topaz?*'

'Yes,' I told him. 'But don't pretend you've no knowledge of her. She wouldn't act like she does if you hadn't.'

'*Act?* What the devil do you mean?'

'Go in and see,' I said primly. 'I'm sure she'll soon tell you.'

I glanced through the mirror hanging near the sink, smugly patting my hair into place and smiling a little at having Matt for once at a disadvantage. I was wearing a yellow cotton dress with a tight waist and full skirt, half-covered by my grandmother's embroidered black satin apron. I knew it suited me and for a wild moment hoped Matt would be so stirred by the effect that he'd send Topaz packing the moment he set eyes on her black face.

But he didn't. Although I left them to themselves, hoping against hope the matter between them might have something to do with Nick Jago or other acquaintances of his from foreign parts, I knew from the tone of their voices behind the door that there was something far more personal going on.

At times, though I shouldn't have, I crept to the crack between the hinges and listened, with a dull, heavy kind of rage welling up in me. She was whining and cajoling, and then there was a muffled sort of murmur, followed by a laugh and a little squeal with Matt's voice shushing as much as he could.

At last I could bear it no longer. I burst in, saying with a harsh edge to my voice, 'Haven't you finished yet? Isn't your business over?'

Matt first looked stupefied, then suddenly violently angry, the hot blood in his face draining away only to return again more vividly as the veins thickened on his forehead.

'Get out, Judy,' he said in the hard, cold voice I dreaded. 'This isn't your affair.'

'It isn't hers either,' I said recklessly. 'What right has she here at all? You tell me that, Matt Thomas.'

He didn't have a chance, because Topaz, drawing herself up to her bulky full height, answered in loud, throaty tones.

'Every right I have, ma'am, seeing as I'm his lawful wedded wife, and Wellington here his true son.'

Wife? Son? For a moment I couldn't accept what she'd said. The room darkened and swam round me; I reached for the table and stood there, propping myself up helplessly while things gradually came into perspective again. It's a picture I'll never forget: the woman, gaudy and formidable in her garish clothes, standing there motionless like some giant, dressed-up creation carved in ebony, with the bewildered, frightened-looking child clutching her hand. Matt, too, was temporarily motionless, as though no word or movement from him could have meaning any more.

Then suddenly the spell was broken. He

strode towards me, taking me by the shoulders and telling me to be still as my whole body shook from chattering jaws to the soles of my feet.

'I can explain,' he said. 'Control yourself. You don't understand ...'

'Understand?' My voice caught in my throat in a harsh whisper. 'Oh I understand all right. I didn't, but now I do ...'

'Judy, Judy ...'

With a tremendous effort I pulled myself away, at the same time giving him such a push he fell against the table, smashing the milk jug that caught his hand and cut it.

Matt lifted the hand to his mouth, watching me all the time as though he could kill me. And I didn't care, not one bit. At that moment I hated him, because I knew with my inherited extra sense and the odious woman's self-assurance that what she'd claimed was true. Matt had married her.

There was a long pause, how long I didn't know. In my overwrought state I could not judge such things. But presently Matt's first anger seemed to die sufficiently, and he said in cold tones, 'Topaz and Wellington will be staying for the night. See a room's ready. I'll talk to you later. Meanwhile ...' he turned to Topaz, 'you and I and the boy'll take a stroll round the harbour. I've a call to make at a dram house. When we get back I'll see you have a better welcome.'

Fury died into amazement in me, as he took the woman's arm pointedly, ushering her and her son into the hall and out through the front door. When they'd gone, the trembling started up in me again. I felt physically sick. My heart was thudding so heavily against my ribs I had to sit down for fear it'd burst. The conceit of him, I thought through my shame. The arrogance and cold-blooded lies. After all he'd said and done to get me to wed him, nothing of it had been true. He'd treated me no better than a harlot ... a whore. A whore as my mother had been.

Oh God! From anger my feelings suddenly turned to despair. I'd never felt so exhausted in my life, and never had my future looked so hopeless. *I'd loved Matt,* loved him. Overbearing he'd been sometimes, but I'd accepted it because he was a Captain used to disciplining his men. There'd been angry times when he'd laid his hand on me, but I hadn't cared because having him want me was the only thing that mattered; and anyway it was true I could be a wild one when the mood was on me and my temper hot. But this! ... *this* ... to have him ordering me about as though I was a servant to dance attendance on that dark creature, the one he'd lusted with before me ... I couldn't, *wouldn't* do it.

Presently, after taking a double dose of the whisky from Matt's desk, I went upstairs and saw that every room except Jane's was in as fine a mess as I could make it, then I locked myself in the one Matt and I shared, flung myself on the bed, and waited.

Perhaps I dozed a bit, I don't know. My head was so swimming nothing seemed real or clear any more. It didn't occur to me that a mistake *could* have been made and that Matt might have a reasonable excuse for what had happened. If I'd started doubting I'd have been nowhere. In the hysteria of reaction nothing registered but Matt's treacherous duplicity. So when, later, I heard the sound of doors opening and shutting below, followed by footsteps on the stairs and Matt and Topaz talking together, I hadn't a qualm about what I'd done, although it hadn't been pleasant throwing grandmother's precious relics about and seeing her best quilts all rumpled on the floor. One or two ornaments had been broken, I knew that; the sound of them smashing was still ringing in my ears. But the loveliest and most valuable, a china angel, was held safe on my breast where I lay. I was pleased about that and, remembering some of the others, felt a slow mounting sadness that brought the threat of tears and a lump to my throat.

Then, keyed up to meet Matt's inevitable reaction, I stiffened myself to coldness again. It was minutes—maybe a quarter of an hour, or even longer, following muffled comments and clicking of latches—before it came.

There was a sudden rattle of the door-knob, a thumping and banging, with Matt shouting, 'Judy, open up. Hear me, you little hell-cat ...'

I didn't answer. I lay there stiff as a ramrod with my heart thudding triumphantly but uneasily until he began again, a little quieter this time, 'Judy, d'you want me to kick the door down? I will, you know, if there's any more of this.'

A pause, and then, 'My God! If I have to

break in you'll be sorry for it. And I mean it. You know me, don't you ... Judy, Judy ...'

There were several more kicks, then an interval of silence, followed by running footsteps that faded temporarily, only to return a moment or two later, then a shuddering impact as something with tremendous force shattered the wood. Matt had burst in, white-faced and strained, one knuckle bruised and torn from the pounding. He had an arm round a piece of iron, and I could see in the lamplight the sweat pouring from his forehead. Just for a second or two he stood staring at me. I forced myself to sit up, both hands across my chest. I remember thinking perhaps he'd kill me and that it really wouldn't matter if he did since there was nothing left for me any more. But he made no movement at first; he didn't even speak; he just let the iron bar fall to the floor, while he went on staring and staring, with a half-speculative, half-condemning look in his eyes. Then suddenly both hands were on my shoulders and he'd forced me back against the pillow, with his face so near to mine his breath was hot on my skin.

'Listen,' he said, 'you know what you deserve, don't you? And any other time you'd damn' well get it. But just for once, by God, you're going to hear what I've to say and keep your mouth shut, even if I have to gag you. Understand? Afterwards ... well, that depends.'

His grip tightened. The nails bit into my flesh as he continued, 'You think I married you when I was properly wed to Topaz, don't you? Well, in a manner of speaking, it's true. But not in the way you ...'

'There ...' I shouted. 'You admit it. I knew ... I *knew* ...'

He slapped my face sharply. 'Shut up, Judy. You know *nothing*, nothing at all of the world beyond your own smug little front door. Think I lived as a monk all those years away at sea? You're no fool. Naïve you may be but no fool. I've had women, of course I have, or I wouldn't know the way to set your pulses hammering the way they do. Any man worth his salt starts to learn things early and takes what he can along the way ...'

'Topaz?'

'Topaz was different. She mattered at the time. She was warm and kind, with a lot of love and laughter in her. We came to a sort of arrangement ...'

Unwittingly I heard myself laugh harshly, sneeringly, before shouting, *'Arrangement?* That's a fine way to put it. I suppose when you married me *that* was an arrangement, too? Very convenient.'

'Stop it,' he said. 'And take that ugly look off your face. I was just trying to explain, trying to get into your stubborn head that marriage to Topaz wasn't the same as yours and mine. Not in any sense. We had a ceremony, yes ... sort of ... to make her feel good, and on account of her folk and the boy, that's all ...'

'Wellington,' I said with dull sarcasm.

'Yes. Wellington. He's my son, Judy, whether you like it or not, and now they're here I'm not having them sent away without a bit of warmth or friendship. I didn't ask them. But Topaz had a bit of trouble, and when Jago let on where I was, she took off the next day to find me. Is that my fault?'

'Yes. *Yes it is,'* I told him, almost screaming. 'Everything's your fault ... *everything.* If I'd known your liking for bedding black women, d'you think I'd ever had given you a second glance, Matt Thomas? You make me sick and shamed. *Dirtied*—d'you understand?—you and your bastard. How many more are there, Matt? One on every island, is that it? Or two? Maybe three—yellow, black, white ...'

On and on I went, shouting and abusing him, lapsing into my native Cornish dialect as the angry torrent of words poured out. I expected him to stop me somehow, to strike me or put his hand over my mouth, but he didn't. He just stood there watching with a look on his face I'd never seen before ... hard and bitter as though the wind had seared it. Then, when the breath had gone out of me, leaving no more to be said, he got to his feet and asked, 'Have you done?'

I didn't reply at first, not until he went on, 'It's settled then. From now on you're going to act sane. No more shouting or abusing Topaz. A little friendliness and decent behaviour. Then when I've made things right for her and the boy and they're off back to where they belong, we can try and forget all this.'

He paused and in that short silence the anger swept up in me again because of the light and easy way he spoke, his casual manner of dispensing with the episode as though it was a mere bundle of rubbish to be dumped and forgotten. Well, I'd never forget. Never, *never.* I wasn't that kind of woman, not the light sort to put up with his cheap trash in my own home. Maybe the same sort of thing had happened to my mother. She could have been like me in the beginning, trusting and ripe for love, believing in a man until he'd let her down just as Matt had now. So I didn't soften or smile or let his lips touch me, though God alone knew that was all I really longed for.

'Get away,' I snapped shrilly when he put out a hand towards my face. 'Don't touch me. I *loathe* you, Matt Thomas. The very sight of you makes me sick—*sick* and shamed that I could've been fooled so long. Kill me if you like, I don't care ... not for anything any more. But get out of here. It's *my* house and I'm not having any foreign whore of yours biding in it ... nor your bastard kin either. It's over. D'you hear? I'm done, *done* with you ...'

Because the tears were so thick against my eyelids I turned my face away, smothering it into the pillow. The silence was deadly except for the clock ticking on the mantelpiece. I steeled myself for an angry spate of words, even blows from him, but nothing came. The pause seemed interminable until, as though from a long distance away, I heard his voice in cold, flat tones saying, 'Very well, if that's what you want I'll certainly oblige.'

I glanced up in time to see his broad

back silhouetted momentarily against the wan lamplight near the door. Then the latch clicked and I was alone, free at last to let the sobs come thick from my throat. In spite of his conduct I knew my words had been unforgivable, the sort most calculated to shame a man to the quick. *My* house. *His* bastards. But I hadn't meant it the way it sounded, and he'd know. In time he'd come round and see things in proper perspective. He must, he *must,* my heart cried all through that long terrible night.

But in the morning I knew I was wrong. When I went down for breakfast, after bathing my face well with cold water, there was no sign of him, nor of Topaz and Wellington.

I asked Jane as casually as possible if she'd seen the Captain and thought she eyed me curiously before answering, 'No. No one at all. But the bedrooms are in a fine mess. Was there trouble last night, mistress?'

'If you'd been back on time, you'd have known there was,' I told her, relieved all the same that she hadn't. 'Quite a scene, in fact. I expect my husband's gone out to ... to ... well, get the p'lice perhaps,' I ended vaguely.

Whether she believed me I couldn't tell. Anyway it was unimportant. Only one thing registered just then: Matt had gone. Perhaps never to return.

For the first time I wondered how I was going to bear it.

CHAPTER 4

Following Matt's departure I seemed to live in a kind of dream, eating, working, and sleeping, hardly aware of it, although when a week had passed and he still hadn't come back it slowly dawned on me that I really was on my own, with no one else to depend on; no one to take me in his strong arms, assuring me all was going to be fine and I needn't worry about a thing; no one to laugh and be with at nights or to flood me with the comfort of just being near; no one to love.

And yet I still did love him. I tried not to. At times I almost made myself believe I didn't, but beneath my cold exterior, memories lay deep and hungry, always waiting for a chance word or act to quiver them to life again. So except when I was tired or in a weak, unsuspected moment, I forced myself to do practical things, making a fetish of work; scrubbing out the house with Jane's help, having the rooms got ready again for sea-faring gentlemen, painting, putting the notice up, and getting sufficient food in and as much prepared as possible for any unexpected call. Every week I took something from the cash-box Matt and I had kept locked away for safety, and this, with what was left of my grandmother's savings, covered immediate expenses. There was no need yet to call at the bank. When I'd anything to put in, I thought, I'd go.

Sometimes I caught Jane looking at me with a queer, questioning look on her face, a sort of resentment, too, that made me realize I might be driving her too hard.

Once I said to her sharply in what Matt had called my shrew's voice. 'What's the matter with you? Work you too hard, do I? Well, if you're not satisfied, say so and go. Anyone who stays with me's got to pull her weight and a bit extra. And don't expect a rise, because the money's not there to give.'

The girl shrugged. 'I'm not complainin', mistress. But when are these gentlemen you talk about goin' to appear?'

'Oh. So *that's* what interests you. *Men!*'

She shrugged. 'There edn' much else round here to scrimp and slave for, es there? An' since the Cap'n left, there's not bin much fun 'bout the place.'

I was about to check her audacity when her looks, for the first time, clearly registered on my mind. She had a plumpish but well-formed figure with a small waist above full hips, swelling breasts under the red cotton bodice, and masses of lustrous black hair framing her vivid face. Her eyes, thick-lashed and dark brown, had a limpid sensuality in them that matched her pouting lips, moist and red as autumn berries.

At the moment she was lovely, tempting to any man with the heat of desire in him. Ten years on, though, she'd be stout and cumbrous and domineering, probably, with no charm anymore to set male hearts afire. Who could blame her for wanting some fun now.

I shrugged, suddenly sorry for her.

'They'll come,' I said. 'If you stick by me they'll be scratching round you like a crowd of sparrows after a tasty tit-bit in no time. Soon as we're known again. But you watch your step, Jane. Keep your head and see you *use* men, don't give them so much as a crumb until you're *sure.*'

'I can look after myself,' she said.

'You may think so,' I said, 'but thinkin' gets you nowhere. Nor dreams either.'

As I spoke it was as though my grandmother was in me, goading me to hard speech and bitterness. What cultured veneer I'd striven for and acquired during my youth and brief time with Matt was suddenly shattered by the crude instincts of self-preservation.

I went upstairs presently and took a good look at myself in the large mirror, with my hair drawn back severely and eyes hard in my set face. It was as though in that short time spring and summer had suddenly withered into winter, leaving a coldness there as hard and relentless as the grey seas pounding against the granite coast. I knew then I'd somehow have to get the hatred out of me and learn, even without Matt, to become a woman again. For what use was life without warmth and joy in it? What glory in fighting a battle that took femininity and beauty away?

I loosened a few silky copper strands of hair about my temples and lifted a hand to my cheek, rubbing warmth into it until a faint colour stained the taut flesh. Then I smiled and youth returned. But the smile was a mockery. Oh Matt, I thought, why did it have to be like this? recalling with an almost unendurable stab of pain the countless times he'd lain with me and loved me, bringing my spirit and body to full, sweet flowering. I think those times were the worst. The times I started remembering.

But after that outburst I made myself more patient with Jane, keeping a careful hold on my tongue. Whatever else I'd lost, I was determined to regain my woman's pride, reserving the shrewish, cold exterior and ways only for those occasions when the sailors started coming back and wanted more of me than they ought. Then I was hard as any man, with a look in my eyes and words ready to set the fear of God into them if they so much as tried the slightest liberty.

So in a way I was two people: one the woman filled with repressed, hungry longing, the other shouldering a man's role because I felt I had to.

Once Jane said to me, 'You're doing too much heavy work, mistress. Why don't you get Boney One-Eye to help with the casks an' liftin'? He's always glad to earn a penny or two, and would be more than willing.'

Yes, I thought, she had a point there.

Boney was a bit of a simpleton, the result probably of too much inbreeding, with a shuffling limp and a rolling glass eye where a natural one had been knocked out in childhood. A 'character', visitors thought him.

But he was more than that; strong as a bull, with a round-shouldered form that reached six feet even then and tremendous arms capable of knocking two men sprawling at one blow. Not attractive in any way, but he could be an asset, scaring troublemakers away; though he was mild-tempered by nature, he'd go all out to protect anyone he'd a liking for, and I knew he liked me.

So I took up Jane's suggestion and hired Boney One-Eye to work several hours in the afternoons and evenings for a sum that wasn't large but sufficient to earn his eternal gratitude and co-operation.

As Christmas drew near sea-faring gentlemen were filling our rooms again, thanks to my grandmother's reputation for providing good fare and the fact that I knew as well as any how to bake and make a satisfying meal for hungry men.

There seemed no reason why life shouldn't continue that way indefinitely except for one thing, a feeling of sickness in me sometimes—physical as well as mental—that made me long to be away, to be rid of tormenting memories and the restricted life of my own small town. Every time there was a thump on the door my stomach lurched, sending my heart bounding and causing a faintness and a terrible longing mixed with the fear it might be Matt. With every vessel that put in to port in the harbour I half-expected to see his familiar form swinging up from the pier and across the sands; and when it didn't, I was both relieved and heavy with disappointment at the same time.

Once I left Jane for a whole afternoon to deal with things on her own and set off for the moors at the back of the town. It was January, and cold, but in sheltered places the pale young fronds of bracken were already showing through last year's decay, and even an odd primrose or two.

At the top of Rozzan Hill I sat on a lump of rock near the cromlech, where two sea-gulls rose squawking into the air. The cold winter light over the sea, Gwythack way, was blinding, and for a moment I felt dizzy, unable to distinguish between the huddled rooftops of Port Einack and Gwythack sands to the right. My heart was pounding. Everything receded into temporary darkness, then I recovered and knew what I'd suspected for the last two weeks was true. I was with child.

How long I stayed there I don't know. I was shivering when I got up at last to make my way down. The wind had freshened, and the cold air blew against my face, with the warning of storm to come. Jane was waiting for me when I reached the house.

'You look all wisht,' she said. 'I was wond'rin' where you bin so long. "Mebbe the buccas've got her," I says to meself, an' me with a houseful of sailormen to deal with on my own.'

I forced a smile. 'Sorry. You get a mug of tea for yourself and I'll carry on from here. A house *full* did you say?'

She nodded. 'But there's no need to fret. The rooms are all straight and tidy 'cept for their bundles and the men's stuff. Well ... I'm not so sure about *men's* exactly. I've got somethin' to show 'ee ...'

She ran upstairs and was back again as quick as the flash of a lamb's tail with an orange shawl over her arm, embroidered in a design of dragons and birds in silver and green silk thread. And I remembered the days when Matt used to come laden with gifts for me.

'Pretty,' I remarked, trying to stab the wave of irrational jealousy suddenly filling me. 'But you put it away safe now, and don't wear it till the one who gave it you's gone. Have no softness for him either, nor feelings of gratitude. Take what you can, but give nothing; that's the way for a woman to get on in the world and be safe. Soon as you show you've a heart, bits of it will be nipped away until there's nothing left.'

In a wave of weakness, much to my disgust, I started to cry. It was the first time I'd given way to sobs since Matt left, and they were great, gulping, shuddering things that shook my whole frame. It seemed they'd never stop.

Jane got me to the kitchen, pushed me into a chair and went for brandy.

'You drink that, mistress,' she said, pushing a glass to my lips. 'And don't you go talkin' about work. It'll be a time before you're fit for anything much from the look of you.'

'I'm all right,' I said, feeling gradually eased by the warmth of the fire and spirit inside me. 'You mustn't fuss. I walked too fast and too quick to the moors and back, that's all.'

'Fiddlesticks,' Jane said, continuing after a

long, shrewd look. 'There's more to it than just the walk, isn't there? An' *you* don't weep for nothin'.'

'No. Not usually.'

'You can't fool me either,' the girl continued relentlessly. 'You're expectin', aren't you, mistress?'

I was suddenly angry.

'What's that to *you?* It's not your business.'

'I reckon it is though,' Jane told me stubbornly. 'There's the future to look to. At the moment Boney One-Eye and me can shoulder what you can't, but after that? We'll have to get extra help then, mistress. Runnin' this place edn' easy. I'm not afraid of hard work like that other one you had, Carmel. But work in the fish cellars would be easier than carrying the load of this place on my own ...'

'I don't intend you should,' I answered tartly. 'And the herring season doesn't start till July or August at the earliest. Still ...' I eyed her squarely, 'if you're trying to tell me you want to leave, do it now so I know where I stand.'

'I *don't* want to leave,' Jane said quickly, 'an' I wasn' aimin' to upset you, but with you as you are we've got to be practical. That's all.'

Practical. Yes. What she said was true enough, and the fact was rammed into me the following week when I had a letter from the bank asking me to call as the manager would like to see me.

Why? I wondered, staring at the piece of paper blankly. I hadn't drawn anything out; it wasn't as though I was owing them anything. Perhaps they'd got wind of Matt leaving and wanted to alter the account in some way. Yes, that could quite easily be the reason. But it wasn't.

When I reached the bank at eleven o'clock the following Monday, I knew as soon as the grim-faced clerk showed me into the manager's office that something was wrong. There was no welcoming smile from the portly figure behind the desk, none of the admiring glances I was accustomed to from men when I wore my best; and I'd been extra careful this time over my appearance, putting on my special, high-necked black dress under a red and black tartan cape and a small bonnet hat with a feather and strings to it. Ear-rings, too; true, carved jet handed down from my great-grandmother who'd been Spanish. I knew this because when I'd done something I shouldn't as a child my grandmother had blamed the foreign streak in me.

'True Cornish we are,' she'd said, eyeing me severely before the inevitable beating. 'Bred true through an' through my girl save for the bit of a devil in you from Grandma Luzana. It was your mother's downfall, but it shan't be yours, even if I wears my own arm away thrashin' it out.'

Sometimes I'd wondered about great-great-grandma Luzana, and when I saw myself through the glass before setting off that day to see Mr Bolus—William Bolus, the bank manager—it *did* seem to me I had an air about me not all Cornish. Maybe it was the new thinness I'd got through fretting over Matt. My eyes looked darker and seemed to flash more in my face which was hollowed slightly under the high cheek-bones and pale, giving me a haughty look that could have belonged to any great lady. And just for a second a queer thought struck me; queer because I wasn't one to delve deep into such things: behind any one face many others could lurk—the faces of those who'd gone before. Nobody was just like anyone else but made up of generations of different people, as my child would be when he was born. I knew somehow he'd be a boy. Like me mostly, perhaps, or Matt, or even the father I thought I'd glimpsed that day at the fair. Above all, though, he'd be *himself*, a human being capable of carving his own way through the years ahead. Oh yes; in those few seconds I wasn't only Judy Thomas but someone possessed by an instinctive culture and foresight I'd never thought I had in me. The next moment it had gone like a flash and I was walking out through my own front door, but with a new courage and air of grandeur that didn't desert me even when I faced the sour Mr Bolus over his desk.

'Good morning, Mrs Thomas,' he said primly. 'Do sit down and make yourself comfortable. What I have to say won't take long. It's about your account here.'

'Yes?' I said, with my chin high.

'You've put nothing in at all lately to help ease payments,' he went on as though he wasn't a human being but some sort of mechanical voice speaking from a primped-up mouth, 'and though we never wish to press such things, it would be a help if you gave some indication of how things are with you. Your current account is also in debit.'

'*Payments?*' I asked, quite at a loss to understand. 'Debit? I'm sorry, I don't know what you mean.'

He sighed before continuing more slowly but with an irritation I couldn't fail to notice. 'The *mortgage,* Mrs Thomas.'

'*Mortgage? What* mortgage?'

'My dear young lady, surely you're aware of what you signed with your husband concerning the house? Your name was on the document as a guarantee that, if necessary—meaning if debts were incurred you couldn't meet—the property would become the bank's to sell as an asset.'

The shock was so sudden that even then I couldn't properly take in what he was saying. I'd always signed what papers Matt put before me as a matter of course because he had a knowledge of such things whereas I'd had no experience of law and banks and the way they worked. I *did* recall, though, hearing him say once, 'If you put your name to this, Judy, it'll mean we can always get value for the house if we want it. It's a safeguard, see?'

No. I hadn't seen at all. *Then.* Now, under the penetrating chill stare of the plain little man confronting me, things began to fall in place, and I felt a mounting sense of shame and disgust at Matt's duplicity.

Fear, too. Fear of the threat to my own home: it could be sold because money was owed to the bank.

The high neck of my black dress seemed

to tighten, half-choking me. I swallowed hard before asking, 'What debts are you speakin' of, Mr Bolus?'

'Interest on the mortgage; in other words, the loan the bank allowed on your property, Mrs Thomas. It comes to ... let me see now ...'

He appeared to calculate, humming and coughing, with his eyes on a sheet before him, although I knew it was all pretence. He had the sum ready like a bomb to hit me. And when he did I nearly fainted.

'But ... but ... why didn't you say so before?' I asked. 'Why did you let me go on so long, believing everything was all right when it wasn't? We had a joint account, too, Matt and me. It was ...' I was going to say 'all my grandmother's savings' but stopped in time, not wanting to shame myself or Matt that much.

'Ah yes. But your expenses during the last year have been so high that any assets you had, I'm afraid, have been exhausted, and more, for some time,' the reasoning, cold voice went on. 'Whilst your husband was working and you were both engaged on what appeared to be a promising project, a little licence was permissible. Now I'm afraid ... well ...' he paused, continuing almost immediately ... 'forgive me for asking this, but I understand Captain Thomas has gone away and that your plans are changed. Do you mind telling me what you're going to live on in the future and how you hope to put back what is owed?'

The blunt question, together with the humiliating knowledge that William Bolus was probably fully aware of Matt's undignified exit—perhaps even of Topaz herself—stabbed me with such anger I got up, suddenly feeling the blood hot in my face as I said, 'Don't worry. Your debt will be paid. I've got quite a lot at the back of me you don't know about. A week or a fortnight and you'll have no need to fret yourself. I'm not one to owe money to any living soul, Mr Bolus. Least of all to *you.*'

Whether my sneer registered or not I didn't know, or why I made it, except to salvage my own pride. He was only doing his job. If he'd been a more approachable kindly sort of man with a shred of feeling in him, I might have acted differently. As it was, all I wanted was to have him squirming like a worm at the end of a line. So I tossed my head and with a tremendous show of bravado went to the door. He was just in time to open it for me.

'Good day to you then, ma'am,' he said. 'I shall expect to hear from you soon.'

'Quite soon,' I said, passing through with the manner of any great madam, as fine as Lady St Heriot herself.

The jet ear-rings jangled against my cheek as I made my way from the square to the wharf. It was a clear day but cold, with the fresh wind slapping my hot cheeks to wild fire. Most of the fishing boats were anchored in the harbour, with a schooner or two and several Breton boats making a splash of colour against the sea. As I walked to the house two fishermen in bright smocks and clogs pushed against me, with a spate of coarse language and ribald laughter. I had a smattering of their tongue, which was not so different from some of the native Cornish my grandmother had known. What they said was ugly and insulting, and just for a moment I forgot my new-found dignity and let fly with a flood of words equal to theirs, at the same time turning and giving the fattest a push that was as effective as a man's because it was so unexpected.

Taken by surprise like he was, the Breton fell back, tripped over the cobbles and landed on his back, to the great amusement of his friend. I watched them for a moment lurch away, leaving the stench of liquor in the air, and when I turned to go into the house, I almost ran into Boney One-Eye.

'Lugger 'en, shall I, mistress?' he said with the gleam of battle in his eye. 'You do say the word, ma'am, an' 'ee'll be sore laid flat as a tumbled pancake, that 'ee be fer sure ...'

'No no, Boney,' I said, putting my hand on his arm. 'Let him be. There are things more important to dwell on than a drunken Frenchman.'

That was true enough, I thought as I went, suddenly tired, to my room.

The wretched loan: how could I repay it?

As I unfastened my dress and let it fall to the floor, my mind wandered this way and that, trying to think out a solution. The night-lodgers weren't an answer, not on their own. I had to have something at the back of me to tide me over until a profit showed—and sufficient profit to keep the odious Mr Bolus satisfied. And I had to have it soon. Quite by chance I glimpsed my own reflection through the mirror: firm, high breasts above a narrow waist from where the starched white petticoat ... my best ... flowed out over rounded thighs. I remembered how Matt had admired my figure and how so many times his arms had slid round from behind, pinching my nipples till I squealed. The mere thought of it caused such a rush of longing I was jerked to sudden, renewed anger. 'Damn you, Matt Thomas,' I said aloud. 'Oh damn you, *damn* you.'

I tore off the petticoat, then picked it up with the dress and put it on the bed. After that I sauntered back to the glass, wearing only my vest and long, frilled drawers. What a sight I was to be sure—me clad like any circus clown yet still wearing the jet ear-rings any duchess could've been proud of. If I hadn't been so tormented, I'd have laughed. Still, thinking of the ear-rings gave me an idea.

Under the bed was a box with other small treasures, mostly handed down to me from great-great-grandmother Luzana. Some I knew were valuable: jewellery, including a small miniature in a fine gold frame that I'd been told was of Luzana herself as a girl.

When she'd handed it to me, my grandmother had said it was nothing she wished to look on again, but if I wanted it I could have it, as one day it might fetch a guinea or two. There were other things, too: a carved ebony rosary on a chain, an ivory statuette, several rings, a bracelet and a shred of chiffon and lace, so old it was almost falling to pieces. Luzana's wedding veil perhaps.

For some unknown reason I'd never shown them to Matt; I had held back perhaps because the extra sense of mine had unconsciously told me they were safer in my own keeping. Until Matt's disappearance they'd been hoarded with other knick-knacks on the top shelf of a wardrobe in the attic. If it hadn't been for my visit to Mr Bolus and wanting the ear-rings, they'd have been there now.

I took a long look first at the small painting, thinking how beautiful great-great-grandmother was, with piled-up black hair, a clear complexion and a double sort of lace frill round her neck above a square-necked green dress very low in the bosom. My grandmother had sniffed when she'd given it to me. 'All fancy bred and furrin she was, poor thing,' she'd said, 'who'd never've seen the coast of Cornwall 'cept for the wreck. Died soon's my mother wuz born, an' maybe 'twas for the best. Such folk doan' really fit in here.'

In my childhood I'd puzzled about her, as I had about my father, from time to time, but I had mostly kept my mouth shut because, although many Cornish families on the far west coast had a Spanish strain in them at one time, Spain had fought the English in drawn-out, bitter warfare and the Cornish had long memories of such things.

So the miniature had stayed hidden away until that day. I held it in my palm and stared at it. A guinea or two; it was surely worth more than that, I thought, as well as the bracelet and rings with the blue and green stones in them. I didn't know much about the value of such things, but it seemed to me if I sold the lot at the antique dealer's in Penzance I might make enough to keep Mr Bolus quiet for a few weeks or months to come. There was Matt's boat, too, which was comparatively new and in good repair. Fishermen were always wanting boats at a reasonable price.

The next day, after I'd helped Jane clean the rooms and seen the sailors safely out, I got Billy Trevean to take me with him to Penzance, with the treasures wrapped up safely in a bag and my heart bouncing as quick almost as his nag's hooves along the moorland road. It was a fine morning, with the wild hills lit to pale gold in the sun and the crows and gulls wheeling over the small stone-walled fields. Once or twice Billy tried to draw me into conversation over Matt, but I held him off with hazy remarks that told him nothing. People could *think* what they liked when I was out of earshot—and I'd no doubt tongues were already wagging about how the Cap'n had taken off—but what they didn't know they couldn't prove. If any fishermen had a shrewd idea, they'd hold their tongues because they were a close, loyal lot and not likely to spread news among the womenfolk.

Once in the town I left Billy to his own business for two hours and made my way straight to Chapel Street, where the shop was. I was wearing my best again, and I smoothed the skirt as well as I could before going in, pushing my hair close under my small hat so's to give me age and dignity.

At the last minute I kept the miniature back, pushing it away in my pocket, and handed only the bracelet and rings to the old man. He was bent, with a wrinkled, yellow skin like creased parchment, a hooked nose and jutting chin. His eyes above the spectacles were shrewd under bushy brows, and when he'd examined great-great-grandmother Luzana's knick-knacks he pretended at first they weren't worth much after all. My heart sank when he said, 'Pretty, but not really valuable, missis. I c'n give you a shillin' or two, maybe a guinea for the lot. But not a penny more.'

Though my heart was sunk like a stone to the pit of my stomach, my head acted quickly. If he was ready to give a guinea at the beginning, I thought, I could surely get four times the amount or more with a bit of bargaining.

So I started off, pretending I didn't care, even gathering the stuff up at one point to go, saying as haughtily as possible, 'All right, Mr Joseph, if that's all you can rise to I'll bid you good day ...'

I was almost at the door after further arguing, when he said, 'Here, wait a bit, ma'am. All right, all right, give me another look.'

After hesitating just long enough to have him worried, I walked back to the counter, and with a bit more humming and hawing and coughing, he put a pearl-handled magnifying glass to his eyes and said, 'All right. How much do you want?'

'Fifty,' I told him recklessly. 'Fifty solid gold pieces, Mr Joseph, and not a farthing less.'

I stood rigid, with my heart frozen from anxiety in case I'd put my foot in it properly and asked so much he'd withdraw any offer at all.

To my great astonishment he agreed as cool as you please, saying, 'All right, missis. You shall have it. Fifty it is. But ...' he said, eyeing me shrewdly, 'you're a hard bargainer, and a woman at that.'

'It's *because* I'm a woman,' I told him, trying not to show my satisfaction. 'I need the money, and I know, too, that what you have there is valuable.'

Still, I was amazed, quite stupefied really, as I walked up the street to the main road with the sovereigns safe in my bag. As I swung along towards the Ram and Bottle where I was to meet Billy Trevean, they clinked whenever I touched them. I was careful not to walk too quickly, in case thieves or cut-throats were around. Penzance on the whole was a respectable place, but when boats were in harbour from foreign parts you could never tell what greedy seaman was lurking round a corner to attack any female for what she had. I kept my face well hidden with the hat perched forward towards my nose and went at a steady pace as though I'd no responsibility or goods on me that any lusting male could want.

When I reached the inn I went through the door to a small parlour past the main bar, reserved, I noticed, for 'Ladies'.

With my background I didn't consider myself a lady by any means, but I *felt* it, so rich was I in pocket and wearing my best black, too.

A number of men, mostly farmers I supposed, were gathered in the taproom as I passed. I deliberately took no notice, but one face stared out from the others and caught my attention just for a second or two. I don't know why—but then it's always hard to explain what makes one certain person seem more important than the rest. There was nothing particularly handsome or striking about this man, except perhaps his eyes that were blue and had a kindly look, and maybe the fact that he was big—a bit portly, perhaps, with huge shoulders a little humped forward like those of a friendly ox. Yes, that's what I sensed—friendliness. Obviously well-to-do from the style and cloth of his clothes, a cut above the crowd gathered round, I thought, and when I heard someone address him as 'Squire', I knew I was right.

Still, it was no matter to me. I went on, without a second glance into the parlour, though I knew his eyes were following me.

There was no one else in the small room, and when a girl came asking me disapprovingly what I wanted to take, indicating I should have asked before I went in, I told her recklessly, 'A small port, thank you,' trying to sound grand, as though it was the most natural thing in the world for a fine lady like me to be taking port at a public house before mid-day.

When she'd gone I looked round. It was a small place and could have done with a good dusting and a window open. The air was thick with the smell of malt. The pictures on the walls were dreary lithograph things of the 'Battle of Trafalgar' and of a dying child saying her prayers before taking off to heaven. The sad yellow leaves of the aspidistra in its large grey-white china pot on the window sill needed a good wash with clean water, just as the dreary lace curtains did. As soon as I'd drunk my port, I thought, I'd go outside again and wait until Billy Trevean appeared.

When I went through presently, the big man was still sitting near the bar-counter, and I noticed how fresh-skinned he was, so pink-complexioned it made his eyes, which were slightly prominent, more blue than ever. He gave a faint smile with a slight inclination of his head as I moved on. Maybe I moved my own just a little, not wanting to appear impolite, but I didn't allow a single flicker of pleasure to touch my lips. Ladies, I felt instinctively, always held off until a day came when a proper introduction arose.

Anyway, it was hardly likely that my path would ever cross the Squire's again, although that, as it proved later, was the wrong conclusion to come to. As things turned out, one day not so far ahead, we were to meet under circumstances I'd never have dreamed of which were to change the whole of my life.

CHAPTER 5

On the day following my visit to Penzance I went to the bank and laid thirty guineas before the manager, having told the owlish-looking clerk behind the brass rails of the counter that my business was with Mr Bolus and no one but him. The high-an'-mighty manager looked more than surprised, and when he'd got over the first shock I could see he was wondering how I'd got hold of the gold and if everything was all legal.

I almost laughed in his face, but remembering my own dignity and my determination to behave as a lady in public, I just smiled, inclined my head, then lifted my skirt in one hand saying, 'There's more where that came from. If you want to see it, contact me and you're welcome.'

Before he could answer I'd sailed to the door and the next moment was outside.

After that I felt better, I had a good bit in my pocket, with the proceeds of Matt's boat, whenever I sold it, still to come. The feeling of being financially all square with things lifted my spirits like wine, until I remembered Matt himself. Then the longing came back, and I knew if he appeared at any of these weak moments I'd welcome him with warmth and tears, all ready to take him, forgetting what he'd done and put me through in the past.

But Matt didn't come back, and when March arrived bringing high seas and gales with sullen clouds giving place to intermittent sunshine sprinkled with fine rain, my heart told me he never would. The house was often full at that time, and Jane and I worked ourselves tired each day changing sheets and blankets, cleaning and cooking and preparing food for the evening.

On the whole the sea-farers weren't a bad lot; loud-mouthed and crude sometimes, but generally well-behaved, considering they were such a mixed crowd—Cornish, French, Welsh, Asian, and coloured men from all over the world. Mostly if any trouble arose it was between the Cornish and the Bretons, because their superstitions and language had much in common; and it was through an argument between a Frenchie and a Plymouth man that faithful Boney One-Eye landed in trouble.

In the morning it was, before the Plymouth boat set sail again that it happened. The Breton was just ready with his bundle to leave the house when the Cornishman strode up from the beach, one fist raised high in the air and carrying something into our yard that looked for all the world like a dead mouse. There must've been bad blood between the two men because I'd heard them arguing the evening before after returning from the dram-house.

As the Breton walked through the door a great fist swung into his jaw; he fell back against the wall, with such rage on his bearded face I thought surely one of them would be killed.

For a few moments they lunged and fought with a fearful thudding of fists yelling and shouting words I didn't understand or want to. Then when I could move I saw something lying on the step and when I peered closer discovered what it was. A hare's pad.

Everything was clear to me then, because anyone with true knowledge of fishing knew that the mere mention of a hare or rabbit when setting to sea or on it meant certain bad luck, just as seeing a clergyman was, at sailing time.

So I guessed the Cornishman had found the hare's foot on his deck or nailed to the mast and had come to revenge himself on the Breton for the ill-wished act.

By then the fight was getting worse. Blood was spurting all over the place, and when I tried to interfere, all I got was a great smack on the ear that brought an unladylike scream from me. It was then Boney One-Eye appeared. Like an immense bull he swung into them, knocking them sideways and not stopping them but pounding each one together and in turn until the oaths and yelling died into a mere sickening, groaning wail.

Jane, who'd come to watch, turned and suddenly fled back into the house. I'd have done the same if only Boney would have calmed down. But it wasn't until the two men were lying in a disgusting state on the cobbles that he desisted and, drawing an immense hand across his wide mouth, said, grinning, 'There, missis. That'll teach 'en.'

What he'd done, I knew, had all been for me. But he'd done too much.

One man, the Breton, was taken to hospital with a cracked skull; the other, minus his front teeth, made straight off to the law and lodged a complaint. The result was that Boney One-Eye had to appear before the magistrate on a charge of assault.

I don't like to remember the occasion now, or the strain it was having to be there, speaking up on his behalf. But if I hadn't, he'd almost certainly have landed up in gaol. As it was, he was let off on the condition he left my employ and went back to live with his old grandmother who kept pigs on the headland.

It was a sore blow to me. Already the child was developing strong in me, and heavy tasks put a strain on both of us. Jane wasn't ready to shoulder Boney's work; even if she'd had the will, I doubt she could have done it.

So there we were, two females left on our own to deal with a house full of strong men each night on top of the rest. I got the temporary help of a half-Irishman, Figgis, who was a reputed beach-comber and a bit else in the smuggling line. His mother who was Cornish, took in washing and lived in a shack in Angel Court off Love Street. Mostly he stayed with her. But he came to work for me only on the condition that apart from board and a wage I couldn't really afford, he had a room on the premises.

In desperation I agreed to allow him a small cubby-hole on the top far-back floor. It was a mistake. Only a fortnight had passed when I discovered him in my own bedroom one night, clad in just a night shirt, staring down at me with a candle in his hand. For a moment I was petrified, aware only of the long, pale face crowned by its thatch of gingerish hair and small, light eyes watching me with a certain look in them.

He put out a hand, touching my forehead and smiling knowingly, 'Pretty,' he said. 'Ah, Sure ye are now ... pretty.'

I suddenly became angry, inwardly cursing myself for forgetting to lock my door.

'Get out,' I hissed. 'You get out *now*. Take yourself off an' never come back, or I'll ... I'll *kill* you ...'

I waited breathlessly for him to move, but he didn't. So I suddenly sat up, took my own candlestick from the bed-side and threw it at his head.

Even then he didn't go, just dodged it neatly; and with the leer fading from his face into a look of hateful concentrated desire, he sprang upon me, half-pinioning me beneath his exposed and lecherous form while the candle fell to the floor and spluttered out. How I freed myself, I don't know; perhaps it was the bite I gave him. The taste of blood was on my lips when I tumbled myself out of bed and raced down the landing to the stairs. I tried to call Jane, but no words came. I knew he was already after me and that no one else would hear because the three lodgers had been deadened with liquor when they'd arrived late that night. So all I could do was run and run, and when I tripped on the stairs I just let myself roll until I landed at the bottom. There was a wrench of pain, a sudden shout from someone above—Jane, I think—and then all was darkness.

When I came to myself it was morning. The doctor was there, and Jane was bending over me.

'It's all right,' she said. 'That devil's gone. You're safe now, mistress.'

Gone? Yes.

But that wasn't all, as I soon found out. The baby'd gone, too—the one I'd secretly longed for, because he'd've been Matt's.

When I look back now on the time that followed it's hard to explain—even to myself—exactly how I felt. Only a drawn-out, awful emptiness seems to register, a loneliness beyond belief, that had no warmth in it or true feeling, just the nagging sensation that somehow I had to go on—though heaven alone knew why, since all that I cared about had been taken from me; Matt, my belief in him, the future we'd planned together, and the child inside me held so near to my heart.

'Buck up,' Jane said. 'There's another day tomorrow and lots after that. Some day you'll find a man worth lovin' an' then you'll wonder what all the agonizin' was about.'

I didn't have to wonder. I knew.

And though her words might make sense, to me just then they were mere mockery. I didn't answer when she was in that mood; I simply went on fiercely with my scrubbing and baking or whatever chore I was doing, until my arms ached and my whole body was so tired I fell into a heavy sleep when I went to bed.

Everything was all grind and rush, taking money in one week then paying out because the new man I'd hired asked more in wages, and on top of that, scrimping myself so I could put a bit in the bank, even though I had to get it out again more often than not.

By July funds were sinking and I told Jane she'd have to do with board and lodgings and nothing else until I was properly on my feet.

I didn't blame her when she said if I couldn't pay she'd have to go where they could. In another month the seining would start, and good money could be earned for a bit in the fish-sheds. She agreed to stay with me until then, and I tried not to plan too far ahead, although when I thought of living as a woman alone in a house full of sailors it seemed to me I'd be better wandering the countryside with the moorland air sweet in my lungs and no niggling debts and worries to load me down; no drunken threats nor lying at nights listening rigid and fearful behind my locked door to clumsy footsteps on the landing and furtive, great hands at my latch.

I wondered about my father again at these times and pictured him travelling from place to place, striding about in great tents or barns, wearing fancy clothes fit for a lord, and everyone gaping at him in wonder, not caring whether he'd a bottle to his lips or not. The idea struck me to set off and try to find him. But I hadn't the first notion where he was, and although I'd never been afraid of a bit of adventure, the thought of footpads, or vagabonds getting me one night in a country lane, revolted me after what I'd gone through.

Besides, there was Matt. One day, surely, I'd see him coming towards me over the beach or down Fore Street, maybe from the Kiddleywink, with the old warm gleam in his eyes and arms all ready to crush me to him.

I'd have gone without a doubt in the world, forgetting his angers and roughness for the sake of all the rest there'd been between us. But of course it was just wishful thinking. In my sad, solemn times the feeling still lurked deep down that he'd gone for good.

So I laboured on, thinking if the worst came I could always join Jane at the fish cellars in August, making extra that way. I'd be stronger by then, and if I couldn't manage the sea-faring gentlemen as well, it would be easy enough to take the notice from the front parlour window for a few months and start with boarders for the winter.

In the end, though, I knew that sort of arrangement wouldn't work. Besides, I'd seen more than I wanted of women exhausted and old before their time; exhausted wives, trying to cope with their homes and families, and spending the night hours salting and bulking fish in guttering candle-light. There was a bit of jollity when the season came to an end, of course; a merry enough 'cellar feast' held in some sail-loft with the women feasting at a good supper, all neat and tidy in their best clothes and clean soggets. A fiddler would be there, and there'd be dancing and a deal of singing. As a child I'd been taken there once or twice, but the thought now held no cheer for me.

The constant odour of fish about the small town, and the smell of drains, especially in the summer, depressed me.

What was the use, I thought one day, of fighting and slaving and wasting my looks for the sake of a grey, granite house that could offer me nothing but hard work and loneliness? I looked at my hands and was affronted by the reddened chaps and callouses. They'd been nice hands when I was growing up, strong but slender, with tapering fingers; hands more suited to rings, surely, than the scrubbing-brush, salt water and fish.

I dismissed the idea of going to work for the seiners and on an impulse decided to get rid of the house for good. I didn't waste any time but got a lift with Billy Trevean the next morning for Penzance. The manager was busy when I arrived at the bank, and by the time I saw him it was almost one o'clock. I didn't waste words, and I didn't listen to any of his mumbo-jumboing arguments either.

'Sell it,' I said, all haughty and sure of myself now I'd come to a decision. 'Call in your mortage thing or whatever it is you've been threatening to do these last months. There'll be a bit left over for me, I s'pose? That'll be enough to keep me till I get a job. And that's all I want.'

I had to sign something, which I did with a flourish; and when I left, it was with a sense of triumph and glee that for once I'd shocked that odious little man into silence.

Once outside I gave way to mirth and laughed aloud. A man turned and looked at me as he passed. I didn't care. For the first time in my life I felt free, with a feeling in me after all that life could still be worth-while and that something fresh and exciting could already be lurking round the corner.

It was, although I didn't know it until early September, just after the house was sold, leaving me a week to pack up and get out.

I was sitting in a coffee shop treating myself to a cup when I noticed an advertisement in the *Cornish News*.

'Young lady wanted,' it read, 'to serve behind bar in respectable Coaching House. Must be of nice appearance and manners, and willing to give extra time when necessary. Good wages and board provided. Apply G Pendelly, Fiddler's Arms, Penzance.'

Nice appearance, I thought ... Well, I had that all right—when I took the trouble. The wages, though not too important at the moment since I'd have a tidy bit in my pocket when the bank paid back what was owed, were still tempting. As for board, that could solve my problem. Without even giving a hint to Jane, I got in touch with the landlord as soon as possible. When he saw me with my chestnut hair becomingly braided yet neat under my small hat and wearing my tartan cape over the high-necked black dress, I could tell after the first few sentences between us that I'd get the job.

That's how it happened, and how, in the middle of the month when the tang of early autumn was in the air and the town was making busy for a fair, I met the fresh-faced, blue-eyed squire who'd taken my attention on the first occasion at the inn.

The Fiddler's Arms was smaller than the other inn I'd visited, and older. Better run, though, as I discovered in my first week there. George Pendelly, the landlord and owner, was a widower helped by his sister Nancy, a well-meaning, portly woman with a neat appearance and a hearty laugh that put me at home as soon as her large hand gripped mine.

'My son Ebenezer's here to assist George when necessary,' she said, 'so you won't be too hard pressed, m'dear. Part time behind the bar, and to give me a help with the baking sometimes, if that's agreeable to 'ee?'

'Of course,' I told her. 'I'm used to cooking.'

'Then there's Polly. Polly comes in daily ... a bit on the simple side but as good a hand wi' the scrubbin' brush as any you do get. O' course ...' she said, eyeing me with the first tinge of doubt, 'the hours can be long sometimes, an' you doan' luke too strong a maid ... If I had of bin here when you called that day I'd have put all such things to 'ee, but as you weren't expected, George—Mr Pendelly—had to do it himself; an' men, though we can't do without 'em, bless their simple hearts, are more like to be took with a pretty face than a strong elbow.'

I smiled. 'I'm very strong. If you knew what I'd got through in the past you'd have no worries on that score.'

'I'm glad to hear et, m'dear. And what, if I may ask, was you doin' afore you did come here, Miss ... Miss ...?'

'*Mrs* Thomas,' I told her abruptly. 'My husband's at sea. And I was running a place of my own. My grandmother's place before she died, in Port Einack.'

'Aw!' she nodded her head knowingly. '*Married*. An' when do he return, may I ask? That husband o' yours?'

I shook my head. 'I've no idea. He's a Captain. We don't see much of each other.'

'Hmmn. Like that, es et?' She shrugged. 'Well, 'tedn' none of my business. All men's much of a muchness underneath, ef you do ask me, an' the sea-farin' ones has a bit more of et than the rest fer sure. Owin' to their trade, o' course. Travel, temptation.'

If she hadn't been so amiable and amusing I'd have resented her curiosity, but it was hard to resent anything about Nancy, her good nature so matching up to her form, which was immense.

When the topic of my past was exhausted she returned to more practical matters.

'Your clothes now ...' she said, eyeing the black frock critically. 'Not quite right for Fiddler's Arms. You'll be needin' somethin' fresh. Two dresses, I'd say. One fer the bar an' another fer cookin' ...'

'Oh, I have a fresh blue print,' I told her, 'and two aprons. And in my box there are some put away ...' I hesitated, wondering how I'd ever be able to bear wearing the colourful finery Matt had ever bought or given to me.

The shrewd little dark eyes seemed to disappear momentarily in their mounds of flesh as she shook her head, saying firmly, 'Naw, m'dear. You shall start all fresh. I've materials upstairs that can soon be fitted an' sewn, so long as you be handy with the needle. Yeller silk, I'd say, fer the bar—customers like to see a bit of colour about—an' grey cotton fer kitchen. An' doan' 'ee start thankin' me. 'Tes all fer good of the house, as you might say. An' I doan' want unhappy memories troublin' 'ee here.'

Probably I wouldn't have much time for remembering, I thought afterwards, as I took what belongings I wanted from the trunk that had been my grandfather's and arranged them on the mahogany chest-of-drawers in my bedroom. There would be a great deal to learn and do, which thankfully was sure to take my mind off things. It was a small bedroom, with sloping eaves, a large bed and chair, and a marble-topped washstand; with the immense wardrobe and chest, too, there was hardly sufficient room left to swing a cat round. But it was well-aired, clean and fresh, on the top floor, with a small window overlooking a maze of roof-tops to the harbour and Newlyn beyond.

There was no picture on the wall, except

a religious text and a faded photograph of a genial-looking old gentleman seated on a sea-wall.

The atmosphere, though confined, was one of care and affection, and I knew with an instinctive rush of gratitude that I was going to like being there, though what I *didn't* realize then was that, in my second week, two well-remembered eyes in a fresh coloured face were to seek mine over the bar counter.

He didn't speak at first; then, as I handed him his whisky, he said, 'Didn't I see you before, quite a time ago, in the Ram and Bottle?'

I nodded, feeling the warm blood course my cheeks. 'Yes, I think so.'

'You remember?'

'I have a very good memory, sir,' I told him unsmilingly, extremely careful to use my best English.

'Do 'ee know Squire Pendruggan then, Judith?' I heard Mr Pendelly say behind my shoulder.

I was spared having to reply by the other man answering for me.

'Oh yes. We're acquainted. And I'm very pleased to see her here. You've good taste, Pendelly. I shall be a frequent visitor from now on.'

After that, the landlord's manner to me changed, becoming almost deferential at times. His sister's, too. Obviously Squire Pendruggan was an important figure in the district. What I didn't know at the time was how important he was going to become to me.

CHAPTER 6

The regulars crowding the bar of the Fiddler's Arms on market day were of a more polite order than the sea-faring gentlemen I was accustomed to catering for in Port Einack. Farmers mostly, their talk was chiefly concerned with cattle and corn, though I soon became accustomed to a bit of ribaldry when the liquor prompted it; an occasional wink from some ruddy face, suggestive remarks in my ear whenever George or Nancy's ear was turned away, and appreciative glances over the counter where I stood in my yellow silk dress, drawing the mead, beer, or the rum, whisky, whatever was asked for.

It didn't take me long to learn what was what, or the price of things. And the jollying of the men didn't bother me at all. Besides, George or Nancy was generally at hand to deal with any argument that might arise; this alone gave me confidence. I felt at ease to flaunt my looks in a proud and dignified manner, knowing well that whatever hot emotions I might rouse, there was nothing anyone could do about it.

Nancy had been right about the yellow silk; it suited my glowing cream skin and chestnut hair. The style we'd chosen together was decently high at the neck, edged with black ribbon, but tightly waisted above a slim skirt draped to the back, so nothing of my figure was lost. Above my grandmother's black satin apron my breasts rose neat yet gently swelling.

I wished at odd moments when admiring male glances were on me that Matt could see me there, walking in one day, and would try to claim me. Already I knew how I'd act: 'Get off back to where you came from, Matt Thomas,' I'd say. 'To your coloured wife and your half-caste child. There's nothing for you here.' With all eyes turned on us, I'd watch him, shamed, shrug his shoulders and take off again. But the triumph in me would be half-agony, too, and I knew it would be a toss-up whether I'd let him disappear forever out of my life or rush after him, flinging myself into his arms.

It was all just a flight of fancy, of course, because Matt never *did* come to the Fiddler's Arms. By degrees I learned not to think of him, although in my sleep sometimes there were dreams when I'd glimpse him walking along a pale beach, and I'd run and run, calling his name. Even then it was no use. If I caught up with him round a headland or lump of rock, the luscious, ebony-dark creature would be with him, staring into his face with her burning eyes. Her shining arms would be round his neck, and he wouldn't see me at all.

Once I found him in a dark sort of cave, just waiting in the shadows, so still and withdrawn I was afraid. Then, when at last I moved forward and touched him, he drew back, staring coldly, his eyes empty and unresponsive. I knew then that my beauty must have gone. In a frenzy of loneliness I bent down where a dark pool, left by the sea, held a glitter of light, like a mirror. My own face stared up at me, older, wan, with fine wrinkles round the eyes and mouth. My hair fell lank like weeds to my shoulders. I knew Matt would never love me again.

When I got to my feet his form was already being taken into the shadows and, even as I watched, completely disappeared. I turned and rushed into the cold evening light, feeling such desolation in me I thought I must have died.

When I awoke, my heart would be racing and my forehead clammy with sweat. I'd get up and go to the mirror with a candle held before my face. The worst part would be over then, because I'd know what I saw was real—a youthful face framed by a tumbling glory of burnished hair—and that the rest was only a bad nightmare. I was still young and lovely, and it could be that one day, somehow, Matt and I would be reconciled.

I didn't believe it, but it was still possible. And when you're young, with life mostly before you, the knowledge of days and years ahead can make the ghost of a chance seem a real probability. In any case my moments of looking back, even in sleep, were rare. Generally I was too tired at nights to be bothered by troubled dreams, and the days were so full, I was no longer consciously concerned with Matt at all.

In quieter periods at the inn I gave Nancy a hand with the cooking and baking. She was so appreciative of the dishes I'd learned under my grandmother's tuition that tasty snacks were provided and served over the counter for farmers and visitors on market day. My own pasties and heavy cake were in much demand, and once Squire Pendruggan said to Nancy with an appreciative gleam in his blue eyes, 'You have a real treasure here, Nancy. If I was you I'd watch carefully or you'll be losing her.'

Nancy, very red in the face, said, 'Both George and I know her worth full well, Mr Pendruggan, sir, but if she does have a chance of betterin' herself we'd not be standin' in her way for sure.'

'Your generosity does you credit,' the Squire said with a touch of irony. 'I must remember it.'

I didn't attach any importance to his words at the time, but looking back I see now it was from that moment William Pendruggan's attentions to me took a new turn. He became more personal, treating me as an equal rather than as a serving girl. I had a growing feeling in me that very soon he'd make me some proposition leading up to a better position in life.

I was right. One evening, on the moment of opening time, he took what had come to be his usual place at the counter, and before anyone else arrived he said meaningfully, 'I've a favour to ask of you, Miss Judith, something I hope you'll comply with, not thinking me too forward.'

His eyes were bright in his ruddy face and so warm on me that I could already feel the blood creeping from the back of my head to my cheeks.

'Oh yes?' I said, trying to appear casual. 'If there's any help I can give you, I'll certainly try, sir. Though what it could be is beyond me ...'

He laughed. 'Not at all. Very much within your capacity, I can assure you. The truth is ...' he leaned forward a little, with a slight wink of one eye, 'I like your pasties, your heavy cake and lardy cake, all the rare little side-lines and cookies of yours, so much, I was wondering if you could supply me with an assortment a woman of your fine talents would choose for a social occasion?'

I stared at him, thinking what a mouthful to be sure; and when he'd finished speaking the breath seemed to die out of him, as though he'd got a great weight off his mind. He wiped his forehead with the fine linen handkerchief from his pocket and smiled.

The smile made him appear younger, and just for a moment I glimpsed him as he must have been when he was in his youthful prime: eager and good natured, with fair hair thick on his head and laughter bright in his blue eyes. His figure would've been straight and slender then, before too much good living had brought the paunch to his form and netted the bluish-red lines under his eyes. He was still handsome in a heavy, middle-aged way, and that day he had obviously been careful to look his best, wearing fawn twill riding breeches with a green jacket, yellow waistcoat and one of the smart brown silk bows and high collars favoured by the gentry.

If it had been any other man but him I'd have

suspected his motive. As it was I could only say, with a pretence of casual interest, 'If you tell me exactly your requirements, Mr Pendruggan, sir, I'll do my best to give an answer.'

'What an agreeable young woman you are, to be sure,' he answered. 'And so self-contained, if I may say so, which is a rare quality in one of your age and looks ...'

If only he knew. I thought, trying to keep my mouth straight. Self-contained? *Me?* The idea was so ludicrous it sent my thoughts flying with a rush to the past, bringing momentarily stabbing memories of wild conflicts with Matt; stormy occasions when our two wills had clashed until I'd been a wild cat at his mercy, then quiet and gentle as a young doe in his arms.

'We haven't much knowledge of each other, sir,' I said, all lady-like, 'but if it's cooking you want, I *may* be able to oblige.'

'Yes,' he agreed. 'And it's like this, Miss Judith. In a fortnight's time I have a meeting at Gulvarrick, for my tenants—mostly small farmers and their wives—at the house. The housekeeper I have is getting old and finds it hard to cater for a number of folk. Now would it be possible, do you think, for you to provide a share of the eatables and bring them up in time for Mrs Poldane to arrange? If so, I'd be greatly obligated. Good fare's appreciated by farming people, and I'd send a man for you with the gig ...'

He broke off, eyeing me with such hope and a sort of uneasy fear on his large face, I had to look away before saying, 'You'd have to ask Mr

Pendelly or his sister as it's them who employ me. There's the question of time and cost, sir. The cooking? Well, baking's no stranger to me. And if you got permission for me to come up to your place on my afternoon off, off-time, it's likely it could be arranged. But you must see I can't say right off.'

He nodded. 'Of course, of course. Naturally I'd have a word with Nancy first. As to the cost ... all materials and time would be well paid for and a good bit over for your pocket. Have no fear, Judith; now you've no objection, I'll do everything in a proper manner and get permission from the Pendellys as soon as possible.'

And that's what he did. I was astonished, at first, to find George and Nancy so willing for me to co-operate with Squire Pendruggan's suggestion. But when I thought things over later, it didn't seem so strange after all. Besides being a wealthy and respected figure in his own right, he was a magistrate, a man to be on good terms with whenever possible. I must say I felt honoured myself, and not without conceit at his praise of my cooking. The thought that I could be wanted because of a certain talent, instead of just my figure and face, filled me with a new pride and self-possession that was obvious, I suppose, to George and Nancy.

'She'll grow beyond us, you mark my words,' George said to his sister once. 'We'll not be havin' the maid with us long.'

Nancy's small mouth became a button in her round face before she remarked, 'Ef 'twas fer her own betterment we'd not have to stand in her way. When times come fer you an' I to tek off fer heav'nly pastures, Ebenezer'll tek over here. An' you never can tell what ideas he'll have fer the Fiddler. So, so long as Judith do know fair an' square what kind of an establishment she's settin' foot in, brother, 'tes all that concerns us.'

'Ah.'

George took a long pull at his pipe, stared at me thoughtfully for a few moments, then said, 'I've heard tell things bean't always so honey-sweet up at Gulvarrick as Squire would have us believe. Oh, a fine upstandin' man *he* be, as we all 'ppreciate. But much goes on there that edn' the way of good Christian folk, accordin' to those who do know.'

As I waited, puzzled, for him to explain, Nancy put in, almost snappily for her. 'Oh, stop makin' such hard bones o' et, man. Squire can't help his wife's carryin's on any more than you can help that bald pate of yours. When he married her she was as pleasin' an' pretty a young creature as any could see.'

'Born the wrong side o' the blanket though,' George remarked, 'as you well know. An' the Maddens was always a crazy lot ...'

'Shsh!' Nancy said reprovingly. 'Tedn' our business to go spreadin' family history, 'cept, of course, what be necessary. Judith, m'dear, what my brother wus tryin' to tell 'ee wus simply that Squire's good lady spends most of the time away, bein' in pore health, you could say.'

'You mean ...?'

Nancy touched her head significantly. 'That's what I mean. An' havin' a lively nature there's times that she makes trouble—distressful trouble—at th' manor, Gulvarrick. Not often, o'course. Some say she's gone for good now, an' fer the sake of Mr Pendruggan, God bless his kind nature, I do pray 'tes so.'

'I think I understand,' I answered. 'But really I don't see it's any of my business. All the Squire wants is for me to take a few goodies up for the tenants' party. As you don't mind, I'll do it. But I'm hardly likely to stay there more than half an hour, just time enough to show the housekeeper what's what. Mr Pendruggan says she's old and can't manage crowds any more.'

'True enough,' George conceded. 'As irritable an old crow as you could find these days. Still, if anyone can charm a smile from 'en, I'm sure it will be you, Judith.'

And so it was all arranged.

I learned later the number of guests expected for the forthcoming gathering would certainly not exceed a dozen and, from the Squire, that a variety of my specialities would be appreciated, with special emphasis on the pasties.

On the evening before the event, thanks to Nancy's good nature, I had the kitchen to myself for making an assortment of gingerbreads, fuggans, saffron and seedy cakes, pies, pasties and bread. I was working to such a late hour Nancy came downstairs from bed to give me a hand.

'You'll be all washed up by tomorrow fer sure,' she said stubbornly, 'an' even ef 'tes your half-day off, there's the mornin' heer to think of. This place edn' all charity, y'know.'

'I don't intend it to be,' I told her more briskly than I felt. 'You'll take half the profit or I'll walk out an' never come back. Forgive me speaking so straight.'

She glanced at me knowingly. 'A real firebrand you can be, I see. Now I'm beginnin' to understand why you an' that sea-cap'n o' yours came to grief. No strong man'll take kindly to a wumman with a likin' fer wearin' the breeches. Still ...' her face had suddenly such a broad beam of mischief on it I couldn't be angered, 'there's plenty deserve more wumman's tongue than they do get. An' I doan' blame 'ee one bit.'

After that I kept silent, knowing that if she referred to Matt again I might fly off the handle and say more than I meant.

By the time I got to bed I could hardly keep my eyes open, and when I slept it was heavily, with no troubled dreams of Matt to torment me and no haunting fears for the future.

At three-thirty promptly the next day, one of the Squire's men, Pascoe, arrived with the gig ready for the journey to Gulvarrick. I was wearing my best sober black, which seemed suited to the occasion and was carrying three immense baskets containing the assortment of food. Nancy and George helped me to get seated safely and as we set off they stood watching and waving, just as though I was destined for some royal occasion.

When I look back now to that part of my life, I never fail to remember their great kindness and how it helped to bring back warmth and meaning to my days. Their two faces, round and bright as immense, polished apples, are as clear in my mind now as on that far-off afternoon which was to lead quite soon to such a change in my circumstances. But then other things stand out, too, things that for as long as I live will remind me of my first sight of Gulvarrick: the heady tang of yellowed leaves already falling to the damp earth; the glittering radiance of the afternoon sky between the networked trees; and, as we climbed higher towards the western rim of hills, the small patchworked fields licked to gold-orange and pale green from the lowering sun.

The hamlet itself was mostly hidden in a fold of the land below the moors, and it wasn't until the trap took an abrupt curve to the right that I had a real view of Gulvarrick Manor, a grey granite building standing at the end of a tree-lined avenue. It wasn't a grand place in the manner of Castlegwarran, but just as old, from the look of it, with a jutting gable at the front, three tall chimney-stacks and two rows of latticed windows stretching under mellowed roofing and eaves. As we passed through the iron gates I saw cattle grazing in parkland on either side of the drive. There seemed a great peace about everything, and I marvelled how it must feel to have such a gracious home in the family, already picturing in my imagination times gone by when peacocks perhaps strutted about the garden and gentlewomen wearing richest velvets and satins strolled with their husbands and lovers under the trees. I'd seen a picture of a peacock in a book when I was a child and always wanted to have a sight of one in real life. But my grandmother had chided me.

'Peacocks?' she'd said sharply, sniffing. 'Doan' you go gettin' ideas like that, chile. *Vain* critters, I've heard tell, an' only fit for kings an' queens an' them born to such frivolities. So just 'ee look sharp and stop day-dreamin' or I'll take my slipper to 'ee.'

But the vision of the peacock had remained, and although I'd kept my vanity a secret, something of it had flowered as I grew up. I'd known that, given a chance, I could learn and act as quickly and gracefully as any fine lady of the land. Perhaps because of my Spanish great-great-grandmother, or of my father who, I was sure, was an actor. Who could tell? The very fact of my mysterious ancestry encouraged thoughts of exciting possibilities, and I was full of them when I stepped out of the gig round the back of the house.

It was quite different there and reminded me more of some great farm house than a gentleman's estate. Two wings of the building jutted out, forming a large cobbled yard facing the kitchens with stables opposite. The air had the pungent smell of animals and hay, and a boy passed by whistling, with two pails on his arm.

My first awe changed instantly to one of more friendly ease. I had no need to feel inferior. To the contrary: as I reached across to the door to give it a sharp rap, laden with one basket on my arm, Pascoe following me with the two others, I could have been any duchess herself, carrying goodies for the poor.

A second or two later the face of a plump, pale girl with ginger hair poked round the door.

'Oh aiss?' she said, screwing up her eyes. 'Wan' Missis, do 'ee?'

'The housekeeper,' I told her. 'I've brought the goodies that were ordered.'

She might not have been a half-wit, but she was certainly simple.

'Aw. Well ... I'll be seein' ...,' she said hesitantly.

'Fetch Mrs Poldane. Quick, sharp, Liddy,' Pascoe shouted. 'Do as you're bid 'fore I teks a boot to y'r tail ...'

Startled by the rough tones which had been so lardy soft to me, I watched the girl scuttle away with the speed of a frightened rabbit.

'Go inside, miss,' the man told me, 'an' doan' 'ee tek no notice of Liddy Bream. Half-baked she wuz before she poked her silly head into the world.'

I stepped into what appeared to be a dairy, with white-washed walls and cool marble slabs below shelves containing honey and bottles of cordial. Cans and milk churns stood in the shadows below, and a large bowl of thick cream. Everything smelt very clean and fresh, and I was grateful for a few minutes to recover myself and see my hair was smoothed tidy under my hat. Pascoe didn't stay; he just dumped the two baskets by mine, then strode away to attend to the gig and horse. His footsteps were still clanging across the yard when Mrs Poldane appeared.

She was a thin, rather bent and careworn woman, wearing a stiff, dull purple dress with a small lacy cap perched on her grey hair. It was impossible to judge her age, but obviously she was getting on and had been overworked in her day.

'You're Mrs Thomas?' she asked rather sharply. Before I could reply, she added, 'And these be the grand pasties and cookies I've heard so much of?'

I nodded uncomfortably, detecting a note of jealousy in her voice.

'I hope they're to your liking. The Squire—Mr Pendruggan—complimented me on the pasties, but I'm sure yours are as good, perhaps better. He was just thinking of it being a little assistance to you, that's all.'

'Hmmn. I'm not dead yet, not by a long chalk,' the woman said tartly. 'Still ...' she added, softening a little. 'I'm grateful for the help all the same. Since Cook left, and with only Liddy and the men to fall back on, I've found these tenant gatherings a bit more than I can handle comfortably. *Appetites* ...,' she flung both hands up disparagingly, 'you'd be surprised what gluttons dependants of that kind can be.'

'I'm sure,' I mumbled, doing my best to appease her.

'Well, come along now. Let's get this stuff

to the kitchen and see what you've concocted. *Liddy!*'

At her sharp rasping command the girl appeared again, hurriedly wiping her hands on her apron.

'Take them into kitchen, quick,' the housekeeper commanded, 'an' stir your stumps, girl. We've a lot to do 'fore evenin'.'

'I'll help,' I said, as the girl attempted to lift a basket in each hand. 'They're heavy.'

'You'll do no such thing,' Mrs Poldane contradicted. 'It's what she's paid for to *work.* An' what she seldom does, let me tell you.'

Thinking that poor Liddy must lead a miserable existence under her shrewish superior, I nevertheless had to watch while the girl carried the carefully packed container through a second smaller room, a larder or erstwhile butler's pantry, and then into an immense kitchen with a great sink under the window, the space of one wall almost completely given to a large Cornish oven and grate, and with two clean newly-scrubbed deal tables in the middle of the room. There was a tall dresser for the china and glassware, and everything was spotless.

'Now,' the housekeeper said, when Liddy had been dismissed, 'let's see what you've brought, shall we?'

I could feel she was impressed by the varied assortment as I unwrapped the food that was all carefully tied in greaseproof paper, but when I suggested the small meat pie would be best eaten cold and not reheated, she flared up saying tartly, 'I know probably far better than you, miss, what's what in cooking, and how to serve a meal in the proper fashion. I'm obliged for the trouble you've put in providing such a spread, but don't try and teach me my own business, if you don't mind.'

Feeling the hot blood flame in my cheeks I somehow managed to restrain a show of temper, and it was good I did so, for at that point the Squire himself came to the kitchen. He was carefully dressed and had contrived somehow to keep his paunch more tucked in than usual, which made me wonder, with an impulse to giggle, if he'd struggled into corsets for my benefit. The housekeeper straightened herself, turning her head sharply in my direction as though she expected me to curtsey. I didn't, of course. I'd never been the curtseying kind and would've found it hard, even for royalty.

'Well, well, Miss Judith,' he said, rubbing his hands together appreciatively. 'What a grand spectacle, to be sure; the odour's already tickling my guts. Yours, too, I hope, Mrs Poldane.'

'Quite savoury,' the housekeeper grudgingly conceded.

'I must be wary then,' William Pendruggan said half-teasingly, 'before I'm tempted to take a bite. And you must have a glass of cordial with me, Judith.'

That he'd dropped the formal 'Miss' for mere 'Judith' didn't escape me *nor* Mrs Poldane. And I couldn't help noticing how warm his eyes were upon me as I answered, 'I really shouldn't. There are things I have to do ...'

'And the first is to have a bit of a rest and

chat after all the labour you've gone to on our behalf,' he interrupted quickly. 'Come along now to the sitting-room. I'll not take no for an answer, so you'd best oblige without further argey-barging.'

That's how it was that five minutes later I was seated in a comfortable room overlooking the front lawn, with a glass of cherry brandy in my hand and facing the Squire. It was a gracious but homely interior, furnished in walnut, with brown velvet upholstery and hangings.

What we talked about is difficult to recall now, although I *do* remember confessing to him that I was not *Miss* Thomas, as he'd supposed, but a married woman with a husband who'd taken off to foreign parts.

'Ah. Um,' he said reflectively. 'Then we're both in the same boat.' His expression darkened with a kind of sadness before he went on, 'Your man is not likely to return in the near future, I take it?'

Resenting the implication yet trying to appear casual, I answered with a lift of my head that made the jet ear-rings swing against my cheeks, 'I've never any way of knowing when his ship'll come into port, sir. He's a much travelled man with a liking for foreign parts or I'd not be serving behind the bar at the Fiddler's Arms.'

'Just so, just so.'

There was a pause in which I began to feel a bit discomforted, so many thoughts seemed to be lurking behind his eyes. For the first time I realized my visit there might have been prompted by deeper implications than just a fine spread for his table and that he wasn't quite the bland, innocent-minded country gentleman I'd imagined.

I got up suddenly, wishing I'd brought the pair of black satin gloves I'd found in great-great-grandmother Luzana's belongings. It's an elegant feeling somehow, putting on fine gloves in a flustered mood—I'd done so before visiting Mr Bolus, and they'd done a great deal to calm my spirit. But there! gloves and cookies hadn't seemed fitted for the occasion, and certainly I'd no reason to feel in any way under obligation to William Pendruggan.

'I really *must* be on my way now, sir,' I said, with my back stiff as a ramrod. 'Thank you kindly for the wine, and for ... for ...'

'For what, Judith?'

His smile was warm and friendly again, changing him back in a flash to the middle-aged, courteous gentleman I'd known before. Certainly, I told myself with sudden relief, he'd suggested nothing improper at all; all he'd done had been to appreciate my cooking and put a bit of money in my way.

Actually the 'bit' was far short of the truth. As I was about to leave the room he thrust a quantity of sovereigns into my hand—far more than was deserved. I drew back, shaking my head.

'No, sir. Oh no, I *couldn't*. Not all that. It's not right ...'

Even as I pushed the money back at him, some of my grandmother's harsh words seemed to ring in my ears: 'Keep yourself to yourself,

Judith. If any rich man comes generous with the gold, see you tek it quick, but doan' 'ee give an inch. That way y'r pocket'll grow an' y'r value spread so quick mebbe 'ee'll net a real fine fish in th' end.'

'Now, now,' I heard the Squire saying reasonably, 'don't underestimate yourself. You've done me a worthy service today, and I pay what's due, no more.'

So I took the money, and when I'd put it safe in the small bag I carried, he lifted one of my hands in his, holding it firmly, before opening the door. I tried to draw it away quickly, ashamed of the slight roughness that still remained from my working for seafaring gentlemen. But it was too late. He'd already seen.

'A delicate hand you have, Miss Judith,' he said with such courtesy my indignation evaporated like a pricked balloon, 'and fitted for different things, surely, than spending your life serving farmers or over the kitchen table ...'

'I see no shame in honest work, Mr Pendruggan, sir,' I told him sharply, 'and if I can please such as you with my cookies, it would be a pity not to use what talents I have, don't you think?'

He laughed.

'Well said, m'dear. Well said. All the same ...'

His tone changed; for a long moment I felt his blue eyes searching mine as though they'd burn to my very soul, and more than that—through my black dress and petticoats to my firm white body that Matt had used so roughly at times and at other times pressed with hungry lips.

In spite of all my resolve to be dignified and remote, my breasts pricked and thighs ached just through remembering. Perhaps William Pendruggan sensed the conflict within me, I don't know. Men so often have an instinct for such things. But he ended the silence by adding, 'If you ever want a proper well-paid position, one of trust and security as befitting your talents and person, Judith, you can have it here ...'

'Oh no. I ...'

'With no strings attached,' he added meaningfully. 'Mrs Poldane is getting on in years, and I've a feeling retirement in a cottage on my estate might be very acceptable to her in the near future. So it's likely I may soon need a replacement.'

I searched his face to find there any indication of an ulterior motive. There was none. I'm sure at that moment he had a purely business relationship in mind. Besides, who was I to blame him if for a second he'd envisaged what life *could* have been had circumstances been different?

Heaven knows I'd done the same thing myself countless times when I'd wandered by the harbour at Newlyn and had seen not Matt but some man with a look of him and an eye for me that had caused an upsurge of passion with the thought, If only we could be close and kill the past forever ...

There was no blame in wanting and not having, only pain. And it seemed sad a generous man as the Squire should have to live always with a ghost at his back. When you're young it's more agonizing perhaps, but with someone of Mr Pendruggan's years the future must have appeared heavy indeed sometimes.

So I said as calmly as possible, 'I'll remember your kind offer, sir, and thank you.'

His reaction was unexpected.

'Thanks be damned,' he said. 'I *want* you here, Judith ... not from any dark intent, but to have a merry face to greet me i' the mornings and a tasty meal on the table without the creakings and groanings of a rheumaticky old biddy to spread depression around. D'you understand, girl? *Life!* It's life I want about me ...'

I smiled, because I understood only too well.

'Of course,' I said. 'And I'll think about it. I really will.'

This seemed to satisfy him, and after assuring him his outburst hadn't in any way angered me, I left and was driven away in his gig back to the Fiddler's Arms.

Naturally in the days that followed I gave a good deal of thought to his proposition, little dreaming then how short a time it would be before I was ensconced at Gulvarrick, after the unexpected death of George Pendelly from a heart attack.

With Ebenezer taking over and Nancy's virtual retirement everything changed. So it was that on a cold December day I set out once more for the granite house beneath the moor, and a new phase in my life began.

CHAPTER 7

I couldn't help feeling a knot of sadness in me that winter day when I left the Fiddler's Arms for good. Although I'd only been there a few months I'd come to think of it as the only home I had, and George and Nancy almost as my own kin. But I was excited, too, and as the gig taking me to William Pendruggan's neared the turn leading to the house, all regrets vanished because I knew a fresh life was starting for me.

I'd taken great pains with my appearance, wearing the black dress but with a froth of lace at my throat that I'd bought some days before. It was Mrs Poldane's last week as housekeeper, and I was determined to be upsides with her and not have her taking too high-and-mighty an attitude, even though she was to supervise and explain my duties before she left. Perhaps it was vain of me. Perhaps grandmother had known my sneaking desire for admiration when she'd taken such a hard hand to me in youth. But good looks, however much trouble they'd been sometimes, were a great help in giving confidence, and as I was to be in charge of the household it seemed only right I should start with no misgivings.

As things turned out there was no need to have worried about Mrs Poldane. When

I knocked at the back door and was shown into the kitchen by Liddy, I knew from one glance at her simple face that something was wrong. The very air held a kind of fear and tension in it that I sensed immediately. Pascoe was quiet, too. He simply dumped my bag, gave me a wry look and said, 'Well, that's that. And let's hope you do have luck here, miss.'

'What did he mean by luck?' I asked the girl, 'and where's Mrs Poldane?'

Liddy shook her head and with a scared-rabbit look in her pale prominent eyes replied, 'She'm gone, she have. Took off.'

'What do you mean *gone?* Mr Pendruggan ... the Squire ... said she'd be here to receive and acquaint me with the ways of the place?'

'But he dedn' knaw, ded 'ee?'

I shrugged helplessly. 'Know what? Oh, for goodness sake, girl, don't just stand there gaping. Go and tell your master at once. I certainly don't intend to wait here like a ... like a ...'

I was interrupted in my hot speech by the entrance of the Squire himself. He looked paler than usual. There were heavy rings under his eyes, giving him a slight air of debauchery that discomforted me. His dress, too, was not impeccable as I'd always seen it but rumpled round the collar with his tie askew and his coat creased as though he'd slept in it.

My heart sank. At that moment he looked almost old, making me wonder with a stab of uncertainty what manner of a post I'd landed myself into. Still, pulling myself together, I inclined my head with what I hoped was a dignified air and said, 'I'm sorry you should have been bothered to have to greet me. I expected Mrs Poldane.'

'Nat'rully, m'dear, naturally,' he said, drawing a hand across his forehead. 'It was right a woman should have received you. But as things are ...' He broke off, glancing irritably at Liddy's simple face so avid with curiosity. 'Go away, girl,' he said sharply, 'Off with you, and set about clearing some of the mess up.' She scuttled off, and following the slam of a door, he turned, taking my hand in his momentarily before continuing, 'I do apologize for this reception, but there was trouble here last night.'

'Trouble, sir?'

'My wife returned,' he said, 'which explains the sudden departure of Mrs Poldane. Or will, when you see the state of the house.'

'Your wife?' I echoed, shocked.

'Yes, yes. It was a complete surprise. And upsetting, very upsetting. But *that's* done with now. And I can assure you, Judith, she'll not return again. It's over. Quite over.'

'I see, sir,' I said, though most of it was a complete mystery to me.

'Come along then,' he told me, opening the door into the back hall where Liddy was on her knees with brush and pan. 'You're owed the whole truth now you've been so kind to come and bide here.'

I followed him up the flagged passage to where it widened and took three ways, branching off in one direction to a wide staircase with a statue at the bottom of a nude female figure holding a lamp, and on the opposite cutting abruptly to the right where several doors indicated reception rooms.

The main hall continued to the front door, which was lit to several colours in the early evening light from a tall stained glass window halfway up the stairs. The whole effect was of bygone days making me feel for a moment I'd really strayed there from another age.

Then Mr Pendruggan said, quite sharply, 'This way, Judith, just so you learn something of what I've had to put up with all these years.'

He flung a door open, held it, and said, 'Please step in. It was once a very beautiful room. The best in the house. My dear wife obviously didn't like the idea.'

I went inside and was immediately horrified, at first unable to accept the evidence of my own eyes. In my time I'd been witness to plenty of rough play from seamen and lodgers, but never anything like this.

Delicate china and glass was scattered, smashed, on the floor; silk brocade curtains had been wrenched from their hooks and lay torn in heaps, ripped mercilessly by a pair of blood-stained scissors. Ink or some other dark liquid had been spilled over the finely upholstered chairs and sofa. A portrait of William Pendruggan stared up from the carpet, from a broken frame. If ever there was devil's work, I thought, this was it. The only apparent decent object left was a large painting of a woman hanging over the mantelshelf.

She was very beautiful: white skinned, black haired, with a pointed, smiling mouth and green tilted eyes which seemed in my first shock of awareness to review the scene with a cold, contemptuous amusement.

The Squire, waiting for my reaction and aware of my troubled interest, said from behind my shoulder, 'Lovely isn't she? Queen of all she doth survey. So very fitting.'

His heavy sarcasm didn't escape me, but I knew it sprang more from extreme pain than anger.

'Yes,' I agreed. 'What ...?' I broke off in confusion.

He laughed lightly, though there was no mirth in it. 'What happened? Need you ask? Last night I was woken from sleep by that ... that vixen's return. For months I'd thought all was well and that she'd resigned herself to being rich chatelaine of her private retreat, which has already cost me, I must admit, more than the estate can properly afford. Still, when a man marries he has obligations, and in the past I'd not chafed unduly when she took it into her head to pay me an occasional wifely visit. Not until last night. Now I know that my first duty should be to have her properly and legally certified.'

I stood mutely with a feeling of shame in me, and pity that a gentleman of quality and such a kindly nature should be put to so much distress.

The pause seemed interminable.

Then at last I said, 'I'm sorry, sir. You must

have suffered very much.'

'Too much to dwell on it unnecessarily,' he agreed. 'I thought it only fitting you should understand why Mrs Pendruggan no longer makes her home here and to assure you there's no fear of her intrusion in the future. With *you,* Judith, to take over, Gulvarrick should have some peace at last. In fact, I'm sure of it.'

Staring him straight in the face I said, 'I'll do my best, but why you should have such a high opinion of me I can't imagine. I'm not exactly a peaceful sort by nature, and I like my own way when it suits me.'

His hand fell firm on my shoulder.

'So you should. So you should, m'dear. What woman of spirit doesn't? Oh, have no fear. We shall get on well.'

His eyes which had been full on my face travelled briefly over my whole form. I couldn't help noticing the quickened breathing beneath his jacket or the way the fresh colour deepened in his cheeks. Best to get things on a right footing once and for all, I thought, before any ideas got working in him which I hadn't bargained for. So I dislodged his hand, drew myself to my full height, turned away and remarked in aloof, business-like tones, 'Now what about me getting a pan and brush and clearing some of this mess up? Seems to me that's my first job here, Mr Pendruggan, sir.'

He looked about to explode.

'The very idea. A glass of wine, or tea first if you prefer it. Then I'll see Liddy gets the bulk under way.'

'No,' I answered firmly. 'Thank you kindly, but I've not come to your house to sit about parlours taking refreshment when there's work to be done. Liddy can help if she's a mind to, and if she hasn't, I'll have to see about teaching her. I'm sorry to disagree with you, sir, but I've never been the idle kind. It's not my way.'

As I spoke it seemed again that my grandmother was at my ear, prodding me. I sensed he was mildly annoyed, though he did his best not to show it.

'Very well,' he said, rather shortly, 'I'll send the girl along. But you'll not be wearing the black dress, I take it?'

'Certainly not,' I answered, 'if someone can show me where I sleep, I'll change into my blue print and apron.'

'Just as you please,' he said. 'Wait here and I'll fetch Liddy. I'm exceedingly put out that Mrs Poldane isn't here to do things properly for her. But last night was too much for her. Not that I blame her for taking off, poor old thing, but ...'

'Please, will you stop apologizing, sir,' I said, growing hot and embarrassed under his gaze which was far too intimate and emotional to suit me. 'I've come to *help* you, haven't I? And that's all I wish to do.'

He turned away, saying half-absently, 'Yes, yes, of course. Don't heed me, Judith, I'm in such a sore distressed state. Excuse me then. I'll send the girl along.'

He went to the door after giving a little light bow, which struck me as strange, me being who

I was, a mere servant to work for him. But then the poor man was obviously suffering greatly from his unhappy experience, and I suppose in my black dress with the jet ear-rings swinging below my chestnut hair, I *did* look rather above my station, especially with my chin up and eyes bright and resolved.

I hadn't enjoyed putting a distance between us. It would have been easy enough to touch his hand gently or to rest a finger or two against his cheek. But pity, as I'd learned, could so easily lead to much more. And a man in the Squire's position would fall easily to anyone showing a spark of warmth.

What a pity it was, I thought as I waited for Liddy, that men seemed always to be either wayward and callous, able to tear a woman's heart in two, then take off without a qualm, or the soft gentle kind needing love above all things but incapable somehow of setting a girl's blood and senses alight. Recalling Matt again made me suddenly angry, with a wild, futile wish somehow to humiliate him and pay him out.

But of course there was nothing I could do. Matt didn't care. His life was far away from mine, in some way-off place with Topaz and Wellington; somewhere I'd never see, nor wish to.

Stupid then to have had such qualms about Mr Pendruggan, when *no* one—Matt, or my grandmother even—was there to criticize or condemn. My life was my own. If a day should come when William Pendruggan wished more of me than to act as his housekeeper, I was free to make my own choice and would do it.

What the answer would be, I'd no way of knowing just then, although when I faced things squarely I knew the problem must inevitably arise one day.

CHAPTER 8

During my first week at Gulvarrick I found the place at the back was larger than I'd thought. Beyond the stables and yard there were outhouses and cowsheds, and the land that side was for tilling or pasture. Liddy, so simple in most ways, had a good knowledge of such things, being a 'small farmer's' daughter, and though at the beginning such matters were a mystery to me she taught me a good deal about country life during her rare gossiping moments. How the Squire, for instance, had practically lost his fine dairy herd of cattle a year or two previously, due to some mysterious disease that she said had been 'wished on 'em by that theer Ettyn'. When I asked her who and what was Ettyn, she announced in dark tones that he lived on 'that theer shamblin' place on hill opposite side of road', that he 'was a queer one an' no mistake, an' that his old Aunty Dorcas was a witch who'd put a curse on Squire'.

Accepting her garbled information as just superstitious or a tale concocted by Liddy to give her importance, I was curious enough to speak to Mr Pendruggan about it one day.

He shrugged. 'She's right about Venn Ettyn,' he said. 'He's an odd fellow, but to his own advantage. Not a fool by any manner of means. The bastard son of a tinker's daughter and some nameless adventurer who paid well to have things kept quiet and get the family well set up.'

'Oh.'

'I'd rather you had no truck with him if you should chance to meet,' the Squire continued with a hard note in his voice. 'He's injured me; not with that ugly old beldame's magic or widdershinning around, but by true cunning, blast him.'

'I'm sorry,' I said, not knowing how else to commiserate.

'At a time when I was at a low ebb, due to my wife's extravagances and ... other things, he acquired Gulvarrick land, and Castle Carnack into the bargain ...'

'A *castle,* Mr Pendruggan, sir?'

'Oh, it's only a ruin, Judith, on the top of the moors skirting the Ettyn place. Valuable though, historically, dating back more than three thousand years.'

'Then why did you let it go?' I asked.

'Money, Judith. Had to. But I thought it was to someone else. Misled I was, up to the hilt. If I'd known it was to *him* ...' He broke off with the blue eyes darkening in his face, which by then was reddened in anger.

'What else has he done to upset you so?' I ventured to enquire, half-expecting a 'Mind your own business, girl.' But Pendruggan was not that type of man. He just replied darkly, 'Things best left unsaid. What I'm pointing out is, the Cranes and Pendruggans are of different clay. They don't mix and never will. Gypsies, the whole lot of 'em, and always will be, in spite of Ettyn's swagger and his noble, rascally kin.'

'Noble?'

'On his father's side, if you can call it in any way noble laying a tinker's wench and siring a bastard brat. The rest of the brood have come out true to type: black-eyed, black-haired, good looking in their dark way, and under their father they worked well, I'll give them that.' He paused before adding, 'I knew Joe Crane. Worked my land, for a time, before he was bribed into marrying Belle Ettyn, Venn's mother. He died though, and since then that unscrupulous elder son's taken over and seen they thrive like devil's spawn. There are six of them now, counting Belle—Venn, Sarne, Flavia, Marcus and Paul. Flamboyant, insolent creatures when they see a chance to throw their weight around. Not that they get it—with me. And I'd be obliged if you were careful to act the same. Keep out of their way, and if by chance you should meet a fiery-haired, tall young fellow in the lane or lurking by the field gate, steer clear. Hold your head high and don't so much as utter a "good day". Will you do that for me?'

'Of course,' I said, thinking all the same how colourful and interesting William Pendruggan had made the Ettyns—or rather the Cranes—sound. Venn especially.

'After your description I don't suppose I could possibly mistake them.'

'Hardly. Not Venn anyway with his flaming red hair. The way he looks could have earned him a part in a play any day.'

'You mean on the stage?'

'That's right. Why? You've no knowledge surely of actors and the profession?'

'No, master,' I told him, 'but my father did. He was a player himself.'

The moment I'd made the statement I could have bitten my tongue out, because of course I didn't *know*. It was only what I'd deduced from observation that revealing time with Matt at the fair.

'Oh *indeed?*' the Squire said, staring at me thoughtfully, 'Now I understand.'

'What, sir?'

'Your strange knowledge of language and putting things that seems odd for a fisherman's daughter. What other girl in Port Einack, for instance, would know how to write her own name or converse with such grace and careful manners?'

I laughed outright.

'My father, as I've said, was no fisherman, sir. But as I never knew him I certainly didn't get any learning from him. I was brought up by my grandmother, and brought up hard. But she had a Bible and taught me early how to speak and make out the long words in it. Then I had a few years schooling and took advantage of what was given. I'm not a reader of books, sir—there's been no time in my life for it—but I've seen that I never forgot what was what in language, so far as it went.'

'Hmmn. I can see you're talented in many respects, Judith. When you arrived here that first day with the goodies, wearing your fancy little hat and ear-rings, you looked as fine and upstanding as any lady of a great house. And I thought to myself, "there's more to her than a mere fisherman's daughter, I'll wager".'

'Maybe,' I told him, adding a moment later, not without a certain conceit, 'my great-great-grandmother was Spanish. I've a miniature put away safely with my belongings. Very beautiful she looks wearing a low-cut green dress, with a gold frame all round.'

He didn't answer for a moment. I wondered at first if he was going to laugh or behave all condescendingly, just as though I was some vain serving girl putting on an act. But he didn't.

To my surprise he took my hand and put his lips to it like any young gallant, sending a hot flush up my spine to my forehead and then my cheeks, which by then must have been blazing red. I reached with my other hand for the square of fine linen in my pocket, placing it to my mouth with the pretence of a cough, then quietly but firmly removed my fingers from his.

He drew himself up abruptly.

'I've been keeping you too long from what you have to do, with my tedious tales,' he said in a changed, formal voice. 'You must excuse me, Judith. Having lacked a feminine ear for so long has made me over-talkative.'

I smiled.

'Nothing you've said has been tedious, sir. It's right I should learn what's what in the neighbourhood, and I'll remember about—what was his name? Ettyn—'

'Venn Ettyn,' Mr Pendruggan said shortly.

'Yes, do that, for *your* sake as well as mine.'

I assured him as best I could to keep his words in mind. Anyway, there was so much for me to do and get accustomed to at Gulvarrick during those first days, I'd little time for wandering about the lanes. Except for Liddy and the houseman Adam, who did the heavy work like keeping the boiler going and chopping wood, bringing the logs in, and making himself useful when he was needed, I was on my own. Adam was a dour, late-middle-aged man fancying himself a cut above the rest, having a room of his own next to Pascoe and his wife, who bedded above the stables and harness-room with their son.

Of course I saw to it that I was agreeable to any of the farm hands if they came to the kitchen door needing anything, and I was always ready with a kettle of hot water to fill their cans, and maybe a pasty or two if I was baking.

'Mrs Poldane never made so free wi' the cow-hands,' Adam said once. 'Kep' herself to herself she did which was right an' proper. No muddying footsteps about when *she* did rule.'

'Seeing that the men are accustomed to have a bite in the kitchen at mid-day when they feel like it,' I retorted sharply, 'and that the floor's well used to boots, I see no reason not to be polite. After all ...,' and I gave him one of my most winning smiles, 'floors only need a bucket of soap and water and elbow-grease to make them shine again. Liddy and I are quite capable of seeing to that, aren't we, Liddy?'

'Yes, mistress,' Liddy agreed, although she

knew full well it would be her job to do the scrubbing. But Liddy, like me, appreciated the sound of whistling and male voices about her. An occasional slap on the back-side and occasionally some ribald well-meaning remark from one of the men led a great deal to changing her from a dull-witted lump of a girl into a country wench with a spark in her eye and an aptitude for a blush and a giggle that made me think she was not beyond catching a husband after all.

Oh, I could have been far more free-and-easy with them all than I was, if I'd had a choice. But as housekeeper I had to keep within certain limits and in any spare moments used the small back parlour which had been Mrs Poldane's sanctum when she presided there. It was a rather cooped-up place having one window facing the kitchen garden at the side, with a view stretching to the moors beyond. Some of the furniture—Mrs Poldane's own—had been taken to her cottage when she moved, but the Squire had replaced it with a rather cumbrous chest, a table and a high-backed embroidered chair that somehow looked out of place with the rest.

'If you want something more comforting ...,' he'd said after I'd first seen round, 'I'll have a rocking chair moved down from the attic. It was ...'

'Rocking chair?' I'd squeaked with laughter. 'What would I want with that, sir?'

There were times later though when I could well have done with it, moments when I was too tired even to fret over Matt and wanted nothing so much as to just lie back with my eyes closed for a second or two, dreaming.

Yes, at heart I suppose much of me was still a bit of a dreamer. With my eyes shut I could float back into the past so that I was no longer Judith Thomas but Luzana of the white hands and raven hair, at whose dainty feet dukes and noblemen paid homage and worshipped.

At other times I was a wild gypsy-girl with my dark chestnut locks free in the wind, skirts flying, and the whole great world of cloud-swept skies and open moorland about me, the smell of heather and gorse sweet in my nostrils, and not a wish for anything but to be alone and free until some legendary lover came galloping over the horizon to claim me. He'd not be Matt either, but something of Matt would be in him—his force and laughter and fiery ways, but not the treachery.

It was at such moments I'd recall the Squire's words about Venn Ettyn, and without meaning to I'd picture him striding the fields or riding his horse with his copper hair bright in the sun. Sometimes the whole family would be there, a dark unprincipled crowd who'd stolen William Pendruggan's land and laid a curse upon his cattle. In my mind I resented them, but at times I was so curious that I couldn't help realizing one day I'd have to see for myself what sort of folk they really were.

I'd no intention of breaking my word to William Pendruggan and becoming friendly, but I'd never been the sort to accept what I was told second-hand without proving it to my own satisfaction. It was this side of my character that had so often inflamed my grandmother's temper in the past.

'Spit of your mother you are ...' she'd said more than once. 'That wayward and wilful it'll land you in some trouble, unless you do take a careful hold o' yourself.'

Well, maybe she'd been right up to a point, but then despite her independence she'd got herself nowhere beyond the fish-sheds and her sea-faring gentlemen, whereas here I was in a position of trust; to all intents and purposes, mistress of a fine house, in spite of the small parlour I had to occupy and the amount of work I had to do.

In February, when the young celandines were already peeping from the ditches and small, fat buds of young green poked from the lean, dark branches of the trees, I decided one afternoon to take a walk out for an hour, leaving Liddy to deal with the tea. Knowing roughly the boundaries of the estate which I'd been told now covered about six hundred acres, I set off from the back, taking a path at the side of the house towards the moors. Over a thick navy alpaca dress that I'd bought in Penzance on the Squire's orders, I wore a tartan cape and nothing on my head but a green scarf tied under the chin. The weather was sharp and windy, but my cheeks and skin glowed from the joy of being alone and able to climb and wander with no one at my back to tell me where I should go.

Half-way up the hill I turned and looked back,

seeing below me the white lane dividing the Squire's land from the Cranes', winding like a ribbon through a crosswork of brown and green fields to the valley below. The land was lush there, good both for arable and pasture, but when I turned again and saw the gaunt stretch of winter moorland ahead, it was as though I was staring at another world.

I hurried on, running sometimes, tugging at clumps of furze and bracken, eager to see beyond the queer tall stone standing stark against the skyline. When I got there I was breathless and stood for a moment or two leaning against the slab of granite. Everything, except for the fresh wind, seemed curiously lonely and empty of life, not even a bird flapping—only great clouds massing like a fleet of galleons from the west. When I looked below the road had disappeared, taking a direct curve to the right. I walked on and presently saw ahead of me what must have been at some remote time a building, although now it resembled more a circle of ancient stone huts gathered round a taller, tumbled wall, strewn with rocks.

With my imagination seething I was trying to picture the folk who'd once lived there, when a bent bedraggled form looking more like a giant crow than a human being lumbered towards me from a clump of thorn screeching such foul-mouthed language I was too taken aback to understand. She was waving a stick and had black button eyes under ragged brows and tangled grey locks. Her bristling chin went up at a sharp angle to meet her large hooked nose. The black shawl was torn above her dragging black skirt. Everything about her seemed menacing and evil, risen from the elements to torment me. I didn't mean to show fear though, not of any mad old biddy, however fierce she might appear. Her bones must be so old and brittle, I told myself; one push or tumble could crack them to dust.

All the same a queer shudder ran through me as she came purposefully on, almost bent double with her gimlet eyes glowing maliciously from her uncomely face.

I stared at her until, the first harangue over, her enunciation cleared a little, and words were spat out in a hiss like venom from a snake's tongue.

'Get 'ee begone, devil's spawn,' she rasped. 'Doan' 'ee come 'ere agin trispassin' on Crane land or I'll be cursin' 'ee to the dark pow'rs that ded breed 'ee ... Cana marel O ...'

She lapsed into a strange tongue in such a wild voice I put both hands to my ears and shut my eyes briefly. When I opened them again she was gone. I moved a few feet towards the cluster of twisted thorn and sloes, and saw then there was the dark shape of a hut behind, and the glimmer of something white; an apron blowing from a line, I thought at first, then realized it was the white face of a goat nibbling at the undergrowth.

There seemed no point in lingering there. In any case, it was time I started back. The light was fading quickly, giving a queer, greenish glow to everything, and I realized that the old crone's accusation of trespassing was probably true. I'd somehow strayed on to Ettyn or Crane property. She must be the ancient great-aunt Dorcas, the 'witch', and the erection of tumbled walls and stone must be all that was left of Castle Carnack.

I made my way back as carefully as possible in the direction I'd come, and as I neared the closest point to the road, I noticed with a lurch someone staring at me from a tump of hill the other side.

The figure was dark and tall in the twilight, but a dying ray of sudden pale sun tipped the crown of his head to fiery red. I stopped, startled for a second, then moved on. When I glanced back he'd hardly moved, but I could feel him watching me and sensed an interest and awareness that, following my macabre interlude with old Dorcas, filled me with a wild, mounting apprehension. Why, I didn't know. Even if he wanted to he couldn't harm me, and there was no reason why he should try. But as I reached Gulvarrick I was remembering what Liddy had said about the spell laid on William Pendruggan's cattle so that the herd had been lost.

I didn't believe in witchcraft or magic. I didn't, I *didn't*, I asserted to myself. All the same, I knew from that moment that I'd watch my step where the Ettyns and Cranes were concerned—for the Squire's sake more than my own.

With a warm rush of sympathy, affection for

the lonely man took root and spread in me, flooding me with a longing to protect and help him in any way I could. And by blossom time, when the young lambs were playful in the green fields and the men were working the brown earth, we came together as naturally as warm sunlight to the thrusting, growing things, all barriers swept away by a great thunderstorm.

The morning had been heavy, with dimmed, lowering skies filled with a heavy sweetness clinging to the lush grass and burdened branches of May. Sprays of late-flowering blackthorn still starred the tender green of hedgerows; bluebells were already thrusting from their shining, speared leaves. Except for the chortling of birds and sounds of men in the yard there was nothing to disturb the silence. Yet the very peace held a restless, uneasy feeling about it that my sharpened nerves were quick to sense.

Several times I paused in my work and went to the back, from where I could see, on the rising ground above the road, a group of men, with a red-haired one among them, working near a barn not far from Ettyn's place. The house wasn't visible, standing in its dip beyond, but the twisted shape of a chimney stuck up like a giant crooked finger in the distance, reminding me somehow of the threatening crone near Castle Carnack. A farm cart of the Squire's set off about eleven for Marazion to collect seaweed for the land. I'd have liked to accompany the man, with my hair loose and an old shawl round my shoulders, longing suddenly for a breath of sharp sea air and glimpse of the Mount. But it wouldn't have been fitting for one in my present position so I controlled myself and busied myself reluctantly with household duties.

Liddy must have sensed my restlessness.

'Anythin' wrong, mistress?' she enquired once, with a sidelong look.

'*Wrong?* What should be? What nonsense's got into your head?'

'Nawthen',' she answered, ' 'cept you do seem to be prowlin' round like a hungry fox.'

I should have been annoyed and told her to mind her tongue, but I didn't. Liddy, though dim-witted in most things, could be uncannily perceptive about others. Besides, although she respected me, I knew well I'd already earned a simple affection from her as well, which prompted her at times to be concerned for my welfare.

So I answered simply, 'I've got a *feeling*, Liddy, that's all.'

'Feelin'?'

'That something's going to happen,' I told her unthinkingly. 'If it was by the sea I'd say there'd be a wreck or something before nightfall. But then ...,' I paused before adding, 'it's just my imagination working. Take no notice.'

Her jaw dropped. I could feel the undercurrent of fear stirring her heavy body. 'You bean't one wi' the sight, be you, mistress?' she said in a deep hushed murmur. 'Not like ole Dorcas.'

I laughed.

'Certainly not. Take no notice of me. I'm not used to this quiet, that's all. So still, isn't it?'

'Ah,' she agreed; 'I know what you do mean. Cows feel et, too. All huddled 'gainst hedges they are wi' their tales flickin' so's to warn off th' devil. Strange, knowin' critters they cows be wi' their mooin' an' munchin'.'

'Yes,' I said absently. 'And now enough of gossiping. Give the big room—the drawing-room—a good clean round today Liddy. Now we've got it straight and tidy again it must be kept that way.'

'If you do say so,' she agreed grudgingly, 'though it's my belief it'll never be free o' the ghost thing.'

'*Ghost* thing? What on earth do you mean?' I asked sharply.

'Her ... the one Squire married,' Liddy replied darkly. 'Why doan' 'ee tek 'er picture down? That's what puzzles me somethin' dreadful sometimes. The way she looks down all sneerin' an' wicked as devil's daughter. I get frit, an' that's th' truth, mistress Judith.'

'Now don't be silly,' I said sharply. 'And put all stupid thoughts of ghosts from your mind. How could ... Mrs Pendruggan ... haunt the drawing-room when she's alive and being cared for in hospital? Ghosts, if there *are* such things, can only happen when people die; and *that's* all stuff and nonsense, too, so try and show a little sense girl, even if you haven't got much.'

Liddy retreated to the kitchen to finish what work she had to do before starting on the drawing-room. But with her words still in my mind, I went for a glimpse of the luxurious interior that had been so savagely ravaged the night before my arrival at Gulvarrick. Mostly I'd avoided it, not caring to be reminded of poor William Pendruggan's ordeal. Now I realized that something of the atmosphere—something dark and fearful—must have lingered in my memory unwittingly, telling me to keep away.

In spite of the havoc which had destroyed so much that was precious and beautiful, the room still emitted an air of haunted elegance. In the yellowing light, sombre dark green and purple shadows lingered about the satins and velvets of upholstery and curtains, throwing gilt and gold into glistening relief from the tall windows. A gilt clock still ticked from the mantelshelf, which was odd, I thought, as the Squire himself must have wound it; and from the wall above, the contemptuous yet beautiful face of his raven-haired wife smiled down faintly, her green eyes glinting with the strange, illusory effect of transient life in them. It was almost as though she was whispering through the shadows, 'Don't trespass here. This place is *mine.*'

Because of it and because commonsense told me it was only my own voice talking, I stiffened my back and waited there, just staring. It was at that moment Squire Pendruggan came in.

There was the creak of the door, the tread of footsteps on the thick pink carpet, and a voice saying behind my shoulder, 'What's bothering you, Judith? There's nothing here for you to worry over. Isabella will never return to torment Gulvarrick again.'

So her name was Isabella.

I turned, with a faint shudder up my spine. 'It seems very sad, sir,' I heard myself saying, 'and I didn't mean to intrude. I've just instructed Liddy to clean round and came along myself to see what was what. I mean ...'

'Yes, yes, there's no need to explain,' he said, with his hand on my forearm. 'I know you mean well, and that's how I feel for you, m'dear. I don't want you to be bothered by anything of the past. It's right for Liddy to give a sweep round now and then, but there are happier rooms in the house for you and I to be concerned with. Atmospheres have a way of clinging, and though I'm not a superstitious man by any manner of means, what I always say is ... let the dead bury the dead.'

I nearly retorted impulsively, Then why are you so careful to keep the clock wound, sir? But I didn't. Deep down I knew: I knew that, whatever fresh life he might carve for himself, for so long as he lived the portrait of Isabella his wife would remain hanging at Gulvarrick, as it had done since the day it was painted.

In a different way it was the same with me, I suppose; until Matt came back, or news of his death or some other strange fate was brought to me, a secret corner of my life would belong to him—a memory unwished for but part of my past which could never entirely be eradicated, because we'd shared it.

I was ruminating over this when Mr Pendruggan said, shortly before the mid-day meal, 'I've the court to attend in Penzance this afternoon, Judith. Would you care to accompany me? Pascoe will drive us, and you could maybe do shopping and stroll round on your own while I deal with the law.'

My heart jumped. The idea of being away from the solitary, heavy air of the countryside for a few hours was just what I needed at the moment.

'Thank you,' I said. 'I'd like it very much.'

So at two forty-five prompt, we set off in the carriage for the town, behind Pascoe, with the two spirited greys in front. I thought the man looked very smart in his yellow coat and stove hat; William Pendruggan also, who had a special, dignified air in a tailed black top-coat I'd not seen before, and a tall, black beaver hat. He had a high white collar that hid any bulges under his well-shaped chin, and I felt proud to be sitting there beside him. When I'd saved enough from his wages, I thought—which wouldn't take long, since he paid me well—I'd buy myself something more colourful than my best dark dress. Yellow silk wouldn't do for outings, being more suitable for the Fiddler's Arms, but a green taffeta costume perhaps could be fitted and made by the seamstress who lived not far from the market.

'What are you thinking about, Judith?' the Squire asked, as the carriage turned at the bottom of the hill into the main road. 'It seems to me there's something on your mind.'

I smiled up at him. 'No, sir. Nothing particular. I was what my grandmother would have called "dreaming nonsense".'

'Ah.'

I turned away, lifting my chin high, knowing I looked well in profile and that his eyes were studying me intently.

'I think the weather's thunderous,' I added, feeling something more was expected of me. 'Will it be hot in court, sir?'

'Plaguey so, I've no doubt,' he said. 'Not good for the poor rascals brought before me.'

'I'm sure you'd always be fair, Mr Pendruggan,' I told him.

'Ah. Um. Maybe, maybe,' he agreed with a hint of embarrassment, 'but folk—even magistrates—aren't all bred alike, m'dear, and when men get testy they don't always see straight.'

His hand touched mine gently, lingering there for a few moments longer than it should have done, but I didn't pull away, not wishing to hurt his feelings and at the same time being careful to show no sign I'd noticed it.

As we neared the town a rush of air, salty, from brine drifted across the harbour from St Michael's Mount, but the sky was still sullen over the harbour, stirring a brooding melancholy in me that, try as I would, I couldn't rid myself of, even when Mr Pendruggan had gone to the courtroom, leaving me free to stroll about the streets. There was no sun to lighten up the shops, and the pavements had a dreary, dusty look, so I wandered down to the beach where the seaweed smell crept pungent and strong across the round shining stones, stretching in a grey curve dotted with black patches and pale sand from Marazion.

It was then I saw someone with a familiar look about him, strolling casually from the direction of Marazion as though he owned the world; a seaman in high boots and a black jersey, dark head turned to the sky as though it was good to have berthed after a long journey. I knew the type and I knew the man. My heart lurched. I could only stand staring for a moment or two, remembering a day when Matt and he had wandered towards the wharf from Port Einack harbour and the way I'd rushed at them with the wild words on my lips because of the hot meal waiting and Matt's lateness.

Nick; as large as life, with a wide grin on his brown face and wry amusement glinting in his black eyes.

'Why,' he said, as though surprised—which he probably was—'if it ain't Cap'n Matt's good lady. Sure nice to see you again, ma'am ...'

Ignoring the proffered hand, I remarked coolly, with dignity I hoped, 'Good afternoon, Mr Jago. I hope you're well.'

There was a flash of very white teeth as his eyes slid over my figure in a way I'd been accustomed to in the old days.

'All the better for seeing you, that's for sure. A pretty woman's a good sight to any man after weeks at sea with nothing for company but bawdy sailors and a load of copra. Put in here to get a few repairs done 'fore rounding Land's End for Bristol.'

'I see. Well, I'll not delay you,' I said stiffly. 'You must have things to do just as I have.'

'Now, now,' Jago said, 'surely there's a

question or two you wanta ask, 'bout Matt an' Topaz? 'Twas a hard thing you did to him, ma'am, when you sent 'em away. Very cut up he was.'

'Oh *dear,'* I said with heavy sarcasm. 'I'm so very *sorry*. It was my own fault, of course, for having believed a word of his lying tongue.'

The last part slipped out bitterly without my hardly even knowing it. I ought to have walked away and let the conversation end at that point but curiosity about Matt kept me rooted there until Jago commented reflectively, 'Sailors aren't like other folks, ma'am. You have to make allowances for a bit of indulgence when a full-blooded man gets a foot on land. It don't mean nothing in the long run ...'

'Except bigamy and a bastard son,' I interrupted harshly. 'And don't try and tell me that ... that *Topaz* meant nothing. He *married* her and when he took me it was in shame.'

'Oh no, there was no shame where you were concerned, ma'am. You sure meant more than all the rest put together.'

'There were others?' I almost shouted. 'Of course there were. I should've known. What's done once can be done again and again ... how do *I* know how many?'

'You don't,' Jago answered shortly. 'And what the Cap'n does away from you don't affect you, I reckon. You should've stuck by him, missis. The fire would've died in him in th' end, and he'd have stayed with you or taken you with him, if you'd played your cards right.'

My blood boiled then.

'I don't *play* with marriage, Mr Jago, and now I'll be going. I've an appointment in the town.'

'No message for the Cap'n then?'

'None,' I said, with ruthless determination, 'except to see to it I have none of his friends spying on me every time a vessel berths in Cornish ports. Good day to you.'

I swept past him, with my skirts raised slightly in both hands, like any modish lady of fashion. I didn't look back, but I could feel his eyes following me and knew my manner had angered him. Well, let him get the message properly over to Matt when he saw him, that was all I wanted. At that moment, despite my proud air, I hated both of them with a force I'd not thought I possessed. My heart was beating wildly against my ribs and in my throat, half-choking me. Dizziness half-blinded my eyes with a mixture of emotions risen like ghosts to torment me; most of all, bitterness at Matt's duplicity and disregard for what he'd done to me. Topaz was not the only one. Jago had admitted it. I was just one of many. A plaything for his use in Cornwall, no more. No better than an ignorant whore or servant girl caught up by his hot, grey eyes and lying tongue.

After a time, when Jago had disappeared, I sat down on the stones to recover myself and gradually my heart eased. It didn't matter, I told myself, as I got up, straightened my skirts and prepared to return to the promenade. In the morning, probably Jago would have gone, and with him the distressing memories he'd revived.

But things weren't as easy as that. Forgetting never is, not for a woman when she's once loved anyone as passionately as I'd loved Matt. An hour later when I set off again with Squire Pendruggan in the carriage for Gulvarrick, a restless unease still lingered, something he was quick to notice.

'You're quiet, Judith,' he said, 'but not restful. The weather is it?'

'I expect so,' I answered, grateful for the excuse. 'The air's so close. Maybe rain would freshen things.'

At that moment it started; not much at first, just occasional heavy drops spattering the leaves and grass. By the time we reached the house the rain had increased, with an occasional low rumble from the west. But it wasn't till late that night that the real storm began, driving against the house with lashing fury lit by spasmodic flashes of lightning. The ominous crack and roll of thunder caused agitation amongst the birds outside and the whinnying of horses from the stables.

I got up from my bed and went to the window. There was nothing to be seen through the streaming glass, only rivulets of water against the black sky, lashed on a rising wind through the moaning, bent trees. Then, when the lightning and thunder struck simultaneously, there was a sudden tremendous cracking and roaring from below as though the house had fallen.

Putting a shawl around my shoulders, I

instinctively rushed downstairs through the intermittent flaring light, towards the drawing-room.

The Squire was there; a broad, strong figure holding a lamp that swung drunkenly in his hand. He didn't move for some seconds, not until I touched him on the shoulder.

'What is it?' I said. 'Mr Pendruggan, what's happened here?'

He turned and stared at me, his usual florid face grey in the lamp's fitful glow.

'Look,' he said, pointing towards the fireplace. 'My God, Judith, she's got her way this time.'

At first I didn't understand. Then, going into the room I saw that bricks had tumbled to the fireplace from the chimney and were lying there with a charred-looking ball of lead or some such metal.

'A thunderbolt,' he said, going forward. 'We've been hit. There's something accursed about Gulvarrick, Judith, something that'll cost me my life in the end.'

'Nonsense,' I said, with a great rush of pity to see such a strong man so crumpled with anguish and fear like a great child somehow, facing a dilemma he'd no way of comprehending. But I knew what he meant, because in spite of the rubble and the tumbled objects about the floor, the painting of Isabella was still untouched in its place on the wall, its glass intact and the lovely face coldly sneering above the mess.

When he didn't reply I reached for his hand. 'Come away, sir,' I begged. 'You can't do any good here. In the morning we can find out just what's happened. But ... there's nothing to be feared of. It's just the storm, Mr Pendruggan, like we used to get at Port Einack sometimes. Only worse happened there sometimes, when men were drowned at sea.'

He looked down at me, and there was such a longing for comfort on his large face, my being went out to him and I knew if he needed me that night, I'd be there.

And so it was. All of what I gave to William Pendruggan, following the storm, could have been Matt's if he'd wished for it. But Matt, tossing me coldly aside, had left only a great empty vacuum where my heart had been, a vacuum waiting for a man's need to fill it.

William's.

Long after the storm had passed, when quietness lay over the countryside and even the wild gulls were still, we lay in his great bed, close together, marvelling that from anguish could spring such a wealth of belonging. His large hands were gentle on my thighs and breasts, his lips stirring a dead part of me to life again. Against my flesh his own pulsed with a desire long denied. And when at last fulfilment took both of us to forgetfulness we slept at peace, his lips touching my hair, my face buried against his shoulder.

CHAPTER 9

I think the next few months were probably the most peaceful of all my life, which shows how many sides there are to loving. With Matt everything had been life and movement, passion and laughter, brightness and the dark; a constant change of moods that had kept me always on the brink of wondering what was to come next. With William it was like the slow waking up of a flower that had been too long in bud; a kindliness that had compassion in it as well as the warm stirring of summer's waking. I didn't feel for him with the wildness that had been only for Matt. Nor did I wish to. William Pendruggan needed me; I was content to give what I could, because he was a good man, and his thought and respect for me helped heal the scars Matt had left behind.

The corn grew strong and straight in the fields that year, and the days were mostly fine, filled with sunshine that ripened the fruit early and brought the grain to golden prime. Sometimes Liddy and I would give a hand to the men in their work. William didn't seem to mind, and I was relieved to be free of having always to ape a lady of fashion.

Then, at nights when my body was tired, I'd go up to bed early, knowing that a little later, when Liddy was safely in her room, William would visit me, staying if he wished, or not, just as the mood took him. But his arms would be strong and warm round me, and as my body felt the deep pulse leap throbbingly to his touch, life would flow rich between us until the summer darkness took us to sleep.

Once as we lay side by side after coming together, William said gravely, 'If I was free, Judy ... if circumstances were different ... I'd ask you to be my wife. I'm sorry it can't be. Sometimes it makes me wonder to myself what right I have to place you in this position ... and you young enough to be my daughter. Did you know that? Forty-five I am, nearly forty-six.'

I laughed. 'Forty-six? Gracious! To think I'm lying with Methuselah himself.'

And he pulled me to him, slapping and caressing me softly, so I wriggled nearer, all cosy and eager for him to have me again.

The right or wrong of things didn't worry me at all. Perhaps it should have done; certainly my grandmother would have thought so. But then she hadn't had much joy out of life, and it seemed to me then that joy in living was what human beings were meant for. If no one else was hurt by it, where could the harm be, marriage lines or not?

It was only occasionally, when William was away in Penzance, that the image of Matt rose again briefly, and I'd think of him with a sudden stab of physical pain more cutting than toothache because I knew if Matt had been true to me I'd have been faithful as I'd promised, until death, and no other man in the world would've dared to touch me. But Matt had betrayed me, leaving me neither wife nor virgin, so why should I sacrifice all warmth and happiness that came my way for the sake of a cold and sterile virtue?

How much Liddy guessed of what was going on I didn't know, but as she slept on the top floor at the other side of the house and was forever mooning round at that time over Pascoe's son who was a sturdy growing lad, I don't think she'd any idea, nor would I have cared if she had.

Adam was different. Adam occasionally threw a dark, suspicious glance at me whenever William and I had been in conversation. Country people, I'd already found, had shrewd minds about such things; but what he didn't know he couldn't prove, and anyway, he wouldn't have risked starting a rumour and losing his job.

I was careful, too, never to give a sign of familiarity towards the Squire on the rare occasions he had company at Gulvarrick. The company was mostly fellow farmers and their wives. But on one special night Lord and Lady St Heriot themselves were entertained to dinner. Lady St Heriot was a tall, pale, elegant figure, wearing a high-necked, grey silk dress with her white piled hair entwined with a ribbon and a rose in it. Her husband, who hemmed and hawed and boomed in a loud voice about nothing in particular, was long-faced, with a domineering aristocratic nose and a high colour at the cheek bones. I had an uncomfortable idea that when the meal was over and most of the wine gone, he'd some proposition to put to William; I guessed it could easily be for acquiring some of the good Pendruggan land.

I hoped not. Selling any of the property that had been in the family for generations—hundreds of years, he'd told me—was a worry to him. But I *did* know, although he never fretted me with financial problems, that money was tight with him just then; he had had to breed a new dairy stock and pay out more than he could comfortably afford for his mad wife, the lovely Isabella.

He seemed his usual, easy self that evening, and I saw to it that nothing could be complained of in the meal, preparing it myself and attending at the table wearing my sober black under a starched white apron with a dot of a white, lacy cap on my head. My hair was drawn back severely and pinned tight. Liddy had smirked when she'd first seen me looking so prim and straight-laced.

'Lawks, mistress,' she'd exclaimed, 'you do look like some schoolma'am 'bout to bring out th' switch.'

'Mind your language,' I'd said, 'or you shall have a taste of it.' Suddenly we'd both burst out giggling.

Oh the dinner was a most proper one in every way, with roast duck, apple pie served with dollops of rich cream, and a special butter-milk cake made by my own hands as an extra. Liddy, due to the excitement of the occasion, was as alert as she could be, waiting in the kitchen with dishes ready to carry behind me into the large dining-room.

When the meal was over Lord St Heriot and the Squire retired to the drawing-room, while I helped his lady adjust a flower on her gown in the small ladies' apartment leading from the hall. Then she smiled at me and offered a coin, which brought the blood to my face.

'No, thank you, ma'am ... mi'lady,' I said with a touch of hauteur. 'It's a housekeeper's business to see Mr Pendruggan's guests are looked after.'

A strange, knowing look seemed to flash across her thin face.

'I *see,'* she said with a frosty smile. 'Your master's extremely lucky to have so competent a young woman at his service, and you, if I may say so, are ...'

'Lucky, too,' I interrupted quickly. 'Yes, I think so, ma'am.'

But a slow anger gathered in me like a sullen cloud that would have exploded if I'd had much more of it. For the first time I recognized how invidious was my position in the Squire's house, and a longing for freedom stirred in me as I remembered against my will my wild days with Matt when I'd been beholden to no one but him. I'd determined never to think of him again, but that evening as I lay lonely in my comfortable bed, I did. I thought of him and was very near to cursing him for leaving me unwanted to find affection elsewhere, in a house that wasn't mine and with a middle-aged lover I could never wed.

Perhaps I was overtired, or maybe Lady St Heriot's condescending manner had shamed my vanity more than I knew. She'd every right, I told myself; I *was* fulfilling a servant's place at Gulvarrick. There'd been nothing wrong in what she'd said. But for that long hour before William joined me to soothe my nerves and longings to peace, I was no longer Judith Thomas, housekeeper to a country squire, but Luzana of the miniature lying in my drawer—Luzana of the slim form and noble bearing, dancing somewhere in a strange land of another age when young gallants knelt before me and rich men drank my toast.

Thinking this way made me feel better. Since childhood I'd learned the value of dreaming for restoring self-esteem, so when William came to my room later the worst of my mood was over, though the soft touch of unshed tears was still moist against my lashes.

'Why, love,' William said, bending over me and touching my forehead with his lips, 'what's bothering you?'

I shook my head.

'Nothing, nothing at all. Perhaps I'm a bit weary. Weariness takes all women like that sometimes.'

He took my chin in his hands and stared long and thoughtfully into my face.

'You mustn't work so hard on my account,' he told me. 'I'll not have it. The meal was excellent ... superb, Judy, but there was no need to go to so much trouble. What you need is more help. I'll have to see about getting another girl in ...'

I sat up abruptly, with my eyes suddenly cleared and my chin out.

'No, sir ... no, William. If you do that I'll get up and walk out right away; you see if I don't. What a way to speak, and with the bad luck you've had to suffer.'

His face softened as he drew me to him, and I was content to relax in his strong arms, but with no waking of passion in me this time, only a great longing for sleep.

He knew and understood. Although there was no intercourse between us that evening, he lay all night close against me, and I slept deeply and calmly until the morning came with the distant sounds of activity from the farm-yard and a cock bravely crowing.

Next day the restless tension had gone, temporarily allaying all conflicting memories of Matt. But in the afternoon when I went to get wild flowers for my bedroom, I was brought face to face with Venn Ettyn. Although my first feeling was of quick dislike, I knew from the very first moment that in some way, however dark, he would play a part in my future.

How could I tell? I didn't even know myself, because the intuitive inner voice doesn't give answers; it only points the way.

Perhaps there'd be a long-drawn out war between us on the Squire's account. Perhaps in some way Ettyn would be to me just a means to an end, a way of buying back for William what had been stolen. I tried to think this was the answer. But no amount of reasoning has any real power against instinct, and my instinct told me to watch my step or I'd be up against something stronger and more formidable than anything I'd had to fight in my life before.

Yes, that's how it was during those first seconds when my eyes met his, tawny gold and staring down on me from a chestnut stallion almost as red as his own hair.

'Good morning,' he said, in a strong, low voice that was more cultured than I'd expected. 'We haven't met, although I've seen you around often enough. Pendruggan's ... housekeeper ... aren't you?'

'That's true,' I answered, trying to ignore his hesitation over the word housekeeper.

'Lucky man,' he said, but without a smile. 'I'm Ettyn. Venn Ettyn, in case you didn't know.'

'I *did* know,' I answered, 'the same as I knew you were no friend of the Squire's.'

'That's not my fault,' he said calmly. 'I don't go in for feuds as a rule. So I hope there'll be none between you and me.'

'If you don't get in my way and I don't get in yours, there's no reason for there to be so long as you behave right to Mr Pendruggan,' I told him. 'And now, if you don't mind, I'll be on my way.'

With my chin high I swept past him, but in a second he'd jumped from his horse and caught up with me.

'Look, Miss Thomas,' he said. 'Or ...'

'Mrs Thomas,' I corrected him, so he'd try no liberties.

'Mrs Thomas or Miss, it makes no difference,' he replied maddeningly. 'I've no personal motive in speaking, except to spare any future misunderstandings about trespassing.'

'I ...'

'Let me finish,' he continued. 'I want you to know you're free to wander about Castle Carnack any time you choose. That part of the moor's legally mine, true. And a good thing, too, or some spineless gentleman could've sold it when his pocket was low, for exploitation and a mint of gold. Land like that can't properly be owned; it belongs to itself, and the last thing I'd do would be prevent anyone with an appreciation of its character walking there. Do you understand?'

'No,' I answered. 'The only time I went there was by mistake, and I was sent off by an old woman with a string of words I couldn't repeat. Your aunt, I suppose?'

'So she says ... several times removed though,' he answered. 'Take no notice of her, Mrs Thomas. Most people don't. I'll have a word with her, but I'd say you were equal to a mad old biddy any day.'

His narrow golden eyes had a thoughtful yet enigmatic look in them before he nodded, took his horse by the reins and started walking back down the lane. But in those brief moments I noticed how high his cheek bones were, the firm clean set of his rather thin lips and a certain remote hardness about him which suggested he'd be a dangerous man to cross.

I went on towards the moors thinking over his words about the land, how it belonged to itself. In a way I understood what he'd meant; wild places, like people, couldn't be claimed or fenced in. Somewhere then behind that cold, rather forbidding exterior there must be a sensitive quality he kept carefully hidden except to those who felt as he did. Me? But how had he known?

I was still pondering about it when I reached a thin copse of trees fringing the moor. I turned and from where I stood I could see the Ettyn farm with its crooked chimney sprawling in the hollow. It looked a queer place, with a square granite front joined on each side by stables or cattle sheds to another back part with an archway in the centre. I recalled what William had said about the house having been enlarged after the family prospered from humble beginnings through 'hush-money' concerning Venn's ancestry; also, Ettyn's allusion to 'some spineless gentleman', by whom he'd obviously meant the Squire.

Neither of these points seemed sufficient to warrant such bitterness on William's part. If he'd *had* to sell land, what did it matter who it went to, be it Venn or someone else who might easily build or desecrate property that had historical or archaeological value?

Whether Ettyn had wilfully meant to imply contempt of William Pendruggan or not, I didn't know. But for the first time I felt a mild stab of criticism for the Squire. Not because he wanted to retain what was his, but because, perhaps, he hadn't fought harder. I'd sensed from the beginning the streak of softness in him which had meant gentleness and kindness as well, and I'd been grateful then, because my spirit and body were still suffering from Matt's hard treatment. In a way we'd both been in the same reactionary state; William tormented by the memory of his wild wife, and myself by the callous indifference of a man who'd deceived me into thinking he was my legal husband when he was no such thing.

I'd been William's prop, just as he'd been mine. There'd been no hypocrisy in our relationship; no shame, only a deep need and capacity for loving and—until the brief meeting with Venn Ettyn that afternoon—no doubt.

Now suddenly, a niggle of discomfiture wormed its way into my thoughts. Summer was already at its height, with foxgloves, wild roses, and lush late bluebells starring the ditches and woods and hedgerows. The heather smelled sweet from the moor, and wild things scuttled through the long, curled bracken. Birds sang, and the wings of gulls were silver-white against the blue sky.

But how long would summer last? And how long would any life with William endure?

I knew full well a woman who loved truly should not question affection in this way, but as a small, frail cloud briefly dimmed the sun's radiance, the memory of Venn Ettyn's youthful figure looking down on me reminded me with painful reality of clear, cold facts. William was already nearer fifty than forty and too well fed to retain his looks for much longer. There had been nights recently when he had been unable to appease the physical ardour I felt for him; nights, to my shame, when I'd tried to pretend with my eyes closed that he was Matt. On the other hand, the great warmth between us had so far kept our feelings for each other a living and firm bond. Would the bond still be there when he was old and portly and perhaps testy with gout?

I knew very well such thoughts were wrong and dishonourable, and recognized that only the sight of the younger man had roused such restlessness in me. If I'd been able to believe in God as the men of Port Einack had done when they set out under cold skies for a night's fishing, I'd have prayed as they prayed, before setting sail, for safety and sustenance. But my God was different; my God was the need to give all I had in human love, receiving my full share in return.

If that was wickedness, then I was wicked like my mother had been, and there was nothing I could do about it or even really wanted to.

When I got back to Gulvarrick with a bunch of bluebells held sweet and fragrant against my cheek, William was waiting for me in the hall. His face was rosy and smiling in greeting, though perspiration trickled in beads down his forehead. Having learned to be discreet, we didn't kiss or so much as touch hands, but I told myself with a rush of relief and wishful thinking that all was well, today was today and tomorrow was tomorrow, with a wealth of tomorrows ahead, each a little life in itself.

I didn't know then, there was no way of telling, how few tomorrows at Gulvarrick there'd be.

CHAPTER 10

The harvest was a rich, golden one that year, accompanied by traditional ceremonies which were an experience for me who'd never known the 'Crying of the Neck', when the last swath was dressed with poppies and cornflowers and carried to Gulvarrick kitchen to be hung up.

William was there with between twenty and thirty men, apart from the household staff; and we gave a fine supper—'the Gooldize'—later, with beef, boiled mutton, fuggans, buns, apple pie and cream, and plenty of cider.

It had been a busy day for me, preparing things beforehand with Liddy, but I wasn't too tired to enjoy the merry-making afterwards and the singing of such songs as 'Green Brooms', 'Here's a Health to the Barley Mow' and 'Harvest Home'.

William was like a great overgrown boy for those five hours, and it was hard to associate him with the correct man of fashion he was at the magistrate's bench. All seemed merriment and goodness and satisfaction with work well done. Manners were easy and free, unrestricted by class or station.

When the last workers had gone home and Liddy, Adam and the boy were safely abed, William took me by the hand and led me to the wide-open front door. Looking out into the quiet moon-bright sky where the stars hung so brilliantly over the countryside he said, 'We shall never forget this night, my love.'

And I answered with a rush of emotion so complicated with happiness and sadness I couldn't rightly understand, 'No, never.'

'Whatever happens in the future,' he continued, 'this has been a rare occasion—one of the rarest of my life—because you've been with me. A man's heritage means a great deal to him, Judith. And for generations ... hundreds of years since the fifteenth century, family roots have been here on this land. Mine, and those that bred me. Yet when I go there'll be no son to carry on.'

I would have liked to say, 'If you have a son by me, sir, would it count?' But the question remained unasked, because I knew there could be no satisfactory answer. In some ways William Pendruggan was a conventional man, and although he cared for me I doubted that a boy born out of wedlock would be to his taste. Besides, I wasn't at all sure I wanted it. Even during those moments of deep communion between us doubt was growing in me, a frail, uncertain shadow telling me of Time's quick passing, how all things must end sometime, and that one day, not far ahead perhaps, my life with William Pendruggan might end.

Whether it was the inner-voice speaking to me or the lingering memory of the old hag's vile harangue and cursing by Castle Carnack, I didn't know. Lying beside William later and listening to his steady breathing above the clock's tick at the bed-side, I told myself it was just overtiredness and that in the morning everything would appear different.

But when morning came the cloud still lingered at the back of my mind. I got up early and went to pick mushrooms in a high field bordering the moors. They grew thick and luscious there following a heavy dew, and the Squire had a great liking for them, although they faintly revolted my taste, reminding me always of poisonous fungi that were said to thrive where the devil trod. This, of course was merely an old woman's tale, and at my age I should have learned to disregard it. But stories heard in youth have a habit of reviving in lonely moments, and I *was* lonely that day. The world seemed so quiet, too, following the night's festivities; all still and perfectly silent under a veil of mist, with nothing but the echo of a cock's crowing from below and an occasional screeching of a gull from the sea.

My basket was almost full when I looked up and saw, with a start, Venn Ettyn walking towards me over the short grass. He wore knee breeches with an open-necked shirt, and his red hair glowed bright from the damp and lifting light.

A strange sort of quiver ran through my body. I wanted to be haughty and aloof and put him at a distance, but it was hard to do that with my heart bounding so fiercely I could hear it thumping against my throat.

'Oh!' I said, pulling the shawl close at my neck. *'You.'*

If he smiled I didn't notice it. I realized intuitively that smiles wouldn't come easy to him. He had a serious alertness, a quick, shrewd turn of mind and body that could have belonged to a fox or some wild creature assessing a dangerous position. His manner when he spoke, though, was entirely civilized.

'I didn't mean to startle you,' he said, 'or to trespass either ... which I'm doing.'

Shaking my loose hair over my shoulders and straightening my back, I asked, 'What is it you want, Mr Ettyn?'

'Do I have to have a reason for talking?'

'No. But ...'

'Of course I do. And I have,' he told me rather shortly. 'Seeing you about so early alone made me think I'd get off my chest what's been nagging me for some time.'

'Really? I can't see where I can come into it,' I replied, 'or what business of yours can possibly concern me.'

'It doesn't,' he replied. 'My business is my own affair. It's yours I'm talking about.'

'But ...'

Without giving me a chance to continue he went on, 'I'm no friend of Pendruggan's, and he's none of mine, because he's wished it like that. But if you ever find yourself in a dilemma, Judith Thomas, remember I'm not far over the way to give a hand. And don't act indignant. You may well need advice sometime, even a place to go to, if things work out as I think. My doors then will be open to you. You can rest assured I've no dark intentions of seduction or of taking a wife. To be frank, women don't greatly interest me, except to pull their weight domestically. You look a strong young woman, if a little wisht and perplexed. But that's to be expected, after last night's festivities. Anyway, that's what I wanted to say—from a strictly business angle, you understand. My farm, Thorncarne, needs a bit of extra help in the house. So if you want a place, there's one ready for you there any day.'

He turned to go, and a second later, before I'd even had time to give a tart answer, he was striding away to the gate bordering the road. By the time I'd properly got my thoughts in order he was already a tall, dark shape receding into the mist clouding his own field path.

As I walked back slowly to the house it was with a queer feeling of perplexity in me. He annoyed me, and I didn't like him; I resented his cold arrogance, which had seemed impervious to any mood of mine. The allusion to not wanting a mistress or wife was, I thought, insulting, although he may not have meant it to be. Obviously my own feelings were unimportant to him. Then why had he been so quick to put his proposition to me? Perhaps he just pitied me, or perhaps he saw a chance of obtaining cheap labour if and when I left Gulvarrick.

But what had given him the idea I might need a haven? Suddenly my circumstances and future seemed shaky and uncertain. I never doubted William's affection for me, nor mine for him. But affection needed roots to thrive on, and I had none in the Squire's household.

As the day wore on, my fears had lifted. I told myself how stupid I'd been to let Venn Ettyn or the old hag on the moors disturb me.

Twice during that week I caught a glimpse of Ettyn's sister, or rather half-sister; once she was going down the lane with a black-haired young man I guessed was one of her brothers. Even from a distance I could see she was handsome and well-formed, walking upright with a bold, free step and swing of her skirts that made me think of a dancer. She was wearing something red at her neck, and her black hair fell to her waist. With the sun on it, it shone bright as a raven's wing. The man had an air of defiance about him, walking sharply with his chin up as though going into battle. He was brown-skinned and gave a feeling of great energy. Once when the girl touched his arm he shook her off. She shrugged, tossed her head and suddenly left him, turning back the way she'd come.

The second time we saw each other was face to face, and in the early morning, too, when I'd gone once again for mushrooms. Whether she'd seen me before I didn't know, but there was a paper bag in her hand, stained with blue juice. I'd reached the moor, and she was hovering by a great bunch of laden bramble on Pendruggan's side of the lane.

That didn't worry me. I was certainly not going to begrudge her a few blackberries, even on William's behalf, but she stepped in front of me abruptly and said in a husky, rather deep voice, 'All's free in the lane, you know. Or didn't you?'

I laughed. 'I'd not thought of it. But I'm sure you're right. They're large here, aren't they? The berries, I mean. I like them, especially with cream.'

My friendliness must have taken her aback. She stared for a moment, her eyes dead on mine. I noticed how large they were, like shining sloes fringed by thick black lashes. Then she said, 'You meet Venn sometimes, don't you? The Squire won't like that. There's a feud, in case you didn't know.'

'It's nothing to do with me,' I told her pointedly. 'I'm just the housekeeper.'

'Oh? Is *that* so?' She laughed cynically, showing a glimpse of very white teeth. 'Sorry. I didn't know. Well ... I must be getting back.'

She turned away and went past me down the lane towards Thorncarne. What impudence, I thought, wishing I'd had a tart answer ready. My hand was tingling from a repressed desire to slap her face. If the rest of the family were like her I could well imagine that the stories of them being a wild lot were true. But one at least wasn't. However strongly he might feel about his own concerns and family matters, he'd an unusual capacity for hiding his emotions. Remembering our brief meeting I could hardly believe that he and the girl were brother and sister. Though both were handsome in their different ways, there wasn't the slightest resemblance in their features or manners. Then I recalled the relationship was on one side only and couldn't help wondering about Venn's father from whom, probably, he'd inherited his strange, almond-shaped, golden eyes, flaming hair, clear-cut profile and aloof way of speech.

Penzance court was held the next day, and before he set off William said, 'It may be a long session, Judith, so I won't ask you to accompany me this time. Perhaps you'll dine with me tonight though. I haven't seen as much of you as I want, recently.'

I smiled. 'Very well. Yes, that would be nice.'

Owing to the conventions and having to keep our relationship so rigidly to ourselves it wasn't often this happened, but once in a while we risked any talk between Liddy and Adam, and ate in the dining-room, instead of my sitting in my own small parlour, which I was beginning to dislike more and more as the days went by.

I arranged a simple meal, but one William liked—roast chicken and fruit pie, followed by cheese and biscuits. I was wearing a dress I'd had made by the seamstress only a fortnight ago; green silk, tight over the bust and at the waist, cut a little lower in front than usual, but quite respectably, showing just the shadow of curving breasts below. I'd pinned my dark russet hair high on top, leaving a few curls to stray against my cheeks. Knowing I looked my best, and feeling William's eyes warm upon me when I took my place at the table filled me once more with a glowing peace, the nearest I ever got to happiness those days. I wanted to please and flatter him, and later to have him close so my flesh and his were fused into the contentment of giving and taking, bringing mutual comfort.

Any restlessness I'd had completely disappeared, and I was content to see him well-fed and mellowed before me, just a little over-flushed, perhaps, from the wine and good brandy, with his senses stirring to physical desire.

The day had been warm and the windows were opened to the freshening coolness of early evening when I heard a commotion outside in the road somewhere; horses' hooves coming to a halt and the sound of male voices overshadowed by a woman's, harsh and imperious.

We were just finishing our meal and preparing to go to the parlour. William jumped up quickly, with a napkin to his mouth. I knew immediately from his stance and expression of his eyes that something was very wrong.

'What's the matter?' I asked. 'William ...'

'Sit down,' he said, more sharply than he'd ever spoken to me before. 'I'll attend to this.'

But he didn't have a chance.

Before he reached the door it opened, and with an outraged flutter of furs, skirts, draperies, and frills, a woman came in, tall and hypnotic in her rage, green-eyed, with two spots of brilliant colour burning her cheeks. She had a muff in one hand and a beaded handbag in the other, which she threw across the room just missing William's face.

'So!' she remarked in a high shrill voice. 'This is what you get up to when I care to take a rest for a few weeks.' The contempt in her voice was unbearable, and I waited for William to crush her, but he merely said, 'Isabella, my dear, calm yourself. There's nothing to be distressed about. Mrs Thomas, our new housekeeper, was merely dining with me for once.'

'Dining? Once?' She laughed. 'Don't be a fool, William. I know you.' And then she turned to me. 'I know *your* kind, too. Do you think there haven't been others of your sort before you, whoring after my husband in my absence?'

She paused, staring at me outraged, and never had I seen anyone so beautiful and at the same time so evil.

I faced her calmly, though my whole body was trembling.

'You don't understand,' I said. 'There's nothing ...' I broke off helplessly, unable to deny so much that was true.

'Understand?' she shrieked. 'I *understand* all right. Get out, do you hear? Get out at once ...'

William went towards her placatingly. 'My love, you've got everything wrong. She means nothing to me ...'

I could hardly believe my ears. The room suddenly rocked around me. I thought I should be sick. I stared helplessly, hopelessly, at William's face, searching for some sign he didn't mean it, that he was merely trying to calm her. But there was none. As he took her hand, lifting one of his to her fevered cheek, I knew I no longer existed for him any more. He was completely besotted, as he always would be when she was about. His eyes, limpid from the wine and the shock of seeing her, were mournful and pleading as a sick dog's. He *loved* her.

In my weakness I clutched at the chair for support and would have sat, but pushing William aside, she clutched me by the shoulder and brought one thin hand hard against my face.

'Did you hear me? Get *out,* this very instant, or I'll have you whipped ... beaten down the road as you deserve ... trollop!'

'William ...,' I begged, but unavailingly. His eyes when he glanced at me were tortured but empty of any response.

'Perhaps it would be better,' he said feebly.

Better? Better? How could it be? How could this man I'd trusted with my body and all I had to give treat me with such callous indifference, such cruel disregard for my feelings or dignity? My throat ached with the tears too frozen to reach my eyes. I could hardly stand because of faintness and the queer, unreal feeling of being in some obscene nightmare. Then, with an effort, I heard myself saying, 'I'll go, of course. Please let me pass so I can pack my things.'

But Isabella rushed by me into the hall, and as I made for the staircase both her arms came towards me in a violent push, sending me crashing with my head against a chest. Darkness filled with intermittent flashes of light blinded me for a moment. I put my hand up to where the pain was and felt a bump already rising. Then William appeared from the dining-room, but I realized he hadn't seen the incident.

'She fell,' Isabella said contemptuously; then,

with an assumption of dignity calculated to impress her husband, she continued, 'Your clothes will be collected and sent on when you let me know your address. Just leave immediately. The mere sight of you here is an affront and a disgrace.'

'But, my dear ...'

'No,' Isabella cried, running towards him and flinging her arms round his neck. 'William, William, I can't *bear* it. To come back and find another woman in my place. Can't you see ... can't you *understand* ...?'

He didn't answer, just fondled her hair and pressed his lips to its satin darkness.

Revolted and cold with a rigid, icy chill I'd never felt before, I lifted my head and dragged myself to the door. Then I turned.

'I wish I could curse you both,' I said, and it was as though someone not myself was speaking. 'But you're not worth it ... either of you.'

I saw William's face flinch before I went out into the autumn night in my green silk dress, taking nothing with me but a vow to trust no man again ... not ever.

How long I walked the lanes that night I don't know. Any sense of time had left me and I wandered in such bleakness and despair that I wanted to die. A mist was rising curling in chill waves round my body, but I didn't feel it; I walked on aimlessly with no thought in me but to be away—anywhere—from that scene of degradation and betrayal. Sometimes I started running and then stopped to regain my breath.

My heart was still pounding against my breast and a sense of hopelessness encompassed me, like that of an animal—a hunted fox—with no place to hide in.

As the excruciating pain in my head eased to a dull ache, I heard a horse approaching, and through my shock a wild hope stirred in me that William had come to fetch me back after all.

But it was not William. When I looked up I saw that the shadowed figure was taller and his face was lit to brief clarity in the wan light of a watery moon. Ettyn.

'So it's happened already,' he said and when I didn't speak, he added, 'Come along, you must be cold.'

I didn't resist when he lifted me to the grey's back and took it by the bridle.

'Put this on,' he continued, taking off his coat. 'No one in our house would relish an invalid to look after. We're a busy lot.'

His voice held no sympathy in it; no emotion, not even anger. I was too exhausted to care, feeling only a sense of inevitability driving me to Thorncarne, something preordained that, had I listened to my own instinct, I'd have recognized the first time Venn and I had met by the moor.

That night I slept by a warm fire on a sofa in some kind of a parlour between rugs and blankets and with a stone hot water bottle at my feet. I recall vaguely a large woman coming in with a bowl of broth that I took automatically with muttered thanks. Her features didn't register except for black eyes peering from a fleshy face, surrounded by masses of dark hair. I knew though she didn't want me there and had no sympathy for me; she was simply doing what Venn Ettyn told her to do.

When I had drunk the soup she took the bowl away, leaving Venn to stir the coal and logs and to bring me a whisky.

'Drink it,' he said in an emotionless, authoritative voice. 'It will make you sleep, and in the morning we'll have a room got ready for you upstairs.'

Even in the state I was, I was amazed at his certainty and assumption that I'd stay there. Obviously though not a talkative man, he was used to having his own way. On the verge of sleep later, I realized something else, too; we had one thing in common—an uncanny aptitude for sensing the future. I *did* stay at Thorncarne.

Why? Who can explain the pattern of life and reasons for doing the most unpredictable things at unexpected times? Certainly not me, and I didn't try.

I could easily have taken off the next morning in search of a post in Penzance or made my way back to Port Einack where humble jobs could be found for minimum payment in the fish sheds, scrubbing and cleaning, or in some third-rate eating house. But I didn't relish the thought. Somewhere at the back of my mind wounds still smarted from memories of Matt which I didn't wish revived.

The Squire was different. All feeling I'd ever had for him had changed that one night to cold contempt. Not hatred—he was too unimportant, too flabby, and poor a creature to hate after the first shock. No doubt we'd meet in the lane from time to time, or perhaps by chance in Penzance. I wasn't afraid of that. It was he who'd played the coward, not me. I was only angered for having so demeaned myself by believing he could love me.

Love? Was there any such thing? It seemed to mean women always giving, and men taking. Well for me all that was over. When I needed something a man could give I'd see I had it if it was offered. But nothing of mine, no secret place in my heart, should ever belong to anyone again. In that way I would be free to take the path most advantageous, and some day perhaps I'd be rich and proud enough to use any man I chose as they'd once used me.

It was with such hard thoughts that I woke on my first morning at Thorncarne, roused by Flavia who looked down at me with a cup of strong tea in her hand. She didn't smile or say anything except, 'Here you are. There's a room ready upstairs.'

'Thank you,' I said, as she reached the door.

She turned, and her handsome gypsy face was hard as stone as she said, 'Don't thank me. Thank Venn. He's boss here.'

The door slammed, and through a rising wave of anger I felt a stirring of triumph also.

If Venn Ettyn wanted me there, I thought, all would be well, and some position would be found for me in the household. Perhaps this was my first step to power.

Instinctively my hand strayed to the gold miniature of my grandmother Luzana still hanging on its gold chain round my neck. I was glad I'd worn it the previous night and was grateful for the feeling it gave me of someone born to better things. Flavia had noticed it, too. In the brief, covetous glance she'd thrown me, I'd seen her eyes on it and known it had set her wondering.

That was a good thing. Wondering could hold envy as well as curiosity, and perhaps a lurking fear.

I didn't expect any affection from the wild, strange family I'd so unwittingly wandered into. But respect? Yes, I meant to have that.

Feeling better for having made that decision and from the stimulant of the hot tea, I got up, tidied myself, and made my way into the hall which, from the sounds of activity at the far end, obviously led to the kitchen.

When I got there the door opened on a long table with the family sitting round, headed by Venn.

'Come in,' he said. 'We've a good breakfast here, and you must be needing it.'

I was aware of one or two faces glancing up, then looking back again to their plates. Drawing myself up straight, I went to the table and took a place indicated by an empty chair.

Little more was said. Any hostility they'd felt was veiled and withdrawn. A friendly word would have been welcome, but as I'd not expected it, I didn't allow myself to be rebuffed.

In this way my life at Thorncarne started, with no indication at all of what the future was to bring.

CHAPTER 11

Learning the ways of the Thorncarne household was a revealing but not too difficult experience. From the beginning it was obvious that what Flavia said was true—Venn was in command. Though I knew I wasn't exactly welcomed by the rest of the family, no one appeared to resent me too much. Belle, who was extremely stout, self-indulgent and untidy, with a bottle of gin she generally referred to as the 'tonic' nearly always at hand, realized quite soon the advantages of having me there, accepting me as a servant to shoulder much of the domestic work. This didn't worry me. Venn after all was going to pay me for my services; not so much as the Squire had done, but then I hadn't the same responsibilities. As it was I was grateful for something to do that was physically tiring, to take my mind away from the torment I'd been through.

There were times when Belle suddenly decided to rouse herself, and then for a brief hour or two everything became an uproar as she started 'tidying up'. Her black eyes sparkled with a dangerous light, her tongue when she used it was a virago's and her broad figure had a frenzy of energy devoted to scrubbing and polishing and sloshing the water round with the smell of carbolic soap everywhere.

'Ma's got a "mood" on,' Sarne would say, with a wink. 'Best kip out of her way or she'll likely give 'ee one.' He was like his mother in looks—or would have been when she was young—black-eyed with hair so dark and curly it had a springing life of its own in the sunlight, reflecting all the brown and deep blue shades of dark mountain pools ruffled by wind and rain. He didn't speak much in my presence; none of them did. But from the beginning his eyes were frequently on me, and I knew Flavia noticed.

Marcus, though nearly four years younger than Sarne, who was only nineteen, was taller and more lightly built than his brother, finer featured and with a watchful quality in his brown eyes that reminded me vaguely of Venn. But his lips had a contemptuous twist, and in manners he resembled Flavia. He was sixteen, and Flavia two years younger. Paul, a broad sturdy boy of twelve, was very like Sarne and openly rebellious of Venn's discipline, which could be harsh on occasion.

None of them seemed to resent the power of their eldest brother, though at times Sarne eyed him with the belligerent glance of a young bull measuring the strength of a future opponent. I didn't see much likelihood of such a combat really coming about. Venn's mentality was the sword-sharp kind; even if his physical strength declined, he would manage to hold the reins not only through his ability but because of his secret heritage and the very material consideration that every month he went to the bank in Penzance where he collected his 'due', as it was termed.

What the 'due' was I'd no idea until Belle let it out to me in one of her drunken, confidential moments.

'His dad,' she said, with a smug sly look, 'his dastardly "high-up son-of-a-bitch dad" ... or you could say his dad's pa.'

I waited, hoping to learn more. But even in her inebriated state Belle was close, and she put her finger to her lips with a shushing sound.

'No talkin',' she said, '*my* secret, only *mine* ... Belle Ettyn's; and to tell the truth, darlin', I've almos' forgot meself. What's it matter? What the bloody hell does it matter s'long as the gold comes in?'

When I didn't answer, her mood suddenly changed.

'And what d'you mean comin' tryin' to worm yourself into family business? Eh? You just watch your step, girl, or chucked out you'll be, same as you was from over theer. An' doan' you try any of your tricks on that son of mine either. A real lovely boy, Sarne is, the pride of his mother's heart.'

She hadn't noticed Venn standing at the door of the kitchen, but I had.

He came in quickly, almost soundlessly, in the strange, light way he had of walking.

'You hold your tongue, Mother,' he said, taking the bottle away, 'and try and *behave* with dignity, even if you don't have any. Unless you show a bit of respect I'll see Judith in your place before you know where you are. Understand?'

She lifted her head, grumbled under her breath, thought better of it and nodded sullenly.

'Just what you say Mr Ettyn,' she agreed with blurred sarcasm. 'O' *course,* darlin'. Who's your poor mother to deny 'ee? Oh I'll be all sweetness to the maid if you say so, even curtsey if you wish.'

Her smile was wide and ingratiating, but her eyes held the brief malice of a viper's, reminding me of the witch-like creature on the moors, and I decided to have as little to do with her as possible.

Interims like this were rare though, due mostly to the fact, I suppose, that the family, knowing their mother's weakness, watched her closely when they were about. In any case her purse didn't allow too liberal an amount of alcohol on the premises. Venn doled out the household income and wages for Sarne and Marcus. Flavia was allowed pocket money, but only on the condition she went to boarding school the following year and helped in the house until then.

'Imagine it!' she said indignantly to me one day. 'A *boarder.* Horrible I call it. Why should I go to one of them stuck-up places where they use switches and make you learn soppy things like sums and bee-*haviour?*' She lifted her chin, smirking. 'I was all right at the village place—the Dame's. What would I want with *more* learning? Oh my! can you see it—*me,* like *him?*'

'Who?'

'Venn, o' course. Didn't you know? He was away for years, right up till he was sixteen. That's what gives him his airs.'

'I didn't know,' I told her.

'He's a prig,' she said, with a sidelong look of her wonderful dark eyes, 'and a bully, for all his cool quiet ways. Don't you go falling for *him,* Judith Thomas, or you'll be in for a nasty shock. In any case ...' her voice wavered.

'Yes?'

'He doesn't like women, and he'll never marry unless it's someone rich who can prosper his bloody lands and herds ...'

She turned away with a toss of her head and swing of hips, almost running into her brother who was coming through the door.

His lips were tight.

'I heard what you said,' he remarked coldly. 'You were shouting, and it wasn't pleasant. If I ever hear you swearing again I'll give you the worst tanning of your life and send you off to school right away. So just remember, miss.'

He shut the door with a snap.

Flavia shrugged.

'You *see?'* She said, but in lower tones. When I didn't speak she added, 'As if *anyone* could tame *me!* If he dared raise a hand to me I'd bite it, *hard.'* And she laughed. 'So I will at school if they bully me.'

'Why should they?' I asked, getting rather bored by Flavia's tantrums.

'Because they're like it ... those gorgios. *I'm* no gorgio; like ma I am, but not so soft. If I'd been her I'd never've let a snooty gago lay me.'

'Gorgios? Gagos?'

She laughed with a natural amusement that changed her suddenly from a wild-tempered young woman into a vivacious and lovely child.

'You don't *know?* Gypsies. Gagos are Romanies, and gorgios the pale ones ... like Venn.'

'Thank you for telling me.'

'Of course, I suppose it's a good thing we *have* got Venn,' she added reasonably, after a pause. 'He does care about us, and he *has* got money ... somewhere. Part of it's in Port Einack, I'm sure. Or else Penjust. He rides there often, and when he gets back he's full of business matters and nothing else ... though no one knows what it is.'

My heart quivered. 'Port Einack. I see.'

'You know it?'

'I was born there,' I said, and almost added, 'married, too.' But I held the words back in time.

Conversations like this were rare at Thorncarne, mostly because time was so limited. Apart from the cooking and housework, there was the dairy to keep clean, floors needing to be washed several times a day following the tramping in of men's boots, and the endless cups of tea brewed during the cold weather.

The house itself was difficult to keep in order, being a curious erection of old and new parts connected by small corridors. My bedroom was in the front part of the house near to Belle's, Flavia's and Venn's.

Sarne and his brothers slept at the back in rooms above the stables connected by an arch.

The cow sheds were opposite, stretching to one side of the original building, and from what I gathered at odd moments Venn meant sometime to have the whole place rebuilt when there were sufficient funds and his cattle of a top breed.

'Thorncarne then,' Sarne told me, 'would be the finest farm in all west Cornwall ... That's what *he* thinks. In the meantime we have to stint and work for almost nothing while he puts the lot away for his own ends, the close fisted b ...'

'He's probably thinking what's best for you all,' I said tritely, not really interested in their family feuds or ambitions. What did it matter to *me*, who would be a mere bird of passage in the end?

'*Best? For us?* You want your head examining, girl. He's a hard one, Venn is. Why do you think he's letting Paul stop school at Christmas? So he can get another hired hand practically for free. That's our fine brother.'

'He needs money for Flavia's education perhaps?' I suggested. 'If she's going to boarding school.'

Sarne laughed.

'Oh *yes*. He'll see Flavia's properly educated just so she can snap up a rich husband later to add to his own filthy lucre. But maybe she won't. I know my sister; she's a wild one, and if the rich milk-sop don't arrive quick she'll most likely bed with someone else who'll land her with a lusty bastard, I'd say. Serve him right.'

I couldn't help a stab of anger, though there was no reason I should, except that Venn had befriended me.

'You're not very loyal to your brother,' I

reminded him sharply.

He turned his eyes full on me, and they were hot as black coals burning.

'Me? If anyone harmed Venn, I'd kill 'im, see? An' we don't need any furriner telling us our business. You don't understand us an' never will I reckon. But ...'

He stopped talking suddenly, while the flame in him died to softness.

'Yes?'

A flush mounted his skin as he turned away saying, 'A lovely woman you are, for all that. I s'pose that's why you got chucked out of Gulvarrick.'

'That's not your affair,' I told him.

'Isn't it? I should've thought it *was*. All of us. Seems to me we've taken you on trust pretty easy-like. One day at the big house, the next here, and no one questioning why. If it hadn't been for Venn ...'

'Hold your tongue,' I snapped. 'I'd no *wish* to push in. If you want to know about me go and ask *him*. Go ... *go...'* I almost shrieked with my voice rising and the breath quickening at my breast. 'Where I come from and what I do's none of your business, as I said. No callous youth's going to be poking and prying and flinging questions at me every time I cross his path, and that's for sure. I'm no soft-bred girl to put up with your cheek and rough tongue, Sarne Ettyn ...'

'Crane,' he corrected me, with his eyes narrowed and a flicker of amusement on his lips. 'My dad was a Crane, though I guess

Ettyn's more to your fancy.'

He strolled away, flaunting his broad shoulders and swinging his narrow hips, thinking no doubt to impress me with the physical magnetism he probably used on any girl that took his fancy.

He didn't impress *me.* I was annoyed and amused in turn by his bravado which had the quality of an adolescent about it more than a grown man's.

Perhaps I felt this because William had been so much older, so cultured and gentle under his large bluff exterior.

William.

Matt.

As memories swept through me I wondered with a wild rush of panic whatever had induced me to stay for more than a single day at Thorncarne. With only a few fields, a patch of moorland, and a road between us it was almost inevitable that sometime I'd meet the Squire face to face. What then?

He'd be shocked, of course; maybe he'd try to explain and console me, if his wife wasn't near. What a surprise he'd get then. Bitterness with a cold sense of revenge in it tightened my lips until I suddenly found myself laughing derisively. I wouldn't speak; oh no. But my glance, or stance, the contempt I felt would be a fire to sear him. I wanted that: to pass him by with my chin up or, if he got in my way, to push him aside like a sack of rubbish to be dumped in a ditch.

In the beginning I'd fretted and shed secret tears over lost tenderness and affection gone sour. But the time for crying was over, and the need for it. This it was that had kept me at Venn Ettyn's place—to show William and prove to myself he didn't matter one jot and counted no more to me than a feather touching my cheek, to be brushed away and forgotten.

As it happened I *did* see him a few days later.

I was walking back from the village after delivering eggs to the shop when the Squire's chaise, driven by Pascoe, appeared coming towards me. Though I kept my eyes straight ahead as they passed, I noticed the erect, elegant form of Isabella sitting beside him, with some ridiculous flowery creation perched on her black head. In an instant of time before the vehicle went by I was aware of William's discomforted face half-turned in my direction and I could imagine the look of pleading in his prominent blue eyes. I knew he wasn't happy. *How* I knew is hard to explain, except that happiness generally has a glow to it, something sensed rather than seen, and all I sensed about that fashionable little entourage was cold strain and unease.

When I remembered our rich contentment together during the golden days of late summer, sadness all of a sudden overcame resentment and I knew I could never actively wish William ill. He would get it soon enough, I thought, as I went through the gate to Thorncarne. Before winter properly set in William Pendruggan would regret the day he took the wild Isabella back to his bed and I'd feel shamed that I could ever have desired to avenge myself.

I was right. A week before Christmas something happened more terrible than I'd ever contemplated; something that for a time was to overshadow all my days at Thorncarne, sweeping any lingering bitterness I felt into a cloud of horror and revulsion.

Even now it is like a monstrous nightmare when I remember.

CHAPTER 12

It happened at night.

I was woken about twelve-thirty by loud screaming and shouting that could have been a man's, or a woman's, or both. At first I thought I'd woken from some sort of nightmare; the moon was full on my face from a chink in the curtains, and moonlight can affect the mind strangely, especially in sleep. Then as the sound continued I knew it was real. The gulls were squawking, too, as though they knew some horror was about. With nerves tensed I got up, threw a woollen shawl that Belle had given me round me, put on a pair of shoes and rushed on to the landing towards the stairs. Venn was already ahead, and his mother peering from her doorway. The ludicrous sight of her registered in the fitful light—great staring eyes under tangled mop of wiry hair resembling some macabre, giant hedgehog's.

'Be careful ...' she screeched to her son. 'You take care an' kip outa trouble, Venn. For heaven's sake ...'

He took no notice, just plunged on through the hall and out of the front door with me after him. The night was still and cold, but I didn't notice it; only the dark shadows streaking like ugly black fingers to the road, and the fear ... the awful, eerie fear of something lying in mortal terror out there. Something hurt and mournful, near to death.

But when we got there and saw the lumpy shape all twisted on its back facing the cold green light of the sky, I knew the terror was over—for him.

William.

His mouth was open, his eyes staring, holding the frozen glassiness of the moon's glare above the slashed throat. A dark stream of blood had spilled over the torn cravat to join a wound near the heart. The knife still protruded, steel-bright and glistening when the light touched it.

Red, black and livid lights burned my eyes for a moment. Sickness gripped my stomach. I put a hand to my head before moving a step closer, wanting to make sure ... to be certain this was really the man who'd once held me warm and close against him, pulsing with life and desire.

There was no mistake. That macabre travesty of a human being was indeed William Pendruggan, and I wanted to shout, 'No, *no.* Get up. It's a nightmare. It *must* be ...' But no words came from my lips. I shuddered convulsively and was unable to control the shaking of my whole frame.

Venn's hand closed on my arm, pushing me back.

'Don't look, Judith. It's no sight for a woman.'

I turned away, hiding my face in my hands, and when I glanced round again Venn had thrown his coat over the mutilated form.

'We must get the police,' he said, 'and

someone should be told at the house ...'

'His wife?'

From his look I knew, as he did, that she wouldn't be there.

'I'll go for Adam,' I said, but I didn't have to. That same moment Adam and Pascoe both appeared from the direction of Gulvarrick, running and stumbling as though their lives depended on it.

The rest of that night is only a confused memory to me now; the police coming, the body being taken away and questions ... questions I couldn't answer because I didn't know, and Venn saying, 'Let her alone. This business is nothing to do with her.'

But it was.

I had to appear with Venn at the inquest a week later and tell the coroner and police all over again how we'd found the body with the knife stuck in it.

'Did I recognize it? Had I seen it before?'

'Yes,' I said. 'It was a kitchen knife, used for vegetables.'

'Of course you were ... housekeeper ... at Gulvarrick ... were you not, Mrs Thomas?'

'Yes,' I answered abruptly, resenting the insinuating pause before and after the word housekeeper, wanting to rush out suddenly from the stuffy place that had the feeling of a prison about it, into air that was clean and free of men's dark, suspicious thoughts.

'You left your situation hurriedly, I believe?' the relentless, superior voice continued. 'Why was that?'

'Do I have to answer?' I demanded with a burst of spirit.

Then someone, I think it was the coroner, interrupted. 'At this point the question doesn't seem at all relevant. Suppose we confine ourselves to essential points?'

Perspiration was gathering in beads on my forehead, and at one moment as the dampness trickled down my face and neck I thought I might faint. Only the steady, intent look of Venn's eyes on my face pulled me back abruptly to awareness of who and where I was.

'Thank you,' I whispered.

Although the sordid proceedings couldn't have taken more than half an hour, including statements from Adam and Pascoe who'd only been roused by the shouting, the time to me seemed interminable. When it was over, following a verdict of 'murder by some person or persons unknown', I was so exhausted my body and mind felt wooden, as though no life or warmth would be there any more.

Before driving me back in the farm-trap Venn forced me to the Ram and Bottle for a stiff drink.

'You did well,' he said, as the spirit warmed me. 'What cold fish those devils can be. Don't think of it any more. Try and put the whole thing to the back of your mind. It's over. Done with.'

'Is it?' I said bitterly. 'I don't think so. Not until *she's* found. His wife. And even then there'll be mud-slinging.'

'What's a bit of mud?' Venn asked, with the first sign of any humour I'd seen in him. 'We have plenty at Thorncarne.'

I tried to smile, but the effort must have been a travesty.

Venn's hand slipped briefly over mine, then he went on, 'As far as I'm concerned, your relationship with Pendruggan, whatever it was, was your own concern. But now you're with us it's the beginning of something fresh. Idle tittle-tattle carries no weight with me, and if my mother forgets herself, in her cups any time, you just tell me and I'll put it right. Flavia, too. She's a sharp-tongued little madam on occasion, but she knows which side her bread's buttered. They all do. Now ... for heaven's sake, why are you brooding still?'

'I must go away,' I said, not knowing what had prompted the thought so suddenly. 'I've *got* to, for a time anyway.'

There was a drawn out silence before he said with his golden eyes blazing and a tightened look on his mouth, 'You'll do no such thing. Or if you do, I'll bring you back, Judith Thomas, however far you go. I'll find you, never doubt it, in the end.'

I turned my head away, not wishing him to see the burning flush mount my face.

'Anyway,' he continued in more remote, cool tones, 'running away would only be a confession of fear; of guilt, in some eyes.'

'What do you mean, guilt?'

'You don't have to be told that,' he replied shortly. A second later he added, 'Come along now. We must get home. There's work to be done.'

He was once more impersonal, as detached as a stranger addressing a mere acquaintance, and a swamping feeling of loneliness descended on me as we drove through the fading light of the cold afternoon back to Thorncarne. Flavia and Belle were lurking about, ready to spring on us for news the moment we appeared.

'What was it then?' Belle demanded in her throaty voice, eyes avid, first on my face, then Venn's. 'Murder, was it?'

'Of course,' Venn said. 'What else *could* it be, with the evidence they had.'

'Do they *suspect* anyone? Tell us, come on, out with it all.'

'Shut up,' Venn answered, quite roughly for him. 'If they do, you know very well *who*, don't you? And the sooner Isabella Pendruggan's found the better for everyone. So stop any wild talk or evil ideas you've got in your head and see about supper. Judith and I are both needing it.'

Grumbling under her breath Belle turned away calling Flavia to follow. Flavia waited behind to tell me that Pascoe had been over with a parcel for me.

'Your clothes,' she said. 'I don't know why you didn't get them before instead of wearing cast-offs. I've straightened them and put them on the bed. But the black dress's torn.'

'Torn?'

Flavia nodded.

'I'm sorry, Judith,' and her tones were

genuine. 'With a mad woman like her, what can you expect? If you ask me it's a good thing she took off. No one could feel properly safe with a creature of her sort about. I hope they catch her quick and put her away for good. Or p'raps she's dead. That would be best of all.'

I shivered, knowing it was true, but the mention of death was hateful to me; I tried to put it aside, thinking that after Christmas, when the new year came, there'd soon be snowdrops pushing through the ground, followed by the tiny yellow celandines, primroses and later the flame of gorse on moors and cliffs above the sea.

During the following week, whenever possible, I got out for half an hour for a wander about the countryside, generally taking field paths at the back of the house, as far away as possible from Gulvarrick. Sometimes though, when Belle could afford a bottle of her 'tonic' from the village, I had to fetch it for her, passing the house in the distance. A shiver ran through me whenever I saw the blinds closed over the windows and the front gates locked. The men, of course, would still be working at the back in the sheds and on the land. Until Isabella was found nothing could be done about selling the place. I supposed everything would be hers, and I remembered her in the portrait, beautiful but cold and cruel, smiling maliciously over the mantelshelf as if to say, 'I've won. All this is mine ... *mine* ...'

But if she'd killed her husband, and I don't think anyone really doubted it, it wouldn't do her much good after all, except for her to be able to brag to any poor creatures wherever she was taken, of her wealth, her power and her cleverness. Was a murderess allowed to inherit? I didn't know. The law was a mystery and a terror to me, and during those strained days following the tragedy I wanted nothing so much as to be away somewhere, hiding like a fox in its hole.

Yet I stayed. What Venn had told me had made sense. Besides, when he was near me I knew leaving him was the last thing I really desired. It was hard to understand myself. And sometimes I was filled with a sort of self-contempt that he should already be so mixed up in my mind with Matt and William. I noticed he didn't care for me at all except as someone he'd taken under his wing, and at times I resented it, especially when I'd taken pains to look my best, wearing my green dress or yellow silk with a shawl over the shoulders ready to fall any moment revealing my cream shoulders and firm neck.

Occasionally I caught his golden eyes glancing at me with an inscrutable look in them, but only for a moment, and at those times I pretended not to see, making a show of turning to Sarne or Marcus, whoever happened to be near. I wanted him to admire and want me, but no more. Just to be *wanted*—the knowledge that I was still desirable—surely that was natural after what I'd been through? If Matt suddenly turned up out of the blue I *knew,* or *thought* I knew, none of the rest would matter. But then Matt would not turn up; I was gradually resigning myself to the truth. And when facts registered the old hatred rose in me, because it was Matt who'd placed me in my present position and Matt who'd driven me to Pendruggan's arms and was now pushing me in a conflict of emotions towards Venn.

Christmas came and went with the usual festivities, although work at Thorncarne continued normally, because of the animals and land. Belle stirred herself to providing good fare, with my help, but there were no carols and Belle refused to have decorations about because greenery, to her, mostly spelled ill luck and mistletoe brought death.

However, with her two sons Sarne and Marcus she got riotously drunk on Christmas Eve. Venn accepted it logically and went out for a walk somewhere, leaving Flavia and myself and Paul to amuse ourselves on our own. I'd have liked to have gone with Venn, but obviously he hadn't wanted me along. Presently I went to bed, removing my yellow dress with a dull feeling of disappointment and betrayal wondering hopelessly if anywhere in the world there was a man worth loving who would love me in return.

Through the mirror I stood staring at my reflection with my bodice and underwear removed, breasts ripe and rosy pink in the lamplight, my rich hair tumbled over my shoulders and back and I knew I was beautiful.

I touched one nipple with the tip of a finger,

remembering how Matt had put his lips to each in turn, sucking their sweetness with his tongue.

'Oh, Matt,' I thought, 'why ... *why* did you leave me?'

I stared and stared, trying to recall every detail of his face, but the image was a little blurred. His dark eyes ... yes, they were clear. But the rest of him—the features, hair and form were Venn's. And I never once thought of William.

With shame and because of it, I put my hands to my eyes and turned away. Then, as the clock struck twelve, I finished undressing, put on my shift and went to bed.

For a long time I lay wakeful hearing nothing but the occasional sound of voices from below, followed presently by Flavia's light feet on the stairs.

Later, much later, Venn's firm footsteps echoed along the landing. I lay rigid, hardly breathing, as they neared my door. For a second, I think, they paused, then moved on abruptly.

I turned on my side, with my face burrowed into the pillow. My thighs and buttocks were leaping with life, my breasts pricking where strong hands should have been.

Oh God, I thought, how am I going to bear it? And I knew for the first time what my mother must have felt; knew and understood, resolving in spite of it to make something better of my life, somehow to control the wild desire for love and fulfilment that could rise in such a torment of frustration, making mockery of all else.

In the morning, following a restless night

that had dulled me to tiredness, I felt more composed, and with so much clearing up to do on top of the usual chores, there was no time for brooding or thinking back.

When afternoon came and Belle had retreated upstairs for her afternoon nap, I grabbed the opportunity to take a walk and, hardly realizing it, found myself making my way towards Castle Carnack.

This time I took a different path, a narrow sheep-track to the left, to avoid direct contact with old Dorcas. Although her shack was visible as I reached the higher ground above the copse of trees, no one seemed to be about, but I had a queer feeling of being watched, of eyes peering from the overgrown windows tangled by briars and gorse. The air was cold but tangy and clear, with no drift of wind to stir the silence. There'd been a frost during the night, and the short moorland turf was crisp underfoot, with a wild tangy scent to it. I stood for a few moments on the fringe of the ancient huts, trying to picture the folk who had built and lived there long ago. Nothing came to me but a great sense of age and loneliness, and feeling suddenly cold I turned to go back to Thorncarne.

As I neared the nearest point to the shack a dark figure darted from behind a twisted sloe and stood screeching at me, but more coherently than last time.

'Trollop!' she shouted. 'Whore. My curses be on 'ee, devil's spawn.'

She spat in my direction, then turned and hobbled away, head thrust forward, stumbling as she went, with one hand on a stick.

As I passed the hut a sudden ray of cold sunlight burst through a thin veil of cloud, briefly lighting her window. For a second I thought I saw another face peering from behind the cracked glass—a pale, ravaged, beautiful face, with narrowed eyes and twisted mouth. The next moment it was gone, and pulling myself together I hurried on, with my heart pumping wildly and a sickening, lurching fear churning inside me.

When I reached Thorncarne I was mostly recovered and said nothing of my experience to anyone. After all, the light could do strange things, and I'd no intention of being labelled by Belle and her family as a half-crazy creature who didn't know what was real and what wasn't. Especially by Venn. Nor did I want to be responsible for any enquiries put to the wicked old great aunt. She was their affair and not mine.

As for her curses, I tried to disregard them, but it wasn't easy. So much that was evil had happened since our first meeting.

CHAPTER 13

In April, shortly after Flavia had gone to school near Truro, there was an accident. Belle sprained her leg through falling in the hall after an overdose of her 'tonic' and had to be carried laboriously up to bed by Venn and Sarne. Once there, and believing she was dying, she expressed moaning admission of her sins to some unknown deity, asking forgiveness with tears and prayers to be delivered to a better world.

Venn went for the doctor. When he arrived the worst was over and the effects of the gin had worn off. Belle, looking overblown but otherwise in robust health, was told no limbs were broken and her heart was sound, but her leg would need complete rest, for a week at least. The limb was bound up, and she was given a sedative. After that she settled down to enjoy a lazy life for a considerable period.

'*You'll* have to take charge now,' she said one day, when I took up her breakfast. 'There's no knowin' how long I'll be laid up. Some do say that once a thing like this happens to a woman o' my age et's the beginnin' o' the end.'

She sighed mournfully, then smiled with the ingratiating look she wore when she wanted something. 'It'll be better for you, I shouldn't wonder. One wumman alone in one kitchen's the right way for harmony in the home. An' I will admit, Judith, you'se a tidy hand with cookies.'

When I didn't reply immediately she paused, drew a deep breath, and continued slyly, 'It's like being mistress for ye. Jus' the men an' you. You'd like that, eh?'

Then I startled her.

'Not on my own. Without you and Flavia there'd be too much for one person—churning butter, scrubbing, cleaning, cooking and running up and down. Why ... I could get an easier job in Penzance *any* day, and for more pay.'

Her face clouded.

'Ungrateful, you are,' she almost spat out. 'What is it you're aimin' for then?'

'A girl,' I answered promptly, showing I meant it. 'Not to live in, if you don't want it, but to come each day and give a hand till supper's over. There's one I know of already—Liddy, who used to work for the Squire. A bit simple she may be, but willing and strong ...' I paused, watching the thoughts milling round behind the shrewd, dark eyes. 'Of course,' I added, 'we could p'raps muddle through for another week if you're likely to be right then. Perhaps that would be best.'

'Oh no ... *no.* I'm too bad for that,' Belle protested. 'On top of the leg, me veins an' all. No, if you *must* have help, spik to Venn. Venn's the one.'

I did, and he agreed. And from that moment life at Thorncarne took on a new importance for me. Liddy was only too pleased and grateful to spend the days working for me, returning in the evenings to the outskirts of the village where her father worked his small-holding.

I must admit I liked the company of men better than women and was always careful to look my best when they came in for meals, especially in the evenings. I generally changed then and appeared at the table in the yellow silk or the green dress with an apron tied at the waist, until we'd finished eating and the meal was cleared away.

After the dishes were washed Liddy left. Although there was still a bit to do in the house, either Venn or Sarne, sometimes Marcus, generally lingered behind a bit to give a hand. I knew they were impressed and liked to have me there. Even Paul, the youngest, who'd by then left school to learn farming, had his eyes on me admiringly when he got the chance, and once he said, 'You're pretty, aren't you? If Venn'd seen you first, p'raps he'd be marrying *you.*'

My heart lurched.

'What do you mean, Paul, *first?*'

A flush crossed his face, which was clear-skinned under his reddish-brown hair but sprinkled by pale golden freckles.

'Oh nothing,' he said, 'it's just ... *she's* after him. Ma said so, and Sarne thinks it'd be good. For Venn, I mean.'

'But who's *she?*' I persisted, with a dull, deepening stab of jealousy. '*Who,* Paul?'

'Miss Tattam,' he told me grudgingly. 'She's got a café or something in Penjust and she's rich. But you're not to say. Promise you won't tell anyone I let on.'

I promised, and presently he went to join Marcus, who was in the cow sheds milking.

When he'd gone I thought back to the occasions that had seemed unimportant at the time, when Venn had ridden away on his horse up the hill and along the road winding below Castle Carnack to the north coast, Penjust way. It had never occurred to me a woman might be concerned. But of course it should have done, I told myself relentlessly. A man of Venn's looks and character wasn't the kind to live a monk's life. But *marriage!* The idea was suddenly so offensive to me, so shattering, I had a wild impulse to rush out into the fields where he was working, as I'd once rushed to Matt when he was late for a meal, crying, 'Is it true? Have you got some female tucked away that you visit every time you feel the need in you? Is that it? Tell me. Tell me.'

But of course I'd no right. I could imagine the cold set of his lips, the narrowing of his gold eyes and the sting of his tongue, which would be different, harsher and more hurtful than that of Matt's hand on my flesh, and I knew I had to control myself or lose his respect for ever.

But after that—I hardly realized it myself—the thought of the unknown woman was always at the back of my mind somewhere, gnawing and biting me, so on occasion my temper grew testy and Liddy learned to know the sharp edge of my tongue. I wished I could see the obnoxious Miss Tattam and judge for myself what influence she'd likely have on Venn. But as he always made a point of visiting her, and not the other way round, it didn't seem possible.

Then, on a fine warm day towards the end of the month, she arrived at the front door in one of those fancy looking traps called a governess cart, wearing a frilly, high-necked, blue dress, with her fair hair showing just enough below a flowery hat to give her a saucy, beguiling air.

Venn, who obviously hadn't expected her, was out in the fields, so when she'd given her name as a 'friend of Mr Ettyn's, Miss Tattam', I had to show her in to the front parlour and chat while Liddy went to find Venn.

I tried hard to be polite and act in a proper housekeeper fashion, but the sound of her high-pitched, silly voice and the superior, prim look of her lips which had a way of pursing up above her rather receding chin somehow infuriated me. She seemed so sure of herself. Although I didn't care for her kind of insipid looks I knew some men might find her attractive, including Venn, who had a caring for defenceless things.

Defenceless? She wasn't, of course. Just cunning and winning, as I discovered ten minutes later when Venn walked into the room, having changed from his outdoor boots and working jacket into a brown coat and fawn breeches, with his bright hair smoothed back as though a wet comb had been run through it.

'Alicia!' he said, striding across the room and taking both her hands in his. 'What a splendid surprise. But why didn't you let me know? I'd have been ...'

What he'd have been going to do I didn't

learn, because she said gushingly, fluttering her eyelashes at him, with a smile on her lips that was sweetness itself, 'Venn dear, I didn't know myself until this morning when a spot of business for me to attend to turned up in Penzance. Naturally though, as I was passing, I felt I had to look in.'

'Naturally,' he agreed. 'I'd have been hellish annoyed if you hadn't.' He dropped her hands as though reluctantly, turned to me and said, 'This is a friend of mine, Miss Tattam, Judith. Judith ...'

'It's all right,' I interrupted. 'We've introduced ourselves.'

Perhaps I spoke more tartly than I should have done. His eyes seemed to darken and narrow slightly before he remarked in formal tones, 'Would you mind making tea for Miss Tattam and myself, Judith, and if you've got any of your home-made scones. I know they'd be appreciated.'

'I'll see,' I told him stiffly, before going out. 'I expect there are a few left.'

At the foot of the stairs I heard a harsh, whispered voice calling my attention and, looking up, saw Belle standing on the landing above wearing a red flannel dressing gown and with two dark plaits of hair falling over her shoulders.

'What do you want?' I asked, irritated by her intrusion at such an unpleasant moment.

'Come on ... up here, 'twon't take a moment.'

Knowing if I didn't she'd make some sort of a fuss I went halfway to the landing where she stood looking like a great fat cat who'd stolen the cream.

'I seen her from the window,' she said. 'That's her ... the one Venn'll take if he's got any sense in his head. Tattam her name is, and they're close, very close.' She paused a second before adding with a sly, conspiratorial look on her large face, 'You din' know, did you?'

'It's not my affair,' I said.

'No?'

'No.'

I turned abruptly and went downstairs to the kitchen with what I hoped was a show of cold dignity. But my heart was pounding. In such a mood I could have walked out and away that very moment and was considering it when Sarne came in from milking.

I was probably making more of a clatter with the china than usual, because there was a knowing look on his face when he grinned and said, 'What's gotten into you, Judith? Upset by that la-di-da creature, are you?'

'I don't know what you mean,' I told him curtly.

'No? But I saw her come. And when Miss high-an'-mighty Alicia Tattam's about we're *all* her servants, in case you didn't know. Even me. Head stable boy I am, which is why her school-marmish cart and nag are at the back having care and rest.'

'Oh, I see. She and Venn are going to be married, I've heard.'

He threw back his head and laughed. '*Belle* wants it, because of the nest egg it'd bring.

Venn? Maybe? I don't know. But he's a wily one, and it's my guess he already gets what he wants without.'

'I see.'

'What's the matter with you?' he asked again. 'Surely you're not sweet on *him?*' Then, when I didn't answer, he said, 'I believe you *are.* My God!'

'Rubbish!' I exclaimed tartly. 'You don't know what you're talking about. And get out of my way, for heaven's sake. I've the tea to attend to.'

After that there was a difference somehow in the relationship between Sarne and me. He seemed more thoughtful, speculative even, and began to take care with his manners. His speech fined down, and his eyes had a hot glance in them sometimes. New sides of his character began to show. He had a knowledge of flowers and butterflies and all wild creatures that surprised and pleased me. Before, I'd imagined him to be a mere handsome, sturdy young farmer, with a liking for a drink in the pub on a Saturday night and a jocular, teasing way with country girls that had them fluttering round at the first glance of his flashing dark eyes. But obviously I'd underestimated his intelligence. He was as good as most vets with the farm animals and able to manage a cow through a difficult birth better even than Venn, which made Sarne invaluable at Thorncarne. Although the sheep there were not much more than two hundred, they needed care and watching through hard winters and the lambing seasons. There was the shearing, too. But it was the herd of Devon cows—Venn's speciality—that demanded most of his attention.

'Venn doesn't understand cattle, not really,' Sarne told me once, 'but he's a great one for wanting the best herd in Cornwall and having a prize bull sometime to start a new breed. Cash. Power. Being top. That's Venn, and o' course you get the best milk as well as beef from Devon stock.'

Such talk of cows and breeding was beyond me, having lived my youth so close to the sea always with the sound of waves breaking and ship's sirens hooting through fog and storm. Listening to Sarne was like learning a new language, but it wasn't the kind to really interest me. Only Sarne himself—and this because I wanted to push all thoughts of Venn behind me.

Knowing he admired me helped. All unthinkingly I played up to the effect I had on him, turning my head, when possible, the way it looked best—just a little tilted up so my neck was arched and full under my dainty chin and pert nose, with my rich hair falling away from the high cheekbones. My eyes—sometimes green, sometimes amber—would be turned away, with the thick lashes shadowing them so he'd no idea of what my thoughts were. I wouldn't even be sure of them myself, only that I felt a woman once more and that my feelings for Sarne carried a faint echo in them of Matt—Matt of the dark eyes and wild temper who'd taken the best I had and betrayed it.

Venn didn't consciously enter into things at all just then, except as a goad to my pride and my wild determination to get the better of the simpering, rich Miss Alicia Tattam.

Later I was to realize that I hadn't behaved fairly to Sarne. I didn't know how he really felt until a night in early June when something happened that was one of the most terrifying events of my life.

The evening was misty filled with the seething heat of young summer and scents of lush growing things filling the still air. After supper, Belle, who was seated on the step of the front door twanging her guitar—a habit she'd learned from her own mother when she was a child—called me aside with a wink and whispered she'd be 'obliged' if I'd go to the village for her 'tonic'.

'I *need* it, luv,' she said wheedlingly. 'Me leg's paining me something awful.'

Thinking she'd never looked more robust in her life, I agreed grudgingly because there was still some clearing up to do after Liddy had left. Still, the fresh air might brisk me up, I thought as I left the house, and the scent of May was heady, almost intoxicating, in the hedges.

As I swung down the lane drawing the richness deeply into my lungs, I kept my eyes determinedly from the side drive of Gulvarrick leading to the stables. Although the Pascoes were still in their quarters above, I'd heard that Adam had gone, and the emptiness of the house beyond always gave me a troubled feeling, reviving all sorts of memories that depressed me.

It was easy enough in the glowing light to put dark thoughts behind me, but on the walk back the sinking sun had gone behind some rising clouds and the mist was thickening, hanging a chill veil over the landscape, muffling trees and bushes into all manner of queer shapes. When I reached the gates I found my footsteps quickening; but for some reason quite beyond my control my eyes went to the drive and then my blood froze. I stopped for a second or two, wanting to move but unable to. It was like being in a nightmare, one of those awful dreams when something's after you and your feet are stuck to the ground. My heart was pumping, and I put my hand to my mouth to stop the screams coming, because she was there by a clump of bushes, all white and still, watching me. Isabella. William's wife.

I don't know how I recognized her; I couldn't with my eyes, not really—she wasn't near enough—but with her figure so blurred and still and white, so menacing somehow, I knew it couldn't be anyone else. She was quite naked, and through her tangled black hair her eyes were watching. I could *feel* them, and sense their burning, mad stare filled with hatred and a frenzy to kill.

Moments can seem an eternity under such conditions, and in that short space of time all sorts of memories rushed back to me: the way she'd ordered me from Gulvarrick, and sent me spinning against the hall chest; her bitter, condemning voice that had turned so quickly to tears and sweetness when William appeared;

most clearly of all, the last time Dorcas had cursed me below Castle Carnack and I'd seen a face watching me from the window of her shack. At the time I'd thought it all my imagination. Now I knew it wasn't—she'd been *there.* All these long weeks the authorities had been searching for her, Isabella Pendruggan had been hidden away with that odious old woman on the moors. How had she managed it? By cunning alone? Or witchcraft? Or was it that something about the old hag had been sufficiently intimidating to put even the police off?

Whatever the answer it made no difference now. Isabella was here, a maniac beyond all help.

As *I* was, if I made a false step.

I knew instinctively that when I moved so would she, and I could be at her mercy, as defenceless as William had been when she killed him. Her nails would be cruel and harsh; in her hand could be a weapon—a knife perhaps, as it had been before, to plunge into my throat. My only chance was to stare her out, to wait a little until my brain worked properly and I knew what to do.

But everything was so deadly quiet and still, so lonely and terrifying, with the mist curdling and drifting faintly in a rising breeze about the wild, naked form by the trees, flapping its coolness against the clammy dampness of my own face. If I'd thought there was the slightest chance of helping her—of anything human to appeal to—I'd have taken the risk and approached her. But I knew there was none. Isabella was a woman no more, merely an animal waiting for the first opportunity to spring.

The tension was unbearable. Suddenly my strength seemed to fail, with a trembling and shaking of my body that took the ground in a rush of darkness from beneath me.

There was a wild scream of laughter as I fell, with one arm reaching helplessly for a tree. The sound echoed weirdly in obscene triumph again and again, until the two burning eyes came down to mine—green no longer, but flecked with red, like those of a wolf—and claw-like, thin hands reached for my neck.

I had a brief glimpse of her white breasts, scratched and streaked with blood, before, in an agony of disgust and a last frenzy for survival, I closed my eyes, bringing one knee up viciously against the cold flesh. At the same moment my voice returned, with a scream higher and more shrill than her own.

There was a scattering of birds from a nearby bush, a sudden release from the frenzied grip and a pause in which Isabella sprang to her feet and darted into the darkening shadows of Gulvarrick.

Almost immediately, another voice, a man's was crying, 'What's up? Where are you? ... What the hell? ...' and then, as Sarne's strong form emerged through the mist, he said, 'My God! Judith.'

He lifted me up and held me against his breast. 'What is it, my lovely? Tell me, tell

Sarne. There, there! It's all right now.'

It was some minutes before I could explain, and when I'd finished he said grimly, 'I always thought that Jezebel was lurking around somewhere. Never you mind though. We'll get her now, and soon. Hush now, hush, darlin'. There, there, it's all right.'

As my sobs ceased I was content and grateful to have his arm close about my waist, helping me back to Thorncarne. So gentle he was, strong and kind, with all the tenderness come to my aid as though I was some defenceless young animal needing thought and care.

Long after I'd gone to bed that night I remembered the warmth in his eyes, the strength of his arms, and something else, too; something unsaid that I knew all the same was there, though I wouldn't admit it.

How could I, when deep down, in spite of all the gratitude and affection I felt for him, I knew it wasn't enough. Yet I couldn't help responding to and being fond of Sarne, but the fierceness and the pain, the wild ecstasy and longing I'd had for Matt, were missing.

As for Venn? I couldn't and wouldn't think of him at all. He meant nothing in my life; *nothing*. Perhaps even then he was holding that silly Tattam woman in his arms; I could just imagine her stupid face as she stared up at him with her prominent cow's eyes.

Oh well, I thought before sleep claimed me, let him have her, and good luck to them. He's a cold-fish anyway.

The trouble was that however hard I tried to

delude myself over this, I couldn't quite believe it. Venn wasn't cold—he was just inaccessible to me.

Somehow that knowledge hurt.

CHAPTER 14

Isabella Pendruggan was found in the early hours of the following morning in an upstairs bedroom of Gulvarrick. She had managed to get into the house through the conservatory door which wasn't securely fastened, and from there to the hall.

When discovered she was strutting about in an embroidered petticoat, with nothing above but an assortment of necklaces and a tall stove hat of William's. Pascoe, who'd helped the police break the locked door, said that when they entered she gave a majestic gesture of her arm, waved a walking stick at the constable and said, 'Arise, Sir Walter.'

If it hadn't been so sordid and tragic it would have been ridiculous and not without a touch of humour.

As it was, my spine still tensed when I thought of it, and I was only too thankful to know the miserable business was at last over.

Later she was taken to an asylum near Bodmin and properly certified; following further police proceedings, which proved her to be William's murderess, she was committed by the judge to a place for the criminally insane for the rest of her life.

When August passed to early September Gulvarrick was put up to be sold. The Pascoes, however, were allowed to remain there until they found other, suitable quarters. William, it transpired, had been heavily in debt, and the house carried a considerable mortgage. If a reasonable price was not obtained from any interested purchaser the bank would put the whole property up for sale by auction.

When I recalled the news I was reminded with a wave of irony how Matt had once placed me in a similar position, and I was swept for a time by the old grief, thinking what a tangled pattern life was and how, if he'd acted differently, we could still have been together and the torturous events of the last months spared me.

Then I pulled myself to the present. Brooding was no use to anyone. The moors lay rich bronze, brown and gold under the skies, there was an earthy tang everywhere and my senses ached for warmth and fulfilment, with a hunger made more intense because of all I'd lost. Sometimes as I lay alone in bed at night on the verge of sleep, half-dreaming, in my imagination Matt would be there beside me and my body would throb as I reached a hand to touch him. Then, when I came to my senses realizing he'd gone for good, I'd think of Venn and behind closed eyes would see his own golden ones staring down at me and the tentative half-smile on his lips before his strong, lithe body bore down upon me, crushing me to him.

When the emptiness of truth registered, I'd feel shamed by my own weakness and jump from the bed, going to the window restlessly to stare out across the fields and moors under the misted moon. I'd realize then the stupidity of wanting the impossible and turn my thoughts elsewhere. Sarne.

Sarne at least was real and strong and true. I never fooled myself that I loved him; I didn't. But a man can mean other things to a woman than passion, and his admiration inflamed my vanity. Let his eyes follow and hunger for me, I thought; let Venn notice and object if he chose. I would go my own way because I was my mother's daughter—and my father's. My beauty was maturing, and freed of Belle's sharp tongue and sly innuendos pride was growing in me again and I walked with my head high, remembering the dark-eyed beauty, Luzana, whose blood ran in my veins.

Once when I was passing the drive to Gulvarrick, Pascoe appeared by the gates and took a small parcel out of his pocket.

'These be yours, I think, Mistress Judith,' he said, handing it to me. 'The wife found 'em when she was clearin' up th'other day. Lyin' on the floor, they were, where you slept. "These be Miss Judith's, surely?" she said. "An' real jet, too".'

He stood watching me as I unwrapped the paper and found the ear-rings I thought I'd never see again.

'Thank you, Pascoe,' I told him. 'I wasn't wearing them the night I left. And everything happened so quickly ...'

'I know, I know,' he broke in, looking slightly embarrassed. 'Jus' you try an' forget it all, missis, as we're doin'. A real bad night it was when Mistress Isabella came back an' that's fer sure. Are ye all right then over theer?'

'I'm housekeeper now,' I answered. 'Plenty to do, but I'm used to work, and if people talk I don't listen. What good does it do?'

Pascoe shook his head doubtfully. 'True enough. But theer's one up theer by Castle Carnack who'll do 'ee harm if a chance comes, so watch your step, ma'am, an' don't go too near.'

'Dorcas?' I said contemptuously. 'What harm could *she* do to me, a rheumaticky old crone like her?'

'She can *wish* 'ee,' the man said darkly. ' 'Specially on account of what's happened to her kinswoman.'

'*What* kinswoman?' I asked, puzzled.

'Didn' 'ee know? The mistress, Isabella. Great-great-niece or somethin' on the other side. Not the Cranes', no relation there; not by blood you could say, but connected. Old Rebecca Madden's great-grandchild from all accounts, and real wild *she* was. Gotten herself hanged for malpractice. Course that was long ago. Long before my time. Things be different now. But blood-ties still count, and Dorcas edn' the one to forget an injury. Funny, esn' et? When Squire first brought that woman to Gulvarrick, she was the loveliest critter you could ever see. So dainty, too, and walked like a princess. Well, I reckon she may've made him think she was because he met her in London, see? Gotten herself a part in a play, actin' or dancin' or some such thing, and he was besotted, poor man.'

'Yes,' I agreed, suddenly understanding so much I'd never known before. 'And he always was. He was the faithful kind, Pascoe. The kind that doesn't forget whatever happens later.'

'Ah.'

When I got back to my own room, I put the ear-rings on and lifted my hair to the top of my head. One day, I thought, when I've got a new dark dress to suit, I'll wear them and perhaps have Venn admiring me.

I didn't even think of Sarne, not until the following evening after another visit to Thorncarne by the odious Miss Tattam. She hadn't stayed long, but I'd had to wait on her again, and once in a fit of temper I had been deliberately if politely rude. When she'd left Venn came into the kitchen. Liddy had left and Belle was upstairs, so we were alone.

'Don't ever do that again,' he said with repressed anger in his voice, his eyes deepening from gold to orange flame. 'Housekeeper you may be here at the moment. But if you throw any more tantrums, I'll ... I'll ... well, please watch your step, Judith, and remember ...'

'I'm a servant in your house,' I interrupted before he could finish. 'Certainly. I hope *you'll* remember it too, and that any moment I choose I can take off, leaving you to find another in my place.'

Without waiting for his reply to my threat I flounced out of the kitchen and up to my room. Liddy had done the washing up and tidied the place before she left, and there were only a few things to see to before bedtime: Belle's hot drink to take up, and leaving cheese and bread laid on the table in case any of the men needed a snack when the evening's work was finished. Sometimes old Ben Couch, the shepherd, who gave a hand as well at other farm work when required, looked in for 'a bite' if he felt like it, but that night I'd seen him leave earlier for his small cottage near the moors.

The air outside had a tangy scent that fired the restless feeling in me to be away for a bit somewhere where I could forget the annoying incident with Venn, or at least get it into some sort of proportion. What did he matter, I thought, as I pulled a shawl round my shoulders? When he'd taken me in, it had only been to his own advantage. The fleeting interest he'd shown in me at the beginning had soon passed with his increasing fondness for Alicia Tattam.

Tattam! What a ridiculous name. And *she* was ridiculous, too, with her simpering, chinless face and squeaky voice. Obviously, though, her insipid looks appealed to some men, including Venn. Unless it was her money. Belle had implied it, even Paul; and Sarne, in no mean terms.

Sarne. How warm his eyes and voice had been when he'd rescued me from Isabella; how strong his arms. No cold-blooded criticism there; no aloof superiority to put me in my place just because I'd refused to kowtow to a frilly, dressed-up creature all aimed to catch a well-to-do husband.

Suddenly I had an overwhelming wish to see him, to have his dark gypsy eyes admiring me and his voice filled with flattery against my cheek, saying things he really felt and that I knew had no guile in them. I so needed support at that time—ballast, I suppose, for any feminine vanity left to me from the humiliating periods of life with Matt and Pendruggan. So I went downstairs and slipped out of the house quietly, before Belle should take it into her head to call me, demanding service of some kind.

Though autumn was well set in, the air was not cold but calm and quiet and filled with the heady smell of dying bonfires and tumbled leaves. Sarne I knew was generally about somewhere at that hour, simply because of the roaming blood that was in him. Like me he had a thirst for freedom and the open countryside. Good worker he might be but at the end of a day he usually took himself off on a wander-round before going in for the night. My inner sense told me we'd most surely meet if I lingered long enough.

I walked on aimlessly towards the moor, drawing all the glowing richness of the evening into my lungs, wilfully dispelling any looking back to another autumn and another life, when Matt and I had been together and no cloud had seemed to threaten our future. All bird-song had died and the light was fading quickly by the time I reached the curve of the lane cutting towards the opposite coast. I waited there for a few moments first looking towards the rising hill tipped by its standing menhir, then turning and glancing back over the stone-walled fields above the lush pasture land. The valley beneath was already shrouded by milky mist. No glimpse of main road or distant sea was visible. I could have been alone in a dream world or on the verge of sleep myself.

But I wasn't. Gradually a shape emerged from the darkening shadow of a wall where a path led through the fields from the house. I'd been that way myself, often, when the barley was high and the root crops and greens thriving. Now much of the ground was fallow and ready for liming. But the air was softly seductive and filled me with expectancy and a curious, glowing warmth.

It was Sarne, of course. He'd seen me and was making his way quickly in my direction. I had an impulse to tease him by going on up the hill just to make him call and hurry after me. Not a nice thing to do, but I didn't feel nice that evening; I had only a longing for comfort and flattery, and a need to be upsides with Venn, though not for the world would I have admitted it. And in the end I resisted the temptation to provoke, and I just stood there until Sarne had caught up with me and was standing at my side with his arm round my waist. His body was warm and I could feel the maleness of it close against me and the pungent smell of dung from the sheds on his boots.

'Hullo, Judy,' he said, with his warm lips touching my cheek. 'Knowed I'd come, did you?'

I tossed my head. 'You've a nerve, Sarne Ettyn.'

'Crane.'

'Crane or Ettyn, what's it matter?' I said lightly, drawing away from him sharply and walking briskly ahead. He sprang after me, quick as a cat, and had me facing him, in his arms, before I could do a thing about it.

'Doesn't it then? Doesn't it?' he said with his eyes burning on mine. 'Want me, do you, as much as him ... Venn?'

His voice was thick, trembling with an urgency that suddenly shook me.

'Sarne ...' I said, trying to release myself. 'Please don't ... I didn't mean ...'

'What didn't you mean, darlin'? No ... you needn't say ... It don't matter ... nothin' but you an' me, love ... shsh ...'

A hand came to my mouth as his lips nibbled my ear, then travelled from there to my throat and neck, while I struggled unavailingly against him, yet with my heart pounding in a torment of bewildered excitement.

Bringing one palm, with all the force I had, against his chest, I gasped, 'Don't ... don't ... please. Oh no, *no* ...' realizing through all the tumult of my senses it wasn't Sarne I longed for, not really.

He muttered something unintelligible before his lips came down on mine, while one strong arm travelled from my waist to the buttocks and lingered there. I knew then it was too late. His touch was already flooding the thrilling, trembling awareness of my deepest sexual and emotional need. As I struggled, almost breaking my back to escape the inevitable, he caught me up and laid me in the bracken, where I lay scared and throbbing with fear and desire.

Even while he loosened my skirt and underwear I whispered my protests, muttering, 'Please ... we mustn't. Oh God, Sarne, stop.'

But his swelling self was already upon me and in me. Although the tears were warm on my cheeks, he neither saw nor cared, but had me as any healthy animal had its mate, in a wave of spreading darkness mounting to a wild and bittersweet culmination. When it was over and he'd eased himself away, my sobs broke free and I wept; hopeless crying that held no relief, though my body was wearied and appeased.

Sarne tried to comfort me.

'Look, Judy, look love ... there's no harm in it. Judy ...'

He bent over me. His face was flushed, with a gratified sort of shame on it, and for a moment I hated him.

My voice was harsh when I said, 'How *could* you? How *dare* you? Go away. Go on. Go back to your cows and your sheds and your ... your Thorncarne ...'

'Aw, stop it,' he said, shaking me by the shoulder. 'Get up, Judy. D'you want the whole place to hear? Here ...' He picked my skirt up and flung it at me, glancing round furtively. 'Put it on. Suppose Venn comes along ...?'

I jumped up in a kind of frenzy, struggling into the garment, while he adjusted his own clothes, drew a hand across his thick hair in an attempt to tidy it and glanced towards Thorncarne furtively.

'I'll be going back,' he said then in a practical, cool way. 'You follow when you feel like it. An' remember there's no need for anyone to know about this. Just keep quiet an' act reasonable. Then maybe sometime ...'

His eyes switched on me again with a wary speculation that made me long irrationally to slap his face.

'Get away from me,' I almost hissed, 'and don't you ever touch me again, do you hear? Not *ever!*'

He shrugged, started ambling away and then turned once briefly and said, 'For a woman who's bin askin' for it for weeks, you've got a fine way of thankin' a man, I must say. Never mind, darlin', the next time it'll be different.'

'Never,' I said, with my temper rising. 'Never, never. There'll be no next time or I'll kill you.'

I knew he was shocked. Or perhaps the cutting, rising note in my voice unnerved him. Because of my anger he'd have liked to sneer and goad and put me further in my place, but he was afraid of being overheard, especially by Venn. So the next moment, with a short embarrassed laugh, he was off towards Thorncarne, leaving me distressed and humiliated by the confusion of my own thoughts.

It was easy enough at first to put all the blame on Sarne, but after the first reaction, I realized with shame that the episode had been more of my own responsibility than his. If I hadn't tempted and lured him into wanting me on account of my own vanity and desire to be upsides with Venn and his wretched Miss Tattam, none of it would have happened.

Now, suddenly, I knew Miss Tattam hadn't been worth it. I should have fought her in a different, more clever way; with my brain instead of my body. Venn might never learn of this wretched incident, but the knowledge would be with me always, sullying any future contact we might have because I could no longer be completely honest with him.

As I walked back through the hushed, misted twilight, desolation filled me; the desolation of knowing that what my grandmother had predicted was true. I was like my mother, and there was no comfort in knowing it, except that I now understood her better and could picture a little of the torment that must have driven her into the path she'd taken. Already there had been three men in my life: Matt, William, and now Sarne. Venn didn't come into it because he'd not wished to. William had scorned me at the moment I most needed him, and Matt ... to Matt I'd been no more than a convenient wife, one of others in any port he chose.

To Matt I'd given my trust and virginity. Matt then was responsible, and it was him I should be hating instead of Sarne. But by the time I reached Thorncarne I'd no energy or desire to hate at all. Tiredness encompassed me. All I wanted was to get to bed and to sleep. I tried to climb the stairs soundlessly, hoping Belle had taken too liberal a portion of her tonic to be wanting her hot milk.

As I passed her door there was a creaking sound and her thick voice calling, 'Es that you, Judith? Forgotten me, have you? Come in here ...'

Wearily I turned the knob and went in. She was sitting up in bed with her coarse black hair tumbled over her shoulders and her pink cheeks flushed red above her three chins.

'You're late,' she muttered. 'Where you bin? Havin' it in the hay somewhere?'

Her voice was sneering, nasty.

A rising of my own temper gave me courage.

'Stop it!' I told her roughly, 'and mind your coarse tongue ...'

'Why, you ... you're ...'

She looked for a moment as though she'd have a fit and was silent long enough for me to say, 'Don't threaten me, Belle. I've had about enough here. It seems to me it'd be better for all of us if I left and went on somewhere else, and if I think the same in the morning that's just what I'll do.'

By the ebbing of colour from her face and her swallowing hard, I knew I'd won. The last thing Belle wanted was to have to shoulder the household chores again.

'No need to tek that line,' she said sullenly, 'but when you're lyin' here all maimed an' defenceless it makes you kind of touchy sometimes, I reckon.'

If I hadn't been so emotionally depleted, I could have laughed.

'You!' I said. 'Defenceless? Don't try and

fool me, Belle, I know what you are. And for once ...'

I paused, as she waited, watching me furtively from her black eyes.

'Yes? What you goin' on 'bout now?'

I smiled falsely. 'For once it would probably do you good to get your own night-cap. Lying about too much can bring on a stroke.'

I didn't wait to hear her reaction. There was no need. Belle had a lusty love of life and would be horrified by the mere suggestion of its coming to a close prematurely. She was still staring at me when I went out, closing the door firmly before hurrying to my room.

Whether she went down for the milk I didn't know and didn't care. I just undressed quickly, washed and scrambled into bed.

Sleep should have come quickly, but it didn't. For hours I lay wakeful, wondering then what the future could possibly hold. Once I got up, lit a candle and took it to the mirror which hung above the primitive dressing table. My hair shone glossy and lustrous over my shoulders, lit to deep bronze, gold, and flame in the flickering light. Slightly slanted above the high cheek-bones, my eyes still betrayed the secret longing in me for the fulfilment of a true love.

But what was love? And what true?

Instinctively my eyes glanced down at the miniature of Luzana on the table. Her face, serene and pure, stared up at me with composed dignity. But who could know what hidden thoughts and longings, what torment, had lain behind the image when the portrait was painted?

No one. It was a reflection, no more; a reflection of a woman who had lived and died centuries before, with nothing to give me but a reminder that something of her ancestry was also mine. And of what use was that when the turbulence of real life was wild inside me, driving me into situations I seemed to have no way of solving without discredit to myself?

Presently I laid the miniature down and went to the window. Outside the mist was rising in a thickening, milky vapour of fog, shutting out the world beyond.

If only, I thought, that evening, too, could be erased. But of course it couldn't, as I later learned to my cost.

CHAPTER 15

In the days following I did my best to avoid direct contact with Sarne, though for a time he hovered about whenever I was near, and I knew from his sidelong glances that he was wanting a chance to approach and talk to me. I pretended not to notice, only answering briefly when he asked a question on some mundane matter that had no bearing on our relationship. Once or twice he followed me across the yard or into the dairy where I was churning butter. I didn't look up, and though he attempted to draw me into conversation I kept my lips firmly closed; presently, after a hot exasperated exclamation, he left, slamming the door behind him.

Whether the others noticed the strain between us I didn't know. But I fancied Venn's eyes were on me more frequently, holding a curiously speculative look that might have flattered me before. Now I reminded myself of the so-superior Miss Alicia Tattam; in any case, through my commitment with Sarne I'd renounced any possible involvement with Venn.

Not that I accepted that Sarne had the slightest claim where I was concerned. To the contrary. No man had any rights over me. I was free. Myself.

Even Matt, through his monstrous deception, had become but a bad memory; a memory that had driven me from one dark mistake into another, leaving me embittered and cold unable any more to give trust or affection.

That's what I gulled myself into believing during those late autumn weeks. As the days shortened towards winter the conviction grew in me that I should pack my things and take off one day, putting Thorncarne and Gulvarrick behind for ever.

But I didn't. Against all commonsense and judgement I stayed. And oddly it was then that Venn started questioning me about Matt and my past.

'It seems wrong you should be forever tied to a man who's deserted you,' he told me bluntly one evening when we happened to be alone in the kitchen. 'A wife with no husband.'

'Oh but I have,' I answered quickly.

'Have you?'

Something in his voice—something doubting and yet warm, filled with a personal interest he'd never shown before—caused me to turn sharply and look at him. There was flour on my arms from the basin where I was preparing for baking, and my hair was damp on my forehead. Trying to tidy it, I said, 'You know all about it. I said he was a sea-captain, didn't I, and had to be away a lot. Well, it's true.'

'Then he's a damn odd husband, that's all I can say,' Venn remarked sharply. 'If you were *my* wife no sea journey or port in the world would keep me away from such a ... such a ... fine woman as you, even if my life depended on it.'

'He has commitments,' I said ambiguously; 'duties that keep him ... occupied.'

'Yes, I know. Such as ... Topaz, perhaps?'

I stared, with the blood suffusing my face in a rich welling tide.

'How? ... You don't know what you're talking about,' I managed to say, with a pretence of wiping my face with a corner of the apron. 'Ridiculous. *Topaz!*'

He got up and took me suddenly by the shoulders. 'Don't play with me, Judith, and don't lie. I know about him, because I've made it my business to. I have, among other things, shipping associates, and news travels. We've a mutual acquaintance by name of Jago. Nick Jago. So there's no point in trying to fool me.'

I rounded on him fiercely. 'Then you'd no right to go prying and poking your nose into *my* affairs,' I said with the temper hot in my eyes and voice. 'No right at all. What my husband does is no business of yours ...'

He gave a short laugh and dropped his hands.

'*Husband?* If I'm not very much mistaken, *that* he isn't and never was,' Venn said shortly. 'Whichever way, I intend to find out, and it won't take long either.'

'You keep your sharp ears and lying, greedy tongue to yourself,' I retorted, quite forgetting any manners I had. 'Keep it for your prunes and prismy mistress, the simpering Miss Alicia Tattam ...'

I broke off breathlessly, thinking he might

easily slap my face, so set and cold his mouth was, though his eyes were hot.

He didn't speak for a moment, then he said, 'For that I should put you over my knee and give you a good beating. It's what you deserve. But ...' with narrowed glance he paused a moment before adding, 'I don't mean to give you the satisfaction. Although we may not appear an entirely civilized household, I'm doing my damnedest, as I've done for years, to make it so. For that reason, Judith whatever-your-name-really-is, you'd best control your temper or else lose the respect of Belle and the whole family. You wouldn't like that, would you?'

'I wouldn't care,' I said stubbornly.

'Oh but I think you would. I think it pleases you quite a bit being, to all intents and purposes, mistress here.'

When I didn't speak he ambled to the door, turned and said, 'And please don't try and run away. We're specially busy on the land this time of year, and wasting time finding you would be an infernal nuisance.'

Giving me no time to reply, he snapped the door behind him and was gone.

To my dismay I found my heart was beating uncontrollably with excitement that was not entirely unpleasant. My legs, too, were shivering slightly from the brief interlude. No one before, except Matt, had aroused anything like the feeling in me, and for a few heady moments my whole body pulsed with new life and potential rapture.

Then, suddenly, I remembered Sarne, and my heart chilled to stony despair. I would never escape what had gone before, I thought with growing despondency. Without constant lying and pretence there was no evading that one fateful evening when, in a fit of jealousy, I'd given Sarne what should never really have been his.

How right I was. Though foolishly I'd not anticipated such a thing at the time, I discovered at the beginning of December I was with child.

One thing was clear to me then: after Christmas, before anyone knew, I must leave Thorncarne. How and where to go was of no account once the first decision was made, although a wild idea was already simmering that when next the travelling players came to Penzance I might join them.

Maybe I was thinking of my father. Or perhaps I just needed to be taken far away from all that reminded me of the past. Whatever the reason, I had somehow to start again and build a new life. I wouldn't give in. I *wouldn't*, I told myself fiercely not visualizing one part of how difficult such a course would be.

Christmas was cold, with crisp frost hardening the ground and undergrowth. Flavia came home for the holidays, with a whole lot of new airs to throw around and a fresh way of speaking that infuriated Belle, who complained that all Venn's high-and-mighty ideas for 'eddication' seemed to be doing was to turn her into a stuck-up little madam.

To me she was the one bright spot during that short period. Sarne was monosyllabic and surly; Venn, rather tight-lipped and watchful; and Marcus and Paul, too involved with the animals to be much about the house. There were no decorations nor holly simply because of Belle's queer superstition that most greenery brought ill luck. But she appreciated my cooking and ate enormously, making the festive season an excuse for taking more alcohol and spirits than usual.

Following these bawdy intervals there was generally a session when she strummed at her guitar for a time before being helped up to bed by Venn and Sarne.

'Ah,' she would say then, or something like it ..., 'what fine sweet sons I do have, surely. My own darlin' ma before me had twenty. An' as she sat of an evening wi' the goats nibblin' the bushes, theer'd be her eldest, a girl, Thisbe, with her own childer roun' her, an' all they others playin' as ma made music sweet 'nough for th'angels o' heaven to hear. We knowed how to live sure 'nuff ... breedin' quick an' jolly like young peas burstin' from a pod. Ah. A grand rich life et was then, an' my pa Petrock was a gorgeous fellow. Brown an' black-haired, with it so thick on his chest he could've been a great bear comin' through the trees. An' we seed the world, to be sure we did ... travellin' an' eatin' in our own time ... great dark hills I do recall, and rivers thick with young elvers ready for a sandwich. This place ...' she said, with a spit of contempt, 'what es et? Nuthen'. An' that red-haired son of mine no better. The image of his pa, he is, the gorgio who laid me. Ah me. Ah me. Real sufferin' I've knowed ...'

Her fat fist would go to her eyes where the maudlin drunken tears were welling.

No one took much notice of her meanderings at these times. How much of it was real and how much her imagination I didn't know. Nor did I care. Belle's past had little interest for me. I was far too concerned and fearful for my own future.

When January arrived I heard that a fair was coming to Penzance at the beginning of February, and it seemed to me this would be the time to leave, before my figure thickened or any tell-tale signs of my condition showed.

I forced myself to look ahead and plan coldly, though I realized it was impossible to predict the outcome. Thoughts of my father had revived again, with the wild notion he could be at the fair with the group of players, strutting about as I'd seen him before when I went with Matt. I didn't doubt any more he'd been my father, though I *should* have done; after all I had no proof, only the memory of that strange, fleeting moment of compelling recognition when he'd paused briefly, with the flask to his lips.

My grandmother's words echoed through my mind again in the chant I'd heard so often during my youth: Your father was a drunkard, and your mother was a whore.

Well, my mother, I *knew,* was dead. But something told me, stronger than any probability, that somewhere my father still lived, in a sphere of existence I'd never known. Drunkard he still might be, but of my blood, without whom I'd never have been born. I was convinced I knew the manner of his life, and in what company. I could picture the journeyings from place to place, by wagon and cart probably, with props and scenery stacked behind; tents put up at fairs and festivals, and acting sometimes in village barns or small halls. I'd once seen a bit of old newspaper pushed away with other unwanted stuff in an attic at my grandmother's house, and because I'd learned to read early it hadn't been too difficult to peruse the print, getting a rough picture of the player's background. Even so, long afterwards the heading of the paragraph was still clear in my mind: ACTOR PROVED GUILTY ON CHARGE OF DRUNKENNESS.

My grandmother had caught me absorbing the smaller print before I could finish reading it, and she boxed my ears soundly. Her narrow face had been crimson as she tore the paper to bits.

'Doan' you ever read such trash agen,' she'd said, with her bright black eyes glistening, 'or I'll tek a stick to your back, my girl, so you'll never forgit.'

I'd said nothing, but I'd seen enough; a photograph of a man with a sword in hs hand, bowing before a fine lady wearing a crown.

At the time I'd not thought the incident important, dismissing my grandmother's anger as just one of her over-sharp reactions when she considered I was prying into affairs that didn't concern me. But during those early months of

1883, the memory returned with compelling significance. Why had she been so heated over such a small incident? There could be but one answer, of course—the notice had referred to my father. So with this fact firmly embedded in my mind, I decided on my first course when I left Thorncarne, which would be to locate the players if they were in Penzance.

If not, well, there was always the Fiddler's Arms. Though I'd only seen Nancy Renalden once or twice since her brother's death, she'd impressed on me that in any difficulty there'd always be a welcome for me at the inn.

'Ebenezer's ways aren't mine, midear,' she'd said the last time we'd met. 'All fer modernizin' th' place he is, and I'm not sayin' he'd tek 'ee on fer any job of work, but I've still a say in th' business when I do want, an' a right to tek in any guest I do choose. No ...?' her expression had been ruminative, a little sad, as she'd paused before continuing, 'I don't altogether hold with many of the changes he've made, but then et's his life an' the future before 'en. A flash brassy bit of a girl he's got behind the bar now. All eyes an' cheek fer the men. She draws trade, I s'pose—of a kind. But not your sort, Judith. You was a real blessin' to us, with that proud look on you an' no nonsense in your eyes. I only hope he doan' wed her. That's my fear, though I shouldn't be thinkin' it. Still ...' She'd straightened up and given me an affectionate pat on the shoulder. 'See you doan' forgit, Judith. Call on me any time you do feel like et, an' 'ee'll be more'n welcome.'

There was great comfort in recalling Nancy's words, because I realized the chances of the players being at the February Fair were doubtful. But if I had to take her hospitality, at least I'd have money in my pocket to pay her for some weeks ahead. During my time at Gulvarrick and Thorncarne I'd saved sufficient for a 'rainy' day, though it had been a problem sometimes keeping the money safe from Belle's notice.

At that period, as January passed to February, her glance, when she wasn't drunk or asleep, was often on me with a curiously probing and knowing look.

Once, when a feeling of sickness had drained the colour from my face before I turned to take her breakfast tray away, she said, 'What's gotten into you, Judith? Been layin' around, have 'ee? An' don't lie to me. I know the look of a wumman when she's bin havin' et. Not Sarne es et? You tell me now ... you edn' bin leadin' my lovely boy into trouble 'fore 'ee's ready, eh?'

If I hadn't been so angered I could have laughed in her face at her allusions to her 'lovely boy'. As it was the words broke from me in a torrent of fury.

'Don't dare speak to me in that way ever again, Belle, or I'll take off after telling Venn the reason why; *then* there'll be fireworks.'

Her mouth drooped sullenly.

'You *will* always put on the drama so. That's your trouble. Thinkin' of you I was, as much as him. 'Cos take et from me, gel, he's the rovin' sort, Sarne is, an' ef you try to chain 'im you'll have 'en wild an' kickin' as any young bull, an' that's fer sure. His own sort he'll find one day ... Romany. An' then there'll be others to follow on. Folk of my own kin—Ettyns, the *real* sort—bred strong an' true.'

'Like Venn?' I said acidly.

She flushed. 'Venn edn' no Ettyn. Not the proper kind. Venn's ...'

'Yes?'

'Hold your tongue,' she snapped, 'an' leave family matters where they belong.'

I said no more, knowing that in spite of her temper my threat about telling Venn had subdued her. I realized something else, too; on one point I'd never get her to speak—Venn's father. And I guessed why. Fear of penury. Although Venn now was independent in his own right and quite capable of supporting her, the habit of years—the dread of disclosing something that during his earliest youth would have cost the family all they had—was still formidable in her mind, a secret to guard until the day she died.

Following Belle's shrewd observations and snide remarks, I kept well out of her way, except at meal times and during enforced interludes when I had to attend to her wants simply because she was too gin-sodden to do it herself. Sarne's sullenness didn't lift, but sometimes I could feel his eyes burning through me, even when I turned away, and knew he was wanting me. Wanting and yet hating me at the same time in the way a man does when he's been denied. I was proud at those times, trying to lash and humiliate him by my scorn.

That I was being unfair, even a little cruel in a physical way, didn't worry me. Knowing I'd mostly brought things on myself only sharpened my anger against him.

Whether Venn was aware of anything amiss between his brother and myself I'd no idea. But in his silent, forceful way he was more attentive. Once as I stood at the field-gate looking at a ewe with her lambs and thinking how innocent were all young things and what a sin they should ever come to be slaughtered, he came up in his quick, light-footed way behind me and said, 'Dreaming?'

I turned sharply, with a bunch of snowdrops I'd gathered held tight at my breast where my cape fell away.

'No,' I said. 'Just thinking.'

He paused for a moment with his fawn's eyes unmoving on my face. Then he remarked with something new in his voice, a kind of wonder, as though he'd never seen me before, 'What a lot you've got to give to life, haven't you?'

'Have I? Perhaps,' I spoke unthinkingly, to break the strange new spell on us both. For a moment something glowing and strong had leapt in me, flooding the world with expectancy and warmth.

Then I'd remembered. Sarne; and the child I carried.

Nothing could have shown on my face, I was so careful to keep it calm and closed with all secrets hid. But Venn looked puzzled. He touched my hand with his, and before I pulled it away he said, 'What's the matter, Judith?

Why've you been avoiding me?'

I laughed artificially.

'Avoiding you? What a thing to say. I've just been busy, as *you* have, about the farm, and ... Miss Tattam, of course.'

In an instant the magic died. His face darkened as my hand was released abruptly.

'Why the devil do you always have to drag *her* into things?' he demanded. 'Am I supposed to consult you every time I meet a friend or business associate?'

'Of course not,' I answered, drawing my shawl closer against the chilling air. 'I'm sorry I spoke.'

I would have moved past him, but all unexpectedly he suddenly caught me by the arm, swung me around and kissed me full and hard on the lips. The world spun round; I almost fell when he released me just as quickly, saying, 'There! And if you ever throw Alicia at me again, Judith Thomas, it's more than a kiss you'll be getting.'

A moment later he'd swung up the path into the lane, and I went to the house slowly, excited and yet hurt and numbed with pain and desolate because the ice had been broken at last and the thing I'd unconsciously longed for had happened—but too late. Nothing could come of it. In a short time I'd be gone. He could think what he liked then and wipe me from his memory like bad things from a slate. Unless Sarne told him, he'd never know the truth. That was something to be grateful for, at least; Sarne, for his own sake, would keep things to himself.

The next week I left, giving no reason for my sudden departure on any indication where I was going, just a short note saying, 'Thank you for all you've done. I shan't be back, so don't look for me.'

It was late at night when everyone had turned in, and no one saw me leave. I wore my tartan cape and a headscarf, and carried a large parcel under my arm containing my three dresses and small personal belongings, including Luzana's ear-rings. Round my neck I wore the miniature on a chain, and I thought as I swung down the lane to the main road, We're together now. You're all I have ..., imagining the lady in the portrait was real and alive.

When I reached the fair-ground the stars were bright in the cold sky, with a thin moon rising above the tents and stalls. There was the sound of grinding music and raucous voices shouting from every side. Hot potatoes were cooking, and through a spurt of flame I saw a goose being roasted over a fire. Further on was a conglomeration of stalls where macabre waxworks were on display, and next to that sat an enormously fat woman side by side with an ugly, misshapen dwarf. I pushed here and there, straining my eyes for a glimpse of 'Moody and Hackett's Theatre' but could find nothing. At last, in desperation, following a vulgar attempt by a beer-soaked lout to waylay me, I rushed into a fortune teller's tent, thinking she if anyone would know if the players were expected.

She was a thin-faced, bent, bedraggled-looking creature, huddled into a black shawl, with red locks straggling over her shoulders from under a spotted handkerchief. There was a crystal ball in front of her, and her eyes were small, dark and shrewd.

'Well,' she said, with an odious, beguiling smile revealing one or two broken yellowed teeth, 'what can I do for 'ee, my pretty dear? Your hand is it? Your hand and fortune for a morsel o' silver ...?'

I offered my palm, with a coin from my pocket, knowing that without it I should get no information at all. To my surprise she paused and, with her eyes narrowing to slits of intense watchfulness, said, 'Go your own way, daughter, and don't ask mine. Your path's where your heart sends 'ee, an' you know it. Interferin' with the darkness an' the light's none of my business, an' it's writ strong in your palm. You be one of the few, girl, one o' the few, so take 'ee off, an' my blessin' go with 'ee.'

To my astonishment she pushed the silver back at me. I hesitated before asking, 'The theatre people ... are they here? Moody and Hackett's?'

She shook her head. 'Not till Corpus Christi, chile, an' death have struck 'en, so I've heard?'

'Death? Who?'

She shook her head.

'I can't tell 'ee cos I don't know. My ears isn' for such as them who strut the stage an' put false notions in folks' heads.' Her chin poked forward from her shawl; her stare was fiery and full of doom. Then she struck her thin breast with a bony fist and said, 'The truth's here, girl. Only here. Ole Becky knows, an' only her.'

What she meant I couldn't guess, only that she wanted to be rid of me. It was as though I'd put some fear in her that even she herself was unable to understand.

So I went to the narrow gap in the tent, pulled it aside slightly and glanced back before leaving. Her eyes were riveted on the miniature of Luzana hanging from my neck on its chain; her whole manner displayed an uneasy caution that puzzled me.

But then, I thought practically as I was caught up again in the throng of sightseers, she might easily have thought I was some person of quality in disguise, gone there to spy and tell tales of her to the law.

Instinctively my hand closed over the portrait before I drew my cape closer about my neck. I hadn't felt tired before, but I did then. Dejection and disappointment at knowing the theatre company wasn't there combined with the pushing and jostling of the crowd enfolded me with a sense of loneliness I'd never felt so acutely before.

Seamen, farmers, shopkeepers, maid-servants wanting to be hired, ordinary townsfolk, soldiers, and a few persons of quality, all mingled together so it was hard to know who was who and what was what. The cheap-jacks were shouting, and pigs squealing. One or two drunks were already fouling the air with their coarse tongues. A passing lout wearing a seaman's jersey and woollen cap pinched my breast as I passed, and attempted to waylay me. I kicked out at his stomach and brought my hand smack against his face. He reeled, spat and muttered a string of obscenities over my shoulder.

I laughed to myself, but without humour, thinking how was he to know my background or the way I'd learned to deal with his sort? Contempt filled me then; self-contempt for having landed myself in the state I was, with nowhere to go and none to care how I eventually landed up, in a poor-house, jail, or even a brothel?

Not that I'd any intention of it being in any of those places. Whatever else I'd lost I still had my pride, and it was fierce and strong in me underneath my depression. All I had to do, I thought as I reached the edge of the field, was to rest a bit, if only for the night, at the Fiddler's Arms, and then make my way northwards where I could find some sort of job, perhaps as barmaid, and earn good money before the child was born. The thought of bearing Sarne's child was still distasteful when I remembered. But a child was a child and would have to be cared for. The funds I had wouldn't last for long, but whatever happened I'd no intention, ever, of taking help from the Cranes or Ettyns.

So I went on and cut my way along a track to Penzance's main street and from there to the Fiddler's Arms.

It was already well past closing time, but Nancy was still up and was so pleased to see me that tears for a moment glistened in her eyes and trembled on her broad pink cheeks, which were bright with delight and mingled with a faint consternation.

'My dear luv, come 'ee in, come in, midear. To see 'ee at such an hour, an' such a cold night, too. What's the matter, Judith, somethin' wrong es et?'

I almost broke down but contained myself in time. 'Not wrong exactly,' I told her, as she ushered me into her own small parlour, 'just unexpected and ... upsetting.'

She made me a toddy and settled me in her best chair by a still bright fire; when we were both contained and ready for talk I explained, sparing nothing except my feelings for Venn, and Sarne's identity.

'I'm not trying to excuse myself,' I said when it was all over. 'I was happy with William Pendruggan. He made up for Matt and other things, and whilst his wife kept away he cared and was fond of me, in his own quiet way. Then, after the tragedy, when I went to the Ettyns—I mean the Cranes—it wasn't too bad until ... until this man appeared ...'

I broke off, waiting for the question that I knew would come.

'Edn' you goin' to tell me who he is, luv? This chap?' Nancy said quietly. 'A man who puts a woman in the family way has responsibilities after all. An' it seems to me ...'

'No, *no,*' I protested, silencing her sharply. '*Never.* Don't press me, Nancy. If you do I'll have to take off immediately. You understand?'

She shook her head. 'No, I can't say I do, midear. But ef you won't, you won't. So we'll let that be. Though what you're going to do ...?'

'I've planned what I'm going to do,' I told her. 'I shall go further up country and get a job for a time. It shouldn't be too difficult, if you'll give me a reference ...'

'Reference? Now don't you ever suggest any doubt 'bout that,' Nancy interposed sharply. 'Such a one you sh'll have that even the good Queen herself couldn' wish for better. As for a bed, you sh'll have one here for as long as you do want. There's plenty of space an' to spare. Ebenezer's took against havin' lodgers an is all fer changin' the front parlour into some sort o' coffee house fer visitors. More cash in et, he says, 'specially with holiday trade increasin' an' all them fancy folk comin' down by steam train to paint the Mount.' She paused, took a deep breath, then went on, 'Have 'ee heard o' the Cap'n, Judith?'

I shook my head.

'No, and I don't want to,' I said firmly, although the mere mention of his name revived something I'd tried to forget, and set my pulses fluttering.

'Ah. Oh well ... that's life, I s'pose. Though I do think et's a pity when a wife an' her lawful wedded gets torn apart.'

'I'm afraid I may not even have been that, Nancy,' I told her. 'His wife I mean. From what I've heard ... I wasn't the only one. In fact I *know.*'

'Dear dear. Dear dear.'

For a moment or two she sat sadly clucking and reminiscing like some lonely old hen bewailing the loss of her chickens. Then suddenly she sat up and with forced brightness said she was going to have a bite and see I had one, before going upstairs to see a room was properly ready for me.

I didn't see Ebenezer that night, he was out somewhere, probably at the fair, Nancy told me, with that 'flash black-haired madam' of his, whom she feared would have him at the altar before the year was out.

'Thinks he's clever, Ebenezer does,' she said as she showed me my room later. 'So he is, when it comes to makin' a show an' gettin' his hand on a bit of money. But women! He edn' got the sense to see further than his own nose. She's shrewd, that one is. Knows how to keep a man sniffen as if he was a donkey with a carrot before 'em. Ah. Maybe she does give 'im a bit of a nibble now an' then, just to keep 'im after her skirts. But that's all. Nuthen' more. An' ef I had my way I'd sooner see 'en fall for one with a bit o' weakness an' love in 'er.'

I smiled, feeling suddenly tired. 'Never mind, Nancy,' I said. 'Perhaps it will work out better than you think. Loving a man doesn't always bring happiness.'

After she'd left me, I thought bitterly of the truth of my own words and how naïve I'd been when I'd taken, on faith, all Matt's passionate avowals, never dreaming that everything between us could be founded on a lie.

That night a wind blew up from the west, moaning fitfully round the walls, swinging the signboard outside so it creaked dismally, reminding me of ships at sea. Although I was tired I found it hard to get to sleep; so many pictures filled my mind, impressions of the past mostly ... sea-faring talk and genial, rough men full of liquor following months on the water, cursing and laughing together as they jostled along the harbour. I recalled watching as a child the fish gutted on the slipway in Port Einack, and the bargaining that went on, then the fish-wives or 'jousters' in their shawls or scarlet cloaks setting out to hawk their husband's fish on foot or by other means, from village to village, with specially shaped baskets on their backs. They wore black beaver hats or bonnets and looked to me like characters from a fairy-tale. But there'd been little of a fairy-tale about life then; and as they grew to be old, those same women had been bent and sombre-looking, bright-eyed still but walking slowly along the harbour looking like weary old ravens ... widowed mostly, and many childless, having lost their male kin at sea.

As I'd grown older there'd been those others—the fearsome, tramping Evangelists, who preached the word of God and hell-fire and damnation in one go. They'd terrified me until my grandmother had lifted a bony fist and struck one of them on the jaw, sending him reeling.

'God I will have in my own home,' she'd said to me afterwards, 'but none o' that squawkin' an' screechin', 'cusin' good folk of evil they hadn' done. An' no interferin' wi' business, mind. Remember this, girl, what you have to do es b'lieve in th'Almighty, but doan' trust 'en too far. Folks like us es meant to kip an eye on our own affairs.'

Incidents like this returned that night in a continual pictured pageant, ending up inevitably with memories of Matt; Matt who'd promised security but had left me as a bird of passage only, to make my way through macabre happenings to a strange refuge in Nancy's house.

I'd seen the bedroom before, but only on quick occasions when I'd given a hand with dusting and cleaning. It was one reserved for lodgers but retaining somehow an odd air of the past, with lace curtains drawn over the pull-blinds, heavy mahogany furniture including a teak seaman's chest in one corner and a daguerreotype on the wall of a bewhiskered, white-haired gentleman with his hand on a Bible, who Nancy had told me was her late husband.

A faint air of moth balls pervaded the air, but it was a homely smell and one I knew well. The large brass bedstead was completed by a feather mattress, and blankets and sheets with an odour of lavender about them.

Oh yes, the room was comfortable enough. It was only my mind that wasn't. On top of everything else I couldn't forget how I'd acted with Sarne, and for what reason.

When three o'clock struck I slept at last and was only woken by Nancy coming in with a breakfast tray. I was grateful, surprised and shocked all at once, because the only other time I'd had such luxury was from Jane when she'd discovered I was having Matt's child.

'You *shouldn't,* Nancy,' I protested. 'I could've come down so easily and saved your legs traipsing up the stairs.'

Nancy tut-tutted. 'You eat and enjoy it, midear,' she said. 'The bacon's our own ... home-cured and cooked, and maybe it'll put a bit of life into you. An' when you've finished ...'

She paused significantly.

'Yes?'

'Only when you're ready, mind, an've got every bit o' that inside of you ... there's someone downstairs waitin' to see 'ee.'

My heart jerked, nearly stopped, then rushed on unevenly.

'What do you mean? Who? Tell me! It's not ... Matt?'

Nancy shook her head. 'I only wish 'twas. An acquaintance o' yours, I do believe; no more. But you should see 'en, girl. That's my advice an' I do mean et. Make yourself all tidy an' grand to greet 'en. There's nuthen' like bein' proud to get upsides with a man.'

However much I pleaded, she'd say no more. After thinking first of Matt my mind turned to Venn; then I dismissed the thought because he'd no clue where I was, and even if he had, he would probably scorn the idea of following. Besides, at that time, he'd be busy on the farm. Sarne? No. I couldn't believe Sarne would be interested in trying to track me down. Jago perhaps?

In a flurry of excitement I managed to eat the breakfast, then washed from the hot water brought up to me, dressed in my best black and went downstairs.

Nancy was waiting in the hall.

'He's in the back parlour,' she whispered. 'Mind. Now listen to what he says, midear. There'll be no one to poke or pry or put an ear to the keyhole ... I'll see to that. Tek as long as you do want, but doan' 'ee act hasty. Consider well what you be doin' before you turn your back on a friend.'

She patted my arm briefly, turned and went a few paces down the hall into the kitchen, closing the door firmly behind her.

I paused a moment, patting my hair to see if it was tidy, then, braving myself to meet whoever it was with dignity and thinking it was surely Jago, I went into the room with my head up, all ready to tell him not to speak to me of Matt. Oh it was quite clear in my head what I'd say and my way of saying it: contemptuously, with a cold sneer on my lips for the way Matt Thomas had behaved.

But I got a shock.

As I shut the door, a figure standing with his face to the window turned, and I could feel the colour draining from my cheeks. Not Jago, not Sarne, or even Matt himself, but Venn Ettyn came towards me, slowly but purposefully, with a grim look about him that sent shivers down my spine and set my legs quivering.

I didn't speak, I couldn't ... not until he said, 'Sit down, Judith.'

'Why should I?' I asked with a spurt of anger.

'I told you not to follow me. There's nothing to say.'

'Sit down,' he echoed, without a smile or change of expression in his voice.

If I could have run from the room I would have. But without upsetting Nancy and perhaps creating a scene, there seemed no way; so I did what he said, and waited, trying desperately to quieten the bumping of my heart. I wished he'd do the same but he just walked to the window again.

Then coming back he stood a few feet away from me and looked down at me saying, 'What got into you? What made you act so childishly and without a scrap of consideration for anyone else? The truth, if you don't mind.'

'I *do* mind,' I answered sharply, jumping to my feet again. 'I have my reasons, but they're my own affair and nothing to do with you. I'm sorry if I've left Belle to cope, but I'm sure she'll manage it. And you've still got Liddy. So *please* ...' My voice faltered as a wave of emotional weakness swept over me. '*Please* ... please, Venn, do leave me alone.'

There was a pause in which he stared at me with a deep, questioning look in his eyes; and in the silence, although his back was to the light, I noted for a vivid moment I was never to forget, every line of his finely carved face—the aquiline nose, the strong, proud chin, the wide brow under the flaming hair and the stern lips that softened as he looked at me.

Then he continued, still in that cold, aloof voice, 'You will go your own way, of course, and act as you choose. If you've no manners at all, or any sense of what is decent behaviour, I can't teach you any. And it's true what you imply; no one is indispensable. Good housekeepers aren't all that difficult to find. However, I'm sure you must admit you owe me *something*. An explanation. And believe me, Judith, I don't intend to leave without it.'

I turned away, but almost before I knew it his hands were on my shoulders, swinging me round to face him.

'Now,' he said, 'are we going to discuss this thing reasonably? Or are you wanting a scene? Believe me, Judith, I'm quite capable of making one—if I have to.'

I made one more attempt at evasion.

'What does it matter? I'm sorry for any ... any inconvenience I've caused but ... and anyway, how did you find me?'

'Commonsense,' he answered curtly. 'You had to be somewhere, and I guessed it was either the fair or here. Besides, have you forgotten what I once said? That wherever you went, however far you ran, I'd find you in the end. Remember?'

Yes, I remembered, and the reminder hurt acutely, because I knew then he'd meant it; I realized too late the implication of his words. However important Miss Tattam had been in his life at that time, I'd been more to him. Perhaps I'd half-guessed it all along and been too proud and stupid to admit it. The episode with Sarne ... oh God, I thought, why had I been so obtuse and weak, so vain and shallow, as to deny my own feelings just for the sake of jealous bravado? Wild I'd been, wild and headstrong like my mother before me, doing things there was no way of putting right now because Venn would never understand.

Through a cloud of confused misery, I heard Venn's voice continuing, but more gently as he lifted my chin with one hand, forcing me to stare straight into his eyes. 'Well, Judith? Darling ...'

I pulled myself away, threatened by a sense of faintness, of the room closing in on me, with no air to breathe. The feeling only lasted a few seconds, and when I'd recovered I was suddenly calm and clear-headed, knowing what I had to do.

'Don't say such things,' I told him in a cool voice that hardly seemed my own. 'I'm not your darling and never could be. I'm a married woman, with experience ... two lovers, and a child in my womb. There! Are you satisfied *now?* Is *that* what you wanted to hear? Is it? Is it? I wouldn't have told you if you hadn't forced it out of me. I didn't *want* to. It'd been better, much better, if you'd left well alone. But you couldn't, could you? You had to track me down and humiliate and bully me, wanting me to creep and crawl and beg forgiveness. And for what, Mr Ettyn? I'm not yours. I'm Matt's, and always have been. And if I have to answer to anyone, it's to him ...'

I broke off with the rising tears in my throat half-choking me, waiting for a spate of angry words to follow.

They did not come. But I could sense something in him crumble and die as his shoulders sagged and he turned, walking again to the window. I remember quite small things now about the interim that followed: the pecking of a sparrow at the glass, and the far away calling of a ship's siren from the sea; the drift of curtains in the wind through a chink between the panes, and laughter from the street below.

When Venn glanced at me once more his face was set, withdrawn and cold; almost a dead face.

'And is this so-called husband of yours the baby's father?' he asked with heavy irony. 'Hardly, I should imagine. Pendruggan's perhaps? But no. He's been dead too long.'

He stood perfectly still for a moment, then suddenly had me by the arms again, his fingers biting into my flesh like iron.

'Who? *Who?*' he demanded, as the tears fell from my eyes, coursing down my cheeks freely. 'You just tell me. Some roving tinker come begging at the door, was it? Or a drunken sailor wanting a bedfellow for the night? Out with it, Judith. My God, if you don't tell me, I'll ...' His grip tightened.

'All right, all right,' I gasped. 'If you must know ... it's ... it's ... Sarne.'

When the word was said all tension went from me. In a daze of sudden weakness I sat down again, with my head in my hands. How long the silence between us lasted I didn't know. Only Venn's voice brought me to my senses, and all anger had gone from it. It was cold and withdrawn, as though he was speaking from a long distance away.

'I see. Sarne. Trust that lusty brother of mine. And trust me to give him the hiding of his life when I get back.'

'It wasn't his fault,' I said. 'It was both of us. Mine mostly. I don't expect you to understand, Venn, but ...'

'Oh, believe me, I understand only too well,' he said with icy precision. 'I should have seen the truth long ago, listened to my wily mother's observations. Well ...' he drew a long breath before continuing, 'there's only one thing to do about it, isn't there?'

'I don't see ...'

'Then let me enlighten you, and keep your pretty, lying little mouth shut until I've finished, if you don't mind. You're coming back with me to Thorncarne tonight, madam, and as soon as possible Sarne will marry you.'

'And do you think I ...?'

'I don't think. I'm telling you. Whether you like it or not, you and Sarne will be married, for the child's sake if nothing else.'

'You're forgetting Matt.'

'I've been finding out a good deal about the gallant captain lately,' Venn said derisively, 'and he's no more your husband than I am.'

As he spoke I couldn't help noticing the twitching of a small muscle near his mouth, almost a wince of pain.

'You've no proof,' I said bitterly.

'I shall have shortly, when the proper papers arrive,' he told me. 'Everything will be quite legal and safely sealed and signed.'

'And because of *that* ...' my voice was sharp with bitterness and scorn, 'you imagine you can force me into taking a man I ...'

'Presumably you must have some slight liking for him?' Venn interrupted coldly. 'I can hardly imagine even *you* lying with one you had no feeling for.'

I didn't answer. What more was there to say?

And so it was on that same morning an hour later, Venn drove me back to Thorncarne into a future I'd no wish for with the last man in the world I'd had chosen as a husband.

Sarne, I think, felt the same way, but he was as powerless as myself against the force of Venn's will to have matters properly legalized and in order under his own roof.

At the end of March I became Sarne's wife, and because of it I learned to hate him as much as I hated Venn, although my feeling for Ettyn was of a different kind and something which at times, in solitary moments, made me cry with anguish and longing for the one thing I wanted and could never have.

CHAPTER 16

I was married in russet brown, with a full cape falling discreetly from neckline to hem, over a dress carefully calculated to hide any perceptible swelling of my figure. Venn, ironically, paid for the outfit, as he did for Belle's, which was of brilliant scarlet silk, emphasizing her enormous bulk outrageously. At first she had refused to attend the quiet ceremony at Bethany Chapel in the adjoining hamlet of Guldron, protesting that the Ettyns had always been good Catholics, whatever the Cranes were, and she'd no liking for heathenism. It had seemed odd to me, laughable really, that considering her pride in Romany tradition she should suddenly discover such a passion for the 'true religion' as she put it; especially as she'd always taken such pains to avoid the slightest contact with 'any o' them clerical black crows'.

Nobody had cared whether Belle attended or not, certainly not Sarne or myself. The quieter the better, I'd thought, and I'm sure Venn was of the same mind. A week before the ceremony, however, Belle had suddenly changed her mind, as I'd thought she might, protesting that it would be an unnatural mother who'd let a son go to the altar without his nearest kith or kin to represent him, most of all her darlin' Sarne, who'd always bin the apple of her eye, so he had.

Under other circumstances I could have got considerable amusement from her motherly concern, but as we set off for the chapel in a respectable cab hired by Venn, with Venn, who was to give me away, beside me, I had a sudden, dreadfully trapped feeling of wanting to be done with them all—free of Belle's coarse absurdities and of Sarne's sullen aggressiveness and, most of all, of Venn's cold determination to have me safely off his hands.

What would happen, I wondered, if I were to jump out then and there, refusing to go ahead with the marriage? At one point I was tempted to try, but as though sensing my thoughts Venn placed his hand over mine for a moment and I heard him saying in a formal, detached way. 'Most brides feel anxious before the ceremony. I'm sure once you're inside the chapel you'll behave in a proper way. Sarne will make a good husband and father if you accept him for what he is ... honest, down to earth and loyal.'

'Yes,' I said coldly. '*You* should know.'

'So should you,' he retorted quickly, 'considering what's happened.'

I had a wild impulse to try, even at that late moment, to make him understand; to cry, Venn, Venn, please don't let this thing happen ... this marriage to Sarne. I don't *love* him, not the way you think. It was *you.* You were the reason, don't you see ...?

But of course he wouldn't see, because I'd learned by then that men had one-track mentalities where women were concerned. If she gave her body she gave everything. The mind and the imagination didn't count at all. Women were just taken and owned, for the bearing of children.

I sat back in a cloud of dejection deepening into dread, as the cab turned the corner to the left, nearing the top of the hill where the chapel stood.

A small crowd of people were waiting when I went in on Venn's arm, but my eyes and senses were too dazed to recognize anybody except one, an old woman seated at the back of the chapel with her chin out-thrust and her eyes black pebbles under her beetling brows. She had an ancient bonnet on her head and a kind of beaded black shawl round her shoulders. Old Dorcas.

For a second my heart nearly stopped. I wanted to turn and rush out, run and run where they could never find me, like a fox to its hole or wild thing to its lair; somewhere far away from the threatening malignant stare of that wretched old witch come to sneer and leer and maybe cast her awful spell over the future. I should have done it long before, I realized in a terrifying fit of clarity. I should never have allowed myself to be so coerced by Venn into this mockery of a union. Why had I done it? Why? *Why?* Unless somewhere at the back of my mind I'd recognized that life with Sarne, despite its difficulties and shortcomings would ensure, at least, proximity to Venn?

Oh God, I thought as I walked on stiffly down the aisle with Venn's arm steadying me; help me, please ... and help my child.

But God seemed far away as I saw Sarne standing ahead by the altar, broad and somehow formidable in his best black, with Marcus at his side. He turned once briefly, glancing at me through narrowed eyes, his face unsmiling but with a sort of relentless power on it that confused me. Why such small things should register so vividly at such a moment I don't know, but it was as though I was seeing him clearly for the first time in my life. And I was afraid.

If it hadn't been for Venn and Marcus I'd never have got through. But once the minister started on the formal ritual, everything became automatic, words spoken in a sort of trance and promises that meant nothing at the time but which were to mean so much later.

When it was all over and we were back at Thorncarne, there were the usual toasts and boring speeches, followed by an ample meal prepared by Liddy. Belle got outrageously drunk, and Marcus and Paul had to half-carry her to the sofa in the back parlour.

After that all became confusion in my mind, although I remember one isolated incident when I turned on Venn, saying bitterly in a harsh whisper, 'I'll *never* forgive you for this. *Never.*'

We were alone for only a moment, which didn't allow me to hear his reply. Perhaps he never spoke at all; he didn't really need to. His face was suddenly white and stricken, as though I'd cut him to the heart.

Well, I hoped I had. Yes, I hoped Venn would suffer, I thought later, as I made my way with

Sarne upstairs to the room prepared for our wedding night. And if he married Miss Alicia Tattam, I was quite sure he would, which was some consolation.

'What you thinkin' about?' Sarne asked as I stood staring through the window across the brown moors. 'Silent all of a sudden, aren't you?'

'Maybe,' I answered. 'It's the flowers. Have we got to have so many? They make my head bad.'

'Never satisfied, are you?' he grumbled. 'Ma goes to a lot of trouble on your account, Judy, yet all you can do is start grumblin' right away. Why?'

'Because I think we should have waited till our own place was ready,' I told him. 'We should've started on our own.'

'Maybe we should've,' he agreed. 'Or maybe we should never've started at all. But then you didn't think o' that, did you, not when you landed us together. Now keep quiet, Judy, an' take that cumbersome thing off. A real brown duck you look an' no mistake. All feathers an' frills hidin' your sweet, tender flesh. Come on now. I didn't aim to wed a nun, darlin'. But then there wasn' no fear o' that, was there?'

He moved towards me purposefully, eyes dark and smouldering in his flushed, handsome face and lips set above the thrusting chin. I backed away instinctively, dodging behind the bed. He laughed softly, before taking off his jacket, tie and confining breeches. Then he approached me almost soundlessly on his stockinged feet, and when he caught me he tilted my face up to meet the hot flame of his eyes.

'Frit, are you, darlin'?' he asked in a thickening, throaty voice. 'Frit of what you had so willing before in the bracken? Remember?'

Yes, oh yes, I remembered, I thought desperately, clutching the buttons of my bodice close to my neck. I remembered and didn't want it again, because my longing for him on that autumn evening had been bred only through revenge and the desire to get the better of Venn.

'Well?' Sarne went on. 'Gone all sour, have you? Now that's not nice, darlin', not to your lawful husband.'

His hand went to my bodice and pulled my own away. Then, very slowly, as though savouring each revelation of my body, he took my garments off one by one, and when I was quite naked he laid me on the bed. I started to struggle, but one hand was on my mouth, the other stroking my navel and thighs.

'Now, now,' he said, with his breath rising and falling quickly. 'None o' that. I've wed you, haven' I? An' you're mine now ...' Unthinkingly, I bit his hand. He struck me once across the face and said in a harsh whisper, 'Any more o' that an' I'll give you something to howl about real an' proper, darlin'. So be quiet now before I forget mysel' an' do what no self-respectin' man should to a woman.'

I lay back with a feeling of faintness on me as he plunged into me, moaning endearments that meant nothing at all but pain, resentment and eventually a wild and bitter fulfilment.

He tried to be kind later, and I pretended to respond, steeling myself to the thought that this was only the beginning; somehow I had to get used to it, to bear it for the sake of the child. I slept only fitfully, and once during the night I felt him turn over, edging nearer and enclosing one breast with his hand.

'I didn't mean it, y'know,' he muttered, 'not about hurting you. I wouldn't really ... not *badly*. You know that, don't you, Judy, don't you? *Don't* you, love?'

I closed my eyes tight, saying wearily, 'Yes, I know. It's all right. Go to sleep, Sarne.'

'Things'll get better,' he went on. 'When the little un comes we'll be a family on our own. I'll be good to you. Only doan' go cold on me, darlin'. I fell for you right from the start. I did, honest. But then you was always hankerin' after Venn ... until that evenin' ...' His voice trailed off. I felt his fingers come to my cheek and forehead gently, stroking the hair away. Then his lips on my temple. 'Forget him,' he said, with his breath warm against one ear. 'He's got a way with him, Venn has; always did have, for women. All that eddication and everything, and having that father ... but underneath he's wild and cold, Judith, an' always on the look-out for hisself. Don't think of him. Push him out ...'

'Oh Sarne, Sarne ...,' I said, with a queer kind of compassion stirring in me. 'Don't go on so. What's Venn got to do with us. He's *nothing*, and if you must know, he never *could* be, to me.'

After that Sarne seemed to relax and was quiet. Presently, by his heavy breathing, I knew he was asleep.

But it was a long time before I got off again. Though my body was tired and my brain was in torment, filling me with contempt that I could have lied so glibly and that from then on I would have to keep pretending and saying things that weren't true, keeping up a front that all was as it should be between Sarne and me when things in reality were so desperately wrong—for me anyway.

Somehow I got through the next two months without any major confrontation with Belle in the kitchen. Things were very much the same as they'd been before the wedding, except for a coolness, more felt than seen, between Venn and myself.

He excused himself from being much in the house on the pretext that he had so much to do seeing to the conversion of a barn into new small premises for Sarne and me. A labourer had been hired to help with the work, and I realized early on that, when finished, the place, though small, would be attractive, with one large room downstairs and two above. But I hadn't really much interest in the project. Everything seemed to have been taken out of my hands, even the daily routine; meals which would be taken, Venn told me, at Thorncarne with the rest of the family, to save me trouble.

I didn't argue, knowing Belle had put the idea into Venn's head, simply because she didn't want the business of cooking herself. After the baby came, though, I determined I'd run my own life as I chose. What did they think I was, I wondered frequently. A lump of furniture to be dumped here, there, and in any place the Cranes wanted, whenever it suited them? A mere cog-in-the-wheel, so one of their breed could bear the family name and grow up to take his share of the work in the future?

When thoughts like this churned my mind I was so filled with fury, I often took off to the moors and Castle Carnack, where I could stand with the sweet air fresh on my face and my hair blown wild on the wind.

I no longer took any notice of, or feared, old Dorcas, though as I passed she'd stand at her door watching, trying to unnerve me by weird incantation in a tongue I didn't understand, her dark eyes peering malevolently from under her crushed-down hat. Once a white cat streaked through the bushes before me, and almost simultaneously I heard a rasping wave of laughter from the door of the shack. White cats, of course, were supposed to bring ill luck. At another time I saw a hare flying over the moorland turf and recalled the old superstition that witches had a habit of taking an animal's shape when it suited them. Although I didn't accept such superstitious nonsense I glanced involuntarily down at my feet and saw the gaping hole of a derelict mineshaft only a few feet away. It was covered with bramble and furze but the shadowed gap was unmistakable, and I knew that another step or two could have landed me with a terrible death. The frail branches and overhanging bracken were certainly not heavy enough to bear my weight, heavy as I was with child, and just for a moment horror so swamped me I had to rest on a rock to collect my nerves.

After that I didn't wander about the moors so much but chose the quieter ways of the valley, which were rich now with bluebells, cow's parsley, and a froth of blossom from the hedges.

By early June our new home was ready for Sarne and me. Moving in was accomplished with the minimum of trouble, except for Belle's interference and her sudden, excessive interest in what was right for her darlin' son an' the child, her grandson, that was so soon to be born. Of me she took practically no notice at all, which unduly annoyed me at first until I realized this was probably for the best.

The baby, a son, was born without difficulty or complication at the end of the month, and from my first glimpse of him I knew he was the image of his father—strong and lusty, with already a thick tuft of dark hair on his head.

Belle was delighted, and so was Sarne.

As for me, I didn't really care. Unlike most women I had none of the passionate mother-love generally experienced after the first shock and weariness was over; only a curious indifference, because he seemed to be no part of me in any meaningful sense but something merely contrived and manipulated into being by Ettyn purpose and for Crane and Ettyn ends.

Sometimes in the days following I felt a pang

of compassion for such a small, defenceless creature. But the compassion amounted to no more than I'd have felt for a newly born lamb or calf, and I knew then, in the queer way I had, that as he grew he'd be drawn further and further away from me and I wouldn't mind at all.

If he'd been Matt's—or even Venn's—but then neither of them had stood by me or wanted from me the most precious thing any woman could give. So I steeled myself to forget the past, living each day as it came, not looking to the future because I dared not.

CHAPTER 17

The baby was named Petrock, after Belle's father, and Sarne, after his own, at Belle's demand. I didn't mind. With the passing of the weeks his likeness to the Ettyns increased, making me feel in a queer kind of way an outcast and merely incidental in giving him life. Belle was enraptured by her darlin' son's offspring, curtailing even her drinking habits in order to give him her full attention. Occasionally I'd feel a stab of resentment, reminding her he was my son, and there'd be a hard glint in her eye when she'd answer outwardly, amiably enough. 'O' course he is. But the spitten' image of your dad, aren't you, my lovely?'

And I'd turn away thinking, let her get on with it. Let her spoil and mollycoddle him with her lollipops and fat chuckles and endearments. Because of him she was more tolerant and easier to get on with in the kitchen, and whenever I wanted to be free I could be, knowing she was forever bursting to have him in charge.

All the same, except for Belle, an atmosphere of resentment seemed to hover over Thorncarne. Sarne frequently sulked, because although I'd learned not to deny him my body, steeling myself to accept his marital demands with as good a grace as possible, he must have known I didn't want him physically; the knowledge frequently goaded him to excessive behaviour. Sometimes I was saddened not only on my own account, but on his also. If we'd not been forced together so inexorably I'd possibly have been able to feel the warm friendship for him that had so often been there earlier. There were moments when I glimpsed a hurt in his eyes and a sullen droop of his lips, and he appeared more of a great overgrown youth than a man. Then I'd remember my first days at Thorncarne, the period when he'd taught me so many things about the countryside and the ways of animals, and later how he'd rescued me from the terrifying incident with Isabella. There was much that was good in him, and I often despised myself for not being able to love him and for my own weakness in allowing Venn to shape our lives so disastrously.

Venn. It was odd how his image overclouded everything, until I remembered Matt and with closed eyes imagined again the hot, hard pressing of his lips on mine and the wild richness of our life together before the appearance that fateful day of Topaz and Wellington on our doorstep. I didn't want to think back, and mostly I didn't, but in my dreams sometimes the whole of my past swept before me like a pattern gone awry. And when I woke up there'd be tears on my cheeks and so strong a longing for the impossible that my whole body ached, though even then I couldn't always distinguish Matt's image from Venn's.

I'd been Matt's wife, though. He'd married me, whatever that legal document that Venn had got from abroad said. And it seemed to me often that one day he'd return, and then the rest wouldn't matter; not Topaz, Sarne, the baby, not even Venn. Wife or not I'd go with Matt, wherever in the world it should be, leaving the past behind like a bad dream.

The next minute I'd know I was wanting the impossible. Matt *wouldn't* return, and all I could do was to make the best of what I had, at Thorncarne.

It was early September when our small home was completely ship-shape, with a patch of field fenced in to make a garden, and flowers and vegetables already planted. I noticed then for the first time how nice the place was: all cream and blue paintwork and rush-seated wooden furniture, made mostly by Sarne himself. Except for making a few suggestions I hadn't taken the interest that most women would have done in the preparations and conversion of the property, and I knew Venn had noticed. It must have been obvious to everyone.

'I hope you approve,' he said coldly one afternoon. 'Catering for a woman's tastes isn't really a man's business. But now you've got your own place, maybe you'll pull yourself together and think of your family for a change, instead of only yourself.'

We were alone, standing near the door, with the tangy smell of woodsmoke drifting over the brown fields and open moors. I glanced up at him, knowing my eyes blazed as hard as the hot, bright gleam of his own.

'It was *your* wish I should marry Sarne,' I

told him, 'not mine. So it would be better if you stopped criticizing and minded your own affairs.'

I turned abruptly to go, but he pulled me back.

'Don't ever say that again, Judith. You *wanted* it. You wanted Sarne—as you told me only too clearly that day at the Fiddler's Arms ...'

I laughed sneeringly. 'Maybe you didn't listen,' I said, 'or maybe your ears want examining, or maybe ... maybe it was just what you wanted *yourself,* Venn Ettyn, so you could be free of any embarrassment and secret hankering you had. Free from wanting me so you could take Miss Tattam with a good conscience. Yes ... *that's* what I think. You're cold and clear-headed, so filled with ambition you doan' care who you break in gettin' it ...' I was breathing heavily and lapsing into the Cornish dialect that came so unwittingly when I was upset. 'Well ... go on, take her. She's got a tidy bit put by, I wouldn' wonder ... her with that shop an' a carriage of her own. Marry her and all that goes with it ... an' I hope you rue it to the end of your days ...'

For just a second I saw the hot blood mount his face and thought he'd strike me. Then, when he moved closer, I rushed away into the fresh new room smelling still of paint and varnish and locked the door.

I rested against it before going to the window. Then, when I'd calmed enough to look out, I saw his tall figure striding across the grass towards Thorncarne.

My legs were trembling so violently I could hardly stand, and there was a heavy thudding of my heart that sent me to a chair where I sat until the sharp pain in my head had eased. I knew I'd behaved badly and that I'd had no right to speak that way. But the outburst had released something I'd been boiling to say ever since I'd agreed to marry Sarne. And now he knew I wasn't so blind or such a fool he'd taken me for. Somehow the knowledge put new life into me, and after a minute or two I got up and went back to Thorncarne, where Belle was stuffing something rich and creamy into little Petrock's mouth.

'Don't do that,' I said sharply. 'You'll make him sick.'

I snatched the baby from her and wiped his mouth. While he screamed and kicked, I heard Belle shout furiously, 'See what you done? All upsettin' him, just when he was nice an' cosy with his grandma, his own bebee. What you know about childer anyways? You with your nose so stuck in the air you couldn' tell the top of his fuzzy head from his darlin' toes, pore li'l thing. A fine state he'd be in ef he was left to *you*, an' that's a fact.'

I walked out with the child in my arms and down the hall to the front door, where I stood for a minute with the cool air blowing against our faces, while his temper gradually died. I was just about to go back into the house when the sound of carriage wheels and horses' hooves approached from the lane, and along Thorncarne's rather rough track—or drive as

Belle liked to call it—a phaeton appeared. It was pulled by two horses driven by a coachman in a yellow coat and tall hat, and when it stopped outside the door an elderly gentleman was helped out. He was elegantly attired in a grey, tailed coat, white waistcoat and collar, and a top hat. Though he was tall and thin, he walked with the aid of a stick.

At the door he paused for a moment before saying, 'Is this the Ettyn farm, young woman?'

I might have resented the 'young woman' if I hadn't been so startled by something about him I couldn't at first place. Then, suddenly, I knew. The imperious manner; the bold, well-formed nose beneath the probing, gold-shaped eyes; the touch of ginger that still remained in the white sideburns and in hair at the temples that must once have been red: Venn, I thought—this could be Venn sixty or seventy years ahead.

The conviction so shook me I didn't reply until I heard him continuing testily, 'Madam, I asked you a question.'

'Yes ... oh yes,' I replied, pulling myself together. 'I mean, our name is Crane. But ...'

'I don't mind a damn about your name,' he said curtly. 'It's Ettyn I want to see—Mr Venn Ettyn, if you don't mind. And I'd be obliged if you'd find him as soon as possible. I've come a confounded long way and haven't any time to waste.'

Angered at his manner I nevertheless managed to show him into the best parlour, saying coolly, 'Do sit down, Mr ...?'

'Sir John Carvellun,' he interrupted, taking a

chair. 'And thank you. It's a tedious drive here from Launceston, and I'm not so young as I was. So excuse an old man's testiness. And by the way, ma'am ...'

'Yes?'

'Keep Crane's widow out of the way, if you don't mind ...' He gave a sudden unexpected wink which completely changed him from a bad tempered, elderly gentleman, used to bullying people around, into a conspiratorial, almost elfin confidant. 'Too ...' he extended both arms significantly, 'large a problem for me to shoulder at my age.'

I smiled at him, nodded and, after closing the door quietly, went to search for Venn.

I found him at the stables with his grey horse, Jupiter.

He turned quickly when he saw me, and in that brief moment between us hostility seemed to die suddenly into an ache and a longing so acute it was as though the earth rocked beneath my feet. Then I heard him say, 'Yes?' in the cold, curt voice I'd grown accustomed to recently.

'There's someone waiting to see you in the front parlour. Sir John Carvellun,' I managed to say coolly. 'He seems to be in a hurry.'

'Oh.'

I watched Venn's face closely for any flicker of expression betraying shock or surprise. There was none. 'Very well,' he said. 'Yes. I was half-expecting him. Tell him, if you don't mind, I'll be with him so soon as these boots are off.'

I waited a second, then against all my better

judgement began, 'Venn ...'

'Don't let us start a discussion now, Judith,' he told me, with his face averted. 'Some other time, if it's important.'

Rebuffed and with a flush staining my face, I turned and walked abruptly back to the house.

What happened between them I had no idea, but they must have talked together for quite an hour. I was on tenterhooks all that time, wondering if Belle would suddenly appear in the hall, demanding to know what was going on and insisting on poking her nose in. Luckily, she was in bed by then indulging in one of her alcoholic stupors, and when Venn came into the hall again after seeing the phaeton off, there was no one but myself about.

I was about to leave for 'The Barn' with young Petrock and was taking my cape from a peg in the hall.

He laughed shortly. 'You must be agog with curiosity?'

'Not at all,' I answered sharply. 'The likeness was unmistakable.'

He looked momentarily taken aback, then remarked, 'Your deductions are for once well founded. That was my grandfather.'

'Oh, I see.'

'We had a little matter of business to discuss, so as my mother doesn't know of it I'd be grateful if you'd keep quiet. And if Sarne asks any questions, the same there.'

'Certainly,' I agreed. 'Whatever lies you wish me to tell on your account I'll naturally oblige since I owe you so much.'

Whatever made me speak that way I couldn't think. Obviously he'd never seek my help in the future, which put a further barrier between us. His lips tightened. For a moment the sable eyes had a fiery glint in them.

'Poor Sarne,' he said. 'I'm sorry for him. And if he has any sense he'll put you over his knee as soon as possible to teach you where you belong.'

I swept past him without a word and snatched Petrock from the wooden cradle where I'd laid him in the kitchen. The little boy, surprised to be woken so suddenly from sleep, started to howl protestingly. Venn came in with a scowl on his face.

'Can't you even manage a child gently?' he said. 'My God, Judith, you act sometimes as if you came from the gutter.'

'And so I did!' I shouted. 'And so I *did,* didn't you know? My father was a drunkard and my mother was a ...'

My voice faltered on the last word, and I rushed out into the cool air, but with my cheek damp against Petrock's flushed, chubby one.

'Don't cry,' I said, with my arm protectively round him. 'Oh baby, don't cry. I love you ... I do, *really*. Believe me. You must believe me. Hush now. Hush, hush ...'

Whether he did or not, I couldn't tell. His small hand was suddenly out and his attention diverted by a butterfly fluttering past his nose. In one second his tears had turned to chortles of laughter, and just for that brief time a stirring of affection flooded me with warmth. But such moods never lasted—because of Sarne mostly; when Sarne appeared it was as though I didn't matter at all. All the baby's attention was for him, and I became merely the source of nursing and feeding him. A means to an end. No more. And I had no illusions about it. I realized that when he was old enough there'd be little of me or my forebears in him—only Cranes and countless Ettyns stretching back into the past when Belle's ancestors had roamed the woodlands and lanes travelling from town to town selling brooms and straw hats and posies made from wild-flowers picked from ditches and hedges.

Somewhere deep down a little of Luzana, too, must lurk. But I doubted it would ever show or that he'd recognize it was there.

When I thought of her I sighed, because instead of raising myself to the life she once must have known, I was gradually becoming a virago, wilder in temper even than Flavia, who'd gone to boarding school to be tamed.

With the right handling, I, too, could have been brought to mind my tongue and act in a dignified manner. William for a brief time had managed it. With Matt I'd been too happy to care about such things. Now there was no one. No one but Sarne, whom I resented and who had no refinement or true sensibility anyway.

As for Venn ... But Venn had never needed me. What warmth he'd felt had been a fleeting as Matt's, and as changeful as a summer wind.

Ironically, at that moment, I realized that

although I was now a legally married wife, my past was no better, in fact, than my mother's could have been.

My grandmother's prediction had come true, simply because I'd wanted love so passionately and when I'd found it, it had been ruthlessly torn away.

CHAPTER 18

The new people who'd purchased Gulvarrick were rich 'furriners' from up country, who'd used the place only once or twice when they'd come to Cornwall for the holidays. For most of the time the house had been left empty with the Pascoes as caretakers, which added to the depressing sense of desolation I always felt when I passed.

Then, at the beginning of October, the 'For Sale' notice went up again, and I remembered how old Dorcas had cursed the house and all who lived there. Sometimes, in my over-imaginative moments I had the queer notion that eyes watched me from behind the closed windows, and I fancied again Isabella's wild shrieking through the trees when the wind blew fresh and cold from the moor. As the light closed to earlier evenings with long shadows clawing from the lawn to the lane, I hurried by, averting my eyes not only because of such queer thoughts but because of the memories when the great house had given me refuge and I'd lain secure in William's arms.

I felt no security at Thorncarne, in spite of the child, who should surely have given me a feeling of belonging. Well, I *did* belong, but more as a prisoner—*Sarne*'s ... Venn's ... and a prisoner of my own emotions, too. Even old

Dorcas wielded a covetous power over me and thought she had rights over Petrock.

Once when I carried him to the border of the moor in a basket cradle and laid it down all cosy in the dry bracken so I could gather a few mushrooms and blackberries, I returned to the place and found him gone. I looked round with sudden fear, wondering if he'd woken and could possibly have crawled out. But the cradle was upright and no undergrowth had been disturbed, except some rush a few yards from the narrow path leading to the old witch's shack.

With my temper flaring I strode ahead, pushing at briars and twisted branches until my hands were scratched and bleeding. When I got to the hovel Dorcas was seated outside on a boulder, rocking the little boy in her arms. She was grinning down at him, showing her broken fangs of teeth, and instead of crying he was gurgling and cooing while she chanted something that sounded like 'Romany chi an' Romany chal ... aiee ... I's thy bebee ... small one dark one ...'

I rushed at her furiously and snatched Petrock from her arms. 'What do you mean, you old witch?' I cried, unable to restrain my words. 'How *dare* you take my child when I wasn't there? Or even touch him? I had the fright of my life. Don't ever do it again, do you hear? Or I'll have Venn send you away from here ...' The breath was coming in gasps from my throat.

Her dark skin deepened to an ugly blackish-red as she got up and taking a stick from the ground waved it in a shaking hand towards me.

'Git off you, harlot,' she shouted. 'Off ... off with ye. An' doan' 'ee threaten me nor try to part me from my lawful kin. This chile edn' your'n by any right o' blood ... Ettyn he be, true Ettyn ... bred of your flesh through lust, no more. An' doan' 'ee threaten me, you daughter o' sin. 'Twas a dark day when 'ee did tempt that knave Pendruggan an' worse when you come to Sarne and Thorncarne. So be 'ee off or I'll call the powers o' darkness upon 'ee, so I will, and would do so now but for that pore li'l gago ...'

Her voice was still rasping after me when half-stumbling, I reached the thin thicket of trees bordering the moor. By then Petrock had started to wail. An owl disturbed, rose squawking from the branches. My pulses were fluttering, and for a moment or two the whole of that wild landscape seemed pregnant with threatening, elemental evil.

'Don't cry, Petrock, please don't cry,' I murmured, with my nerves tensed almost to screaming point.

Perhaps he sensed something of my distress. I don't know. But presently he quietened, and holding him closely I made my way back to Thorncarne and my own home. It was only when I got there that I realized I'd left the blackberries and mushrooms behind.

Halfway through the month I was on my way to the village one morning when I noticed that the 'For Sale' notice had been taken down from Gulvarrick gates.

Over the mid-day meal which we usually took together in the large farm kitchen, I mentioned it.

'Someone must have bought Gulvarrick,' I said as casually as possible. 'The notice has gone.'

'Yes,' Venn agreed.

All eyes turned to the end of the table where he was seated in his usual place. His expression was enigmatic, but I could tell from that very blankness he knew something.

'Well?' Belle questioned sharply. 'Who is it? Aren't you goin' to tell? Come on now. Out with et. After all, it's a matter o' importance ... to all of us. The family.'

'Why should it be?'

'You know well enough why, Venn Ettyn. Folks's over at that theer place haven't ever bin to Cranes' advantage. So doan' be so cagey. Spit it out.'

Venn shrugged, then said calmly, 'You needn't worry. Gulvarrick's going to no strange owner. Briefly, with a bit of a loan, I've decided to buy it for myself.'

The silence was electric.

'You *what?*' Belle gasped at length. 'Now look here, Venn, stuck up and proud as you may be, but I'm your ma an've every right to know what you've bin up to.'

'You've no right at all,' Venn told her coldly. 'I've managed to keep you in comparative idleness and comfort for the past ten years or so, so don't try throwing your weight about now or you may find yourself considerably worse off.'

As usual the threat quietened her.

There was a silence from everyone, until Sarne said reasoningly, 'All the same Venn, it's nat'ral we'd like to know. Unless you've got some plans for et you don't want us to hear about.'

Venn laughed shortly, then replied, 'I've no dark secrets in mind about the place. Rest assured, it's merely that the land's good and I want more for grazing. The house has a certain value as a property. What I shall do with *that* eventually, I've not made up my mind yet. It'll mean more work for all of us if the deal goes through, and new hands to be taken on. But extra labour will put more in your pockets. So when everything's properly settled I hope you'll go along with me and pull your weight, the whole lot of you.'

When the shock of his news had abated, Sarne said slowly, 'The land may be good ... in parts. But a whole lot of it's moor. An' what do you aim to do with the rest, Venn? Plough it up? This talk 'bout grazin' ... we've enough surely? The herd's doin' well, an' as for crops ... Black Mill has just about all the oats an' corn, an' where would you think to market more potatoes or greens? Tell me that. Or is et,' his eyes paused significantly before ending knowingly, 'is et that you be wantin' to live like a lord surrounded by idle ground in a fine, lonely mansion just for the power an' look of et?'

Venn threw him a dark glance.

'You don't know what you're talking about.

Has it occurred to you that when my new breed of cattle's established we'll need far more space simply because the beef and dairy produce will be so much in demand? There'll be calls for it right up beyond Devon into the midlands. And when farmers and judges come down for a look themselves they'll expect to see round more than a few hundred acres Take it from me, it will be worthwhile if we tackle it.'

'We?' Marcus questioned doubtfully. 'Oh, I don't know, Venn. There'd be so much more to pay out, wouldn't there? I mean ...'

'Yes?' Venn's voice was sharp.

'Well ... it's quite a business *now,* getting to market and all that. And the problem of sending meat up country ... It seems to me there'd be nothing but work.'

'And you're frightened of that?'

Marcus's thin, out-thrust jaw tightened. 'No. But there's other things in life besides farming. It'd be nice sometimes to be able to have them.'

'Such as?'

'Readin', an' goin' around a bit for pleasure instead of driving great carts of stuff to market. An' music, too.'

Venn's voice was contemptuous. *'Music?'*

'Why not?' Belle's voice shrilled out. 'We come of a musical fam'ly. Never a day did pass when I was young without a bit o' fiddlin' or strummin' the guitar ... an' my pa Petrock had the sweetest voice of any man you could hear; high as a lark's et was bustin' wi' joy one moment, then downcast so deep you could feel all the dark sadness of the world in et. Ah but they doan' sing the same any more. Often I do think that when Petrock Ettyn went to his grave he did take a deal o' richness with 'en. Poor, poor Petrock. A good man he wus, an' a fine father. But then ...' with her voice harsh and her dark eyes suddenly sharp as swords on Venn's face, 'you wouldn' know 'bout that, would you? You with such gorgio in you, you haven' a first inklin' 'bout the sweetness o' lyin' in the grass o' nights, with the bird music rich an' wild from the trees, an' the grasshoppers chirrupin' so mad you could hear the rushes sighin, so you could. Lordy me! I tell you, Venn, livin' aint got into your bloodstream yet, an' et strikes me often it never will, so cold an' wilful you be, an' eager to have the power in your fist.'

After that long oration Belle drew a deep breath, sighed with satisfaction and took a deep gulp of wine.

Then, when silence was restored Venn said pointedly to his youngest brother. 'What do you think if it, Paul?'

Paul shrugged. 'I dunno. Farming's all right to me. I'll help as much as I can. You an' Sarne knows best, I suppose.'

The rest of the conversation that mealtime was desultory, with nothing settled—verbally. But I could tell from Venn's cold stare and determined expression that in his mind everything was, and that none of the others, whatever they thought, could do a thing about it.

Belle soon went upstairs for her 'lie in' with a bottle of her tonic secreted in her pocket.

The others left for the sheds and fields, leaving Liddy to clear away the pots and deal with the washing-up.

I was setting off for 'The Barn', with Petrock in my arms, when Venn joined me at the door.

'You didn't say much,' he said, as we walked across the field. 'Don't you approve?'

'It doesn't matter whether I do or don't,' I answered promptly. 'I know nothing about it.'

'It could make a difference to your life though,' he continued, with his head turned upon me more closely than I wanted.

'How?'

'There'll be longer hours for everyone if I go ahead. Sarne won't have so much time for you and Petrock.'

I turned sharply to meet the cold yet burning stare of his eyes. Then I laughed, sneeringly hoping to hurt him.

'Dear, dear. How unfortunate.'

'Look, Judith ...'

His hand was on my arm, and I flinched, not because of the pressure, which hurt, but because of the wild emotions it roused in me. I pulled myself away fiercely.

'Don't touch me, Venn Ettyn. And don't consult or order me about over anything—not *any*thing. You've done enough already, it seems to me. So just go ahead with your plans and leave me out of them. I'm nothing to you or you to me. Understand? I detest you. And if you want a woman's advice, get it from your ... your mistress, Alicia Tattam ...'

I broke off, frightened and yet triumphant to see the white rage on his face and in his golden eyes. There was a pause between us that was almost electric; then, with his fists clenched at his sides, he said through his teeth, 'You little vixen. For two pins I'd ...'

'I know. I know what you'd do. Underneath you're as savage and wild as Sarne, but with less excuse. But you can't, can you? You can't strike me or do a thing about it because someone would be sure to see and I've got Petrock in my arms, so leave me alone.'

I flounced ahead, feeling him staring after me, though I didn't turn to look. I knew my words must have outraged and humiliated him in a deeply personal way, and when the first reaction had faded and my temper cooled, I wondered if I'd said too much.

For some days after that he was careful to avoid me and we had no contact at all.

During that brief interim I did my best to be nice to Sarne, and in bed at nights I let him have me willingly, stifling any lingering hankering I had for Venn or Matt. Sarne was a lusty, down-to-earth lover, and as I lay afterwards with his warm, deep chest close on my breast and his thighs still pulsing against mine, I was able to fool myself into believing he was all I wanted and from then on things would be different between us.

They weren't though. In the morning all was the same as it had been from the beginning, and in spite of the ardour in his dark eyes and the warmth of his voice when he said, 'It was good last night, wasn't it, love?' I knew I lied when I answered, 'Of course, of course.'

'An' you'll never go cool on me again, darlin' ...?'

'Not often, anyway,' I prevaricated.

'You're all I have, y'know,' he said. 'All that really matters, you an' Petrock.'

At that moment I really believed him. What I didn't know then, was that he was all *I* had, too. Three days later Venn informed everyone at Thorncarne that the deal concerning Gulvarrick had gone through and that he proposed to marry Alicia Tattam, who later would live there with him, as his wife.

CHAPTER 19

I told myself I'd always known; I should have expected it. From my first meeting with Alicia Tattam it had been clear to me she was determined to have him. But my mistake had been in letting Venn *know* I knew it. In throwing her name at him in angry moments I'd probably strengthened the suggestion in his head.

Anyway it was no concern of mine; he was free to marry whom he chose and in choosing Alicia he'd proved to me once and for all that he *was* out for power, wanting to amass all the cash he could so he could establish himself as squire of the district instead of William. In the beginning, when he'd told me land couldn't be properly owned, that 'it belonged to itself', he'd been talking merely to impress me, else why should he have gone to such pains to buy Gulvarrick? I couldn't really believe he found the insipid Miss Tattam so intriguing.

And she wasn't innocent at all. There was a hardness of expression sometimes, when she was off her guard, that any *woman* who had an ounce of feeling and intelligence in her would have recognized.

Whether Belle sensed it I didn't know. The two of them had little contact; but if she did, the knowledge was more than recompensed by the triumph she felt in seeing my nose put out of joint.

One afternoon, shortly after Venn's revelation, she said to me smugly, but with an underlying sting in her words, 'When Venn's married and takes himself off to that big place with his fancy wife, there'll be more room here, an' you'll be able to give proper time to Sarne an' the darlin' child, so you will, for sure. A nice little cosy fam'ly we'll be then. Cranes by name but Ettyns through an' through. Ah. All for the best, I'm thinkin'. I always knowed that Venn would marry rich. Didn' I tell 'ee then? Didn't I?'

'I don't know,' I lied. 'I forget.'

'One thing's for sure though,' Belle went on as though she'd not heard me. 'He's not goin' to push my darlin' boy *too* hard, not while I've breath in me body. Marcus now, he could easily shoulder a bit more. Too high an' mighty with his book learnin' for my likin', although o' course he's real gifted for music. But just because Venn's got a loan from that ... that stuck-up, nosey Lord, don't mean we're all goin' to go through the mill for 'en. Venn's shrewd. A mean head on him sometimes. Let him repay things in 'is own way.'

I had a barb and I threw it.

'As you're talking of his grandfather,' I said, 'there shouldn't be much trouble, I'd think.'

Belle's jaw gaped.

'You *knowed?*'

'Yes. He told me. What's more I saw the old man when he came visiting that day.'

'Well! I do think you might've said,' Belle protested.

I shrugged. 'I didn't think it was important. Of course, if I'd known you were such friends ...'

'Friends?' Bell snorted. 'The likes o' him an' the likes of us doan' mix ... 'cept in the manner o' duty, o' course. An' the ole man knows he owes us quite a lot. Ef it hadn' bin for that randy gorgio son of his, I'd never've had to go through the sufferin' I did, an' that's for sure. Mind you I'm not sayin' Rupert hadn' a way with him. That's what they called 'en ... *Rupert.* But then I was a real beauty in my time. You should'a seen me then, Judy—all black hair an' red lips, an' the lashes was so thick on my cheek they could've swep' a carpet. Slim as a larch I was, but wi' firm breasts like young apples stretching my bodice. An' the summer night, 'twas so rich an' sweet. Ah me. Just achin' for love everythin' wus, an' Rupert so thick wi' liquor from Corpus Christi Fair we wus down in the grass 'fore you could say boo to a goose. I do remember, though he did come once or twice the next month to see ef I was all right, an' his eyes wus real adorin'. But when he found I wasn' ... I never seed 'en agen.'

'Oh. I see.'

'He be dead now,' Belle resumed after a moment, 'an' I shouldn' wonder that Venn doan' come into money when th'old tyrant goes. No heir, they say; no heir but Venn ... and him born the wrong side o' the blanket. Makes you think, doan' et, how the virtuous do seem to perish often an' they bastards go on? But then edn' that how kings comed into being? Most o' them in the old days, I've heard tell, were love-childs born of mistresses or whores. Meks you laugh, doan' et, when you do consider how strict the Romanys mostly be over morals an' breedin' wi' their own kind, and the high-ups so ready for a luscious roll in the hay any time with a tasty piece just so long as et's kept sly an' secret in the cupboard. Why, I've heard tell ...'

What else Belle had heard, I didn't want to hear. She'd obviously had just sufficient of her tonic to make her talkative and would probably go on reminiscing to herself for some time after I'd left.

As the days and months passed, bringing Alicia more frequently to Thorncarne, I kept out of her way as much as possible, because the triumphant glint in her sly eyes got on my nerves almost as much as the condescending way she sailed through the house, smiling at Venn's family only because it was expected of her. I had a shrewd idea that once she'd safely 'netted her fish', as my grandmother would have put it, she'd put a wedge once more between Gulvarrick and Thorncarne, and we'd see little of either of them. I could imagine her parading round the estate in her fancy finery and saucy hats, bowing to farm-hands and workers, and doling out presents occasionally in the manner of a queen bestowing gifts on lesser mortals.

For a short time my dislike and contempt of her seemed to draw Sarne and myself more closely together. He was amused at my barbed observations, saying more than once, or some such similar remark, 'Snap out o' it, Judith. She edn' worth a crack of your little finger. One look at yourself in the mirror should tell you that. An' what's it matter if Venn *does* land himself with a shrew? Tame him a bit maybe, although I've got a feelin' when it comes down to it, the boot'll be on the other foot.'

I thought so, too, and though the idea should have cheered me, it didn't. The picture of Miss Tattam and Venn reigning at Gulvarrick, where I'd once presided and later seen such anguish and tragedy, was offensive and filled me with disgust.

Sometimes I'd escape alone to the moors and, ignoring her presence, would pass old Dorcas's shack, cutting straight up to the summit where Castle Carnack stood grey and windswept by the four winds. A sentinel, it seemed to me, of ages long gone and of a future ahead that I should never know. With my face against the cold stone I'd feel my blood stir. Here lovers must have lain and hard battles been fought; countless armies and generations of men and women must have trodden the short turf and gone about their everyday tasks, loving, giving birth and, in their time, dying. What mattered it then that one woman like myself should have got herself so stupidly enmeshed in a pattern of existence she didn't want?

Sarne? Venn? William? Matt? They were incidental in the long pageant of time and eventually would be written off as just shadows to fade into forgetfulness.

Matt. It was only when I remembered him that my own despondency truly registered. I wasn't really the depressed kind and could generally shake myself out of a mood when I'd a mind to. But occasionally the memory of him swept through me with such sudden pain, the present was swamped into unreality and I was that girl of years ago, riding with him in Billy Trevean's cart to the fair, with the laughter rich in us and all those young pigs screaming behind.

It wasn't really so long ago, but when I came to myself again it seemed a lifetime. So much had happened to me since, and maybe to him also, I'd think, recalling Topaz and Wellington. Were they still with him? Or had he shaken them off as he had me, for some other, more exciting future where he could take what he fancied and then pass on? And suppose sometimes his ship was to berth at Newlyn or Port Einack? Would he take the trouble to come looking until he found me? And if he did, what would I say?

My thoughts became such a whirl when I considered the possibility there was simply no answer, and I'd be left with only longing in me; the longing for a fruitful happiness that seemed forever beyond my reach.

I was dreaming this way by the great boulders one late afternoon when I heard the sound of hooves galloping behind me from the direction, cross-country, of Penjust.

I stopped and turned as the horse came to a halt and the rider dismounted. Venn.

'What are you doing up here in the cold?' he said, his face whipped to a fine colour from the stinging wind.

'I'm used to the cold,' I answered sharply, 'and I don't feel it. Anyway, I don't see it's your affair.'

His eyes seemed to kindle and darken again, holding all the colours of the dying evening.

'Need you snap so?' he said sharply. 'You're becoming a real little virago these days, and I don't like it, Judith. What I want and mean to have, dammit, is harmony in the home.'

'Then go ahead wanting,' I told him, 'and maybe you'll succeed. You generally do, don't you? Anything you have a hankering for, you see you get. But don't include me in your greedy plans, Venn Ettyn. I'm not your servant, even though you gave me shelter and got me bedded with your brother. You haven't *bought* me ... neither you nor any of your precious family, so leave me alone if you will. I'm not interested, nor ever could be, in your aims and paltry ambitions.'

In a second he had me by the shoulders and was forcing my chin up to meet the fiery, tightened blaze of his face. Then his lips came down to mine; gently at first, then hot and demanding, as all the sweetness of my heart and body seemed to leave me suddenly and flow towards him.

'You little wild-cat, you ...' he muttered breathlessly, once, before his mouth once more was crushing mine, and then, suddenly, as his arms fell away, 'Well? Satisfied now are you?

Isn't that what you wanted?'

I lifted my arm quickly and dealt him a stinging blow across one cheek. The hot feel of my palm against it relieved some of my tension and anger. And if he struck me back I knew I wouldn't care.

But he didn't. His only reaction—outwardly—was to say, contemptuously, 'And what a hypocrite into the bargain. A hypocrite and a ...'

'Whore?' I said, my voice shrill and bitter on the rising wind. 'Say it! *Say* it if you like. It's not true, except for what *you've* done, you and Sarne. And for that I hate and *loathe* you, Venn Ettyn, do you understand? Hate ... hate ... *hate.* Don't ever touch me again or dare to come near me ...'

My own words died on a torrent of abuse. But his own were more cold and deadly than the brooding black line of massed clouds rising threateningly along the horizon.

'Don't worry,' he said, as though he was addressing some despicable stranger. 'I shall never intrude wittingly into your presence again. And I would be grateful if it's the same with you.'

A second later he had mounted his horse and was galloping along the track leading to the house.

Little more than a month later, with Christmas over and spring ahead, he married Alicia Tattam and brought her back to Thorncarne.

Gulvarrick was not properly decorated and in order to her liking so for the next two months she was to be part of the farm household, something, I think, as objectionable to Belle and the rest of the family as it was to me.

Flavia, who was home for the holidays, showed open hostility from the start.

'What a pompous, stuck-up creature,' she said scathingly. 'And no chin either. It won't last, you'll see. There'll soon be fireworks, if I know my own brother. And ...' with a glint in her eye, 'I think I do, better than the rest of you. Oh my! What a lark. Don't worry, Judy, I know you feel the same way, and whatever happens we're in for a bit of fun ahead.'

Fun? I thought. Well, maybe, for her.

But for myself, I'd have called it by another name.

CHAPTER 20

Strangely, Alicia Tattam's presence at Thorncarne seemed to draw Belle and I closer together. It was quite obvious to us both from the beginning that she was the complaining, whiny kind who took pleasure in seeing the worst of things rather than the best—except in Venn's company, of course, when she was all smiles and flattery, going so far as to say what a nice family he had, which quite sickened me.

She didn't do much about the house either, except to put on a frilly apron in time for meals when she knew the men would be back, pretending she'd been busy half the morning but that didn't matter at all, thank you, when there was so much to do.

'Many hands make light work,' she remarked more than once in Venn's hearing. 'I know I must look an awful sight, but you'll forgive me, won't you, darling. When we go: to Gulvarrick, it will be so different.'

She didn't look 'a sight' in the implied sense at all, which she well knew; just innocently beguiling and pretty in a naïve way that didn't fool me for a moment. There was nothing in any way simple about Alicia. Underneath she was as hard as nails and as wily as a snake, and I was surprised Venn could be so deceived.

What he *really* thought about her I couldn't

guess. Except under provocation he wasn't one to show his feelings. But occasionally I caught a veiled, calculating look in his eyes that made me wonder if caring for her was all pretence or if he was congratulating himself on the fine bargain he'd made. There was just no way of telling. Anyway, I told myself abruptly, it was none of my affair and I didn't care either way.

'She'll lead old Venn a dance all right,' Sarne said to me one evening as we undressed for bed. 'Still, he asked for it.'

'Oh?'

'Thinkin' he can own the world. Well ...' he came over to where I was sitting by the mirror and planted a kiss on the back of my neck, 'there's something *here* he'll never own, eh, darlin'?'

I wriggled my shoulders impatiently. 'Oh, for heaven's sake, Sarne, do leave me alone a bit. I'm brushing my hair, can't you see ...?'

Through the glass I saw Sarne's face darken. One hand enclosed a thick fistful of my tumbled locks, the other caught my neck and cheek, forcing my head round to face him.

'Leave you alone?' he said. 'This edn' the time to tell me that, darlin'. Quite some days et's been since I had you ...'

'Had me? *Had* me?' I said shrilly. 'What a way to talk. Crude—that's what you are sometimes, Sarne—downright crude and ... an oafish.'

A dangerous light flooded his gypsy eyes.

'Oh *ho*. I *see*. Now I'm beginning to understand what's gotten into you. It's that brother o' mine, Venn, edn' it? You've a hankerin' for his lordly ways an' to have *his* arms round you, I shudn' wonder. I always guessed et but put it aside, because I was so mad for you. But after tonight, darlin', there'll be an end to your sneaky thoughts an' lustin' for another man. Git up, Judith. Git up an' tek what's bin comin' to you for a long time ...'

For a moment I didn't move, simply stared at him, shocked, until he suddenly jerked me up by the neck of my shift and tore it from me savagely, one arm enclosing my waist and buttocks, the other divesting me of all else I wore except my stockings and shoes. Then he lifted me up, his lips hot and moist on my lips, shoulders and naked breasts.

'You're never goin' to forget this, darlin',' he muttered before carrying me to the bed. 'If I was in my senses I'd tek a dog-whip to you, but not this time ... This time I'll have you sweet an' luscious as any husband has a true wife. An' you'll like it, darlin'. Not a moan from your pretty mouth or mebbe I'll kill you instead.'

I struggled briefly against him but knew it was no good. I knew, too, that he meant what he said, and I could only shiver with a feeling of revulsion and shame as he fell on me and took me ruthlessly time after time, with a savagery that held all the beastliness of lust and nothing of love.

When it was over he got up suddenly, strode to the mirror and stood there admiring his own physique with the pride of some arrogant stallion having accomplished what he was bred for.

Then he came back to the bed, stood for a

moment looking down on me, laughed shortly and said, 'Move up, I'm ready for sleep, an' don't you dare try any scene like runnin' away or I'll have the hide off your backside as if you wus a nipper.'

With my senses strained and terrified I edged to the side of the bed, feeling cold, so cold it was, as though the blood was frozen in my veins.

I knew then what hate was—real hatred—and determined that whatever happened he should never touch me again. Never, never. I'd rather die.

In the morning, as usual, he tried to make up; he even attempted an apology. But my voice was a sneer when I said, 'If you dare ever lay a hand on me again Sarne Crane, I'll kill you, and myself as well perhaps. And I mean it. For the sake of Petrock I'll stay here ... for a bit anyway, just so no one knows the shame of things. But from now on I belong to myself and myself only. So if you want a woman, find another. There's plenty of your kind around ...'

'But Judith ... Judy ...'

'Shut up!' I shouted. 'You contemptible cur.'

His face whitened. As I drew my wrap round me his jaw came out, and looking round wildly he seized the first thing that came to his notice—the miniature of Luzana lying on our dressing table.

In a fury of rage he picked up the precious relic, high above his head, and flung it to the stone floor. There was the sound of splintering and it was done. After he'd kicked the pieces with his foot he moved to the door, slammed it and went out.

When he was safely away I knelt down and retrieved the splintered remains. Most of the portrait was smashed beyond mending, but the face still was intact, and it seemed to me that the huge eyes stared up at me with pity and understanding. I held it automatically against my breast for a few seconds, then put it away in a drawer.

When the first reaction of the terrible scene had subsided I found my heart was still pumping painfully and my legs were shaking. Mingled with the misery and unhappiness though was a queer kind of relief. It was done at last. My mind for the first time since our marriage was free and completely clear. Sarne would never lay a finger in passion on me again. And he, realizing it, never did. To all intents and purposes our marriage, except for Petrock and dark memories, was as though it had never been.

It was cold that spring, the spring that Venn married Alicia Tattam, and my heart and my senses were cold, too; so frozen that even the rush and bustle of getting Gulvarrick ready and the commotion of the wedding itself didn't warm me. I'd done more than my share of making curtains, stitching cushions and adding bits of embroidery to the pillowslips because Alicia had set her heart on them. Most of the cooking, too, was done by me at that period, but I refused point-blank ever to take step inside the house. Though Belle nagged at me over this, Venn took a stand.

'Leave her alone,' he said. 'Judy's done more than the rest of you put together to have things in order. There's no need for her traipsing about the place. One of the men and Liddy can do the scrubbing, and it won't hurt you ...' he added with a meaningful glance at Belle, 'to cast an eye on things if you can stir yourself to move sufficiently across the road.'

Belle glared.

'You haven' any respec' for your ma at all,' she remarked tartly. 'Sometimes I think there's nothin' o' me in your veins at all, Venn Ettyn.'

'And sometimes I think so myself,' Venn replied.

I didn't attend the wedding, having the legitimate excuse of having to be at Thorncarne to see to the reception. I was glad of that, though I probably goaded Liddy almost unendurably by my feverish mood and frenzy to have things exactly right and ready some time before the guests returned from Church. Why the marriage hadn't been at Penjust I couldn't imagine. Brides were generally wedded in their own parish, as I well knew. But then Alicia, being what she was, probably wanted to show off Gulvarrick to her friends. I could so easily imagine her prancing round, displaying the estate with a casual air as though she'd been bred and born of the gentry. She hadn't, of course, though she might well have deceived Venn or any other man into thinking so. Where she came from originally no one seemed to know, and if Venn knew he didn't say. But at odd moments when she was excited or annoyed, a common strange accent cut her refined tones, and I'd felt like saying, 'For heaven's sake, be what you *are.*' I could have put up with her so much more easily if it hadn't been for her simpering pretence.

As they were not going away for the honeymoon—Venn was too busy with farm affairs—Alicia's dress had been fashioned both as a bridal and a hostess gown. Pink silk, with a small hat, all pink flowers, on her fussy, fair curls, with a silly piece of veiling just covering her eyes. She made a great show of lifting it from those pale blue orbs when they came into the hall and smiled up at Venn with the sweet, sentimental gaze of someone about to take off to more heavenly spheres. Venn bent his head and dutifully kissed her; then, as they passed on, his eyes momentarily fell on mine, and I wondered if he was recalling another, different kind of kiss—the one he'd given me those months before. I looked away with my chin up and lips set. In my green days I felt confident and assured. But depression soon engulfed me; and it was all I could do to see the day through with dignity and a show of indifference.

The rest of the family seemed to enjoy the occasion, except for Sarne, whose face, sullen and glowering, was forever on me when I was in the room. As always when he drank too much he became verbose in an ill-humoured way, with the high colour suffusing his face.

I knew I'd have to be clever in getting to the Barn before him so I could safely lock myself in the room I now shared with Petrock. This was one of the rare social events when I sensed he'd 'put me through it', as he'd threatened in the past. Normally all that was over now. He had another woman somewhere in the village, which had simplified matters and made me thankful to be safe from his unwelcome attentions. Only Petrock kept us living under the same roof, and Petrock hardly seemed my son at all. Since learning to toddle and speak his first baby words, it was Sarne he turned to, Sarne he loved and Sarne he wanted to be with. At first I'd been mildly irritated. Now I didn't care at all. They were as like as two peas in a pod, or would be when the little boy was older. Even then their tastes seemed similar. Sarne bought a colt from a wandering tinker one day, which he bragged might be a winner once he'd been broken in properly. When a month had passed he rode it wildly over the moor, and a few days later, with the child seated before him, he gave Petrock his first experience of riding horseback. The child had squealed with delight when they'd set off, and although I'd remonstrated, Sarne had simply ignored me with a sneer, telling me to keep my snivelling woman's fears to myself. I'd fretted all the time until they arrived back safely, but it was the fretting of any adult for a defenceless, small creature more than mother-love. Although I tried, it was hard to feel affection for a child who obviously had none for me.

So my son was gradually left more and more in the charge of Belle or his father, and following the wedding I slipped off whenever I could from Thorncarne, making my way on foot to Penzance and Newlyn, where I spent all the time I had wandering along the harbour, with my eyes fixed on the sea and any ships berthed there. Hoping for the impossible; for a glimpse of Matt swinging across the sand, his dark eyes dancing and alight for me and his footsteps suddenly quickening as I ran to meet him, to be swept up into his arms.

The thought of his closeness, of his laughter rich and warm against my face, would fill me with such longing my body relaxed and was alive again, like the earth suddenly flowering after a long and bitter winter. But so soon it would pass, and as the clear spring sky faded to the green of approaching evening, melancholy would enfold me again and I'd make my way back to Thorncarne, knowing that only emptiness waited; the emptiness of a loveless life.

Until May came there wasn't much peace at Thorncarne. All the landwork was rushed and late. The extra men hired by Venn were hard pressed getting Gulvarrick land into order, with acres of parkland fenced in for pasture and a part of the low moor cleared and ready for ploughing later. A stream was diverted from the top side of Gulvarrick property to Thorncarne. Sarne, Marcus and Paul worked overtime with crops and vegetables, employing a local youth to help with the animals and milking and getting produce to market. On top of this had been the sheep shearing, which Paul had grumbled about, saying the old shepherd could have been better employed elsewhere and that, with so much to deal with, the sheep be sold to help cover the cost of the new venture.

Belle, as the novelty of having so many men about wore off, became increasingly short-tempered. I didn't blame her; our work was doubled with muddy boots forever cluttering the kitchen and endless snacks of pasty and cocoa or beer being served out at any odd hour.

Before the proper rush started Alicia and Venn had moved to Gulvarrick, but when anything was wanted Thorncarne was expected to provide it. Resentment churned in me. I would have sneaked away one night if it hadn't been for Petrock. But the child kept me chained there. What vestige of duty I felt was for him; however little he mattered, I didn't mean to have myself condemned as a bad mother. In a way my own coolness towards him made me all the more attentive so I could feel right with myself. And at the back of my mind always was the tormenting thought of Venn and Alicia; of her white body lying close to him at night in the bedroom, most probably where I'd lain with William. I could imagine her face turned towards him in the sweetly simpering way she had, and his lips coming down to her pink mouth. I never let my thoughts stray further than that. I doubted she had the passion in her to satisfy Venn and couldn't see him being content with a cold wife. As a mistress she could probably have inveigled him into believing whatever he wanted, because she was so mad to catch him and would gain considerably by the union. But *marriage!* Once wed, I'd a shrewd idea, he'd been in for a shock.

Nothing was obvious though. During the summer when we were forced to meet, she was all smiles and condescension; Venn, polite but guarded, though his eyes sometimes had a puzzled, enigmatic look when he glanced at me. Occasionally she drove herself along the moorland road to Penjust where she was still part owner of the café. The other part, through agreement, had been sold to a man called Joshua Leeds from up country, who'd taken on the management with the proviso that Alicia should be consulted over any major changes. That there would be any wasn't very likely, as the business was a little gold mine in the summer when guests and Americans toured Cornwall or stayed in the district, and I had to admit on the one occasion I visited the place that it was attractive in a rather arty-crafty way, with black cats dancing along the frieze, and pottery and curtains all designed with various species of felines. There was a fish tank, too, in one corner, where exotic breeds swam in green waters under artificial lighting. Oh yes, it had its own refined kind of charm, which an astute businessman like Joshua Leeds must have been quick to recognize and snap up when the chance came along.

I met him twice by chance. He was a smart, black-haired, rather flashy figure, with a fine moustache, revealing splendid white teeth when he smiled. Because a woman is quick to sense such things, I could tell he had a particular feeling for Alicia; whether financial or personal I couldn't judge. But there was no doubt they knew each other well. At one moment I caught him all unawares whispering something in her ear. Whether the quick flush mounting her cheeks was because of him or because she suddenly glanced up and saw I'd noticed, I couldn't be sure. Her manner to me, a moment later, was tart and dictatorial, as though I was a servant. I don't even recall what she said, but it was all I could do to keep my hand from slapping her face.

After that any pretence of understanding or friendliness between us was non-existent. Alicia Tattam and I—I could never bear to think of her as Venn's wife—were coldly formal to each other but with an inward hostility which gradually seemed to penetrate and drive the wedge more firmly between the two households.

Gulvarrick and Thorncarne were rivals and enemies once more, as they'd been for so many years during William's life and even before that. Every time I passed the big house I could feel a cloud of enmity rising to meet me. It could have been my imagination, of course, but even Belle sensed something.

'You can't kill the past,' she said once. 'Et's there always like a sleepin' gurly ghost ready to spill good blood wheniver th'moods on et.'

I shivered, remembering William's death, and moved to get out of the room, but Belle's voice stopped me at the door.

'Another thing ...' she continued. 'The owl's bin callin' over our own chimney for many a night now. An' 'twas callin' the evenin' young Petrock was born. Owls edn' a good sign. Any chile born in ear-shot of et's doomed to disaster unless the Holy powers do think otherwise. So jus' you tek good care of 'en, Judith Crane, so the darlin' boy doan' suffer.'

I shook her words off for just what they were—mere superstition.

But as it happened, and tragically, the portent this time chanced to be true.

On a fine summer evening when Sarne, worse for liquor, returned from the kiddleywink in the village, he announced riotously that he was going to have a breather on the colt and take his son with him.

I gasped.

'You *can't*. Not a *baby*. Besides, he's just off to bed,' I protested.

Sarne grinned, not pleasantly, swaying on his heels.

'He's my son, edn' he? An' over a year old now. Besides, can't you trust me to mind my own?'

His hand grasped my bodice, shaking me so my jaws shook. I could smell the liquor hot on his breath. Then suddenly he gave a push and released me.

'Get him dressed, Judith, in case I forget myself and that you're my wife. But then ...' he paused maliciously, 'you edn' much o' one, are you? Well then, you just do as I say an' be quick about it or you'll be sorry.'

'Do it yourself,' I snapped. 'I won't be party to such a murderous suggestion.'

He lurched forward and smashed his palm across my face harshly. I reeled and fell against the bed, but the next moment in spite of the pain I had caught the little boy up into my arms.

'Sarne,' I begged, 'be reasonable.'

But he was beyond reason and in a few seconds had torn the child from me and was wrapping him in a blanket, to the cooing delight of his son.

The rest now registers only as a nightmare. How long it took them to be away on the colt towards the moor I never knew. All I remember clearly is the terrible scene hours later when the mount returned, dragging Sarne behind by the stirrups, his face and head smashed and covered in blood. He was quite dead.

There was no sign of Petrock until his pathetic little body was found in the early light of dawn lying cold and lifeless in a tangle of bracken near a ditch bordering the Penjust road.

I wanted to cry with my lungs and eyes and heart and all that was in me for the helpless little victim of a loveless marriage. But I couldn't. All feeling in me seemed frozen beyond the relief of emotion, and it was only Belle's sobs that filled the whole of that day in the dreadful agony of loss and bereavement.

CHAPTER 21

I was a widow and alone.

After the first grief of the funerals was over a cold, veiled hostility seemed to fill Thorncarne. Although following her days of crying Belle made no open condemnation, I knew from her eyes when she looked at me that she blamed me for the deaths of her son and grandson.

Venn, trying to be more considerate, suggested that I move back into the house, where at least I'd have company, but I refused. Only at the Barn could I unleash my own emotion and feel safe from the sidelong, bitter glances of Belle and Paul. Paul, who so resembled Sarne, had deeply admired his brother, and following the tragedy he seemed to assume his mantle which unnerved me.

Mercifully for us all the extra work at that time prevented emotions getting openly out of control. At nights I was so tired I fell almost immediately into a drugged kind of sleep, never stirring until morning. When I woke my body was ready again for the endless routine, though mentally I felt cold, in a kind of meaningless dream where the past and the present were curiously intermixed.

Just occasionally the need for action revived in me, and I knew I must get away—anywhere—and somehow start again.

Once I even flung a few things into a bag and sneaked out into the fading twilight, thinking to put Thorncarne behind me for ever. Venn prevented me by appearing, as if from nowhere, from the shadows of the trees.

'Where do you think you're going, Judith?' he said. 'Come along now, none of that.'

His hand closed on my wrist like a jailer's. I shook myself free.

'Leave me alone,' I said. 'It's none of your business.'

'Yes it is. Apart from not wanting any connection of mine wandering the lanes like a ...'

'Mad woman?' I interrupted. 'Is that what you're thinking?'

'I didn't say so. But you need a home and you've still got one. Besides ...' he paused before adding more tartly, 'we're short handed enough as it is now without another taking off leaving the rest of us to bear the brunt of it.'

In the ordinary way my temper would have flared, but it was as if all fire had died in me; like a dead thing with no will of its own I allowed myself to be led back into the house.

Naturally, as the weeks passed an unhappy sort of normality returned, although with Sarne gone and Venn over at Gulvarrick I knew nothing would ever be the same again. I missed little Petrock, too, but not as I should have done. I had no strange longing to hold him close in my arms; none of the natural yearnings of a normal mother in the same situation. I grieved, yes, as I'd have grieved for any child so tragically deprived of life. But it was as though he'd never been a real part of me. What I missed most were the daily habits of feeding, washing and dressing him; carrying him over to the house in the mornings for Belle to croon over as I busied myself in the dairy or with cooking and cleaning the house; later settling him for his afternoon rest, leaving Liddy and I free to prepare the endless snacks for the men.

I could sense Liddy's disapproval in the period following his death. When I was sharper-tongued than usual she'd glance at me almost furtively with a touch of fear in her eyes, as though I was some abnormal monster relieved to have got the child off her hands.

Once, when she cowered away, I said curtly, 'Whatever's the matter with you? Seen a ghost or something?'

'No ... no,' she stammered. 'Not yet. But them's about edn' they? I told 'ee before missis, when you was over at Gulvarrick ... There be a curse on us all from up theer ... on the moor.'

'Stop it!' I cried. 'Hold your tongue, for heaven's sake, or I'll send you packing without a penny in your pocket, and then your father'll take a strap to your back. Is that what you want? *Is* it? Is it?'

My voice must have risen more shrilly than I'd meant. A moment later Belle lumbered into the kitchen, jaws out-thrust, eyes blazing with temper and curiosity.

'What's up?' she demanded. 'What's going on now?'

Liddy had started to moan and wail, with her apron to her eyes and shoulders heaving up and down heavily.

'She be goin' to send me away,' she said. 'That's what she did say, mistress. Wi'out a penny jus' becos of what I told her 'bout the curse on Gulvarrick ...'

Belle, glaring at me maliciously, said. 'She's sendin' you nowhere, girl, without my sayin' so. I hold the reins here an' doan' you go forgettin' et. Ef anyone goes, 'twon't be you, an' that's for sure.'

What they said after that I didn't know or care. I flounced through the door and, leaving work and duties behind, rushed out as I was without cape or wrap, taking the track directly to the moor. I noticed nothing and was aware only of the dead, damp smells of autumn filling the air, mingled with the dying scent of woodsmoke from the valley. Old Dorcas was nowhere visible when I passed her shack, though one of her goats was nibbling nearby. On I went, climbing and pulling at furze and dead bracken until I reached the highest point of the moor.

From there I could see glimpses of the northern coast, where Port Einack lay hidden below the sweep of rocky hills, and southwards to a complete vista of Mounts Bay with the Mount rising like a medieval castle opposite the old town of Marazion. Further away to the west sailing ships were thick in Newlyn harbour. Long-liners, I guessed with an odd merchant vessel or two put in for repairs or fresh water before turning course to the toe of

Lands End for Padstow and Bristol.

A vivid memory of Matt rose to torment me, and I knew I had to get away. There would never be anything for me at Thorncarne again except hatred and unease. Belle and her sons disliked me. Venn had no need of me except as a hired hand. His life, whether for good or ill, was with Alicia at Gulvarrick. I owed him nothing. It was rather the reverse, since he'd forced me into such a disastrous union with Sarne.

Automatically I unbound my hair, which was already drifting in tendrils against my eyes, and let it fall free and thick about my shoulders. With the abandoned gesture life returned in a stinging glow of freedom. I lifted my arms symbolically to the sky and a crowd of gulls rose screaming and circling above Castle Carnack. I'll find Matt again, I thought. Somewhere, somehow, we'll be together again, and all the rest will pass like a bad dream.

I was turning to go down when the sound and crackling of undergrowth disturbed made me look round sharply to my right. To my dismay I saw Venn approaching. A gleam of light touched his bright hair to copper. His eyes were blazing in his set face.

'Why are you up here?' he demanded. 'Don't you realize the natives are talking already? What sort of name are you going to get if you're caught acting so strangely in such a wild place? Answer me, Judy. What's the matter with you? Haven't you done enough already to get the neighbourhood against you?'

I laughed in his face. '*What?* What have I done? You tell me that.'

'Nothing that I can prove,' he answered, 'or that I believe. But others don't think that way. Simple folk like Liddy and Liddy's family are putting it around you were responsible ...'

The blood froze in my veins. 'For what? Sarne's death? Petrock's? Is that it?'

When he didn't answer I continued sneeringly, but I felt suddenly tired. 'Oh let me pass, Venn. If folks want to believe such evil, they will, and it's nothing to me. Witches aren't burned any more. If they were, your malicious old great-aunt would've gone to the stake long ago. Just leave me alone. That's all I want.'

'Judith ...' he caught me by the arm, 'I'm thinking of *you.* You're all I *have* thought about, God knows, for longer than I care to remember. All right, all right ...' he said as I started to protest, 'the whole thing's a mess. The past, the future. And no one can put the clock back. But one thing's sure. I *need* you, heaven help me. I think I always have. There's some sort of dark magic about you ... something I can't explain. But ...'

'Don't try,' I said harshly. 'Don't touch me ...'

'Even in my dreams ...' he went on, with his nails biting into my flesh, 'you're there. Always. An obsession—a torment—call it what you like ...'

Against my will the laughter suddenly rang from my throat again, peal after peal in wild contempt. From a cloud of darkness the world reeled, until his lips closed hot upon mine. For one heady second I responded automatically, then managed convulsively to break free.

'You're like all the rest,' I shouted, with the rage rising wild and bitter in me. 'You want, you *want. Men.* You're all the same, but I'm no one's plaything any more, Venn Ettyn. I'm myself, my own keeper ... free ... *free* ...'

I rushed past him down the hill towards the house, only slowing my pace when I'd reached the trees fringing the moor.

In the last half-hour the sky had darkened with the queer yellowish tone of approaching thunder. An odd sort of desolation encompassed me, the feeling of foreboding and doom I'd been so quick to sense as a child before a wreck or disaster at sea. The wind, with the characteristic unpredictability of Cornish weather, had suddenly died into an eerie stillness through which no living being seemed to move, not even the quiver of a last dead leaf falling from a tree. Looking back once I saw no sign of Venn nor of a gnarled black form watching from above. Yet the whole atmosphere emitted a brooding watchfulness, as though a hundred unseen eyes peered from behind rock and bush, foretelling evil.

I tried to push such thoughts away, and when I reached Thorncarne Belle's grumbling voice helped.

'Where you bin?' she said. 'Always pushin' off you are now, jus' when there's so much to do an' everyone so sad still 'bout my darlin' boy an' his little chile. 'Tesn' right, an' that's God's truth. Sometimes I do think et's a stone inside of you instead of a heart.'

'Why don't you get Alicia to lend a hand now and again?' I asked coldly. 'The men aren't all *our* concern. And if I leave you'll have to be getting someone anyway.'

Belle's black eyes suddenly flashed, not with anger but fear.

'You edn' goin' is you, Judith? You wouldn' leave me here alone with such misery in me an' no way of handling things on me own ...?'

'Oh, I think you'd manage,' I told her unfeelingly. 'A little less weight would be better for you, and as I've said, Mrs Venn Ettyn's got duties, however much she likes to shirk them.'

'Her!' Belle almost spat the word out. 'She edn' no good to anyone. I've bin hearing things too, with these sharp ears of mine.'

'Oh?'

'They bean't hittin' it off as they should,' she resumed, with all her rancour towards me apparently gone. 'A flighty one she is an' cagey with her own money. Besides, that black-haired, fancy fellow's hangin' around more than he ought to. Venn should use his crop on 'en, if what I heerd be true; an' her, too. But oh *no*. Such an independent clever one he is. Won't even listen to his old mother—not that I'm *that* old, mind you. When I get all dressed up you'd be surprised what a fine figure I can make o' myself.'

'I know,' I agreed, thankful to have her in a better temper. 'I saw you at the wedding.'

'That?' She laughed scornfully. 'That's nuthen'.

You just wait, my girl.'

I didn't have to wait long. That same evening Belle appeared at the evening meal with her thick black hair intricately plaited and arrayed on top of her head. Immense brass rings fell from her ears. Over the crimson bodice stretched to bursting point across her enormous breasts, several strips of coloured beads jangled. And to hide her thickened waist a multi-coloured, fringed shawl had been draped and pinned, showing layers of frilly black silk beneath.

Everyone stared as she settled herself like some ancient queen on a creaking chair at the head of the table.

'My! Ma,' said Paul, 'you do look grand.'

'An' so do I feel.' Belle retorted promptly. 'My great-great-grandfather was a Romany Chal, an' doan' you go forgettin' et. It seems to me we bin forgettin' the good things for too long. So tonight let the grievin' end, an' God's peace be on the dead. Tonight is for the livin'. So let's drink to et. Liddy ...' she shouted, 'bring out the wine. The one brewed by my own hands from the elderberry flower. Sweeter than champagne it be, an' far more potent. Hurry, girl, an' be quick 'bout et.'

Liddy scurried off like a frightened hare and after some minutes returned with the nectar.

How long the drink had been corked I couldn't guess. But it was certainly strong, and Belle took liberally of it.

'Drink up, all o' ye,' she said more than once. 'A real fairy brew this is, an' fit for kings an' queens. Tek enough of et an' all the sweet pastures o' heaven will open to ye surely.'

Eventually she became so drunk she fell off the chair in a heavy stupor and had to be carried up to her bed by Paul and Marcus.

Undignified as the little scene had been, the humour of it made me feel better, combined, I suppose, with the effects of the wine itself.

That night I slept well. But when I woke the feeling of approaching disaster had revived in me, and by the end of the week, whether through coincidence or intuition, the strange sense of oppression was proved to be well founded. One of Venn's prize heifers became sick, and although rinderpest wasn't at first suspected, the dread disease was proved by veterinary tests as one by one other cattle went down.

By the end of November his precious herd was practically extinct, which meant that financially he was at a great loss. Although we had little to say to each other at that time, I couldn't help admiring his stoicism and will to go on, despite the tired lines of strain indenting his lean cheeks and the set line of his jaw which told so much more than any words.

'We shall just have to economize and work harder,' he said firmly to us all one evening. 'That means tightening our belts and having less in our pockets. Farmers before have had to start again and make a success of it. This is what I aim to do.'

'And Alicia? That wife of yours?' Belle queried. 'Is *she* content to pull her weight, or do you aim to keep her there in luxury, playing what fancy games she likes on the sly?'

Venn's lips hardened tighter.

'Alicia will come over here to live,' he said, 'and will do what I say; with her own bit of money, too, if necessary. I shall put up Gulvarrick for rental and gain a bit of cash there.'

After this curt, down-to-earth announcement he went to the door, turned and said before leaving, 'I take it I can depend on you all?'

Just for a second his eyes were on my face.

I didn't speak. The rest mumbled a sort of grudging acquiescence, and I knew then that for a time I would stay, but only for a certain period, until work was in hand again and the new organization of Thorncarne properly started.

When that day came I would be off as I'd planned, looking for Matt. And if I didn't find him, there was always my father, providing he was still alive.

CHAPTER 22

As soon as possible, a 'To Let' sign was put up by Gulvarrick gates, and in January Venn and Alicia moved to Thorncarne. The big house once more stared with its empty eyes of windows across the fields and lane; it was as though the greedy ghost of Isabella reigned there once more, exerting her malicious spell again on the deserted rooms and corridors.

Alicia was careful not to show too much resentment at her compelled exit from the place she'd been so proud of. But behind the façade I knew she felt bitter and humiliated by Venn's action, and from her sidelong, calculating glances sometimes and the set of her small mouth when she was off guard, it was clear to me some plan was brewing. In the house she was more of a liability than a help, though she made a great show with the sweeper and duster. From the start Belle disliked her, and if she hadn't been afraid of Venn's reaction she'd have let her temper fly many a time. As it was she retreated into sulky silence when her daughter-in-law was about, and what grumbles and gossiping went on was between her and Flavia.

Flavia, who'd left school at Christmas, seemed mildly amused by the situation.

'Just wait,' she said once, when the three of us were in the kitchen. 'Venn's more than a match for that stuck-up little creature any day. It won't last, of course. Anyone can see that.'

'I dunno 'bout that,' Belle told her grudgingly. 'She holds more strings than she ought to, what with that café place and money in her pocket. Venn says he'll use et, if he has to. But he won't. He edn' that sort; too proud in a stand-offish way. No, you mark my words, milady Ettyn'll go on haven' her jewellery an' fine clothes an' all she wants while we slave here from mornin' till night workin' to put the gold back in that son o' mine's pocket.'

'Well,' Flavia said, with the sophisticated shrug she'd learned at school, 'maybe it won't be for long. *Some*one will take Gulvarrick off his hands sooner or later, and things will brighten up.'

'How d'you know?' Belle snapped. 'That place edn' many's choice, 'specially with Venn hangin' on to all but an acre of the land. A bad name et's got now, as you well know. Bad things've happened there from the start, an' go on doin', I shudn' wonder, till the day o' doom.'

'I don't think so,' Flavia said knowingly, staring at her reflection through a small hand-mirror she carried in her reticule. 'I heard them both talking the other night in their bedroom—you know how the sound carries from their room to mine ...'

'And you listened, of course?' I interrupted.

A spark of the old, wild Flavia glimmered from her dark eyes as she confessed impishly, 'Well ... wouldn't you? I mean, life's quiet round here. Of course I did.'

'Hmn. An' what was et then?' Belle enquired eagerly, 'What's this news you're so mad to tell. Come on, spit et out.'

Flavia wrinkled her brow and put on a show of great thought before remarking in a newly acquired theatrical manner, 'It was Venn I heard first. There'd been a sort of murmuring between them, then he said, in a *very* lordly way, "*Certainly not.* Leeds is the *last* man I'd have using my property. So get that out of your head once and for all, Alicia."

' "Oh, but *Venn* ..." she said, all sweet and sickly, "*darling,* it would mean *so much* in your pocket. And just now when you want money so badly to help with the wretched loan. Don't you *see?* We wouldn't have to meet him—not *much* anyway. And he'd be busy all the time with his fine friends. It's a *marvellous* opportunity ..."

' "No," he said, "and that's final." '

'*Leeds,* did you say?' Belle asked. 'Isn't that the black-whiskered, flash-looking chap she was goin' with 'fore she hooked Venn? Well, Judith? You knows. That was the name, wasn't et?'

'Yes, I think so,' I said. 'Joshua Leeds. He part owns the café.'

'That jus' *shows.*' Belle said with the colour bright in her cheeks. '*Shows* what a madam she is, wantin' to get her fancy man a hold in fam'ly affairs. Still ...' she sniffed, 'Venn'll have none o' that.'

'Don't be too sure,' Flavia remarked knowingly. 'From what I've heard, Gulvarrick's a real white elephant now, after what's happened there; Madness, killings and all the talk of curses and a ghost.'

'Where did you get that from?'

'Everyone knows,' Flavia answered. 'In the district anyway, and news travels. If Mr what's-his-name Leeds offers a high enough rent, Venn would be soppy to refuse. That's what *I* think. Besides, if he's going to have his friends there, or guests or whatever he calls them, it'd bring a bit of fun and life to the place. Just think! Carriages and chaises driving up the lane, fashionable ladies from London and young gallants. Oh my! What a change.'

I couldn't help laughing.

'How your imagination works, Flavia,' I said. 'Even if it was true there'd probably not be any gallants or high-born women at all. Just as likely they'd be testy old men with their fat spouses come to take a rest cure in Cornish air.'

'I don't think so,' Flavia said. 'Too many hills. No, I think if Mr Leeds takes on the house there's sure to be excitement and fun going on. I've got a hunch—here,' she said, pointing to her head where the lustrous hair was piled high with a red ribbon, 'and I bet you it's true.'

As it happened it was. A few days later Venn revealed that Flavia's hunch *was* right. It would be better for the property to be occupied, he said, and the monthly sum to be contributed by Joshua Leeds would be considerable and a great help in reducing the loan.

'And enlarging your herd again, of course,' Marcus said dryly.

'It's not so much a matter of enlarging as starting once more from scratch,' Venn told him, frowning.

'I don't see why the cattle side's got to be so important,' Marcus replied. 'You could have the same trouble all over again, even if you do get it built up. Why couldn' we concentrate more on the vegetables?'

'Because there's not enough money in it. The grain pays, but vegetables only just about cover their cost, when you consider time spent in transport and labour.'

'Flowers then?'

There was a pause before Venn exploded.

'Flowers?'

'Why not? They do it in the Scillies, and with the railways getting easier with faster steam trains there's going to be a fine trade for 'em in London. We've enough land now, and sheltered fields below the ridge. They'd thrive, daffs and those anemones.'

'I must say you're not without ideas. But no. Unthinkable.'

'Bees then,' Marcus continued determinedly.

'Bees? Whatever for?'

'Mead.' Marcus said. 'All that's needed is fermented honey and water, and I've heard it's a rare drink. We could start a brewery of our own. Make a big name that way ...'

'Ah,' Belle interposed, ' 'es got somethin' there, Venn. A touch of the real Ettyn in 'en arter all.'

Such notions, of course, died eventually in thin air, as Venn's enthusiasm and determination to win the hard chore of cattle breeding increased. Alicia took no part in such arguments and seemed unconcerned about the future now that her point concerning Joshua Leeds had been won. Her interest in her appearance, however, seemed more excessive than usual. Whenever she got the chance she'd be preening herself before any available mirror, and as the days passed even the minimum of housework she'd undertaken became Flavia's responsibility.

'You wait though,' Flavia said. 'I'm not going on this way forever. What did Venn send me to school for, if it was only to wait on that silly besom? Never mind, it won't be for long. When her fine Mr Leeds gets to Gulvarrick, I'll p'raps catch a rich husband.'

'And perhaps you won't,' I reminded her.

'Well, a lover would do,' Flavia said, dimpling, but with a sidelong flash of her dark eyes that told me she might mean it, 'so long as he's wealthy enough.'

'Lovers come and lovers go,' I told her bitterly. 'Don't land yourself in a mess, Flavia.'

'I don't mean to. What do you take me for? A ninny? I'm not such a fool as ma was. Although, when you come to think of it, she's not done too badly, has she? Not with a son like Venn and that ha-ha-ing stuck up old grandfather of his in the background. Fancy! If he wasn't a bastard he'd be in for the title one day. And it wouldn't surprise me a bit if it wasn't arranged somehow. Most things can be done with money, you know. Anything can be bought, even a swanky handle to your name.'

Her cynicism surprised but didn't shock me. Flavia had always been down-to-earth, a quality her sophisticated finishing school seemed to have fully endorsed. In some ways though, she was still remarkably like Sarne; especially in looks, though she had finer features. She seldom referred to her brother, which struck me as strange at first until I realized the blow of his death had struck deeply. The nearest she came to discussing the past seriously was one late afternoon when we walked together to the village with eggs.

The air was tangy and fresh, faintly suggestive of a hundred wild-flowers and growing things blown on the wind from the hills, and for a time we hardly spoke, though I could sense her mind travelling back over the years into secret places I'd no knowledge of. Then, suddenly, she said, 'You shouldn't have married Sarne, Judith. You weren't happy, were you? You couldn't possibly have been.'

Trying to keep the edge off my voice, I said, 'What makes you say that? Has Belle been talking?'

'No, she would have if I'd listened. But I didn't want to know. It's just ... Sarne had a lot of feeling in him, and it frightened him. He was always like that, even when he was young. So he turned to bullying sometimes. I expect you found that out.'

'Yes.'

'He needed someone weak and soft in his hands ... someone he could tend and look after. But you're not like that, are you? You're a wild one. Sort of independent and hard, when you feel like it. Sarne wouldn't've liked that at all.'

'I've never blamed Sarne that it didn't work out,' I told her, 'and as you say we shouldn't have married. It was Venn—because of the baby. He forced us.'

Flavia turned her head sharply, and the look in her eyes was cold, as cold as the fading greenish light over the horizon.

'Nobody could force you, Judith, unless you were agreeable,' she said. 'Not even Venn. But maybe it was *because* of Venn you did it—to be near him.'

Her words held such truth they shocked me.

'Don't speak such lies, Flavia. You know nothing whatever about it.'

She laughed shortly, without a trace of humour.

'Oh, don't try that on me. One glance at your two faces when you're near each other says enough without words. Still, there's no use fretting or going too sour on things. In the end it'll come out as I say—three or four lives wrecked because of ... well, *because.* I'm not blaming you for seducing Sarne; Sarne was quite capable any day of taking any woman he fancied, including you. You *could've* stopped him, though, if you'd tried enough. But when you didn't, you could have taken off somewhere further away than Penzance, where Venn was sure to find you. It was the first place he'd look, and you must have known.'

'I never really thought,' I said truthfully.

'No, of course not; you wouldn't. Because it wouldn't suit you to. No one likes to find their weak places.'

'Oh, Flavia, I wish you wouldn't bring up the past. Let it rest, can't you?'

'I suppose so,' Flavia agreed grudgingly, 'now I've got things off my chest. I had to speak, Judith, because I loved Sarne. We were close.'

The subject was dropped then, and in the weeks following everyone was so agog with curiosity about the approaching new tenancy of Gulvarrick that the tragedy of Sarne and Petrock receded sufficiently for all barbed comments and condemning glances in my direction to be forgotten. Every week Belle, wearing complete black and looking enormously resplendent in her gypsy fashion, visited the churchyard with flowers for their graves. Just for appearance's sake I accompanied her occasionally at first, then dropped the morbid habit, which seemed to me hypocrisy and an insult to blossoms cut down before their time. They couldn't help the dead, and I couldn't bring myself to mourn indefinitely a man I'd never loved. I'm sure Belle thought me hard, and possibly I was. But without hardness it would have been impossible to go on there, and I think Flavia understood.

'Oh, take no notice of Ma,' she said, sensing my mood one day. 'She loves a good weep almost as much as a drink. Deaths and weddings go to her head like wine.'

I couldn't help a smile. 'It's you who are hard, it seems to me,' I said.

Flavia shrugged.

'Well, you have to be in this life, if you're going to keep your looks and catch a rich husband.'

Her words, so reminiscent of my grandmother's, startled me.

'Even with looks you can't be sure of that,' I told her.

'No?' Her eyebrows shot up over her large dark eyes. 'If you're clever you can. Brains count, too, you know. I'm surprised you made such a mess of things, Judith. When I first met you— Do you remember? You were housekeeper at Gulvarrick—you kind of awed me. You seemed so sure of yourself and educated. I never thought you'd properly fall for Sarne, not ever.'

'Things were different then,' I answered. 'I had William.'

'Oh, *him*. Pendruggan. But you hadn't, had you? Not in a real way. How could you, when he'd a wife?'

'I don't want to talk about it,' I said abruptly.

'Sorry. All the same ...' She waited a moment, then continued, 'Where *did* you get your learning, Judith?'

'Learning?'

'The way you can speak when you want to and put on the fine manner? What you told me about Port Einack and your grandmother, it doesn't fit somehow.'

'When I had a chance I used to read,' I answered, 'and I *did* have some schooling. It was always my idea to better myself. But then there's the wild side in me, too. Mostly, I suppose, underneath. Although ...'

'Yes?'

'I had a great-great-grandmother somewhere. She was Spanish and must have been a lady. I had a miniature of her ...'

'You mean the one you used to wear?'

'Yes.'

'Where is it now?'

'Broken,' I told her. 'Sarne did it.'

'But *why?*'

'Temper and jealousy. Oh, I can understand it. I wasn't very kind to him. But please don't let's bring Sarne up again. It's over now. I don't want reminding. And if you keep harking back I won't tell you anything at all, and I mean it, Flavia.'

'All right, all right, you needn't get so huffed. I didn't mean to dig. It was thinking of those rich people started it.'

'The sooner they come then, the better,' I said. 'Then you can start spreading your net.'

She frowned, grimaced and walked away, looking back over her shoulder and saying, 'I've heard it won't be long now. Mr Leeds is supposed to be moving in next week, and I've a hunch it's true.'

It was. On a cool spring day a one-horse phaeton arrived, depositing Joshua Leeds at the front door and then drawing into the side lane, where Pascoe and his wife, still caretakers, waited to receive the man and have the animal stabled.

Venn went over shortly afterwards to welcome Mr Leeds—though 'welcome' was possibly the wrong word—and when an hour had passed and he still didn't return, Belle flung off her apron impatiently and waddled to the gates of Thorncarne. She came back five minutes later, disgruntled and muttering under her breath.

'Talk o' work an' all pullin' our weight,' she said, 'ef et's goin' to be this way from now on we'll be shoulderin' Venn's share as well as our own. 'Tesn' right. That's what I do say.'

Alicia, who'd just come into the kitchen, jumped up immediately.

'I'll go and fetch him,' she announced, taking a mirror from her pocket and dabbing her pert nose with rice-powder. 'Anyway, Joshua is *sure* to want to see me, being an old friend of his and also Venn's wife.'

Belle threw up her hands above her head as Alicia's slim form glided through the door; the movement could hardly be called walking since her step was so soft and soundless, her body from the waist held remarkably erect and her head tilted slightly backwards showing her profile to best advantage. Though her features were small it was already obvious that in a few years the lines from chin to neck would become creased and even perhaps scraggy. Venn would find out soon enough the type of woman he'd married. I thought with a tinge of triumph. She'd said she was thirty, but I guessed forty was nearer the truth. How long then could the façade of living together continue? And what pleasure would their intimate life contain when she either cringed away from him in bed or forced her thin body upon him when it wasn't wanted.

Well, he'd asked for it, I told myself ruthlessly. If he'd not forced me into marrying Sarne everything could have been different. In time maybe I'd have forgotten even Matt, or at least put him so far to the back of my mind he couldn't intrude in any real way at all. As it was with the onset of long summer days I found my thoughts constantly turning to him again.

By then the first of Joshua Leeds's 'guests' had arrived at Gulvarrick, and most of them of a type, though of varying ages; elegant, frock-coated gentlemen of worldly or artistic professions, accompanied by ladies of high fashion wearing luxurious clothes, mostly with voluminous bustles trimmed with bows and an excess of beribboned drapery. From my brief glimpses I noted how painted they were, with vivid lips and a high colour filmed by powder white. They either rode in carriages or kept within the precincts of Gulvarrick, but occasionally a couple could be seen wandering about the lanes and a trill of affected laughter could be heard on the air.

Flavia was impressed, though I knew instinctively, despite their air of grandeur and fine manners, few were well-born ladies but belonged, I suspected, to a far older profession. As I couldn't prove it I kept my mouth shut, merely telling Flavia that true aristocrats never dressed in that manner.

She tossed her head. 'Pooh! what do I care?

They have fun and wealth and lovely clothes, and I wish I was one of them. Mr Leeds must have grand connections anyway. Do you know, Judith, I met one face to face yesterday—a gentleman, I mean. He was alone, and very good-looking and young. He had a gold pin in his tie with a diamond in it, and a watch-chain with lots and lots of little trinkets on it. Rings, too. And his coat was black velvet ...' She broke off, breathless.

'What a lot you noticed in such a short time,' I said ironically.

'Oh, it wasn't so short really. We discussed things.'

'What things?'

'He wants to paint me,' Flavia said, all innocence but with a rich colour in her face. 'Imagine it.'

I did.

'Where? Without your clothes in his bedroom?'

'Certainly *not.* The garden somewhere—with wild roses in my hair. He wants a fresh model, you see, for some exhibition in London, and his first words when he saw me were "At *last.* I've found you at last, my wild wild flower." '

She giggled, but I knew the laugh was all pretence. In reality she was tremendously impressed.

'You watch your step, Flavia,' I said sharply. 'Words like that mean nothing.'

'Oh, stop it, Judith,' she retorted quickly. '*You're* not the one to talk. I've got my head screwed on all right, and I don't intend *anyone* to mess up *my* life. If a man wants me enough he'll marry me without having to. I'll see to that.'

What Venn thought of the showy, constant comings and goings of Mr Leeds's visitors, I couldn't imagine, though I overheard Belle saying to him one day, 'No conscience, you haven't, Venn Ettyn, lettin' your place to such as they. Not a moral between 'en, as any true woman wi' eyes in her head can see. An' to think you had us charrin' an' slavin' for the likes o' they. Why your grandfather Petrock would have spit in 'ens faces for the very shame of et.'

'I'm not my grandfather,' Venn replied shortly.

'No. More's the pity. It's that pompous old head-in-the-air Carvellun *you* favour,' Belle said sharply. 'An' ef you asks me, he'll be one o' the first to go visitin' there, I shouldn' wonder.'

'Where he goes has nothing to do with me,' Venn told her, '*or* you. And see you mind your own business where Gulvarrick's concerned. Joshua Leeds is the tenant and has every right to invite what friends he wishes to the house.'

'Even Flavia, I suppose?' Belle suggested slyly.

'*Flavia?* What do you mean?'

'Keep your eye on her. That's all,' Belle answered smugly. 'All that eddication you've given her's put a whole lot o' fancy ideas into her head you doan' know about. An' doan' ask me how I know. We Ettyns've got the pow'r of et, remember.'

How the conversation ended I didn't hear,

but a mood of quietness was on Venn for the next few days, whether on Flavia's account or Alicia's I couldn't know. Perhaps both. Once more discord seemed to be raising its ugly head between Gulvarrick and Thorncarne. It seemed to me sometimes the very bricks and mortar of both houses were imbued with hatred for each other. Alicia, particularly, seemed edgy and rather short-tempered. One day I saw her slipping over the lane to Gulvarrick, dressed far more flashily than was usual at that time of the day in bright blue silk and with a pink and blue lacy thing perched on top of her head.

She was just sneaking towards the side gates when Venn appeared from the fields. He stopped a moment when he saw her, then in a few seconds had caught up with her and taken her arm. She made an attempt to free herself but didn't succeed and a moment later they were both on their way back to Thorncarne.

Flavia told me the next night she'd heard them quarrelling.

'Venn doesn't usually let fly,' she told me, with a wink, 'but last night he did. Oh my! I wish I could've seen. I didn't hear much, but it was enough. "You'll do as I say, madam," he told her, quite clearly, "or I'll send the whole lot of them packing. You too." '

'She didn't like that. There was a sort of murmuring and wailing, and argument and sound of a slap, then, suddenly, everything was quiet. Poor silly thing. And poor Venn. I bet she gives him a thin time in bed. Well, they've asked for it, haven't they? Both of them.'

I didn't answer. However titivating Venn's private life with his wife might be, I didn't want to think about it.

On the other hand the *ménage* at Gulvarrick did intrigue me a little. Since William's death I'd kept the secret vow I'd made never to enter the place again. But when Joshua Leeds stopped me in the lane one afternoon and suggested I might like to take a glass of cordial with him that same evening, I found myself hesitating only for a moment.

'Very well,' I said, lifting my head with a touch of bravado. 'Thank you very much.'

'Six thirty then?' he said. 'Or shall we say seven?'

His dark eyes were ardent on my face. I could sense his admiration for my lustrous hair and rounded, slim figure, though my dress was only of green cotton, with a tartan cape blown back in the wind over my shoulders.

'Seven would be better,' I told him. 'I have duties at Thorncarne, as you must know. Or hasn't Alicia told you?'

At the mention of Alicia's name he frowned thoughtfully, but only very briefly.

'Yes, yes, of course,' he answered, 'and seven would be an admirable time. Till tonight then.'

He touched his tall hat, inclined his head slightly, turned and a moment later was gone.

As I walked up the path to the house I wondered why on earth I'd agreed to the invitation, which was a silly thing to do in the face of Venn's inevitable disapproval. Then, with a stab of guilty pleasure, I knew the answer lay there. Venn. It would give me tremendous pleasure to defy and thwart him, and if I wished to have a drink with Joshua Leeds there was simply nothing he could do about it.

CHAPTER 23

I knew I would probably be a quarter or even half an hour late for Joshua Leeds's invitation, as Belle would not be upstairs with her tonic before seven, or the men about their evening work again until that hour. It didn't worry me. Experience had taught me that a little waiting did no man any harm and that he generally respected a woman more for not appearing too eager.

I dressed myself carefully in the simple-styled black I'd got to replace the one Isabella had slashed. It was high in the neck but fitted round the bust, with a full, draped skirt gathered to the back trimmed by small green and gold bows. Black, I thought, would be in contrast to the over fashionable, brightly shaded dresses worn by most of Gulvarrick's guests. I meant to show Mr Leeds from the very first that I was no light woman available for his pleasure.

I wore my hair simply, too, combed to the top of my head, where its curls were tied by a green ribbon. The effect was lady-like and in no way obtrusive, especially with the dark shawl draped over my shoulders.

As I glimpsed my reflection before leaving I had a momentary pang, remembering Luzana's portrait, which should have been suspended over the bodice. I thought I looked a little like her, and the idea filled me with pride, dispelling briefly my wilder image—the one that Matt would have recognized, and Venn, too. Just for a second I wished Venn could have seen me, so aloof and self-contained, with a film of powder subduing the fresh glow of my skin to a more delicate pallor. But of course any meeting would have involved an argument, which was the last thing I wanted just then.

So presently I left the Barn and slipped quietly down the field bordering the house and across the lane to Gulvarrick, cutting from the side drive along the path to the front entrance.

Confused emotions filled me at the sight of the gracious exterior; memories of my first days there, and the months following when William had given such courtesy and love, soothing my shame of Matt's betrayal. When I reached for the bell-pull it seemed for an instant I was summoning ghosts of the past to life again but when the door opened, it was Mr Leeds instead of William Pendruggan who was waiting behind the man-servant to receive me. Before taking his proffered hand, I noted in a flash how changed the familiar hall was; there were flowers everywhere, with a new, highly-polished, walnut table under the mirror, and instead of the heavy decorative scheme of oak and dark cream, the walls had been painted pale blue and ornately lightened with gilt. The air held an aroma of scent and roses, and luxurious persian rugs covered the flagged floor.

Joshua must be very rich, I thought, and

I wondered how much his 'guests' paid to stay there.

From a dazed dream I heard him saying, with his hand enclosing mine, 'You're late, ma'am ... Mrs Crane, or may I call you Judith?'

Trying to ignore the pressure of his fingers, I answered, 'Mrs Crane might be more befitting, Mr Leeds, as my husband died so recently.'

'Ah yes, of course. We must observe the proprieties, must we not ... for the moment.'

I didn't answer but was aware of his glance travelling insidiously from the top of my head downwards, noting, with a look I well knew, each curve and line of my figure.

'Well, never mind,' he said, alluding obviously to my lateness. 'Women are habitually unpunctual creatures, I've discovered—especially the attractive kind.'

I managed a chilly smile.

He lifted the shawl from my shoulders. 'May I put this away for you ...?'

'I think not,' I said, retrieving it. 'The air's sometimes cool at this time of the year.'

'Not at Gulvarrick,' he told me more curtly. 'As the house is now run for visitors, warmth is essential. Still, just as you prefer. Shall we go into the drawing room? It's my private room whenever I choose, have no fear. Most of my guests are playing cards or out; I wouldn't wish to burden you with their company.'

I followed him meekly into the room I'd once known so well, and I felt a nervous lurch in my stomach as the door closed on the elegant interior. Not the faintest sign of past tragedy or vandalism remained. A few extra pieces of valuable furniture had been added: two Louis Quinze chairs, a pair of silver candelabras and a delicately carved, marble statuette of a female figure on the chest. I suppose there were other changes, too. The decor had been lightened, and everything was very highly polished. Otherwise ... things seemed the same. Even the portrait of Isabella.

It was still there, hanging in its accustomed place above the fireplace, with a strange cutting life about it that sent me suddenly cold. Under her sneering half-smile I felt a wave of sudden apprehension, almost faintness, as my hand closed on the arm of a chair. Then I heard Joshua Leeds saying, 'Do sit down, Mrs ... Crane.' Was it real or only my fancy that his voice held a faintly taunting note?

'Make yourself comfortable, and we'll celebrate.'

'Celebrate what?' I managed to ask, pulling myself together and taking a nearby chair.

Under the raven moustache his teeth gleamed. His dark eyes were full of mockery and a certain anticipatory pleasure.

'Your return, my dear lady. I understand you were in a position of some importance here before the late Squire's death, and I have hopes you may be induced to return in a similar capacity for a betterment of salary and circumstances.'

Dull rage mounted in me. It was all I could do to control it and reply, apparently equably, 'Indeed? What makes you think I should be at all interested, Mr Leeds?'

He turned his back on me momentarily, opened the cabinet, mixed a drink, poured it, and with two crystal glasses containing an amber liquid returned and handed one to me saying, with a brief bow, 'Your health, and mine, madam. A toast to us both and to the future.'

He held his glass to his lips and took a liberal sip, while I pretended to do the same, but when his eyes turned away I poured what I could on to the gold carpet near my chair, contriving to hide it by my gown.

We chatted for a few moments about mundane topics and polite trivialities, though I knew he was debating with himself all the time how best to broach again his outrageous suggestion. I gave him no encouragement, and at last, taking the initiative, he said, pulling a chair nearer to mine, 'Now perhaps with this good cordial to warm us we can really talk.'

'Certainly,' I agreed. 'Please begin.'

Quite clearly taken aback by my cool manner, he proceeded to outline his plan for me to take charge of Gulvarrick's domestic arrangements. Not only would my presence be required when he was there during the summer months, but throughout the winter period I would be needed as caretaker when he would, of necessity, be in London. The salary he offered was high, excessively so, and my duties, I realized also, would cover a wide range.

I pretended to consider the matter while he toyed with the stem of his glass, clicking it occasionally on the surface of the small table.

'Well?' he said, leaning towards me. 'Has the idea any interest for you?'

'Oh indeed yes,' I answered with a polite, fine-lady manner I'd cultivated for such occasions. 'I'm *very* interested, Mr Leeds.'

'Ah.'

He relaxed, with the colour deepening in his cheeks and the ardour returning to his eyes, which once more had a sidelong, appraising look in them. His hand patted my own intimately, a gesture I allowed only momentarily before drawing mine away.

'Then ...?'

'I'm interested,' I said, 'because it seems so strange you should offer such a splendid post to *me,* when you could take your pick from so many other more brilliant women. I come from a simple fishing family, you know, or didn't you realize that?'

'It makes no difference, my dear, *what* your background is,' he said, with patronizing familiarity. 'You are a fine woman to look at, and from what I already know of you we should get on splendidly ...'

I jumped up quickly, with cold contempt blazing to a fierce anger inside.

'You're insulting, Mr Leeds,' I told him. 'I'm not the kind of woman you think, and I certainly wouldn't sell myself to *you* or any other man. What you've heard about myself and Mr Pendruggan I don't know. But he was a gentleman, which you certainly are not. Our friendship was something very rare and quite precious. I should never have accepted your invitation to call; I realize it now. So if you'll excuse me ...'

I swept past him towards the door, but before I reached it he had caught up with me and turned me sharply to face him.

'I'll make you pay for this,' he said in a low, furious voice. 'One day you'll regret those words.'

I laughed, and if he'd delayed me further all manners would have deserted me and I'd have spat in his face.

But he didn't. And as a parting shot, with my hand on the door knob, I said cuttingly, 'Why don't you ask Alicia Tattam, Mrs Venn Ettyn, to give her services? I'm sure she'd handle the post very well indeed. Especially since you already know each other so well.'

I didn't hear his reply, or even if he gave any. The next moment I went down the hall towards the front door, which I slammed sharply behind me.

Walking quickly back to Thorncarne I realized that my one object in agreeing to visit the house must have been just what I'd so effectively accomplished: to get my own back on men—on *any* man who dared to assume I was there for his pleasure. In snubbing Joshua Leeds I'd released a resentment that had been building up in me since Matt's duplicity had so altered my life. In future, I told myself, there'd be no more humiliation, no easy loving nor trust in male promises. Flattering words could be lies, and the body mean betrayal.

Well, my body now, was my own. Never again would I allow violation by a lover. If Matt returned, perhaps ... But Matt would *not* return.

The old refrain was beating through my mind, a constant echo as I reached the gates of Thorncarne, and I was so possessed by it, so fierce with pride, that I didn't notice Venn's static form waiting dark by the hedge.

He stepped forward quickly, and my heart raced.

'Where have you been?' he said quietly, with a dangerous undercurrent in his voice.

For a moment I paused, in order to gain equilibrium. Then I replied coldly, 'I think that's my affair.'

'Not entirely,' he answered. 'As an employee you were neglectful in taking off tonight. Alicia had an unnecessary amount of chores to tackle ...'

'Poor Alicia,' I interrupted. 'I hope she's survived.'

'And don't take that tone with me, Judith. Ever since I brought her to Thorncarne you seem to have been anxious to provoke her whenever possible. And I don't like it. It's difficult enough without ...'

'Without me refusing to be a door-mat,' I finished for him spitefully. 'Too bad. Well, there's a remedy for that, isn't there? As I'm under no obligation to you, or you to me, I can easily leave and go back to Penzance, or elsewhere if I choose. I expect that's the answer.'

I swept past him, with my chin up, and as I did so caught my foot on a stone and half-stumbled.

He gripped me by one arm, held me rigidly for a second or two, then said in relentless, cold tones, 'Oh *no.* You're not getting out of things so easily. And I'm not letting you go until you've told me where you've been, though I've a shrewd idea already. So don't make a scene. It's no use.'

'Very well,' I answered. 'I'll tell you if you take your hand off me. I won't be bullied, Venn Ettyn, especially by you.'

The pressure of his fingers relaxed and fell away.

'So?' he queried.

'Oh, there's no secret about it,' I told him casually, walking on. 'Anyway, by some means or other I expect all Thorncarne already knows. Joshua Leeds asked me over to Gulvarrick for a glass of cordial and a chat. We had it, finished our little talk and I left. Are you satisfied now?'

'No. May I ask what you talked about?'

'You can ask, and as it happens I don't mind telling you. I was offered a post as housekeeper at Gulvarrick. Quite revealing on his part, I thought.'

The tension between us became almost unbearable. For almost half a minute he didn't speak, then he said with no trace of expression in his voice, 'And your reply was?'

'No,' I told him. 'Rather stupid of me, wasn't it, considering the high salary offered. But then you see my duties would have been rather varied, and as I pointed out, I don't happen to be that kind of woman. And now, if you don't mind, please leave me alone and stop this questioning. You've no right over my actions; only one man has that—and he's not here. If he was ...'

My words dried up ineffectually.

'If he was you'd be off with him like a shot, not caring a damn that he'd double-crossed and deceived you time after time, I suppose?' Venn said harshly. 'Can nothing on earth drive that dastardly sea captain out of your head?'

'No, I don't think so,' I answered, feeling suddenly emotionally depleted and miserable. 'If things had been different ... perhaps. There's no way of telling, because you married Alicia, and as you said before that day on the moor, there's no way of putting the clock back.'

'Judith ...'

He touched my arm gently, but at that same moment a white-clad figure came gliding across the grass, looking ghostly and unreal in the quickly fading evening light. Alicia. Her voice though was tangible enough and shrill as she exclaimed, 'Venn, where have you been? I've been looking *everywhere.* Oh!' Her tones hardened with contempt as she said, 'I *see.* Judith. It would be, wouldn't it? Not content with marrying and killing off one husband, she has to go lusting after another ...'

I could feel the blood drain from my heart and my face whiten as Venn's hand struck her hard across one cheek.

'Hold your filthy tongue, madam,' he said in deadly cold tones, 'or by God I'll silence it for you with my own hands. Get back to the house now, and don't ever dare to speak in that way again or it will be the worse for you ...'

I don't know what happened after that and didn't wait to hear; I rushed ahead down the path to the Barn, where I locked the door behind me and stood there, shuddering, with my back against it before going up to bed.

I lay for hours that night, wakeful and uneasy, with the place crowded, it seemed, by ghosts from the past—Matt, William, Isabella, Sarne, little Petrock and Venn—all of them symbolizing somehow a pattern of unhappiness and destruction in my life.

There seemed no end to it and, in my tired state, no solution for the future. At last, too weary to think any more, I slept. In the morning everything appeared the same as any other day except for the dark rings under Alicia's eyes and the strained, tight set of her mouth when she looked at me.

What else had happened between Venn and her during the night I couldn't guess and told myself I didn't care.

But I did. And realizing it made me long all the more feverishly for a sight of Matt again.

CHAPTER 24

The atmosphere at Thorncarne following the unpleasant scene with Alicia and Venn became tense and silent when I was present, filled with veiled hostility from Alicia and withdrawn detachment from Venn who was seldom in the house and appeared entirely concerned with the land, where he worked as hard as any hired hand and gave all his spare time to matters concerning the herd.

Sir John Carvellun called once before Christmas, but his visit was brief; when he left I could tell from the thrust-forward set of his head and quick gesture of his hand as he swept at the undergrowth with his cane that he was not pleased with the outcome. Everyone, even Belle, was aware that Venn's plans weren't progressing as favourably as he'd hoped.

'He wanted too much,' she grumbled one day when Flavia and I were in the kitchen. 'Too big an opinion of 'esself, that's the trouble. Things wus better when we were poorer an' afore he took on all that theer land. As for 'Licia!' she sniffed. 'Ef you asks me, all she thinks of is gettin' across to see that fancy chap or away to her la-da-di café. Well, her room's better'n her company for all the use she is.'

It was true that Alicia *was* becoming more preoccupied at Penjust these days. If I'd liked her better I'd not have blamed her. In such a sour, difficult atmosphere it wasn't easy to relax, and I wasn't at all surprised when she announced one afternoon that she was going to spend a few weeks away attending to business.

'Returns haven't been so profitable this summer,' she said in a practical off-hand way, 'and Joshua thinks it would be a good idea to keep an eye on the new manageress for a bit. I shall have a room above the café but will come back at weekends, of course.'

'That's very thoughtful of you,' Venn said coldly.

Alicia, shrugging her shoulders, flung him a withering glance before gliding to the door.

'Someone must have an eye to business,' she said pointedly. 'I don't intend to spend my whole life stinting and scraping and working my fingers to the bone simply to help breed some overweight, smelly prize bull. There are better things to do.'

The door clicked behind her. Flavia burst into laughter.

'I think that's *marvellous,'* she said, maliciously, with an impudent flash of her eyes towards Venn. 'I wish I'd said it. Alicia *does* hit the nail on the head sometimes, I'll say that for her, although of course I can't stick the sight of her really.'

'And because you can't stick the sight of her, is that why you visit Gulvarrick so often?' Venn remarked darkly.

Flavia flushed.

'No, it's not the reason, and anyway it's *my*

affair. You shouldn't have sent me to boarding school, Venn, if you hadn't planned something suitable for me afterwards. Before I went away life here seemed all right, but you can't expect me to be content now with just messing about the sheds in farm boots and washing dishes in the kitchen. Education doesn't fit you for such things.'

Belle entered the scene at that point.

'Eddication?' she said. 'Who's on about eddication now? I told 'ee, didn't I, there was no sense in et. You shoulda' listened to me, Venn.' Her eyes rounded on her daughter, with the fire in them that must have set hearts aflame when she was young. 'Well? What you bin arguin' 'bout? Not in trouble, are you?'

Flavia glared. 'Oh my God, what a mind you've got.'

'Mind?' shrieked Belle. 'You *dare* talk to your ma like that. Jus' let me catch you an' I'll give you such a hidin' you won't sit down for a week ...'

Her face was beetroot-red, and seeing that she meant it, Flavia darted out in a flash with the darting comment, '*You!* Don't make me laugh. You couldn't catch a broody hen.'

Belle flopped heavily on to a chair, breathing quickly, while she waved a plump hand before her face saying, 'That girl's beyond me. A real termagent. No respec' any more, not for anyone. There was always a bit o' the devil in us Ettyns, but nowadays et seems to me Flavia's got nuthen' else. Nuthen' at all. Jus' sly, wicked devilment. An' I can't control her, Venn. Ever since those primpin' fancy women an' fellas came to Gulvarrick she's bin sneakin' off at all times ... dead o' night or early mornin', et doan' matter. Et's for no good. You ought to do somethin'. She's your sister arter all. An' 'twas you made her what she is, I'm tellin' you.'

But there was nothing short of locking Flavia up that Venn could do, or anyone else. The old feud and rivalry between Gulvarrick and Thorncarne had started up again with renewed intensity. I sensed though I said nothing, that tragedy was already brewing. The very air was full of it that winter; a sort of doomed, brooding challenge waiting for some quirk of circumstance to set it alight. I didn't feel involved personally, except at odd moments when Venn's strange golden eyes seemed to sear my body and my very soul. Unhappiness, like a cold shroud, kept him silent, but I knew he wanted me and was determined that for once in his life this was something he'd never have.

Christmas that year was a joyless affair, and I was grateful when the enforced festivities were over. Joshua Leeds was still at Gulvarrick with one or two of his visitors. When he passed me in the lane, walking or in his chaise, I was aware of the hostile contempt on his face and sensed he would have done me harm if he could. I felt a wry, negative sort of pleasure in recognizing his frustration and was always careful when we met to appear unruffled and only half-aware of his presence.

With Flavia, of course, he was quite different and at pains to show her devoted attention.

There were gifts, too, including a ruby ring and a necklace that she showed only to me before secreting them in a drawer upstairs.

'Ought you to accept such things, Flavia?' I said once, on a cold, late evening in January when she'd stolen quietly from Gulvarrick to the Barn.

She was looking especially lovely in a dark skirt covered by a red and cream paisley shawl, with a red flower in her black hair.

A momentary downward pout curved her luscious lips. 'Why not? He's a gentleman. I like him, and ... and he's very fond of me, if you must know.'

'Oh, I don't doubt that,' I answered, 'in his own way. He's fond of Alicia, also, remember.'

She flushed. 'That's different. Because she's useful. But he doesn't really *care.*'

'And what's caring, Flavia?'

She shrugged. 'Oh, *you* know. You must ... you've been married, and ... and Venn, and everything.'

'Venn and I are nothing to each other,' I told her coldly.

'So you say. But then you won't admit things. I *do.* That's the difference. Joshua *loves* me, you see. I suppose I shouldn't say ... He made me promise not to, until things were right.'

'Right? What do you mean?'

'For our marriage,' she told me with a dreamy look in her face. 'That's it. *There.* My secret. Oh Judith, I *shouldn't* have told you, but isn't it just the most wonderful thing ...?'

How could I say it wasn't, when I'd felt

exactly the same way before Topaz appeared that day in Port Einack? Besides, it wasn't my affair. All I could reply was, 'I suppose it *could* be, Flavia. But men, remember—some men—can make a woman believe *anything* until they get what they want. And Mr Leeds is a man of the world, so much older than you. What about that young man, the artist, who wanted to paint you?'

She shrugged.

'Oh *him*. He was young and ... and sentimental. He hadn't any *passion* in him. It was nice to be admired, but my heart never beat quickly or ... or anything else ... You know what I mean. You *must*.'

Yes I did, and it disturbed me.

'So you mustn't say anything. If you *do*,' she added darkly, 'I'll run off; elope or something. I might even kill myself.'

'Don't be ridiculous,' I said sharply. 'You're far too fond of living and your own skin. The trouble with you is you shouldn't be here at all. You should be on the stage, like my ... my ...'

'Your what?'

'My father,' I told her.

Her eyes widened. 'Your *pa*, did you say? *Really?*'

'Yes.'

Although I had no proof to offer, saying it helped steer her thoughts away from Joshua Leeds.

'But, Judith, how exciting! Where? London? Does he know Mr Irving, and Ellen Terry? Why didn't you tell me, *why?*'

'Oh, it's a long story,' I prevaricated. 'One day maybe I'll explain more. That's *my* secret anyway. So now we both have one. But about Henry Irving ... no, I shouldn't think they met. All actors and actresses don't get to London, you know.'

I thought of the travellers, the strolling players who went from place to place giving their shows in tents at fairs or in village halls and in barns; of one in particular—a slim man with tilted green eyes and a proud way of walking; a man with thick chestnut hair greying at the temples and a fine voice speaking dramatic lines fit to move an audience to tears. I remembered the flask, too, and my mind went back to my grandmother's words: Your father was a drunkard, and your mother was a ... Just for a moment I had an overwhelming wish to be away from the Barn, Thorncarne and, most of all, Flavia's company that had revived the past so acutely.

I stood up suddenly.

'I must get back to the house, Flavia. Belle will be wanting some nightcap or other, and if I were you I'd get up to bed before she sees you in that fancy rig-out.'

My voice, even to my own ears, was sharp and cold, as I'd intended it to be.

She scowled. 'Oh, very well, if *that's* how you feel ...'

'It is. And I don't want any more of your confidences about Mr Leeds. It puts me in a very difficult position.'

'Why? Who with? *Venn*, I suppose.'

I didn't answer, and a moment later she'd left, with a flurry of skirts and tumbled locks, leaving a trail of perfume behind. When I went to the door I found a red flower on the mat. The carnation from her hair. I picked it up and held it to my nose briefly before going out. Such an exotic, sad-sweet smell it had. Like loving, somehow, or the shadow of love with passion already fading. When I reached the path I threw it down absently and drew my shawl close to the neck. The air was cold, with massed clouds rising from the west to dim the winter stars.

I let myself into Thorncarne silently. All was quiet, and there was no light in Belle's room. Obviously she had already had a more-than-liberal nightcap and was probably snoring away on her bed. Marcus and Paul, I knew, must be asleep by then, and there was no sign of Flavia. The men, too, had left.

It was only when I was on my way back to the Barn that I looked round and saw Venn's figure standing motionless by a field gate. My gesture had been involuntary, perhaps instinctive. I paused a second, and the sight of his set face washed pale in a brief drift of moonlight through the broken clouds seemed to call all the life from my body.

I waited, trembling, wondering if he would move or speak, but he didn't. After that short, watchful interlude between us, I turned and hurried away to the silence of my own small home. I couldn't understand myself or the conflict of my own emotions, and that night my dreams were dark and confused; of wild seas breaking on a gaunt shore, and of a shape gathering force against the winter sky as it drove towards me, with great wings flailing and falling in the wind.

Venn? Matt? Or some immense bird risen like a giant phoenix from the past? I struggled to free myself, and my arms were before my face when I woke up suddenly, with my heart beating wildly and my forehead damp with sweat. Gradually my pulse steadied, and when I went to the window it was already dawn, with just a touch of crimson to the east, heralding rain.

All that day I did my best to dispel the lingering effect of the nightmare, telling myself it was nothing but a dream—the pasty I'd had at the evening meal must have disagreed with me.

But it was more than that, as I well knew with my strange sense of foreknowledge. It was not until February though that it happened, and by then the young celandines were peering gold from ditches and hedges, and the first lambs were about the fields. The blackthorn was already blossoming white from lean dark branches, and sprays of young, frail green poked up from last year's decay. A season of promise and spring ahead, yet that very anticipation of beauty filled me with queer foreboding.

Superficially, relationships, though frequently strained, were comparatively normal. Flavia appeared more reflective than usual perhaps, and Belle sharper-tempered because of Alicia's too-frequent absences from household duties. My silent contacts with Venn remained unchanged. Marcus and Paul were too involved with the land for conversation when they returned to the house at night, and Liddy, was the same simple, boring creature she'd always been.

But inwardly I was waiting, always waiting and towards the end of the month my 'sixth sense' was proved correct.

One morning it was discovered that Joshua Leeds and the last two of his guests had left Gulvarrick during the night, taking their belongings and most of the newly acquired, valuable accessories of the house with them.

An envelope had been pushed under the door of Thorncarne, containing a brief note to Venn with a cheque for the rental of the house up to date.

'I think this should more than cover any debts incurred,' it ran. 'I shall not be returning, so there is no need for further correspondence between us. Remember me to Flavia.'

It was signed, 'Yours, Joshua Leeds.'

Everyone was surprised, and during the first reaction no one except myself noticed Flavia's eyes close briefly and her rich colour change to a sickly, greenish pallor. She left the room almost immediately, and as soon as possible, without causing attention, I followed.

I found her in her room lying on her bed, face downwards and sobbing uncontrollably, with her hands clawing the pillows.

'Flavia,' I said, touching her on her shoulder, 'Flavia, please don't. What is it?'

After a minute she controlled herself, turned over and faced me, with a wild, bitter look in her eyes.

'The cur,' she said. 'The dirty lying bastard. I should've listened to you. I should've known.'

'But ... well, you'll get over it,' I said tritely. 'In time.'

'In time? Oh yes. Maybe,' she sneered. 'But it'll be too late then, won't it? *Won't* it?'

'What do you mean?' I asked, though a dreadful suspicion was filling me.

'Mean? You should know. His *brat.* That's what I mean,' she said fiercely, quite forgetting her newly acquired veneer of manners. 'Joshua Leeds. Need I spell it out?'

I shook my head.

'No. No, of course not. But it's not the end of the world. For heaven's sake, Flavia, don't get so ... so hysterical. It's happened to other women, even me.'

'You?'

'Yes,' I said dully. 'When I was Matt's wife. Or thought so. You must pull yourself together now, and later we'll talk about it together. Promise?'

She nodded. Whether she meant anything by it I didn't know. But that night proved my worst fears. Flavia disappeared. She left no note and no clue at all of where she'd gone. All her clothes were still hanging in her wardrobe, and her bed in the morning had not been slept in.

It seemed to me then that while Gulvarrick and Thorncarne stood facing each other over the lane, there'd be no peace at either place. Once more I began to yearn for Matt with all my heart, and I longed to be away.

CHAPTER 25

For the whole day Venn and Paul searched for Flavia: in Penzance and the station first, thinking she might be attempting to follow Joshua Leeds; then, when this failed, over the moor, helped by Pascoe and a man. Belle was sullen and frightened because during the afternoon her odious great-aunt called, muttering forebodings and omens of death. Old Dorcas looked terrible, swathed in a black shawl and dragging skirt, with her hag's face thrust forward level with her shoulders and her wicked crow's eyes gleaming button-black through straggling grey hair. Gold rings tinkled incongruously from her ears, and under the shawl strings of glass beads glimmered, somehow accentuating her macabre appearance.

I wouldn't have stayed a minute in her company if Belle hadn't suddenly suggested tea.

'Get us a pot, Judith,' she said. 'Old Auntie's got a real climb back, an' the wind's blowin' cold from the hills. You'd like a cup, wouldn' 'ee, Aunty dear?'

Old Dorcas nodded. 'Providin' I do bless it fust,' she muttered. 'When those from over theer comes 'vadin' Ettyn land, a real wish es needed to kip devil off.'

Her glance sought mine maliciously.

I turned away, feeling only contempt and dislike. When I returned with cups and saucers, a tea-pot and a jug of milk, Belle said grudgingly, 'Put et down, Judith, an' sit ef you like. Want a cup do ye?'

'No,' I told her. 'Not now.'

As I went to the door and opened it, I could hear the old woman's voice droning some ancient ritual in a foreign tongue. I glanced back and saw her thin, veined arms and gnarled hands outstretched over the table. Her eyes were closed, but Belle's were raised upwards, her hands clasped over her enormous bosom which was heaving with emotion.

As quickly as possible I slipped out, closing the door with a sharp snap behind me. Then I hurried to the Barn for my cape. Dorcas's one reference to Gulvarrick had given me an idea, and I was surprised no one had thought of it before. In the ordinary way, of course, Pascoe's wife would have been over to the big house to see things were in order when the place was empty. But this was no ordinary occasion, and when her husband had told her of Flavia's disappearance she'd probably been too preoccupied to bother with dust sheets and cleaning. Besides, there were so many nooks in the building where a distraught girl could hide, it was hardly likely a glance through would reveal anything helpful, even if she was there.

If? But she had to be; it was the only reasonable place left, I told myself, as I crossed to the drive. I walked sharply, skirting the yard and stables, to a side door leading into the conservatory. The lock was shaky there, as I knew from experience. A good rattle would move it, and once in I could force my way through the dining-room into the hall.

The business of entering was quite simple, and once in the hall I paused for a moment or two, listening and trying to ease my tensed up nerves. How silent the house was; no sign or sound of movement except the rhythmic ticking of the old grandfather clock near the foot of the stairs. The stone corridors, divested of their newly-acquired and brief luxury, seemed curiously, eerily deserted. No breath of wind or life stirred the brooding shadows of falling evening, and yet the very quietness held a waiting, watchful quality, as though ghosts of the past lurked in every corner and doorway, aware of my presence yet uncaring of what I found there.

I went on, looking into each room in turn, even the drawing-room, where the green twilight struck weirdly through the great window across the mocking, pale countenance of Isabella, staring contemptuously from its frame. Once, after searching the kitchen I returned to the staircase and called softly but clearly, 'Flavia, are you there? Flavia, it's only me ... Judith.'

There was no reply. So I went on, half-running up the spiralling stairs till I reached the first landing.

It must have been instinct that sent me first to the large room overlooking the garden and hills; or perhaps merely habit, since some of my quietest, most comforting moments had been spent there with William. With my hand on the door-knob I had a second's reluctance before entering, and yet I knew in my bones something of importance waited; something to do with Flavia.

I was right. She was lying face down on the large four-poster bed—the bed that had once been mine and William's—in a spreading pool of her own blood. I went over to her and touched her on her shoulder. At first she didn't stir, and I thought she was dead. Then I realized that, though cold, she was still breathing. I took her gently by the shoulders and eased her body over towards me.

'Flavia,' I whispered, 'Flavia ... it's only me. Look at me ... please.'

Almost miraculously her large eyes opened, and never had I seen such blind misery.

'It was better this way,' she said faintly, 'much better. I didn't want his bastard, not after ... after ...' Her voice died as the slow tears welled and trickled over her cheeks.

Then I understood.

'What happened?' I couldn't help asking. 'Did you ...?'

She shook her head.

'No, not that. I suppose it was shock or ... or ...' She gave a moan of pain.

I held her close to me, gripping her hand hard. Then when the pain had gone, I eased her back.

'I'm going for help, Flavia,' I told her presently. 'You'll be all right if you just rest and stay there until I get a doctor. But you mustn't move. Understand?'

She nodded dumbly and after a few minutes seemed to settle again to sleep.

An hour later she was back at Thorncarne, with Belle fluttering and fussing round as though she was a distraught hen who'd lost and then found her only chick. When the doctor arrived he confirmed that the worst was over and that after a week's rest in bed with nothing to worry her and plenty of nourishing food, she should be fit as a fiddle again.

Well, I thought later, he was probably right. Flavia was young and strong physically. But emotionally? I doubted she'd recover so easily. My prediction was correct. In her wild, impulsive way she must have cared for the odious Leeds far more deeply than the rest of the family had imagined. When she was properly round and about again she was mostly listless and uncommunicative, pretending everything was all right but showing clearly it wasn't. In the beginning she was generally lingering about at post time hoping obviously for a note from her errant lover. At last, however as the truth sank in that she never would and that there was no way of contacting him, even if she'd a mind to, she became restless and short-tempered, forever roaming the moors or going to Penzance on any flimsy excuse.

Eventually, on Venn's suggestion, she procured a job with a milliner's in Penzance, where for a moderate salary she was taken on as a trainee in the art of hat making and also as a model in the shop for two days a week when special customers called for appointments. It was the latter proposition that tempted her to accept, and I'd no doubt that with her looks she'd prove successful.

So with Flavia's absence from Thorncarne in the daytime and Belle's increasing interference once more in the kitchen, I decided there was nothing there for me any more. Alicia's veiled hostility when she was about the house and Venn's ironic comments combined with the searching, hot look in his eyes whenever they fell on me filled me with mounting, resentful unease. I could sense danger around me and was weary of it. All I had to do then, I decided, was to choose the most propitious time for leaving, and the sooner the better. For too long the war between Gulvarrick and Thorncarne had bruised my life. In depressed moments I could see it stretching on and on, years ahead into some unhappy future when one or both places would inevitably be destroyed. Marcus and Paul were already arguing with Venn about expenditure and possible prosperity in some other line rather than cattle. Flower growing was still a priority in Marcus's head, and Paul was taken up with the idea of bees and of establishing a brew-house for mead. Meanwhile Gulvarrick, the 'white-elephant', was left on Venn's hands, and I couldn't pass it at night without a shiver and recollection of past tragedy.

So one morning at the end of May when Venn was away, I told Belle of my decision and that I had already packed to start off immediately.

Her under-jaw dropped momentarily, and I

could see at first she didn't believe me.

'Go?' she said with bemusement on her large face. 'What d'you mean? Why? *Where?'*

I didn't waste words. 'I need a change, that's why. And don't say you'll miss me, except as a spare hand with the work. Liddy can do more than she does, and your fine daughter-in-law. I owe none of you anything. Nor you me. I don't expect the wages due so that should leave no ill-feeling between us.'

'But *where* you goin'? That's what I wanter know.'

'To relations,' I told her, thinking of my father. 'I'm not entirely alone, you know.'

'No, I didn',' Belle said sullenly. 'An' et seems to me a dirty trick, when Venn's away up country messing about at them cattle shows an' such like. A whole fortnight I'll be alone here ...'

'But with Marcus and Paul and Liddy and Alicia, not to mention the men.' I reminded her calmly. 'Oh no. You won't be *alone,* Belle, especially with your precious great-aunt to weave a spell for you any time you ask.'

Belle's eyes narrowed.

'Now doan' go speakin' ill of any Ettyn, Judith,' she warned. 'Ettyns doan' tek kindly to that sort o' thing, so jus' you remember.'

'I could hardly forget,' I answered. 'And I know, too, that Ettyns are quite capable of looking after themselves.'

She was still grumbling when I left the kitchen and returned to the Barn for my shabby valise and the few things I treasured—a silk shoulder shawl from William, the broken portrait of Luzana, underclothes, two print dresses, and bits and pieces I'd collected during my stay there.

Half an hour later I set off, wearing my black dress and jet ear-rings, with my one small hat pinned to my curls to secure it safe from the summer wind. Although the day was quite warm I let the tartan cape fall loosely from my shoulders to save carrying it, and when I walked through the field gate to the lane there was no one to wave or wish me goodbye. I did not look back, nor did I glance towards Gulvarrick as I passed; I went straight ahead, chin up, strong with pride and defiance, although if I'd let it my heart would have ached.

In less than an hour I'd reached Penzance, and for the first time true realization of my actions registered. I had no idea of my way or destination from there, or what work lay ahead of me. So I rested for a moment or two on a seat overlooking the harbour towards the Mount and Marazion, with my glance instinctively turning to Newlyn harbour. Sails were thick and bright under the morning sun, and I knew presently the long-liners would be setting out for a day and night's fishing, perhaps more.

A merchant vessel or two were also anchored there, and the smell of brine was driven from the sea, salty and fresh. A feeling of strange, half-forgotten familiarity crept through me. It seemed then that the recent months and years must have been some kind of dream and that I was waking at last from the nightmare of Matt's desertion to reality. It could not be true surely, that I'd actually married Sarne, borne his child and then lost them both in such a brief time, or that Venn Ettyn for one moment had made me forget my allegiance to the first and only man I'd ever truly loved, Matt Thomas?

And yet it was. In a sense I was a widow for a second time, and the future, though exciting, held for me a sudden qualm of fear.

I got up from my seat automatically and walked up Market Jew Street towards the town centre. It was then, halfway up, I saw the hoarding on a granite wall. With my breath quickening I read it twice before accepting the evidence of my eyes.

MOODY AND HACKETT'S THEATRE, the print ran; and underneath:

Two theatrical performances by the famous company will be given daily during the first week of June at Dingley's Hall, Hayle. Five to seven o'clock, and eight to nine, excepting Sunday. Do not miss the chance to see first rate shows of splendid drama and hair-raising excitement.

Moody and Hackett's.

My heart slowed and missed a beat before the true import of the words sank in, leaving but one thought in my mind. *My father.*

I realized then there was only one thing to do, and without questioning the wisdom of it, I set about finding transport. I knew I could have walked, if necessary, but I was already tired and wanted to look my best on arrival.

Luckily I found a farmer driving his cart back to the town following market. He was not averse to accepting my company, especially when he saw the coin in my hand. So presently we were jogging along the road past the wide estuary of the river, glistening bright as glass under the sun, facing the old church spire of Lelant church over the water.

I was aware of him turning to look at me once or twice, intrigued possibly by my appearance and unwillingness to talk. It was a silent drive, but the silence filled me with such a wild, anticipatory flood of emotion that it seemed, briefly, all my life I had been waiting for the moment ahead, when I was to face, hopefully, with the one being I'd dreamed about so often when I was a child.

CHAPTER 26

Dingley's Hall stood beyond the Town Square up a side street of commercial and private dwellings which, in spite of the sunlight, had a rather drab appearance. The building itself was larger than most, set back between a public house, The Pirate's Rest, and a patch of waste-ground joining a cobbler's. Hoardings and advertisements were plastered above the entrance, and activity was going on round the carts and vans huddled on the dreary-looking stretch of yellowed grass. Already a small group of sightseers had gathered to watch what was happening. There was a good deal of shouting and banging as props were unloaded and carried laboriously to the back of the building. My heart sank a little. I'd expected something more glamorous. But of course industry, not glamour, was Hayle's main characteristic. The large foundry had brought considerable employment to the district, and the only trade of a more adventurous type was shipping, due to Penzance's safe harbour on a dangerous and treacherous coast.

As I stood tentatively for a few moments, wondering how best to present myself, a young boy nudged me with his elbow saying, 'Go on, missis. Actress, are 'ee?'

I looked down sharply and saw a pale, thin

little face staring up, eyes alight with admiration and awe.

'Yes, yes, of course,' I lied.

'They're all roun' back theer,' he told me. 'Up an' roun', 'ee can't miss et.'

'Thank you,' I said. 'Thank you very much.'

I walked away holding my head proudly, thinking if a youngster could be so impressed I must look the part already. But when I entered the dingy hall, no one took a second glance at me, there was so much shouting and jostling and cursing interspersed with occasional laughter as the properties and crates were dumped near the cramped stage.

It was not until a stout, blowzy-looking woman with frizzed red hair bumped into me and almost knocked us both flying that I made any contact at all.

'What do you think you're doing?' she said irately when she'd picked up the scattered objects, including a cardboard crown, from the floor. 'And *who* are you anyway?'

'You don't know me,' I said quickly, 'and I'm sorry I was so clumsy. But I was wondering ...?'

'Yes?' Though she had been mollified by my apology, her voice was still sharp.

'I'd like to see the manager of the company. Do you think I could?'

She laughed ironically. 'Oh yes, love. You can *see* him, for what it's worth. But if your business is important you'd better tackle Lavinia. Lavinia Gold ... she's Will Hackett's better half, and what *she* says, goes. Take my word for it.'

‘I see. I’m ... well, thank you,’ I answered rather feebly. ‘Where can I find her?’

The woman waved her free arm towards the stage.

‘At the back ... in the wings, if you can call ’em such. More like the black hole of Calcutta, if you ask me. I’d rather work in a good tent any day. These joints are blue murder when you come to moving about. Now let me pass, love. And ... good luck to you,’ she added as I moved on. ‘You’ll need it anyways, with Lavinia as she is.’

Oh bother Lavinia, I thought, walking purposefully to the far end of the hall. I could be a match for any ill-tempered actor’s wife if I had to be, but obviously if I wanted work—*any* work with the company—it was up to me to be as agreeable as I could.

I found the all-important Miss Gold seated before a cracked mirror in a cubby-hole of a place so odorous with the smell of dirt, beer and perspiration that I held my breath for a second or two before rapping sharply on the door. Without turning she said, ‘Come on, come on. Put it down and get on with things. Then stir your stump and tidy up this stink-hole ...’

‘I’ve come to see you, Miss Gold ... Mrs Hackett,’ I said loudly and clearly. ‘I can see it’s a difficult time but it’s important.’

She swivelled round in the chair, displaying a painted, plump but lined face under a mass of brassy yellow hair. Her eyes, blued above and below, must have been beautiful once, and her features, despite the sagging flesh, were still good. I couldn't judge her figure under the gaudy wrap but guessed she was statuesque, of good build, and would be a force to reckon with under any conditions.

'Well?' she rapped out. 'What d'you want?'

'A job,' I answered. '*Any* job, if you have one.'

'Ha.' I could feel the blue orbs assessing me shrewdly before she continued, 'And what in God's name makes a girl like you want to work with *this* joint? Hey? In trouble are you? Or in hiding? On the run? Is that it? Come on, out with it. We're having no troublemakers at Moody and Hackett's. On the level we are, so just you take that in and remember.'

When I'd managed to convince her I was not a thief or a murderess, or with child, at last she said graciously, 'Well, I dunno. Maybe ...' Her voice trailed off calculatingly.

'Yes?'

'Can you act?' she asked abruptly.

Deciding it was best to be quite honest from the start, I answered, 'I never have, not professionally. But when I was a child I'd read and try bits from Shakespeare. We had an old book in the attic; a Bible, too. That's how I came to read.'

'I see.' Her tones were dry.

'If you could give me a chance ...'

'Oh, the *chance* is there,' Lavinia said suddenly. 'In fact we lost an insolent baggage only yesterday. Walked out with a sailor and left us high and dry, she did, the hussy. I'm not saying we couldn't get along without the part. In fact Will was goin' to write it out for tonight—and I don't mean Will *Shakespeare* ...' She laughed shrilly at her own stupid joke. 'Anyway, we don't go in for such highbrow stuff. *Shakespeare!* My God! The gags and curses would soon be flying ... except for Bottom, of course ... the ass in the *Dream.*'

'Oh.'

'Which you'd know very well if you had any knowledge of the theatre at *all,*' she told me witheringly. 'Still, anyone with an ounce of commonsense could master *this* role, I reckon. Not much; just a line or two, with a few bobbings in and out. A maidservant ... that's the character.'

'It would suit me,' I remarked.

'Would it? I'm not so sure. You've got a cool, haughty look about you, and we've no room for any of that here. I'm the only one allowed airs and graces in this set-up. What I say, goes. D'you understand?'

'Perfectly,' I assured her.

'Hmm. Very well then. Mind you, don't expect high wages ... Your keep will take most of that. And, of course, I'll have to ask Will, Mr Hackett. Mr Hackett's owner of the company since Fred Moody's death last year, with me as partner naturally, being his wife.'

'Naturally,' I echoed.

So a little later I was pushed into an ugly, dark grey dress with a mob cap on my head, and a paper was put into my hand with my lines in the play written on it. By then the two little cubby-holes on either side of the stage were seething with activity. Boxes were still being unpacked and bits of furniture being carried out to the 'set', as they called it, while the stage manager, perspiring and grumbling, was yelling at the top of his voice for this and that to be changed, and what did they think they were doing, with the performance to start in less than an hour?

Less than an hour? My heart sank as I studied my short script. Although my entrance and exit were marked I wondered desperately how I was going to judge the times correctly without a rehearsal.

'You'll have to use your "common",' Lavinia told me cryptically. 'There's not much light in the miserable place, but get the hang of the thing into your head now. Remember, you're my *maid.* See? And I'm the faithless wife whose husband returns to the castle when she's a lover with her. Frank Wingsley plays the lover, young Lord Tarren. There he is, that tall fellow with the yellow hair.'

Looking across the stage I saw a good-looking man who could easily have been Lavinia's grandson.

'Oh. I see,' I said lamely.

'Yes. Well ... there's no need to go on "seeing",' she retorted tartly. 'Just keep your eyes to yourself, now my girl. Moody and Hackett's doesn't allow flirting around among the cast. Bad for morale. *Now.* Listen to me, and listen hard or you'll be out on your ear. When you rush in—it will be from the other side—you'll have to look scared. Scared and as simple as they come. "Oh, my lady!" you'll gasp. "My lady ... my lady ... we're undone. He's *here ...!*" '

'I tear myself from my lover's arms then, stagger a little and ask breathlessly, "Who's here? Tell me, girl." I grasp you by the shoulders and it's then you flinch and wring your hands. "Your husband," you cry, "Sir Alfred ..." '

'After that I shriek to you to delay him, and you rush off, while I hide my lover in a wardrobe.' She paused a moment, then said, 'Got it?'

'I'll do my best,' I told her. 'So long as I know which side to come from ...'

'Over there, of *course* ... the way you go off. Will will be waiting to dash on a moment later for the grand finale when he stabs Lord Tarren, so don't get in his way, for God's sake.'

'Will?'

'Hackett, of course. My husband. He should've seen you, as I said before I took you on, but ...' her mouth and eyes narrowed perceptibly, 'he had other business. So I've got to take you on my own responsibility. Oh, and that reminds me—push your hair back.'

'My hair?'

'That's right. All of it ... Shove it under your cap, so no one can go thinking you're some paramour or other come wandering where she shouldn't. Besides, *I'm* the *femme fatale,* remember, and no one's eyes are going to stray from me for *one* moment. If that happens you're out. So don't try any sly tricks of stealing my thunder.'

After a few more promises and an injunction to get myself behind the stage and see Lily made me as plain as she could, Lavinia dismissed me with a wave of her hand to go in search, presumably, of her missing husband Will Hackett.

I turned towards a gap in the curtains leading backstage, but before I'd penetrated the narrow, dark space the fair-haired young man who was to play Lord Tarren appeared suddenly from the side entrance. He was wearing yellow breeches and a canary-coloured coat with a cravat.

'Hello,' he said, with his blue eyes upon me appraisingly. 'What have we here? And where are those gorgeous curls I noted but a few moments ago?'

He pulled my cap off and laughed. I snatched it back from him.

'If you don't *mind,'* I said caustically. 'Lavinia, Miss Gold, has just offered me a part, and as I want it I intend to look just as she wishes.'

He shrugged. 'Oho! I *thought* so. And so you willingly obliged. Well ... maybe it's for the best. Our esteemed miss *is* getting rather long in the tooth, and apart from her crush on me, she undoubtedly wants to make sure her errant husband is kept well and truly to heel. So act your part, sweet nymph ...' with a wave of his hand, 'no doubt we'll meet some other time when the lady can be her own fair self.'

He ambled away with the cocksure swagger of a handsome young gallant who was already certain of future conquest. At that moment I felt only contempt for his attitude, and a dull mounting anger.

Lily was busy in a cubby-hole behind the stage, and I discovered she was the same woman who'd first directed me for my interview with Lavinia. When I explained what Miss Gold wanted she proceeded to work quickly with make-up, aided only by an oil lamp flickering from the draught caused by a hole in the roof. The air was close and stuffy with the odour of grease paint and perspiration. But even under such conditions it wasn't too difficult for her to make me sufficiently plain and unattractive.

'There,' she said appreciatively, when the task was finished, 'that'll please our Lavinia. Now all you have to do, dear, is to learn your lines, and remember, if you forget I'll hiss loud enough from the wings for you to hear. Just act simple-like but dramatic enough, and everything will be all right.'

By then I was getting nervous. It wasn't easy to find a spot with sufficient light for me to read my brief script, and already chairs were being pushed closely together in rows across the floor of the hall. Two or three curious sightseers were lingering at the far end, ready to grab front-line seats when word was given, and I could hear a male voice outside shouting 'Moody and Hackett's! Get your tickets now and have the thrill of your lives watching the celebrated actress Lavinia Gold, and William Hackett himself, in the tragic drama of *Love in Despair*. Come on, come on ... before all seats are gone ...'

On and on it went, while my palms and back grew rigid and damp with apprehension. There was a lot of murmuring and confusion as the small cast took their places in the improvised wings.

When the curtain went up with a rattle, I felt a touch on my shoulder and heard a voice saying quietly in my ear, emitting the heavy smell of spirits. 'Aside, girl, for my first entrance ...'

I stepped back, involuntarily glancing up. My pulses quickened as my eyes in the blue light met his.

He had an aquiline face with high cheekbones, and his eyes were faintly tilted, holding a green tint. The auburn hair was greying at the temples, and he carried a flask in his hand.

In those few electric seconds an awareness—an intuitive recognition—passed between us, whether conscious on his part I didn't know. But my legs were already trembling when his fine voice rang across the stage, commanding instant applause.

Drunkard he might be, I admitted, but he was also something else, far more important. A fine actor. And not only that. I had found my father.

CHAPTER 27

My début as an actress that first night with Moody and Hackett's travelling theatre company is like a dream in my mind now. I remember being half-pushed on to the stage by Lily in the last act and an awful moment of apprehension when my mouth dried up before I managed to gasp out, 'Oh my lady, we're undone. He's *here* ...' followed by strong hands digging into my shoulders as Lavinia cried melodramatically, 'Who's here? Tell me, girl ...'

'Sir Alfred, your husband,' I said. 'Sir Alfred.'

'Shut up,' she hissed in my ear, then very clearly, clear enough for any Sir Alfred to hear, 'Go ... go ... delay him somehow ...'

I didn't wait to be told a second time but scurried off, almost knocking over Will Hackett standing in the wings.

'Not bad,' Lily said afterwards, 'but you changed the lines. There's only *one* Sir Alfred. And you say "your husband" first. Still, it don't really matter, but Lavinia's very strict over words. And another thing ...'

She eyed me shrewdly.

'Yes?'

'You let your cap slip. Don't you go letting Frank see you that way ... Frank Wingsley. Lavinia and him are very close—her private property you might say—and she wouldn't take kindly to a younger woman stepping in.'

'She's got a husband, hasn't she?' I remarked. 'And Frank's so *young*. Surely ...'

'That's the point. Don't talk so soft,' Lily interrupted cuttingly. 'Our Lavinia was quite a beauty in her day, and it goes hard with a woman like her when the wrinkles and fat creep up on her. Don't let her hear you call him Frank either. *Mister.* It's Mister Wingsley where you're concerned. As for Will, her husband ...'

She shrugged.

'Yes? What about him?' I asked more sharply than I'd intended.

'He's a good sort. Willing to overlook Lavinia's little ways. Besides he's got what you could call compensations.'

'Meaning?'

She winked and lifted one hand to her lips significantly.

'The bottle. Could have bin a fine fine actor if he'd given his whole heart to it, but I reckon being married to 'Vinia stopped all that. Always the limelight, that's her; although, of course, she makes good use of what he can give ... his name and all that. In the old days long before Moody died they was an up and coming company. Even had a show near Lunnon at one time. Yes, I sometimes think, it was a pity he ever took up with her. But don't you let on, mind, or I'll scrag your hair out.'

I laughed. 'I'm not a fool. Why would I?'

The words came out unthinkingly, but inwardly I was harking back to childhood days, remembering my grandmother's bitter words and picturing my mother as she must have been when she first met my father—fresh complexioned, raven-haired, with dark-fringed Celtic eyes and a wild heart beating beneath her white breasts with love for William Hackett.

Oh yes, I was sure of it: Will was my errant father. I knew it, as I'd known it when my inner voice had told me of mysterious, unknown events about to change the day's routine.

I said nothing to Lily though, knowing that some day, quite soon perhaps, proof would come and the pattern emerge naturally so Will and I could face each other with only the truth between us.

Another hour passed before the show ended and Lavinia found time to give me a word.

I hoped for encouragement but got none.

'You'll pass,' she said cryptically, 'if you pull your socks up and try to get the words right. My God, it's not *much* to ask. And your cap! Didn't I tell you to keep it straight on where it should be, with no hair showing?'

'It slipped,' I told her.

'Then see it doesn't happen again or you're fired. And your skin was wrong. See Lily uses more yellow on you, and a few spots here an' there would give character. *Character!* That's what's needed, see? We're a *theatre* company, and Moody and Hackett's hasn't room for amateurs. *Room.* Ah, that reminds me—you'll be sharing a bed with Lily while you're with us. So don't go getting any fine ideas of having a place to yourself. You're lucky to be with us at all, let me tell you, and finances only just cover. That's what you've got to accept if you follow the finest profession in the world.'

After this tedious and really rather laughable oration, Lavinia turned away, stared at herself through a chipped mirror and proceeded to slap and dab cream over her face with a vigour that told me she was none too pleased. Then I went in search of Lily, wondering if she'd heard the news of sharing her bed and thinking I might possibly tell her that as I was used to camping out, I'd take a rug or something and sleep under the trees.

But she'd have none of it.

'If Lavinia says you share with me, that's what you'll do,' she told me. 'Hey, come on, love, they're stinking, stuffy holes, these digs, sometimes. But maybe we'll have luck this time. And if I snore, just you give me a dig and I won't complain.'

Lily's description of stinking stuffiness proved to be true, and her snoring was awful. Once in the night I got up and tried to push the small window open, but obviously it hadn't been moved for years. The air was heavy with the lingering aroma of stale, sweaty bodies mingled with camphor and alcohol. What furniture there was was so cumbrous and worm-ridden with age I had the absurd notion at one time that murky secrets of some former tragedy could easily be hidden behind the door of the vast wardrobe. Only a threadbare mat lay alongside the bed, leaving the stained, shabby oilcloth bare.

After a poor night's sleep I was thankful to get up and dress, though Lily woke irritably, enquiring what the hell I was doing when breakfast in the parlour wouldn't be ready till nine.

'You sleep on,' I said. 'I'm going for a stroll.'

Mumbling something unintelligible, she turned over on her stout side and was already snoring when I opened the door as quietly as I could and went downstairs.

The parlour, I supposed, led off the cramped passage on the left. There was a faded lithograph of Queen Victoria hanging in the hall and a few coats suspended on a peg, and the flagged floor obviously hadn't been swept yet. But as the door was slightly ajar a drift of wind penetrated the stuffy interior, and I could hear the mumbled sound of voices and pottery clinking from the other end of the corridor.

With great relief I slipped outside into the narrow street, making my way eventually to the harbour.

The air was still cool, holding the salty sweetness so poignantly reminiscent of the past. I recalled the day following my grandmother's death when Matt had so valiantly rescued me from the louts of drunken seamen and swept me into marriage. Looking across the bay to the west I could glimpse the dark shape of a mine-stack on the distant headland of Pedninta and could visualize only a few miles beyond the jutting arm of rock my birth place, Port Einack, with its twisting streets and fishing fleet.

Although much of my youth had been grim, I realized with a flood of memories, there had been merriment as well; hours when the children of the town had crowded, singing, into the seining boats as they were pushed and pulled across the sands to the water for launching. Once out at sea the fishermen had had their own fishing 'stems' marked by poles on shore, a necessary arrangement to prevent overcrowding at one spot when the school of pilchards was sighted.

And what excitement when the huer's trumpet rang loud and clear through the summer air with his cry of 'Heva, heva!' as the vast crowd of fish moved in a reddish cloud under the surface of the calm Atlantic.

For that brief interval I was a child again and could almost hear my fierce old grandmother's voice saying gruffly, 'Go on girl, join 'em. Have your bit o' fun wi' the rest. 'Tedn' much of et here for 'ee.'

I smiled, thinking to myself how often a soft heart could beat beneath a rough exterior. In her way, I knew she'd cared ... perhaps even loved me.

Now there was no one.

Abruptly I pulled myself from the past to the present. There was no point in looking back, especially at such an hour when breakfast would soon be waiting, followed by a morning's rehearsal in the stuffy hall.

Lavinia had insisted on this the night before, telling me I must be more careful of my position off-stage, as I'd almost knocked poor William out before his most important entrance.

Poor William.

Yes. Poor, I'd thought, sympathizing with him for being married to Lavinia and hoping, perhaps stupidly, that it might give him a little warmth to find he had a daughter.

If. A small word but it meant so much. Lavinia obviously would do everything to discredit such a tenuous and unlikely relationship. But I knew that if I was given the chance of getting to know him, of our having a few precious minutes alone together, the unknown bond must surely prove stronger than a jealous woman's possessiveness. And anyway, I told myself reasoning as I walked back to the dismal lodgings, Lavinia's real interest was the young dandy, her stage lover, rather than her husband. So perhaps a private meeting with Will Hackett would not be too difficult, providing I bided my time and chose the moment wisely.

Lily was already seated at breakfast with Charlie, the stage hand, when I went into the musty parlour. The lace curtains were grimy where the yellow blinds had been pulled up, and a tired aspidistra in an ugly china pot strained its flat, dejected leaves against the glass. Lily, in what morning light there was, looked puffy-eyed and overblown, with too much paint on her face. Charlie, who was a balding man about forty, had his eyes avariciously on his plate and was clearly conscious only of food.

The meal itself was plentiful but not to my liking; strong tea with a little milk, whey, followed by boiled fish that smelt over strong and a dish of 'roast' that the landlady told us was quite a delicacy.

My stomach lurched because I guessed from the look of it, and its odour, that it could well be young 'saul' or seal, which revolted me. I'd always loved the gentle creatures and in spare moments as a youngster had frequently wandered to Clasna Cove where many of them bred and bore their young. Sometimes I'd sung to them, and they'd had no fear but stared doe-eyed only a few yards from the rock where I perched. So when I pushed the dish away something must have shown on my face.

'What's the matter?' Lily queried sharply. 'Not sick are you? Can't afford sickness here. Lavinia'll never have that.'

'I'm all right, just not hungry,' I answered.

She shrugged. 'That being the case I'll get on with it then. What about you, Charlie?'

Charlie glanced up and took the portion left when Lily had refilled her plate.

'I think you're a bit soft,' she continued between her munching. 'You'll be hungry afore the morning's over, and weak stomachs don't make for good acting. That's what Lavinia says, and I reckon she's right.'

Realizing she could be, I managed to stuff a few pieces of bread and fat—it could hardly be called butter—into my mouth. The bread was stale, and the fat strong. But after two mugs of the steaming tea I felt fortified and ready for the morning's work.

Later, when the company had gathered for rehearsal, at the first opportunity my eyes strayed automatically towards William Hackett. Even before the first act started he was already imbibing from his flask, but he was apparently so used to alcohol it no longer obviously affected him, except for an occasional faint stagger in his walk. He had a fine voice, as I remembered from my first visit to the players with Matt, and there was something tragic and lonely in his eyes, a kind of hunger that filled me with pity. I wondered if perhaps he had really loved my mother or if it was just that he'd had so much experience of the world he'd wearied of it because there was nothing else for him to savour.

He turned at one time, as if impelled, to glance at me, and for a second the arm with the flask fell to his side. Our eyes met. I fancied I saw him flinch. Then it was over. He looked away, straightened up and marched towards the wings. At the same moment I heard a voice behind me saying, 'Interested, are you, in that old reprobate?'

I walked round and saw Lavinia's handsome protegée and stage lover staring down at me with something warm and intimidating in his eyes, which both annoyed and irritated me. I knew it so well, that certain look men have for women—*any* woman of looks and sexual appeal.

'I don't know what you mean,' I said coldly. 'So please let me pass. I've my lines to go through.'

'Dear, dear!' he tut-tutted. 'Such vast, lengthy lines, too.' Suddenly he started to laugh. 'Don't try your innocent airs on me, my dear. They won't work, I assure you. I know women too well.'

I was about to lift my head and haughtily pass by when a sly hand touched my waist and travelled upwards to one breast, which he squeezed subtly yet firmly like some delectable fruit ripe for bursting.

I pulled myself away savagely.

'If you do that again,' I hissed fiercely, with the hot blood mounting my cheeks, 'I'll tear your eyes out.'

His jaw dropped and he was still staring at me as I marched back-stage. *That* will teach him, I thought triumphantly. He'll know better in future.

But I guessed, all the same, I'd made an enemy. Lavinia was waiting for me in her cubby-hole.

'Where've you been?' she asked suspiciously. 'You should have been prompt. You've a good lot to learn, my girl, before the afternoon's performance. Last night you muddled through, but it was only a muddle, mind you. You've got to be sharper on the up-take and know the exact moment to be ready.'

I assured her I'd do my best, and five minutes later the tiring business of rehearsing began.

The day's pattern was the same during the whole of that week until Saturday, when three performances were given; one in the morning and two in the afternoon.

If Lavinia had nothing to grumble about, she searched round and soon found a reason, and all the time there was a watchful, suspicious glint in her eyes whenever she looked at me. I realized it was due to my looks and youth, and although her possessiveness was chiefly concentrated towards Frank Wingsley, she also resented any contact between myself and Will Hackett. Her handsome stage lover made no further advances to me—publicly. But if we passed in a crowd or in the darkness of the wings his hand would touch me furtively where it shouldn't have, and being tired through the week's work and tension, I'd have difficulty in checking a shout or scream.

But somehow I managed to keep things on a more-or-less even keel, and at the end of the matinee that last day, Will said with a smile, when Lavinia was out of ear-shot, 'You've done well, my dear. You have the makings of a fine actress.'

'Thank you,' I answered, with my pulse quickening. 'It's good of you to say so.'

There was so much I wanted to say to him then; questions, and matters concerning my background ... leading to the one, final issue between us that might prove my secret hopes. But just as he was continuing, 'I hear you were born not far from here. Is that true ...?' Lavinia appeared on the scene.

'Will,' she cried in high-pitched tones, 'you might see that comp'ny get on with things. Charlie's a real pain-in-the-neck these days, and with all the packing up later and Corpus Christi ahead ... Hey! You've not been at the bottle already have you?'

What he answered I didn't hear. Only one thought properly registered—something in the rush and flurry of my début as an actress I'd forgotten, or rather pushed aside—that Moody and Hackett's was to be one of the Main attractions of the great fair which was held at Alverton thoroughfare, Penzance. Lily had told me tents would be put up in a field for the company to sleep in, with a large one erected for the actual performances. I'd thought it all sounded rather exciting and picturesque when I'd first heard, but the true implication of the event hadn't properly sunk into my head until Lavinia's sharp reminder.

Suddenly I was nervous. Would I be recognized? Would anyone from Thorncarne be there? Venn perhaps? But no. Venn would probably still be away up country, and I doubted Belle would have the energy to get there. In any case, with my sallow make-up and the spots, and my hair pushed away under the ugly cap, probably no one would notice me, especially as I was on the stage for such a short time.

It was all fuss, flurry, hard work, sweat and swearing following the farewell show at Hayle that evening. Later there was no time even for any refreshment except a mug of beer or a strong cup of tea. Lavinia was a screaming fury most of the time, bullying the cast unmercifully, including Will, who at an opportune moment retreated quietly into a corner for fortification from his flask. At one point I made an attempt to join him, but was spotted by Miss Gold, who yanked me back by the neck of my dress to help with the packing.

'No one idles here ...' she shouted. '*No one,* d'you hear? We've a hell of a lot to get through before midnight, and this scenery and props don't move themselves. We're a *team*, understand? You included, and if you don't like it, get out. There are plenty of girls with more talent than you who'd give their eyes for a chance with Moody and Hackett's.'

The problem, I gathered later, was to get to Alverton and more or less sorted out before Sunday morning, since Sunday had such a deep significance for the natives; moreover, Lavinia pointed out, Moody and Hackett's had its good name to keep up in religious circles. Actually I didn't believe she cared a fig for the religious aspect: it was chiefly a matter of obtaining the best site on the field before anyone else got there first. Since the actual fair didn't start until the Wednesday I didn't see what the great rush was about.

I hadn't anticipated that two days were needed in order to get the tents set up and rehearsals under way again. Besides the play I was in, a new one was being performed, which meant lines had to be learned quickly to be perfected for the opening of the fair. In this—*The Tragic Bride*—I was grudgingly allowed to be a gypsy girl who foretold disaster, though Lavinia informed me my skin was to be dyed brown and my hair, which should be black, hidden away again under a scarf.

I nearly shouted at her, 'Why? *Why?* Gypsies aren't all ugly? Why've I got to look drab and dowdy all the time?' But I had sufficient self-control to keep the hot words back. I *knew* Lavinia was growing more jealous every day.

That night, after the cramped journey in a cart, followed by others containing scenery and props, I was once more made to share sleeping quarters with Lily in a tent too small for comfort. At least I'd been able to see a chink of starlight through the flap which moved intermittently in the soft night wind. When Lily was snoring placidly and heavily beside me, I released myself from the pressure of her body, easing away gently to the furthest point possible where the tarpaulin was pegged to the grass.

The air drifted cool and sweet from outside, and as my nerves and limbs relaxed I was caught up once more into a drift of memories which gradually closed over me like the rhythmic flowing and ebbing of a calm tide.

My last thoughts before I slept were of Matt and Venn, who gradually, as I lost consciousness, became fused into one.

When I woke it was daylight, and from somewhere in the town I could hear the sound of distant church bells.

Sunday. A day of rest for the townspeople. But I guessed there would be little for me. And there wasn't.

CHAPTER 28

The fair lasted four days, and all that time I saw no one I knew. There was little time or chance for it anyway, with the bustle and jostling of the crowds round the side-shows and boxing booths, roundabouts, menageries and various stannins. Every afternoon and evening the theatre was packed and when the last show was over heavy business was still being done round the stalls where gingerbread, shellfish and cakes of every kind were sold, including hard-boiled sweets and even home-brewed beer. The thoroughfare was almost completely blocked by stannins on either side of the main street, and drunkenness following the festivities was not only accepted as a natural outcome of the convivial occasion but expected. In the morning, I'd heard, it was not unusual for intoxicated bodies to be found lying in a helpless condition on the pavement.

Throughout this confusion, Lavinia proved herself the martinet and 'real trooper' as characteristic of one born and bred to the theatrical profession. Never once did her energy flag or her discipline let up. At that time I admired her, though with admiration was a fierce dislike of her attitude to Will. She obviously despised his weak qualities—most of all his addiction to drink—and no longer noticed his innate sensitivity and artistic worth.

There were times when I could have shrieked at her, Leave him alone, can't you? He's worth two of you any day. But somehow I restrained myself, knowing I must keep my hot temper in check until the moment came for me to ask, 'Look at me please, Will Hackett, do I remind you of anyone? Do you think it possible I could be your daughter?'

I rehearsed the scene many times to myself when I was not too weary to concentrate. At other moments when I lay wakeful in the small tent, too tired at first to sleep, my mind would wander from Will to the past again, and in my imagination I'd be lying in Matt's arms, though the eyes staring down at me before sleep properly came would be Venn's.

It was all very confusing. I was grateful for the chance Lavinia had given me with the company, but as the week drew to its close a good deal of the glamour and excitement of acting had already faded for me and nostalgia swept through me when I recalled the country sounds and scents of Gulvarrick and Thorncarne, but most of all, further back, of days when I stood at the door of my grandmother's house in Port Einack waiting for Cap'n Matt to return.

These moments of retrospection were few, of course, in the rush of Corpus Christi; and generally, after a brief pause, on the fringe of the crowds I'd be aware of someone watching me, and on turning would be discomforted to see Frank Wingsley staring at me from a few yards away. His glance was always the same, reflective and desirous, mingled with something else—hate. And as I walked away I'd wonder with a stab of unhappiness if I'd ever be free of the jealousy of others.

Will, though, was different. In sober periods his green eyes would stray to my face intuitively, and I'd try desperately to convey a message—*the* message, and questions I had no chance to put, simply because of Lavinia's constant watchfulness.

Then, on the last day, Saturday, following the early performance, when Lavinia was closeted in a private session with her paramour, I wandered to the edge of the fair-ground, Plen-an-Gwarry, for a few moments of silence and peace. The afternoon had been hot, but through a gap in the hedgerows the air blew with sudden freshness from the sea, stirring the grass and bushes, and shivering the petals of pink dog-roses in their glossy foliage. Sadness engulfed me; the sadness born of realizing just for those short, few minutes the beauty and quiet of nature. I heard no one approaching until a voice behind me said quite close to my ear, 'Pleasant, isn't it, to get away? A rowdy business, acting.'

I looked round sharply and to my amazement saw Will Hackett standing there, still in his fancy theatrical attire.

I gasped.

'I didn't hear you. I thought I was ...'

'Alone? Yes. But no one's alone here, my dear. There are eyes everywhere watching us, didn't you know?'

I shook my head.

A faint smile tilted his lips, a smile I seemed

to know from very far away—almost in another life—unless I'd seen it occasionally through the glass, on my own mouth.

'Then why are you here?' I asked.

'Ah.'

Suddenly he started to cough, and when he put a handkerchief to his lips I saw with horror that it was faintly stained with blood. I lifted my arms ineffectually in a motion to help, but he waved them away and presently he'd recovered.

'I must apologize,' he said as the natural colour returned to his face. 'Just a touch of asthma or a summer cold maybe. I've suffered this way for many years, which is why I'm rather a slave, you could say, to my fortifier, the flask.'

He took it from a pocket and quaffed some down. After that he looked better, though the shock and worry still remained with me.

'Now,' he said, while I was wondering how to broach the subject that had been on my mind for so long, 'there is something I should have spoken about before this, but as you know circumstances aren't easy.'

'No.'

'When I first saw you,' he went on, '—and you must forgive me or at least understand why I have to speak so bluntly and quickly—you reminded me of a ... a person I knew very well in the past. A girl.'

'Yes.'

'I see,' he glanced away before continuing, 'you've a quick mind and have already been putting things together, I suppose?'

His eyes now had a tortured yet appealing look in them. I wanted to comfort him, to rush into his arms and lay my head against his breast, but a trembling deep shyness kept me back. The pause between us seemed interminably long before he took a step forward, placed two hands on my shoulders and asked quietly, 'Where were you born, Judith? And what was your mother's name?'

With my eyes steadfast on his own golden ones I replied, 'My mother was a fisherman's daughter, and she died when I was born. I never knew my father or where he came from. My grandmother brought me up, and then ...'

My voice faltered as I remembered Matt. But it was not Matt who brought the lump to my throat. I was aware only that the moment of truth had at last arrived. In a moment I would *know*.

Then, before he could properly speak, something terrible happened. Immersed as we'd been in each other and the emotional significance of that short confrontation, neither of us had heard footsteps approaching over the soft grass behind us.

Just three words had left Will's lips—'Judith, I'm your ...' before Lavinia's voice, strident with fury, shattered the air. Her hard hand struck my cheek as she shouted, 'You whore! You lying little cheat. Get out! Get out! Do you hear ... and never show your face again or I'll *kill* you ...'

She was breathing heavily. Her face was deep

red, the colour of beetroot.

With my palm to my bruised cheek I said coldly, 'You don't understand. Will's my ...'

'Your lover, you lusting slut. I know, I know ... so don't try any games with me ...'

She broke off, struggling for her composure, and it was then that something else far more dreadful shocked us into silence, a terrible rasping cough that broke from Will's throat with a stream of bright blood staining his cravat and the yellowing grass at his feet. I rushed to his aid as he fell, but Lavinia pushed me away roughly.

'Get away, you strumpet. Get Charlie ... or a doctor—a vet would do, from the menagerie. Fetch him ...'

I turned to go, but in the brief instant before I left I knew it was no use. As the coughing died Will's eyes gave me one long significant look, as though all the life left in him was concentrated and held there, speaking the one thing that had been secret for half his life. Then his head fell back and I knew he was dead.

I didn't appear at the show that night. Whether or not the performance was given I didn't know. Shortly after my father's body was carried away I walked automatically from the fair in a numbed kind of dream, too shocked still to grieve or to make any kind of plans. I had none of my belongings with me, nor did I care. It was merely through instinct that I found myself eventually at the Fiddler's Arms, and when I asked for Nancy I was told by the pert barmaid she had died the previous month.

Still dazed and only half-comprehending, I took the road leading out of Penzance towards Newlyn and found there a granite house with a familiar type of notice in the window, which read 'Boarders and Sea-faring Gentlemen Welcome'.

I felt my pocket in a daze and found there a few coins which I guessed would see me through two or three days. Afterwards? But I was still too exhausted by tragic events to visualize further than that night.

I knocked on the door, and presently it was opened by a buxom, kindly-looking woman who seemed at first concerned at my lack of luggage or any credentials.

'Tedn' really a place for young women on their own,' she said doubtfully. 'An' you do look real done up, that's for sure.'

'I'm tired,' I admitted. 'I've been with the theatre ... at Corpus Christi.'

'Oh. One of *them.*' Her voice was more than ever doubtful.

'Not any more,' I told her. 'The work didn't suit me.'

'I see. So you be lookin' for work.'

'I will be,' I told her, 'in a few days. I can pay you till then.'

From her face I could see a plan was already brewing in her mind, and was not surprised when she said suddenly, 'Oh well then, you'd better come in. There's a room vacant, as it happens ... till next week, mind, when a ship calls. As for work?! 'Tedn' all that hard to get a job here. Maybe I can think o' somethin' myself when I give me mind to it.'

And so it was that I found myself once more in the environment I'd been born to, without husband, protector, wealth or any real friend in the world; not even the portrait of Luzana to sustain me. But it was only the next day, when I woke to the sound of ship's sirens in the harbour and the chatter of men below, that the ironic truth really registered. Since my early youth I'd been day-dreaming and searching for the key to my parentage. Now, when at last I'd found my own father, it was through me he'd died. If I hadn't forced my way into Moody and Hackett's, there'd never have been that ghastly, fatal scene in the field and even now he could have been with his company preparing for the next show.

Everywhere I went, I thought with a stab of melodramatic self-pity, I seemed to bring tragedy and unhappiness—to William, to Sarne, to Venn who in his bitterness had married the scheming Alicia, and now to my father.

I got up with a feeling of dejection and put on my corsets, underclothes and cotton dress, wondering how I was going to explain to my new landlady my lack of clothes or luggage. As things turned out I didn't have to.

'You said you was with the players,' she remarked with a sidelong glance over the tea-pot half an hour later. 'An' though I've learned not to be too pryin'—wouldn't be to my advantage—it's clear to me you didn' leave 'em in good feelin'. You, was et? Or them? You'd better out wi' it, midear. Ef there's anyone likely to come makin' trouble I should know of et. This is a respectable place, an' I don't want any bickerin' with the law ... *or* thievin' vagabonds thumpin' my door down.'

I laughed bitterly.

'You needn't worry about that. We disagreed on a personal matter, that's all. My father died suddenly, and after that there was nothing for me.'

She raised her eyebrows.

'Oh! Your *father.* Actor, was he?'

'Yes. A very good one, if he'd had a chance.'

'Hmmn! I did think you had an air about you,' she said reflectively, 'when I first seed you standin' there at the door last night. The trouble is, that work I was tellin' you of ... It wouldn't do for 'ee after all, I'm thinkin'. The work here's hard; no prancin' or fancy airs wanted, just a bright smile now an' then an' a quick hand at cookin' an' with the scrubbin' brush. I'm a widow, you see, girl, an' can't afford to dole out charity ...'

'Do you think I'd expect it?' I queried quickly. 'I'm a working woman ... always have been. Until my husband left me and went away to sea I'd helped my grandmother in Port Einack run a boarding house for sea-faring gentlemen just like this ... only rougher and with less room. After that ... well, it doesn't matter. I've no references, of course, but I can assure you I'm no criminal. The one friend I had in Penzance, Nancy Renalden, who'd have spoken up for me, died recently, but her son Ebenezer would tell you that I worked for a time at the

Fiddler's Arms, and there were no complaints, so ...'

'That's enough. That's good enough for me, midear,' the woman interrupted quickly. 'Any friend of Nancy's be a friend of mine, an' I don't doubt 'ee at all. As for work ...' she eyed me with renewed astonishment, 'to think of et ... that you was born to the trade, so to speak. What I can't understand is ...'

'There's a lot you wouldn't understand about me,' I interrupted, 'and things I prefer to keep to myself, if you don't mind. *Personal* things.'

'Oh. I see.'

Her mouth tightened momentarily, then suddenly she smiled.

'Very well, I won't be pokin' into business that don't concern me. If it's all right with you an' with me, then we can get down to things straight off. Your name is ...?'

'Judith Perryn,' I said automatically.

'An' mine's Beth ... Beth Tregurze. Run this place I have, for thirty years since Amos, my husband, died. O' course, we don't get the seamen you'd have in a place like Port Einack, but enough one way and another. And, o' course, there's generally a few visitors wantin' rooms and those interested in the fishing. Painters, too, on occasion, so I do like to have the place neat an' tidy always. No rough characters allowed. Oh no indeed.'

'I understand,' I said. 'And if you give me the job I'll do my best.'

'That's all right, dear. I b'lieve you,' she said.

When further details of wages—which were higher than I'd hoped—were settled, Beth said, eyeing me critically, 'You can start Wednesday next week, bed and board provided nat'rally. But you do need something fresh on your back, don't you? That print's shabby. Besides, it's my reputation always to have everythin' an' everyone lookin' as smart an' welcomin' as possible. Got anythin' in your pocket, have ye?'

'As I said last night, I can pay,' I told her. 'But if I've got to have clothes ...'

'Ah well, no matter. You shall have somethin' in advance,' Mrs Tregurze informed me, 'enuff to get what you do want. It'll be taken off your wages, o' course, by degrees, so you don't feel it too much. Will that suit?'

'Thank you very much,' I answered.

So it was settled. Little did I dream that in little more than a week I should see Matt again.

CHAPTER 29

My first week at Newlyn brought no surprises, and I fitted into the routine with the queer feeling of stepping back in time to an old, familiar environment, though in a different area and with boarders of a more polished type. These included a sea-Captain and his Mate, a commercial gentleman and an elderly, thin wisp of a woman who'd come, she informed me, to savour the true atmosphere of Cornwall and to paint. Her sketches were delicate, small water-colours of views and of wild-flowers, which were minute in detail and exquisitely done. There was also a Methodist minister who apparently knew Beth quite well and had stayed there before. A very different *ménage* indeed from the roistering crowds I'd grown accustomed to in Port Einack.

During my few days of freedom for shopping and growing accustomed to my new surroundings I made friendly contact with most of the guests and fancied at odd times the Mate eyed me speculatively, as though he'd seen me before. Then I realized he was mistaken; his apparent interest was merely the usual look of most men at a good-looking woman.

On the Monday following my flight from Moody and Hackett's, I went into Penzance and purchased some clothes; underwear, two frocks, a blue-sprigged print, and a dark rust-coloured satin simply cut in the manner of the times but with no pretensions to high fashions. I felt, curiously, that I never wanted to wear black again—perhaps because it was a sign of mourning, and the last thing I wanted just then was to mourn *anyone,* even my father Will Hackett.

In spite of the tragedy and my disastrous past, life was stirring in me again. It would have been fitting to show sadness, but I'd had enough of it. I was still young; my body was a little fuller perhaps but still erect and gently curved, and my skin was clear and cream against the rich texture of chestnut hair. And my lips—oh my lips like my heart were still ripe for the touch of a man's mouth bruising my own, and I longed for the feel of strong arms about me and the warm smell of rough male skin against my cheek and body. There were times as I stood half-naked before the mirror in the bedroom Beth had given me when a faint shame stirred in me for feeling so. But I knew I was beautiful; my breasts had developed, tilting like pale golden pears above the slim waist and flattened stomach, and my arms, though full, were richly rounded, glistening satin-smooth in the light. I wished, irrationally, my father could have seen me then and could have known that the daughter he'd fathered had survived, if only as a symbol of the love he must once have felt for my mother. Whatever fate had divided them, I knew instinctively it had not been entirely of his making ... nor of my mother's. Life, as I'd learned by then, had its own way sometimes of making mockery of human plans.

My new employer was obviously a little shocked at first by the clothes I'd chosen.

'But, my dear,' she said when she saw me in the sprigged cotton which was cut square at the neck and flowing in full lines from the tight bodice, 'won't that get messed up too quick? I mean, it's more of a *lady's* dress ...?'

I smiled. 'Not when I'm wearing the apron. And I've even bought a cheap cap for my head. Besides, this frock will wash quickly.'

'Ah, but the ironing and starching ... We doan' have much time for that sort o' thing, except sheets and such like,' she said grudgingly. 'Are you sure you do realize what's on our hands here, Judith?'

'Quite sure,' I answered. 'Tomorrow I'll show you.'

And I did. All that day I scrubbed, cleaned, cooked, waited at table and even undertook a little extra washing.

Beth was amazed.

'My dear life,' she exclaimed, 'you're a worker an' no mistek. An' still lookin' so fresh as a daisy ... except for your hair which is a wonder of waywardness if I may say so ...'

'Ah well ...' I laughed, 'I must get the cap on, so no one sees it at the meal tonight.'

'I doan' know, Judith ...' She studied me reflectively. 'If you pinned it a bit tighter on top 'twould give a certain elegance, I s'pose, an' guests such as we have at the moment do like that. If you could arrange it all neat I doan' think the cap's necessary at nights.'

So that evening I wore the rust-coloured satin gown with my thick hair pinned as tightly as possible away from my face.

Later, when the meal was cleared away, Beth invited me into her own sitting-room leading off the kitchen for a sup of her elder wine before retiring.

'You're a real wonder, to be sure,' she said with true admiration in her voice. 'A young woman like you could go far. What brings you to this sort of thing? That's what I keep wonderin' ... but then, as I said, 'tedn' my business.'

'No, not really,' I agreed. 'But I did tell you I was born to it. The rest, well ... it doesn't really matter. I'm trying to forget a lot of things in my life; please understand or try to. One day perhaps ...' My voice wandered away uncertainly as fleeting memories clouded my mind.

She must have noticed because she said suddenly, briskly, 'Forget et, girl. I shouldn' be raisin' things you've no wish to recall. Instead I should be thankin' me stars that such a blessin' as you've crossed my path. The last girl, Thamsin, was a besom ... all sharp tongue an' sulks, an' pryin' an' preenin' 'erself just to catch a sly look from the men. *Any* man. That was Thamsin. Queer when you think o' et that she should walk out the day 'fore you came. The good Lord musta' bin at the back of et, that's what I do think. All the same, midear, I'm not goin' to let you overwork yourself. That would be stupid on my part. Mrs

Adam shall still come three mornings a week to do the real rough. And you must have an off time ... Fridays would suit me. Afternoon an' evenin', to give 'ee a bit of leisure. Does that suit?'

'Of course,' I told her. 'But there's no need.'

Still, I was grateful, and when Friday came along that week my heart was quickening and my step was lighter as I hurried two steps at a time up the stairs to my bedroom at the top of the house. It was a nice bedroom, small but clean and sunny, with cream-washed walls and a brass bedstead with a patchworked quilt covering the spread which was bordered with crochet lace. A yellowing oleograph of an elderly gentleman wearing a seaman's cap with his hand on a Bible, probably Beth's father or grandfather, hung on the wall above the marble-topped wash-stand, and a rather large wardrobe faced it on the other side of the room. There was a ewer and basin, and hand-made rag rugs on the floor, partially covering the brown oil-cloth. Nothing artistic or even smart, but everything was spotlessly clean and somehow cheering and peaceful.

I washed, then changed quickly into the rust-coloured satin, tidied and pinned my hair securely but not too severely on top of my head, and took a thin bronze-shaded shawl I'd bought on my shopping expedition at a reasonable price because it was slightly damaged; then, when all was quiet, with the guests gone out or retired following the mid-day meal, I went quickly and softly downstairs and out the front door.

I had no plans and was content just to be free of duties and worries and nagging memories which for the first time for many months seemed dispelled as effectively as the brush of a leaf on a summer wind. The air, though warm, was fresh, and the waves glistening in a froth of white round St Michael's Mount across the bay. Penzance lay in a quiver of heat a mile or so ahead, and I went that way naturally, wishing to wander the wide sea-front, away from twisting streets and narrow buildings huddled over the water.

When I reached the harbour several large vessels were at anchor intermingled with the rigged sails of fishing boats and half-steam craft about to berth or move away.

How things were changing, I thought absently. Soon, one day, I'd heard it said, the beautiful merchant vessels still coursing the ocean with their sails outspread to the wind like those of gigantic proud birds would be gone. The sky would be darkened instead by smoke coiling above the horizon where squat steamers moved quickly and more powerfully than their earlier rivals, to foreign ports and lands. A completely different world it would be then ... like life. Like my own, which had gone from love to love, place to place, in an ever changing pattern of cause and effect, of circumstances so frequently in opposition to human will. It was strange how far my mind wandered in those few brief minutes. I wasn't by nature given to philosophising. But as the summer wind flapped my face it was as though I was no longer myself but a mere figment of history ... the relic of some vast dream moving ethereally across the great panorama of world events. I felt a little light-headed and withdrawn from myself, conscious of occasional forms passing by, but as shadows merely removed from reality. Then, quite suddenly, as I turned to walk on again, my heart started a terrific pounding, thudding against my ear-drums and breast, and my head momentarily went giddy, unable to accept what I saw—a strong, male figure moving towards me through the sunlight.

Even from those few yards away I knew his eyes glinted black under his thick dark hair, his skin was browned from sea and sun and his firm lips rich with a lazy smile over strong white teeth. He was bareheaded, wearing an open shirt over seaman's breeches.

Matt.

For a moment I had a wild impulse to run and hide myself—*away, anywhere*—to escape this meeting which for so long had lain at the back of my mind and in my dreams, taunting me. So many times I'd rehearsed what I'd do or say when and if we were ever face to face again. And mostly I'd seen myself cold and haughty, shrugging my shoulders with contempt and passing by with a sneer. But it didn't happen like that.

All of a sudden, in a few strides, he was before me, his hands on my shoulders and his head thrown back, with a gusty laugh ringing from his throat. Then he said, slipping an arm round my waist and almost squashing the breath out of me, 'Hullo, wife ...'

He was about to kiss me when I tore myself away, and in spite of the wild thrill coursing through my body, the pulsing about my thighs and the weakness of my knees, I said sharply, 'You've a nerve, Matt Thomas. Let me alone. I want none of you.'

His face sobered at my tones. His arm fell away, and I fancied he looked slightly shamefaced before he said, 'Come on now, Judy. That's not true, and you know it. We both know. Didn't I tell you I'd never let you go ...?'

'Yes. So you did,' I replied tartly, walking on, 'but that's just what happened, isn't it? So don't start now trying to walk into my life again as though nothing has come between us all these years. It has, and a very great deal. I'm no longer your wife. I never was, as all the evidence showed. So just leave me alone. I don't want to talk or have anything to do with you again.'

'Don't you? Don't you, love?'

His hand touched my arm just below the shoulder, squeezing it gently. I could feel the strength ebbing away from me, as his old magic flooded me with such yearning for love.

I could hardly hear myself insisting, 'No, no. I don't. You behaved so badly I've cursed you to hell many times, and nothing in the world, ever, will change that.'

'Maybe not. But cursing can do a deal of good on occasions,' Matt said with maddening calmness. 'Remember the times we yelled and fought each other when we were wed, Judy? The time you scragged my face and I smacked your beautiful bottom?' He laughed. 'What a hell-cat you were. And how you enjoyed our fights.'

Confusion stained my face red. 'I ... I ...'

'Shut up, love,' he told me. 'And drop the fine lady stuff. You're no lady nor ever will be. It's me you've had and'll always want till the end of your days. Same with me. Why else would I come from the end of the world searching for you? Fun, eh?'

'Because you had a cargo to unload or pick up, I suppose,' I said quickly. 'Don't play with me, Matt. You can't fool me any more. You did once, but that's all over now. I've had a life, and still have, of my own. I've borne a child to a husband you never knew, and ...'

'A child? *Husband?*' he echoed.

'Yes.'

'But ...'

'They're both dead now,' I told him, 'and I don't wish to talk about them.' I stopped abruptly, facing him with my cheeks flaming. 'I don't want anything to do with you at all, Matt Thomas, as I said. And I wish you'd leave me at peace. It's the least you can do.'

There was complete silence when we walked on together again and yet so apart. I was aware of a curious loss, of something that had probably died long ago and I'd never known it.

After a time he said more quietly, 'I guess there *are* some things in the past I should apologize for, and I do, Judy. But you were no saint, were you ...?'

'I didn't lie or pretend or take what wasn't mine. I didn't act as though I was free to marry when I wasn't. If I'd known about Topaz ...'

'All right, all right. I should've said, and I didn't. But it was because you were so helpless an' needing a husband, and because I wanted you so, dammit. God help me, Judith, I've never longed for a woman as I did for you from the first moment I set eyes on you. *That's* no insult, is it? Maybe I shouldn't have gone to the lengths I did to get you; it was a risk on my part, as things turned out. And in the end I'd've had you anyway ...'

'You ...'

'Because you were lusting with your whole pretty little body for me,' he said ruthlessly, ignoring my attempt at protest. 'So don't play the prude, darling.'

I shut my lips tight, then said coldly, 'Have you finished?'

'No. First of all Topaz. She's dead of the fever. Last year it was, and though we'd not bedded together for quite a time, I was sorry. She was a real, warm, kind woman in her own way, with no airs or graces or the tedious habit of going cold on a man when he needed her.'

'How nice for you.'

'Yes. Yes ... she was a comfort, and I never tried to disguise it. But it was different with you. You meant something I'd never had before in all my life, Judith Perryn. An' that's why I'm saying now, marry me. Marry me again with everything straight and legal between us and I'll show you the whole world. With you beside me we could ...'

'What a nerve,' I interrupted and could have laughed in his face.

'Of course. We're a pair, you an' me. Rightly or wrongly, I married you once, and however much you spit and scratch and try to deny it, the bond's still there.' He paused before saying more gently, 'That's true, isn't it, love?'

My head swam suddenly with such a conflict of emotion, of longing and anger, desire and contempt, I had no way of answering him or saying what I felt, because I didn't rightly know myself. One part of me still responded to his animal charm, while the other rejected it, knowing something was lacking. But what? *What?* Morality or legality no longer mattered to me that much. It seemed to me any fine pride I'd once possessed had been so bruised and humiliated in the last few years it was up to me to take what warmth and comfort I could without too many scruples. Since the day Matt left me I'd secretly yearned to have him back. Except for Venn, no man had counted at all in that way, and Venn had merely despised me, forcing me on his brother with the ruthlessness in him I'd had at last to accept. Oh no, not Venn—there was no love there nor ever had been. When he'd kissed me even his eyes had been cold fire, bitter with accusation and contempt.

I shivered as a thin cloud furred the sun's warm glow, but it was a shiver of the spirit more than the body.

Matt's hand enclosed mine. 'Well, Judith?'

'I don't know,' I said desperately. 'Even if we ... even if I *wanted* it, how can I say yes, Matt? It wouldn't be sense. There's so much in between. Things have happened. I'm not sure I could be the wife you remember any more ...'

'I'd hope not,' he said wryly. 'You were a little devil. All the same you need me, Judy, and I need you. For God's sake, now stop the talking. Come along ...'

He tugged my hand, swivelled me round and started walking sharply up a street cutting to the town centre. I didn't resist, strangely, but went along with him, suddenly willing, with my hair all blowing wild and the strengthening wind beating against my satin bodice and swirling skirt.

'Where d'you think we're going?' I got out at last, when I'd found my breath.

'My lodgings,' he said, tersely. 'And I'll behave, Judy, and put plans all properly before you. Everything fair and square from now on, that's me.'

I didn't know whether to believe him or not; I was in such a torment of surprise still and bewilderment, of shock and indecision. Until then nothing had properly registered, and although Matt was real enough—the strong grip of his hand and the hot flame of his eyes on me; the old swagger and mockery and maddening conceit of the man—half of me seemed to be in a dream. A dangerous dream though, that was drawing to an end, to the inevitable wakening.

Gabriel Street was dark and rather narrow,

suddenly steepening halfway before a glimpse of the main road could be seen. At this point we turned the corner of an alley where a taller building was huddled between a small inn and an ironmonger's. Lace blinds were drawn over the windows and its aspect wasn't inviting. The interior held the same quality of drab respectability, pervaded by an odour I couldn't quite place—of soap mingled with polish, perhaps cooking from the kitchen and a sultry, cloying, sweetish perfume heavy in the air.

After our mounting two flights of stairs bordered by wooden banisters, Matt ushered me into a room. It was comparatively large, with a plant in a pot by the window, a small table and chairs beneath, with a wardrobe facing a chest where a man's knick-knacks—Matt's obviously—were carelessly arranged, including brush, comb, books and a wallet. His Captain's hat hung on a peg with his coat, and boots stuck out from under the bed where a shirt and trousers had been thrown haphazardly. There was a second door—or what must have been a door at one time—near the chest, painted dark brown to match the woodwork and mahogany furniture. A man's room, in which he could take his meals, if he chose, and follow his own pursuits in privacy.

'Sit down,' Matt said abruptly when I'd taken brief stock of the surroundings. 'Not exactly elegant or suited to ladies' comp'ny, but it suits me fine, especially for any length of time. And I'm here for a week before I take off again.'

'Where to?'

'Bristol and Cardiff. Good mixed cargo. But the *Fair Susan*'s getting on in years, and a leak in the hold has to be properly seen to before we take Land's End. Still ...' he eyed me contemplatively, 'we didn't come here to discuss boats, I reckon.'

'No,' I answered. 'You talked about plans. But I don't see ...'

'Oh shut up, sweetheart,' Matt said, grinning. 'You never *did* see straight, nor ever will, I'm thinking, except when it suits you. It's just forgetting you're good at.'

'What do you mean?'

'Stop it, love. You know what I mean. You, me, what we had, and what's coming. Why, you don't even seem to recall what I told you just now about proof. Didn't I tell you everything was going to be fair and square from now on?'

'So you *said,'* I answered warily.

'Here it is then.' He went to the table, took a sheet of paper from a book and handed it to me, saying, 'A letter from Nick Jago telling me of Topaz's death from the plague, and about Wellington going to her aunt's. There's a newspaper paragraph inside, too. Read it, Judith, just to prove to yourself I'm a free man come to claim you. Go on. Don't sit there looking as though you'd seen a ghost. Afraid are you?'

His voice was suddenly sharp. I looked down at the cheap paper, reading what lay before my eyes with a strange feeling of disinterest, then unfolded the crumpled cutting of newspaper giving an account of those dead of recent fever in Jamaica including one Topaz Thomas and her sister Amber.

I had no reason to disbelieve either Jago's account or the paper's, and was surprised the news didn't excite me more. Once it would have; once my first reaction would have been: Now I'm free. Now Matt can marry me. Ironically, though, perhaps because I'd lived with disillusion for so long, it didn't seem to matter much any more.

Absently, I handed the paper back to Matt.

'Well?' he said. 'What about it? Have you gone dumb all of a sudden or are you just being mean, trying to pay me out?'

'Don't be stupid,' I replied, jumping up with a flash of anger. 'What do you expect? D'you expect me to cry, "Oh Matt, how wonderful. Now we can *really* be married and be all cosy together without a thing in the world to worry about. Thank you, Matt, for being so kind and thoughtful." Is that it? Is that what you want me to say?'

'*No.*' He took me by the shoulders, pushing me roughly back into the chair again. 'All I want is for you to see sense, Judy, to have you warm and soft in my arms again, with the future bright for us both and no regret or shame for the past. No barbed jibes, nor harsh tongue, no lies nor pretence. Just you and me. *Marriage,* Judy, *true* marriage. That's what I want.'

I closed my eyes while a wave of weakness and indecision swept over me. Matt's lips came hot on mine, gently at first, then firm and demanding, with his tongue seeking mine. There was the sound of footsteps on the landing and then a knock on the door. Matt jumped up as I confusedly straightened my hair. A second later the door opened revealing a black-haired, stout but still shapely woman wearing a flower-decked hat and blue silk gown under a grey lace shawl. For a moment I could sense Matt's embarrassment and was aware of a kind of sly amusement in the woman's rather prominent blue eyes.

'Hope I didn't intrude, Captain,' she said calmly. 'I came to say I'll be out for an hour or two, but I should be back by evening. If there's anything you want in the meantime ...?'

'Nothing, thank you,' Matt answered quickly. 'Judith, this is my landlady, Mrs Baragwanath. Elizabeth ... meet Miss Perryn, a friend of mine.'

The woman held out a plump hand which I was forced to take, though my instinct was one of immediate hostility. There was something cunning and avaricious about her I didn't like. Something else, too: a sort of complacent power that suggested she knew more of Matt than she'd have me believe.

When she'd gone I asked, 'Do you know her well?'

Matt shrugged. 'As a good cook and convenient acquaintance, no more.'

'Convenient acquaintance? What does that mean?'

A look of anger crossed his face, but his voice was even when he said, 'Just what it sounds like.

Her room suits me. She's not on points about hours or having no visitors. She looks after the place well and is willing to turn an eye when I want it. You don't get many like her around.'

'No, I'm sure not,' I said wrily.

Suddenly his good humour returned.

'Judy ... my own sweet, I do believe you're *jealous*. Jealous of a middle-aged, stout old cow like Fanny ...'

'Fanny, is it?'

'That's what she calls herself. I don't know. It could be Jane or Ruth or Harriet or Lisa for all I care. What's it matter, love? Oh Judy, relax. So many questions. They bore me, always did.'

He went to the wardrobe drawer and took out a bottle of whisky, poured a dram into the glass on the wash-stand, then pushed it into my hand.

'Drink it up, and stop nagging. We've *plans* to make, Judith. So forget the rest. Brooding over old things brings no joy to anyone. And for all your wild ways you were a gay one when I had you. That's what I'd think of those long days behind the mast with never a woman in a hundred miles to see ... your spirit and laughter and courage in getting to grips with things.'

With the glass held absently in my hand I watched him lift the bottle to his lips and take far more than seemed necessary for the occasion. Then he came back to me, put one hand on my shoulder and said, 'Look at me, Judith.'

I turned slowly, raising my face to his. The dark eyes were glowing down on me. There was the old whimsical tilt to his mouth that roused so many memories a kind of dizziness swept over me, reviving a longing I'd no power at that moment to resist. A little earlier I might have swept the glass from his hand and flounced out in revenge for past injury. But now I'd no wish to. I simply stared in a kind of dream, realizing he'd already accepted that he'd have his way, and I half-believed it myself.

'Drink up,' he said, with one hand moving caressingly, insidiously, from my neck to shoulders, the bottle in the other. 'A toast, Judith, to the future.'

Mutely I obeyed him. The liquor was strong, burning my throat. I coughed and put the glass down.

'What is it?' I asked. 'Vodka?'

He laughed, went back to the chest where he replaced the bottle, then relaxed and drew me to my feet.

'Something to put the heart into you and make you see sense,' he said in warm, slightly thickened tones. 'Now, love, don't try any of your fighting and scratching. You're a grown woman, and the childishness is over. You want me still, don't you? And I'll wed you as I've promised, sure I will. Soon's we set sail on the *Fair Susan* next week; a *sea* wedding, with no crowds or prying eyes or religious ballyhoo to put the fear of God into a woman. Yes, that's how we'll have it, love ...'

His arms tightened round me. His face was hot and redolent with the spirit he'd drunk as his mouth closed on mine. I could feel one hand fiddling with the waist of my dress at the back, and when I tried ineffectually to dislodge it, the pressure increased. His large palm and fingers travelled the curve of my buttocks, lingering there for a moment, thrilling at first but then sickening as disillusion swamped me. Then his hand fell away abruptly; I was swept from my feet and held so close I could feel the thudding of his heart against mine and the heat of his body enclosing me in a steam of male desire.

This was the Matt I'd thought I'd loved for years, and yet he wasn't, because I knew his own appetites came first and always would. The 'marriage' business meant nothing—*nothing*—except a means, whether he admitted it or not, of satisfying his own insatiable sexual greed.

I kicked wildly, crying, 'Stop it, Matt, *stop* it ...' but he merely laughed.

'Why, love? Why should I? Aren't you my wife any more then? Haven't I some rights after the way you shamed me and chucked me out before Topaz's very eyes? Oh no, you're not getting out of things so easily now. *No* woman treats Matt Thomas the way you did without paying for it. And by God I'll have you now, if it's the last thing I ever do ...'

He pulled the skirt from my bodice and thighs, and with a hand over my mouth he carried me to the bed and flung me down, one arm pressing me hard into the mattress, the other unbuttoning himself so he was exposed and lusting, his face suffused and swelling from desire and the drink he'd taken.

I kicked and pounded him with my fists, tightening my thighs as he tried to get into me. O God, I thought; Oh God ... save me ... I no longer wanted him. Any longing I'd felt, or brief, renewed passion, had died incongruously into just one emotion—hate. I hated him for his bullying self-esteem and crude, sexual hunger, and for his arrogant assumption that he could lure me with lies and meaningless promises into becoming once more his whore and light-of-love. As the breath tore at my ribs and the sweat poured off me, I knew desperately that if he had me then any decency for the future or self-respect left to me would be gone and I would be better dead.

How long the sickening conflict lasted I don't know, but suddenly, with his flesh close against me, I gave a terrific jerk and buried my teeth in his arm.

There was a yell of pain. His grip slackened momentarily. I half-lurched and rolled from the bed, rushing towards the door. But he was there before me, wild-eyed with fury, his own blood trickling down his arm. I turned and rushed in terror towards the other door, throwing my weight against it, one hand on the latch. To my relief it opened. I shut it quickly behind me, gasping for breath. The next moment he'd burst in. I dodged behind the sofa, and as he flung himself over, struggling on his stomach towards me, I leapt off and ran back to the door. But it was locked. I turned quickly, standing with my back pressed against it, and noticed in that short respite of fear a whole number of things before Matt swaggered towards me: the sofa was in reality, a single bed with a rumpled pink spread over it, and the whole interior of the room was fussily feminine, with even a frilled dressing table. There was a low chest with ornaments on it, including a carved jade Buddha and something that looked like a Chinese dagger. A pair of lacy bloomers lay on the floor, and a woman's ornate Eastern wrap hung on a peg. The air was heavy with scent, the scent I'd noticed when Matt's landlady had looked in. A pair of sea boots stood against the wall.

In a flash I understood, and any lingering shadow of feeling I *might* have had for Matt buried at the back of my mind was suddenly so cold and dead I could no longer even feel hate.

With cool precision I moved quickly and snatched the dagger, my hand instinctively touching the blade, which was sharp—very sharp.

Then, as Matt approached, and clutching it firmly, I held my arm out and with my eyes icy on his said, 'If you try to touch me again, Matt Thomas, I'll *kill* you. I swear I will.'

My voice in my own ears sounded venomous, with the hiss of a serpent's poison in it. He recognized it and knew I spoke the truth. For a second he faltered.

'Look here, girl, have sense. I was only ...'

'Filth, that's what you are, Matt Thomas,' I told him. 'A low-down, sneaking, thieving cur. Unlock this door, and get me my skirt. And don't try any tricks or I'll stick this thing through your heart, as sure as God's my witness ...'

Whether I really would have done or not, I never knew. The thought of it made me want to vomit. But thankfully the test didn't arise. Matt's face suddenly paled. I watched him swallow and the fight go out of him.

'All right ... all right ... no need to get huffed ... Put that thing down, Judy. *Down.*'

'Not until I'm dressed and out of this door and the next,' I told him. 'Go on, get my clothes, Matt, before I change my mind and finish you like the pig you really are.'

My legs were trembling when he brought me my skirt and shawl. He threw them at me; and all the time, as I pushed my legs and feet through the skirt, I had my eyes on him and the dagger ready. In the same unswerving way I edged my toes into the shoes, watchful of any move he made towards me. By then, though, I knew the worst was over. Desire in him had had its own culmination, and he was limp with derisive contempt for himself and for me who'd forced him into such ignominy.

When at last I reached the front door, with the shawl over my shoulders and my damp hair pushed from my forehead, I turned and flung the dagger as far as I could up the stairs. Matt was watching me from the top of the first flight. A muttered oath left his lips as he moved to pick it up.

I gave a short laugh, slammed the door and walked resolutely into the cool air blowing from the harbour. During the interval with Matt a summer mist had risen over the sea and was spreading its thin veil over the town, creeping like a shroud up streets and round corners as though to dull reality into some kind of dream.

For a short way my legs moved mechanically. Then, as I reached the main road I stopped for a minute, leaning against a wall to avoid a threatened lurch of sickness and faintness. When I'd recovered I went on again, crossing the road blindly, only half-aware of someone shouting as I missed a phaeton's wheels by inches. Occasional figures, like shadows, passed and were quickly swallowed up in the deepening fog. I made my way automatically ahead, taking the road not to Newlyn but to the hills, impelled only by instinct.

There was a dripping wetness round me; moors, bushes, and huddled trees all swamped into a desolate nothingness which seemed to me then the end of all things. I had no plan; my mind and body were too dulled and tired to think and my spirit so filled with despair I wished, at one point, I could die.

But death doesn't come so easily. And though darkness fell when I stumbled into a void of ditch, light gradually filtered my senses once more, and stretching an arm out I could feel the cool, sweet touch of grass against my flesh and the evening mist wet on my cold face.

CHAPTER 30

I lay for a moment in a half-dream until the memory of what had happened jerked me to my feet in a panic of revulsion. My dress was torn and gaping at the waist, and soiled and damp from the long grass and misty air which was turning from fog to thin rain. I was shocked not only by the state I was in but also from realizing I was not far from Gulvarrick. In my fury, anger, and terrible disappointment I'd walked the opposite way I'd intended, partly, I suppose, because of the strong drink Matt had given me. I stood stupidly looking at the dress and was bending down trying to adjust it with a pin from my bodice when a queer sound like the rasping and rattling of dry twigs behind me made me straighten and turn round sharply. Through the swirling vaporous air, a bent old figure in crow's black was staring from a hag's face, beady eyes burning coal-bright and gnarled jaw out-thrust beneath the hawk nose. She was leaning on a stick with a bottle under her arm and appeared more like some malicious creature of the elements than of flesh and blood.

Dorcas.

'So et's you be, et?' she muttered. 'I knowed one day sure 'nuff 'ee'd come wandrin' the roads agin to torment Ettyns.' She waved the stick threateningly. 'Git off then afore I calls the doom on 'ee, same as the devil in you murdered young Sarne and Flavia, an' the babe. G'ron ... skit ...'

Once I would have been frightened. Now she did nothing but anger and depress me, so ugly was she with her lips bared above her broken teeth.

'Don't you ever dare say such a thing again,' I said moving towards her, 'do you hear? You're nothing but a slatternly old mad woman pretending to be a witch. You've no power ... *none,* over me. And if you mention the word murder again I'll have the law on you, do you understand?'

Probably my voice had risen. Her jaw dropped; the arm holding the stick was shaking as she put it down. Some of my fury must have penetrated her warped mind, but her voice was still aggressive as she said slyly, 'Ee wudn' do that. Your kind's no truck wi' the law, unless et's one with 'es pants down.' Her laugh was vile.

'You filthy creature,' I said and that was all.

I was turning to go when she clutched my arm suddenly, thrusting her face upwards towards my chin. In spite of the mist and rain, and my own utter weariness, the concentrated hatred in it startled me.

'You'd best not threaten Ettyns either,' she muttered. 'There's power in the blood you's no knowin' of, so you tek care an' doan' come roamin' these parts .. nor lookin' for Venn neither ...'

'Why should I look for Venn? He's nothing to me. I've a good post Newlyn way ...'

She grinned maliciously. 'Then be off to 'et quick, 'cos Venn's goin' 'way. So there edn' a thing but ill for 'ee here.'

Without waiting for a reply she turned and shuffled off into the grey mist, leaving me staring after her, with my heart suddenly turned to stone.

Going away. 'Venn's goin' 'way.'

Was it true? Or had she merely been meaning to taunt and hurt me? How could I tell? There was no way of knowing.

But it seemed when at last I freed myself to turn and take the lane leading back to the main road, something in me died for the second time that day. First when I'd found that the Matt I'd loved had never existed, and then ... Venn. Perhaps since the time I'd met him near the moor during my early days at Gulvarrick, he'd really come first and I'd not accepted it. Would I have fought Matt so hard that afternoon if it hadn't been for Venn? A last desperate attempt to keep faith somehow, even through the tangle of his union with Alicia? I didn't know.

But my heart was heavy as I dragged myself back to Penzance. The evening was closing in, and the town and sea looked desolate in the shrouded rain. If it hadn't been for the fear of running into Matt, I'd have called at a public house for a drink. But every quay-side eating house, small restaurant, kiddleywink or lamp-lit bar filled me with dread. So with my feet aching and my thighs heavy with weariness I somehow eventually arrived at Newlyn. Beth was in the hall when I entered the house.

'My dear luv!' she exclaimed, throwing up her hands. 'What a sight you are, to be sure. What's the matter then?' She took my two shoulders, staring hard into my face. 'Not a man, es et? You ed'n been assalted, or ...?'

I managed to smile and say as convincingly as possible, 'No, *no,* nothing like that. I had a bit of an accident in ... in Penzance. I was crossing a road and a cab nearly caught me. I slipped on the cobbles. It shook me, so I ... I went for a meal somewhere afterwards.'

'*Where?* Where did you go?' she persisted.

'Oh, I don't know what it was called, I really don't,' I protested, hating having to lie so glibly. 'I can't remember. A little place, near the main street ...'

This appeared to satisfy her.

'Well,' she said, 'it could've been the Dolphin, or Stevens'. But you should'a come back and got freshened up. Now you get to bed an' I'll bring 'ee a hot drink. Soon's you get them wet clothes off the better. I doan want a sick wumman to nurse on top of all the work an' that's a fact.'

The conversation ended there.

Later, as I lay in bed waiting for sleep it seemed to me that everything else had ended, too. All chance of happiness or fulfilment with the one man who could have meant everything to me.

Venn was going away. Venn ... Venn ... His name was still in my head with aching reiteration when at last exhaustion took me to unconsciousness.

When I woke in the morning I was thankful for the long day's work ahead which would include, as well as the changing of the sheets and preparation for new arrivals, cooking, and seeing all the rooms were in order, the necessary business of mending my dress and attempting to clean it fit for wearing in the evening.

It was as well I did so, because the following evening, Sunday, an elderly gentleman called at the boarding house; a man with a bright face, golden eyes and grey hair still tinged with a hint of red. Sir John Carvellun.

I was in the kitchen when he arrived. Beth, who was in the front of the house, opened the door to him. Although I didn't recognize his voice I could hear the murmuring of conversation followed by the tread of footsteps down the hall. The door of Beth's private parlour clicked open and shut again. A second later, with a bright colour on her round face, she came into the kitchen.

'There's an elderly gentleman ... quite old ...' she said in awed tones. 'Askin' for you he is, Judith ... It must be you, although he called you Mrs Crane ... *Mrs* Judith Crane. Sir somethin'-or-other he called himself, and he described you exactly. "A handsome young woman," he said, "clear skin, and that shade of hair you can't help noticing, not brown, not red, but a bit mixed. She walks well," he went on before I could get a word in, "and I've been trying to get in touch with her. Is she here?" Well, what could I say, but it sounded like a new help I had. Wish I could remember his name ...' she broke off, screwing her brows together.

'Carvellun? Sir John Carvellun, I expect,' I said.

'Dear luv, yes, that's it. I didn' know you had such fine friends, Judith, or you was married ...'

'I'm a widow,' I told her shortly. 'Sir John's an acquaintance of my ... my late family.'

'Oh. I see.' Beth drew a deep breath and remarked, 'Well, you'd better tidy yourself quick and get into the parlour ... I shall have to see to the meal myself tonight. Hurry then, it doesn't do to keep the gentry waiting. I'll see you're not disturbed.'

I combed my hair up properly, pinning it with curls on top of my head; then I took off my apron and decided I'd cleaned and mended the rust satin sufficiently so it didn't show. Wondering what the old man could possibly want with me and how he'd discovered my whereabouts, I went into Beth's small sitting-room.

Sir John was standing with his back to the door, staring through the window which looked out on the moors stretching over the crest of the hill towards Lamorna. He turned abruptly as I entered closing the door quietly behind me.

'Ah!' he said, striding forward with his hand extended. 'So it *is* the lady I've been searching for.'

He was looking immaculate in grey, with a white front, white winged collar and pale grey silk bow-tie with a diamond pin. Small trinkets glowed from the watch chain across his stomach. He had a grey top hat in one hand and was wearing white spats over his shoes.

'I'm ... glad to see you, Sir John,' I said, letting my fingers rest in his for a moment. 'Please do sit down. May I take your hat and stick ...'

'No, no. I shan't keep you long,' he told me, easing himself into Beth's best maroon velvet-covered easy chair that had little frills round its legs and an antimacassar draped over the back. I took the one opposite. 'Now ...' he leaned forward, 'I expect you're wondering how I found you?'

'Yes,' I admitted. 'I didn't expect to see anyone concerned with Thorncarne again.'

'Didn't you now? That seems a pity, I think.'

'I don't ...'

'No, of course you don't understand,' he finished for me. 'And I hope you won't be annoyed by my intrusion or the way I managed it.' A brief twinkle lit his yellowish-gold eyes that were so strangely like Venn's. 'The fact is ...' he continued almost immediately, 'I happened to notice you one afternoon recently and thought to myself ... Ah, that's the young lady from the Ettyn farm. You were walking back from Penzance burdened with such a load of parcels I'd a mind at first to have the chaise stopped and offer you a drive back ... to wherever you were going. Then on second thought I suggested my man keep track of you, so I had your address for a more opportune moment ...'

‘You mean you spied on me?’

He nodded, smiling mischievously. ‘Wicked of me, wasn’t it? But for a good end, my dear. A very good end ... where *I’m* concerned.’

I was quite at a loss.

‘If there’s anything I can do for you I will, though I really don’t see what.’

There was a perceptible pause, then he said very seriously, ‘Please go back to Thorncarne, my dear.’

I could feel a flush of resentment creeping from my spine to my face, and suddenly a sense of being trapped and on the verge of being plunged back into a past I really wanted to forget.

‘No, no,’ I told him, shaking my head. ‘I’m sorry. That’s one thing I can’t do, and I don’t see what ...’

‘... right I have to interfere,’ the old voice interrupted reasoningly. ‘I quite agree with you. It isn’t *my* affair either, in any definite sense. But where Venn is concerned ... Well, as you must surely known by now from Belle Crane’s loose tongue ... I have obligations. Yes?’

I nodded. ‘I’d heard he was your grandson.’

‘And I’m not ashamed of it,’ the old man said a trifle belligerently. ‘He’s turned out well, far better than I’d have expected, considering the rough start he had. The point is something’s gone wrong up there, at the farm, and he’s talking of taking off to Canada. *Canada,* of all places.’

I tightened my lips and managed to say coolly, though my heart was chilled with a sudden mounting sense of apprehension and loss. 'But surely that's his own affair. Perhaps he wants to make a new start in a land where farming's so prosperous ... Perhaps he needs to have Alicia on his own. They've not been married long, and things haven't been easy for them ...'

'Her?' The old man jumped up with the temper bright in his eyes and cheeks. 'That strumpet! She's *gone,* madam, didn't you know? Taken off to some cheap, flashy no-good in London who was her partner at that ... that café place of hers. Good God! Until he married her I'd respected him for his sense. But one first glimpse of her was enough. You fool, I thought; you bloody young fool.' He coughed, 'Excuse the language, ma'am, I just can't abide fools.' I was silent while he recovered himself, then he continued with a hint of slyness, 'If it had been *you* now, things would have been different.'

His words roused such longing, such acute pain in me, I said sharply, more sharply than I'd intended, 'Sir John, please don't try and get me to plead with Venn to stay at Thorncarne. I'd be the last person to do it, and the last he'd listen to. Venn and I mean nothing to each other. And I can't understand why you wish to prevent him doing what he wants.'

'Don't you? Then I think you should. As his only relative I feel ...'

'He has his mother,' I interrupted sharply, 'and brothers.'

'*Mother?*' He almost spat the word out. His voice was fierce when he said contemptuously,

‘That stout overblown creature isn’t his *mother*, madam. Not by blood, that is ...’

‘Please,’ I began, aware of his embarrassment, ‘don’t go on. You shouldn’t tell me things you may regret afterwards. It’s ...’

‘Fiddlesticks, ma’am. I don’t need you to teach me my own business. Besides, it can’t come as any great surprise. His mother was a different kettle of fish altogether. Stupid and headstrong, though; a silly bit of a humble-born chit with damn fool notions of being a great actress.’

He paused to get his breath back, then added grudgingly, ‘She left home and burned her boats thoroughly. Her parents were the prunes-and-prismy religious kind, all fire and damnation to an erring daughter. Consequence was she got herself bedded with my rascally son, the young devil, and cost me a pretty packet into the bargain.’ His voice softened. ‘He got killed, y’see. Shock it was, a very great shock.’

‘It must have been.’

‘Well, maybe I could have handled things better,’ the old man continued reflectively. ‘Looking back, I’m not exactly fond of the role I played. But that’s life, I suppose. Time’s a mellower. Trouble is you don’t know it before it comes. Still ...’ He sat up straight. ‘Where was I now? Ah. Yes. The baby. Rupert’s and hers. She didn’t want it, and my poor wife refused to have anything to do with the affair. Proud *she* was; a duke’s daughter. Family honour and all that, y’know. So the girl was paid a generous sum to forget about it, and that's where Belle Ettyn came in. She was camping with her family on Carvellun land at the time, and as she'd just lost her own child she was persuaded to take the baby—Venn—for a considerable financial consideration, of course. No doubt she made an excellent wet nurse.' His tones were dry. 'A month or two later we heard the girl, the natural mother, had died, so Belle was temptingly bribed into keeping and bringing up the boy as her son ... on the condition of secrecy, of course, which she swore to in an affidavit ... though God knows if she properly knew what she was putting her mark to.' An elfin grin momentarily transformed the old man from embittered memories to amused anticipation. 'A real character though, in her way, with the knack of loving, however primitive it may be. And there's no doubt when he was small she was fond of the little fellow. Oh I kept my eye on them, you understand? Saw she got a good husband in Crane, who was well paid, too, incidentally, with a small farm and a certain security for the future. Belle never suffered for anything she needed. But Venn ...' he sighed, 'Venn's different.'

Of course he was, I thought sadly, remembering his pride and fierce dedication to family, the family he'd been landed with. No wonder he'd fought so hard for power and roots, when nothing really was his own. No blood kith or kin except this fiery old aristocrat who'd renounced him.

Well, perhaps renounced was hardly the word,

since at this late date Sir John was obviously concerned.

I didn't know what to say, and after a dragging pause I heard the old man remark. 'So perhaps now you understand more what I'm asking, my dear.'

I shook my head. 'No. I still don't see where I come into it.'

'Now now I won't accept that, not at all. You're an intelligent young woman as anyone with half a glance would know. And don't try and make out you don't know what I'm talking about. I watched your face once when you passed Venn, and that alone would have been enough to show where the land lay.'

I flushed.

'Venn, too,' he resumed insistently. 'Do you think he'd be talking of taking off to Canada if you were still at Thorncarne?'

I jumped to my feet suddenly, with a wild mixture of emotion flooding me; confusion, anger, rebellion, intermingled with a sudden, irrational hope. Yet I didn't mean to be played with ... used as an intriguing toy for this lonely old man's benefit, just to have his grandson to his side. If Venn had loved me it might have been different. But he didn't, or he'd never have intimidated me into marrying Sarne.

I answered ruthlessly, 'You're mistaken, Sir John. Venn has no interest in me. *None,* in the way you think.'

He shook his head meaningfully. 'Believe me, he has. And more than interest, I do assure you. Mind you, I'm not pleading for him ... He can damn well plead for himself, if you give him a chance. But he's a proud, wilful character, my dear; a chip off the old block if ever there was one. That's why I want him here, partly, in the old country. So in a way, it's myself I'm pleading for. You see ...'

'Yes?' My voice was sharp.

'I've a mind to make him my heir. He's all I have. Legitimacy of birth ... no, that's beyond my power as the law stands. But heir to my estates, my name, and all I have ... *that* can all be legally his, and a fig for conventions. Anyway, tongues soon stop wagging when there's wealth and prestige enough. And from what I've seen of him, Venn has a manner and bearing no one would sneer at.'

'Yes,' I agreed, 'I'm sure you're right there.'

'But he's all damn set on getting abroad unless there's something more than I can offer to keep him.'

'Why don't you go on trying,' I suggested mercilessly.

'Damn it, girl!' He jumped up abruptly. 'Have you no heart? Do you think I'd go to all this trouble if it didn't mean all that's left in the world to a childless old man, and more to Venn? He *loves* you. Take that in, can't you? I know people; at my age I *should;* and I know, too, from words dropped here and there by my grandson, he thinks more of you than any man should of *any* plaguey woman. But everything's gone sour on him lately: the herd, the farm, his tom-fool marriage, and now you. There's nothing for him at Thorncarne unless you go back. Once you're there things'll sort themselves out, and you two can get to grips together, even if you go to the devil in the meantime. Sorry I've had to be so forthright, ma'am.' He mopped his brow with his impeccable silk handkerchief. 'You must forgive me. Not so young as I once was, and this sort of thing upsets me.'

I hadn't meant to give in, but the last few words weakened me and suddenly I found myself saying gently, 'Very well, if you think it will help, I'll return ... for a bit anyway. But I can't promise anything, about Venn I mean. I don't really think my presence will make any difference. And there's something else ...'

'Yes?'

'Mrs Tregurze, my employer. I've had wages in advance, and apart from that, I owe her a certain loyalty. She's been very kind to me.'

'My dear girl, Mrs Tregurze shall be more than amply rewarded. I do assure you. If you let me speak to the lady, we'll settle things here and now. And then, at the first opportunity, I'll send the chaise to take you back to Thorncarne.'

As easy as that, I thought with irony. A stroke of the pen, a wave of the hand from a powerful old gentleman and everything could be settled as though no impediment existed or ever had.

But of course this wasn't true. No good, ever, could come from future contact with Venn. Only pain. And I wondered how I'd endure it.

All the same, when the next morning arrived I found myself setting off once more for Thorncarne, only differently this time; in Sir

John Carvellun's carriage, with his man seated in front, stony-faced and impersonal like a uniformed wax-work figure, except for the occasional flick of his whip and an automatic sound from his throat as he drew the horse to a halt at the gates of the farm.

CHAPTER 31

No one appeared to be about when I walked up the path to the house, but I guessed some curious eyes had seen me. The door was unlatched as usual, and an air of emptiness hung about the hall. I paused irresolutely by the kitchen, wondering whether to go back quietly and down the side track to the Barn. Then I remembered I hadn't a key; following my leaving it would probably have been locked up or perhaps used by Flavia or one of her brothers. So I went into the kitchen and was taken aback by its untidiness and neglect. Mugs and an empty jug stood on the table with a few messy-looking plates. There was a pile of washing-up in the sink, and the floor was filthy. No window was open, and the air stank of cooking and onions. That slut Liddy, I thought. Where was she?

I put the paper bag containing the new dresses I'd bought, on a chair, pulled off my shawl and was staring and wondering how and where to begin when the outer door opened and Marcus came in.

'You!' he said. 'We didn' expect you, Judith.'

'Obviously not,' I answered tartly. 'What does *this* mean? All this filth and ... and ...' I broke off, at a loss for words.

He looked a little shamefaced.

'I know. But there's more than Paul and me can tackle. Liddy's gone, and Ma says she's sick of cleaning up after us. Flavia shuts herself up in the Barn when she comes back from work ...'

'Oh does she!' I exclaimed.

'Well, you did take off, and what with the crops and animals and haymaking ... And it isn't as if Venn cares. He's going away. Canada, he says, so the farm'll be ours. I wouldn't mind that so much, if it was smaller, because Paul and I plan to go in for bees and flowers and such like with a few vegetables thrown in. But until Gulvarrick's sold there's just too much on our shoulders, Judith. And if Venn's goin' to leave all the settling up to us, like selling the cattle and the whole change-over from one type of cultivation to another, we can't afford help, that's for sure.'

'No,' I said more quietly. 'I understand that. But ... I don't think Venn would leave you in the lurch when you need him.'

'Oh I reckon he will,' Marcus said, slumping on to a chair. 'Venn's changed. Everything's gone sour on him. 'Licia's gone to that cheap smart fellow in Lunnon, Liddy's left, and with *you* taking off it was the last straw.'

'But why Liddy?' I said. 'You should have kept her, for the time being anyway.'

'Ah. Yes. But Venn wouldn't pay out for her; he said she wasn't worth her keep. All for economy he is now. For our sake, he tells us, so's we know what we're in for when he's gone.'

A weight, like lead, seemed to hug my

heart, chilling my whole body. 'Perhaps it won't happen,' I said. 'People sometimes say things they don't mean.'

'He doesn't. Venn's stubborn. Once his mind's made up, it sticks. Anyway ...'

'Yes?'

'Where've you been, Judith? Why did you go like that? So all of a sudden, tellin' no one but Ma.'

I hesitated for a moment before answering recklessly, 'I suppose, like Venn, I wanted a change. I've had it and now I'm back.'

'To stay?'

'Until you can get along without me,' I told him. 'Then we'll see. No promises for the future, Marcus. Promises can be broken and I'm not the kind to be tied down forever.'

'No. Neither was 'Licia,' he said dourly. '*Women!* Ha. I reckon I'll never marry, seeing what happened to you and Sarne, and Venn ...'

I was about to tell him to hold his tongue when heavy footsteps along the hall predicted Belle's approach, and a minute afterwards she pushed in, pausing with her hands on her hips in astonishment. Then she said with a righteous show of indignation that I sensed disguised vast relief, 'What's brought *you* back agen then, like a hungry dog after a tasty bone?'

I laughed. 'Need you ask? All this ...' waving an arm round. 'Is *this* the bone for the dog, or the carrot for a donkey? Because that's what it seems I am ... coming back to such disgusting conditions. A real *donkey.*'

The old familiar flush stained her already bright cheeks.

'Now you look here, Judith Crane—and doan' fergit you're still my daughter-in-law—'ef you so much as spik another word 'gainst Thorncarne, I'll tek a rollin' pin to 'ee, so help me gawd ...' She broke off breathlessly, then continued, with the pleading wail in her voice that fooled no one, least of all myself, 'Oh you doan' know what et's bin like, Judith, everythin' dependin' on these pore weak shoulders o' mine, an' Venn bein' so nasty just at a time when a hand's needed. But then, that's him all over. A real gorgio I bred, an' that's for sure. When I think o' the night his stuck up pa Rupert mounted me, I could vomit. Sure I could.'

'Then don't think of it,' I said pointedly, 'and don't imagine things. Bedded you may have been, but if I were you, I'd be careful of names.'

Marcus, sensing some sort of confrontation, left the kitchen leaving Belle and I facing each other.

'What you mean?' she said. 'Bin gossipin', have you, whilst you bin away? Concoctin' things I never did say?'

'Oh no,' I assured her. 'No gossip, and no blame to you. But I know the truth, Belle, never mind how. Venn's not your son at all. So why let him get you so upset?'

For the first time I saw her colour pale.

'*How* d'you know?' she demanded. 'Who's bin talkin', Judith? Come on now ... I wasn't to tell, see? Ef I did breathe a word I'd be turned out wi' no penny to my name, not a one. Me an' my darlin' childer.'

'Sit down,' I said. 'And forget about it. *No* one knows but me ... and Sir John. *He* told me and I certainly shan't repeat it. In any case it wouldn't matter now, would it? It's so long ago, and such a ... such an old story, really. What does it matter who Venn's mother was. To Venn? I don't think so. He's probably known for a long time. Another thing ...'

'Yes?'

'Sir John's glad for you to keep the farm. It's yours legally, yours and your own children's. So for heaven's sake, calm down. *I'm* tired, too. What about a cup of tea?'

'Ah,' she agreed. 'Tea. Wi' just a nip o' tonic in et to give us strength.'

This allusion to her booster, the remedy for all ailments and unpleasant situations, almost made me smile, and presently everything was so unexpectedly cordial between us, chiefly because of the new scapegoat, Alicia, that it seemed my hasty departure had been worthwhile.

Until I thought of Venn.

The idea of meeting him again filled me with nervous dread. Something about him—his coldness and hardness—had always set me on edge, and his spasms of kindliness sent me into a whirl of emotional conflict and unease. I'd never really been able to assess what he was thinking or planning. Except for odd moments when the barriers had been broken by a chance impulse ending in hasty words, he'd shown little warmth towards me. And yet I'd never forgotten what he'd said more than once when I'd threatened to go away: 'Remember, Judith, wherever you go and however far you run, I'll find you.'

But he hadn't. He hadn't even looked for me this last time. Because of Alicia, probably, and fretting for her. One day, perhaps, they'd come together again, I thought as I cleared the tea things and started preparing for the evening meal. Alicia was a sly madam. She might even have laid a trap for him, hoping to ensnare him to her side again just through making him jealous. After all, Venn wasn't the meek-and-mild sort to be cuckolded by any man, least of all a cheap opportunist like Joshua Leeds. He had a fierce pride ... and it was pride surely that was driving him away now, so he could put all wretchedness and cheapness behind him, leaving him free to start again.

Including myself.

The possibility that the mere sight of me might fill him with dislike and irritation was almost unbearable; and during those hours before I saw him that evening, I was hot with sudden anger at the old man, his grandfather, who'd inveigled me there. He'd only done it for himself; he hadn't cared about *me*—I'd only been a convenience, the alluring, sexy tit-bit to keep the grandson-by-blood in the vicinity of the aristocratic family fold. What a farce. And how easily I'd responded to the part, like any melodramatic heroine out of a Mrs Henry Wood novel.

However, if I was to play such a role, I thought rebelliously, I'd play it as best I could.

I'd more or less given a promise to the old gentleman, and I gulled myself it was for this reason I had to look my best, not accepting the truth was very different.

I *loved* Venn Ettyn.

Not as I'd thought I'd once loved Matt, but with my whole heart and body. Physically? Oh yes. Without the flood of desire there could be no love. But it was far more than that. I respected as well as wanted him. The hours of passion and a touch of gentleness, the pride and the graciousness perhaps might have been mine but for my bitter, sullied past. I ached so intolerably that I knew I had to smother it under a show of brilliant bravado and, if necessary, scorn.

When the meal was prepared and in the oven, I went out to the Barn where Flavia was already titivating herself in the room that had once been mine.

She was so astonished to see me that all she could say was, '*You!* Why didn't you say you were coming back? I could've ...'

'Don't worry,' I told her. 'I don't want this place. I'm only staying for a time anyway, and I've arranged with Belle to have *your* old room at the farm. But there are some oddments of mine in the dressing-table drawer. Cosmetics mostly ...'

She made a move. 'Oh, Judith! I used a bit. I'm sorry. I didn't think you'd want them. Anyway, you never *did* make up, not much, did you?'

'Hardly ever. Just a little on special occasions.

And somehow ...' I swallowed, 'this is rather special, to me. I feel a bit embarrassed walking back like the prodigal son ...'

Flavia dimpled. 'Or daughter. Poor Judith. It's not like that though, is it? The prodigal son had feasting and wine and a great big welcome. But *you!* D'you know what you're doing, returning to this dump with all that hard choring lying waiting?'

'Yes. I'm quite aware of it.'

'Then I think you must be potty,' Flavia said tersely.

'So do I,' I agreed in false bright tones. 'But here I am.'

'Why though? *Why?*' Flavia insisted. 'Oh, come on, Judith, tell me ...'

'Later. There's not time now. Let me take my things, if you don't mind. I need pins, too, and the bunch of ribbons ...'

'All right, all right. Get what you want. And believe me, whatever the others think about it, I'm *glad* to see you. It's been one long, sullen bore here lately. If it hadn't been for my job taking me away in the daytime I wouldn't have stuck it, I can tell you ...'

On and on she prattled while I searched the drawers for things and the underclothes I needed. Then with two parcels under my arm I went back to Thorncarne and deposited them into the room next to Belle's.

I unpinned my hair, letting it fall thick and flowing over my shoulders. Then I washed from the water ewer, thoughtfully put ready by Belle, tidied my rust satin dress and tucked the high neckband away, pinning it carefully so my neck showed firm and clear. The next thing was to tie my curls on top with a golden ribbon and add a little cream to my face and rose-shaded balm to my lips. 'Crushed Geranium', they called it, and it was supposed to soften with 'healing properties to beautify'.

I'd used it only once before, when I was entertaining at William's, and had felt very daring. But this time its insidious, faint perfume and an exotic sense of being up-to-date with current fashion gave me a confidence reinforced with defiance.

Let him see me as I really was, I thought, when I went down to the kitchen ten minutes later. Let him think just what he liked of me ... regard me at least not as a nonentity but as a woman of independence with a mind of her own and a past that was *her* affair only and with any future she wanted to choose.

Oh yes. My mind was full of high and mighty ideas as I walked in, with my head high and my bodice slipping just a fraction lower than I'd intended. Marcus and Paul were already at the table, and Belle, looking exceedingly high-coloured and with a cloth in her hand, was hovering by the stove.

'I *do* think you might'a come down a bit earlier, Judith,' she said, looking up and eyeing me disapprovingly. 'You've had high time to get yoursel' tidy an' titivated up. An' after leavin' us as you did do without so much as a thank ye' or proper reason; with all the load o' the farm, too. Et's thoughtless an' real ungrateful, that's what

I say!' She sniffed. 'Gratitood! My Gawd ... et seems to me there's no such thing now'days.'

'Oh yes there is,' I told her blandly and cattily. 'And you can show a little to me, Belle, by lifting the dish out of the oven, carefully though, with the cloth, and carrying it out to the table, if you've the strength. If not, one of us will come to your aid.'

I could hear Paul sniggering, and when I glanced round I saw him dig Marcus in the ribs. Both were about to explode with laughter.

Belle glowered. 'You've got a sauce, Judith Crane. First dolling yourself up like as ef you wus any fancy tart, then makin' fun o' me in front o' my own fam'ly. I'm not your servant an' doan' intend to be either. If 'ee didn' come back to lend a hand, what wus et fur, eh?'

'Come on, Ma,' Marcus said suddenly, 'don't argue. We're hungry. Let *me* get the thing out an' for the love of Pete stop bickerin'. It's bad enough having Venn as he is without two females spitting an' scratchin' like a couple of wild-cats.'

Belle stalked back to her chair at the top of the table with her head held high above her two chins. Once again I imagined her as she must have been in her youth before easy-living and laziness crept up with her. Even now not a single grey hair tinged the lustrous, if untidy, black locks. Her bold eyes were as black and gleaming as ever, and her golden skin, without its unfortunate high flush when she was angered or upset, was still clear of blemish.

Flavia came in a few minutes after, throwing

me a knowing look as she said over-casually, 'Venn's late.'

'Venn! Him. He doan' care 'bout any o' us,' Belle retorted nastily. 'Likely as not he's gone sniffin' arter some other fancy wumman to 'comp'ny him to Canada in 'Licia's place.'

Although I didn't for a moment imagine this was true, the malicious remark angered me. I knew she'd said it to get her own back against me, but her words still rankled.

'Oh, I don't think so,' Flavia remarked airily. 'More likely he's on the track of some prize brood mare to sail with him over the ocean waves. Can you imagine it ...' she giggled, 'Venn nuzzling his darling in the hold ... Bear up, my love ... steady now, steady. It'll soon be over, and then we can start all over again. A queen you shall be among the cattle of the world ...'

She broke off as Venn entered. Obviously he guessed or had heard the trend of conversation. But when he saw me sitting there in my usual place his face seemed to flinch momentarily, and a little of its colour faded. Then he said stiffly, 'So you're back. What a surprise.'

'Yes, I'm back,' I echoed calmly, though my heart was bounding painfully under the rust satin. 'Have you any objection?'

He shrugged.

'Whether I have or not is of no account,' he said, tearing his eyes away. 'I'm sure Belle will be grateful.'

So it was going to be like that, I thought; no welcome, just cold, aloof informality. I'd have preferred a few hot words and curses even. If he'd attacked me at least contact would have been established. But of course with such a crowd of Cranes watching and eager at any time to savour a hot-blooded scene he'd be very careful to keep any feelings he had for me to himself. So, buoying himself up with the thought and conscious that in spite of his chilly manner his eyes strayed frequently to mine while the rest of the throng were eating, I was not too downcast and made the most of turning my head at its most elegant angle, knowing I looked my best.

I'd hoped for a few words with him before going to bed that night, but when he met me in the hall on his way to the sheds all he said was, 'I meant what I said. Belle will be grateful. The family have missed you.'

The family! The *family,* I thought, with an irrational, rising surge of emotion. As if I cared for the *family!* Didn't he *know?* Couldn't he understand even the first thing about a woman's feelings, especially mine?

'I've simply returned to take Alicia's place for a time, until she gets back,' I answered.

He laughed shortly.

'Alicia's gone for good, as you must very well know, and at the end of next week *I* shall have gone, too. So naturally your help will be appreciated. Good night.'

He passed on, leaving me mutely staring after him for a moment.

At the side door he turned and added, 'I wouldn't start dressing up here if I were you. Marcus is only concerned with bees, and Paul's already enmeshed with a village girl.'

The latch of the door clicked, then snapped to behind him. Fury was wild and hot in me, but grief and a terrible sense of loss and aching disappointment were stronger. My eyes smarted with unshed tears as I later made my way to my room. Why had I been so stupid as to believe that beguiling old man, I wondered as I undressed for bed. I'd been his last card obviously, just a pawn to use in a reckless bid to get what he wanted. And I'd been a fool to believe him. I, Judith Perryn, should have had sufficient sense and experience of men to know that one like me of lowly birth, who'd been bedded by three men already, would certainly not appeal to someone in Venn's position, with an inheritance and fine name for the taking.

Love. What a mockery it was, I thought. Whether Venn took off to Canada or not didn't really matter. I was already so far apart from him the whole world must be between us. Where *I* was concerned it would be better indeed if he did leave, and as soon as possible. Then I could start once more and make my own plans. Go back to Port Einack, perhaps, and live with my own kind ... The stench of fish on the salty cobbles and in the sheds, the incessant sound of waves breaking on the shore and high shrill crying of gulls about the ship's masts ... That was where I belonged and should be. I was no lady nor ever could be. Luzana was merely a myth, a dream and relic of the far past. All I'd aimed and tried for had ended in defeat. I'd poured scorn on Matt, but Matt with his lust for living was the best I was fitted for and deserved.

Matt. As I closed my eyes before sleep, trying to picture him during our first days together. I imagined his hands once again against me, in desire. There was still time; his ship didn't sail for some days. He wouldn't deride or scorn me if I appeared at his lodgings one evening. There'd be no need to explain. He'd just laugh and pull me to him and give me a slap or two maybe, then take me with the passion that had so inflamed me when I was young.

Oh yes. If I needed him, he was waiting, and I knew it.

But I didn't. The memory now repulsed rather than inflamed me. The last thing I wanted was ever to see him again.

For the first few days after my return Venn and I had no contact except at meal times or when others of the family were present. Then one late afternoon when I'd been to the village delivering eggs and cream, he cut into the lane from the fields and caught up with me. There was a fine rain falling; the kind I liked to feel on my face, laden somehow with the fragile, far-off scent of heather and wild flowers from the hills. Soon high summer would be fading to autumn, but just then it was as though spring's whisper was everywhere and I wanted to unloosen my hair and let it drift free in the gentle air. It was at that moment I saw Venn and heard him say, 'What's it like, being back?'

Staring straight ahead I answered, 'Just as I

thought. No different from what they always were.'

'Except that you've more on your hands,' he remarked in expressionless tones, 'and more power with Alicia out of the way. Don't let any of them take advantage when I've gone, though. You must keep a steady hand on the reins or young Paul will be throwing his weight about. Far too much like Sarne for my liking.'

I turned sharply to face him then. 'Oh, have no fear, your precious Paul will be quite safe from me. After Sarne I'm not likely to fall into temptation with another brother.'

I could feel rather than see him flinch.

'There was no need to say that.'

'No, I'm sorry.'

'Are you? I don't believe you've ever been sorry for anything in your selfish young life,' Venn retorted bitterly. He added quickly in more casual tones, 'By the way, how did you find your gallant sea-captain? Was the tête-à-tête enjoyable? Or could it be that you found the experience a little disillusioning after all?'

'What do you mean?' I heard myself saying ineffectually, trying at the same time to get my shocked thoughts into some sort of order. 'I don't know what you're talking about.'

'Don't lie,' Venn said curtly. 'It doesn't suit you, and you're very bad at it into the bargain. Thomas. Matt Thomas—is he well? But I'm sure he must be, and quite pleased with himself, considering all things.'

'*All* things? Just what are you implying by that?'

'No implication. *Fact,* Judy. I was in the Fiddler's Arms the day after your visit and heard quite titivating details concerning your ex-would-be husband and how he'd escorted a certain "pretty little bit" to his lodgings at Fanny Baragwanath's. Oh, believe me, the description fitted you down to the ground ... "pert nose, juicy figure, with a fine way of walking and a proud air about her". I won't repeat the rest because it wasn't all so fine-phrased or complimentary. However, I *do* know it was you.'

'And if it was? What then? My affairs are nothing to do with you,' I flashed at him. 'You've no right at all to come questioning and probing and criticizing my actions. If I want to see Matt I will, without your permission.'

He suddenly caught my arm and swung me into a dip of the tall hedges by a field gate.

'I know that, damn well enough. Everything *you* want goes. What *you* hanker for, you get, whatever the cost. All your life it's been the same, hasn't it, Judith? Men ... men ... *men.* Sensation and the gratification of knowing no one can resist you. That's all your sordid little heart needs, isn't it ... the lust of power and having any male within reach at your feet. Well ...' he released me suddenly and said cuttingly, 'get on with it. Have who you like, *where* you like ... except at Thorncarne. There's one here who can very well do without you. But leave Paul and Marcus alone, or I'll come back from wherever I go, and when I've finished with you, so help me God, you won't know yourself.'

I stood dumbly for a moment, too shocked for words, my throat swelling with anguish. Then forcing myself to move I rushed after him, crying, 'Venn ... Venn ... you don't understand. It wasn't like you thought. I didn't want Matt ... There was nothing ... *nothing.* Please ... please. It's *you,* Venn ...'

But he didn't hear, or if he did so he didn't appear to; he just strode ahead into the thickening rain. And presently I stood still again, with my heart pumping and the tears in a thick ball at my throat, choking me, until at last they fell, streaming from my eyes in such a torrent of unhappiness I thought I must die.

But grief does not kill.

The days passed slowly. Mechanically I continued with my work at Thorncarne, whilst Venn went about hard-faced, preparing for his departure to Canada at the end of the following week.

A bleak sense of desolation seemed to encompass the house, subduing even Belle's high spirits and intermittent tempers to dulled acquiescence. I half-expected Sir John Carvellun to call, but he didn't and I guessed that Venn must have informed him he was sticking to his decision to leave.

One chill evening when twilight was falling I felt I could bear it no longer and on impulse, without shawl or cape round my shoulders, made my way towards Castle Carnack, keeping well to the left in order to avoid any contact with old Dorcas.

The sky was already a luminous green, with

the first star hanging over the ancient stones. Everywhere was very quiet and still except for a bird crying from the distance. I lifted my hand to a slab of rough granite, and life from the past seemed to flood through me, giving some sort of peace. Presently I lay down, covering myself as best I could with tangy sweet heather. I was cold and didn't know it, lost to the world, which seemed very far away. As I slept the hosts of the past seemed to gather round me, and the great wings of nature enfolded me to forgetfulness. My last conscious thought was that if this was dying I was grateful. There was darkness and peace, and freedom from the long hurt of caring.

Then suddenly I woke, disturbed by the crackling sound of twigs breaking, belonging not to the past but to the present. I opened my eyes, shivering. Outlined against the indigo sky a darker shape stood looking down on me, blotting out the rest. Venn.

As he helped me up, putting his coat round my shoulders, my head was suddenly against his chest and his arms round me, as he scolded, 'You little fool, you. What d'you think you're doing? Trying to catch pneumonia? You should be spanked for this. What the hell am I going to do with you?'

I didn't know, and I didn't care. It was enough for me at that moment to recognize the concern in his voice and to have the troubled, searching look in his eyes blazing down on me.

We walked back down the hill with hardly

a word between us. After the first outburst he became withdrawn again, and his voice was cool and controlled when he said, at the gates of the house, 'It would help a good deal just now if you could manage to control the dramatics. And for heaven's sake, get yourself warm and dry. We've enough on our hands at Thorncarne without having to mollycoddle a wayward girl back to health. Your place here is to help, not act like some stupid child wanting to make a scene every time she's thwarted. Understand?'

'Perfectly,' I answered in a voice I hoped was as controlled as his.

But I didn't feel it. My heart was racing, my senses wild and confused. One moment I'd thought he really cared; the next it seemed I was to be no more than a chattel in his household. Well, if that was so, I'd play the part, I thought with a touch of malice. Venn Ettyn in future should have all the servitude and bowing and scraping he wanted. When he passed me, I'd curtsey; when he spoke I'd be careful to answer with an exaggerated *'sir'*. When his eyes sought mine I'd look downcast and demure with my lashes brushing my cheeks. Oh yes, he'd soon see what a paragon of good behaviour he had on his hands.

The idea was quite stimulating until I remembered with a stab of pain how little time there was before he left for Canada.

CHAPTER 32

I didn't see Venn again until early afternoon the next day. He was late for the mid-day meal, which enabled Belle to retire for her 'nap' with a bottle of her tonic under one arm before he spotted it.

'You tend to 'en, Judith,' she said. 'For all his tedious habit o' jumpin' on others ef so much as a minute o' workin' time's lost, he's the fust to want attention hisself whatever the time. That's gorgio for 'ee all over. Seems to me now he's decided on it the sooner he takes off the better. A real tyrant Venn can be on occasion. An' that 'Licia hasn't done him no good either. Nor you,' she added darkly at the door. 'It seems to me sometimes I've missed a good bit goin' on under me own nose that I should've had the sense to tumble to right from the start. An' when I recall that lovely boy o' mine, Sarne, I do think sometimes Aunt Dorcas was right 'bout many things. There's bin a curse on this place since you stepped over the threshold. That's what I do say.'

'Then be sure you know who laid it,' I retorted tartly.

With a glowering look in my direction, Belle turned, muttering under her breath and the next moment was moving ponderously along the hall and upstairs to her bed.

Marcus and Paul were already at work in the fields with the rest of the men when Venn came in.

He glanced at me briefly, then turned away, saying casually, 'Sorry I'm late. Hope you didn't keep anything hot. A snack will do. Cheese and bread, if there's nothing else.'

I didn't curtsey as I'd planned, realizing such a gesture might be overdoing things, but merely remarked in quiet, servile tones, 'Oh a proper meal is waiting for you, Mr Ettyn, sir. And it's been no trouble, I can assure you.'

I went to the oven and with a cloth in each hand lifted the dishes out and put them on the table. Then, still without glancing directly at him, I asked, 'Is there anything else you require? Wine? Whisky, sir?'

For a moment there was no response. Then I heard him burst out explosively, 'My God! What act are you putting on *now?*'

I turned my head provocatively over my shoulder, smiling slightly, relishing his discomfiture and knowing at such an angle I could look my best.

'Only trying to be polite and remember my position here,' I said. 'Surely that's better than having *you* remind *me.*'

'Judith!'

His golden eyes darkened as two spots of colour mounted his high cheekbones.

'Yes, sir?'

'I suppose this is your idea of a game ... trying to goad me. You just don't seem able to act like a rational human being over anything at all.'

'No,' I agreed over-sweetly with a mock sigh. 'And for that I also apologize ...'

'Apologize? *Apologize?*'

He jumped up suddenly, darted round a corner of the table, and before I could do anything about it had taken me in his arms and bent my head back, kissing me so hard I thought my neck would snap. Then he released me just as quickly, turned me round by the shoulders and gave me a sharp slap and a push towards the dairy.

'If you wish to behave like a serving wench I'm sure you won't mind my treating you like one.'

I looked back before flouncing to the door. His glance was set and unsmiling, although I sensed a wry sort of amusement behind the façade. He was *mocking* me, I thought with a flash of temper; and for a hot second I had a burning desire to rush at him, bringing my hand smartly against his face. Instead, all unmeaningfully, I bumped into the dresser, knocking a bowl of stewed fruit to the floor. The glass was shattered, leaving the rich liquid to spread in a flood of crimson under the woodwork.

I stared stupidly for a moment, irritated by my own carelessness. Then Venn remarked, 'There's a cloth in the bucket under the sink, I believe. The quicker it's cleared up the better.'

I started to say, Do it yourself, but stopped in time, resuming cuttingly, 'I quite agree. And I'm really extremely sorry such a mishap should occur in your presence. How lucky for you that you're leaving so soon for Canada.'

'Indeed?'

Something in his voice startled me. For a moment I was caught off guard and stood foolishly staring as he continued, 'But I'm not.'

'You're ... you're *not?*'

'You heard me. I've changed my mind. My presence here is needed, obviously. So get on with your work, Judith, before my temper gets the better of me.'

I obeyed him mutely, angered yet with an overwhelming relief drowning all other emotions. And when later the truth properly registered I knew nothing else mattered, nothing in the world except the time and chance somehow to get things right between us.

But was it possible? Later when I thought back over the short, childish interlude, my doubts revived and I felt a wave of dull depression. Most probably I'd made a good deal of nothing at all, I told myself relentlessly. Venn might not be going to Canada, but this didn't mean his change of plan had anything to do with my presence at Thorncarne. Alicia might even be returning to him. Or there could be some other woman. How did I know there wasn't?

I didn't. Like the air of a pricked balloon any optimism I'd had vanished. I suddenly felt older, with the black memory of the past risen again to torment me like a dark cloud obscuring all hope of happiness.

After that I put on no pretence nor teasing

airs but continued my work about the house mechanically in a mood of silence, much to Belle's surprise.

'What's the matter with you, girl?' she asked one day. 'Sick or somethin'?'

'I'm all right.'

'Well you doan' seem et, an' that's a fact. A real dumchat you are these days, an' no mistake.'

'Dumchat?' I echoed. 'That's a funny word.'

'All me own,' Belle told me complacently. 'Made it up. A real clever one I was as a chile for spinnin' words out of me own head as swift an' shinin' as a spider's web. Why, I recall my own grandfather sayin' my tongue had a magic 'bout et fit for any book that there Shakspir did write. "But you stick to proper Romany, chile," he telled me. "Romany's the speech of kings." An' I remember ...'

With some quick excuse I interrupted Belle's reminiscences and left the kitchen quickly before she could start on another of her long orations. I had an hour to spare before starting to prepare the supper, and longing for a brief spell of solitude, I went out through the side door and took the path skirting the fields towards the Barn. Flavia was not yet back, and in the dying rays of the sun the dwelling had a dejected look, reminding me acutely of life there with Sarne and little Petrock, which seemed now to belong to another world—another life even—and yet it was comparatively such a short time ago. A host of regrets, interspersed by a few rare, rich moments flooded me with an awareness of my own shortcomings and the irrational impetuosity that had first driven me into Sarne's arms. I knew the fault in the beginning had not been entirely mine but was the consequence mostly of Matt's betrayal, followed by William's, and later events mingled with my blind unacknowledged longing for Venn.

So the pattern had been woven. Sarne and Petrock had died; Venn seemed more remote from me than he had ever been. I should never have contemplated it could be different. He had principles; I, intrinsically, had none. My place was not at Thorncarne in proximity with Venn but miles away on the gaunt north coast where I had been born, with the harsh winds stinging the rocky coastline and the smell of salt always in the air. As I stood there with the cool early autumn air fanning my face I knew my future was already ordained.

I would return to Port Einack.

How quiet the evening was; and how sad, with the shadows encroaching as the yellowing sky deepened above the fields and distant moors. The men were mostly at work on Gulvarrick land, except for Paul and the boy busy with milking and about the sheds. The heady scent of woodsmoke was tangy in the air, and a lone gull rose suddenly from a bush nearby into the sky. Glancing up I saw burnished leaves and berries on a bush almost touching my head; and lifting my arm I broke one or two sprays free, thinking vaguely how adept Nature was at reviving old memories and dead desires. The berries were so beautiful, so rich and colourful, even though they heralded the winter ahead. On impulse I decided to go to the churchyard and place them on the grave where Sarne and Petrock lay. I had visited there only twice since the funeral, because it had never seemed important to me to make a show about those who were gone and because merely thinking of them had always depressed me. But now, somehow, with my phase at Thorncarne ending, my fears were gone and it seemed the right thing to do.

I set off, walking fairly quickly by the hedge towards the lane leading under the brow of the hill to the church. Twilight had already fallen when I got there, and the air was already chilly. The gravestone stood not far from the gate, just a single slab of polished granite with their two names engraved on it—In loving memory of Sarne Crane and Petrock his son—followed by dates that seemed to me quite unimportant.

I knelt down and placed the berries in their sheaf of leaves on the brown earth. A bird twittered from somewhere nearby, and as I got to my feet again something broke in me and softened so that the tears gathered in my throat, then flooded my eyes for a moment before coursing slowly down my cheeks.

I think I whispered, 'Forgive me, please, for not loving you. I did try. But please forgive me ...' although it may have been only my thoughts speaking.

I stood for a few seconds as a new strange kind of peace enfolded me, a peace that held no future or plan in it, with no regrets any more for the past nor ambition for what lay ahead.

Then, as the frail wind rose, flapping my skirts about my thighs and whipping my hair free about my forehead, I turned to make my way back to Thorncarne.

It was at that moment I saw Venn. He was walking towards me, silhouetted tall and strong against the deepening light, his head held proudly with an air of purpose about it that I recognized only too well. At any other time I'd have rushed willingly and oh so gladly into his arms. But just then I wanted only to pass and avoid him, because I knew it was no use. He might desire, even pity, me, but the love I so desperately desired wasn't his to give—to me.

My emotions had been too widely squandered. Already I had lain with three men who had left me forever sullied for the one I knew I had been waiting for all my life. No. If I hadn't Venn's respect, I had nothing.

So, as the gate clicked behind me, I merely said, 'Hullo, Venn,' and would have passed him without another word if he hadn't suddenly stopped me.

Putting a hand on my shoulder, he said, 'What is it, Judith? I watched you come up here and then I followed. I couldn't help it.'

When I didn't answer he lifted a hand and touched my cheek very gently, saying, 'Tears? But did you care so much then ... for Sarne? I always thought ...'

I shook my head.

'I never cared for him at all, not really. That's what I am, Venn—a cheat ... a loose woman, if you like. Understand, will you? I'm not worth bothering about. So let me go please. Just forget about me and leave me alone.'

I attempted to free myself but couldn't. Suddenly his arms were round me and my head was close against his coat, while he said, 'Oh *no.* Not *this* time, my love. This time we're going to come to terms and have everything straight between us. Maybe in your young life you *have* done a few things no really nice girl would do and maybe I'll have to keep the reins on you for quite some time ahead, but I think I can do it. In fact, I'm damned well going to. Do you know why? Because you love me, and I feel the same way about you, even more. So when I'm free, as soon as the divorce is through, we'll be married. In the meantime I shall go to London and stay there till everything's settled ...'

He broke off, allowing me just sufficient time to ask meekly, 'And me?'

'You'll stay at Thorncarne and behave yourself,' he told me. 'There's going to be no chance from now on for idle tongues to get wagging concerning either you or me. Understand?'

I nodded.

And then he kissed me. Not wildly or roughly this time, but with infinite gentleness and all the compassion I so desperately needed just then.

Presently, with his arm round me, we walked on, down the lane back to the house.

EPILOGUE

The weary period of waiting was over. The divorce went through, and on a fine spring day in April Venn and I were quietly married in Penzance. We left that same afternoon for his grandfather's place, Rosemerrick.

The house, a gracious mansion, stood on the southern Cornish coast, a few miles from Launceston. Although it was dark when we got there, I felt with my deepest instinct and whole heart that at last I had come home.

Later though, as I stood with Venn at the bedroom window overlooking the wide wooded bay facing Fowy, a feeling of unreality spread through me and my hand tightened on his.

'I can't believe it,' I said. 'I'm dreaming. I must be ...'

Venn didn't answer for a moment; then, very softly, his lips touched my shoulder. I could feel an arm gathering me close and a hand untying my frilly nightdress at the neck. He turned me to face him, his golden eyes darkening upon my own. My pulses leaped as his mouth closed on mine in a kiss which held not only desire and passion but also all the warmth and tenderness man could ever have felt for woman. Then he lifted me up, and the silly garment fell to the floor, leaving me naked and longing to give all that was in me. To give and to receive.

My breasts and thighs ached with desire as he carried me to the bed. And while I lay waiting, wonder filled me that man's body could be so tensed and strong, with such a pride and power about it. I realized I'd known nothing of true passion until then.

A moment later the warm flame of his maleness was on me and in me, and the thrust of love became one with both the spirit and the flesh. Our union was complete, bringing certainty and the thrilling awareness that never again would our lives be parted.

'I love you,' he whispered when we lay at last relaxed and at peace. 'Do you understand? *Love.*'

Fondling him and edging closer again I murmured coquettishly, just to inflame him a little, 'What do *you* think?'

He drew away momentarily, staring me hard in the eyes.

'Damned if I know, but one thing's sure—there's no escape for you now, my darling. For good or for ill you're mine, and if I have to tame you, I will.'

I sighed rapturously. 'That's all I wanted to know. You see ... you're so much *above* me, Venn, in every way. I'm just a ...'

'Shsh! *I'll* tell *you,'* he interrupted. 'An adorable wild-cat, like I said. And don't ever change, because that's the way I like you and will do until the day I die, my dearest love.'

I whispered, 'Oh Venn, darling Venn, nothing's counted in my life ever ... until now.'

He smiled, and his smile was the gentlest

thing. I knew then the past didn't matter, but only the future, with Venn and I making the best of our lives together, begetting, as time passed, children to follow us and take their places in the new century ahead.